Piers Anthony was born in Oxford in 1934, moved with his family to Spain in 1939 and then to the USA in 1940, after his father was expelled from Spain by the Franco regime. He became a citizen of the US in 1958, and before devoting himself to full-time writing, worked as a technical writer for a communications company and taught English. He started publishing short stories with *Possible to Rue* for *Fantastic* in 1963, and published in SF magazines for the next decade. He has, however, concentrated more and more on writing novels.

Author of the brilliant, widely acclaimed *Cluster* series, and the superb *Split Infinity* trilogy, he has made a name for himself as a writer of original, inventive stories whose imaginative, mind-twisting style is full of extraordinary, often poetic images and flights of cosmic fancy.

D1586336

By the same author

PIERS ANTHONY

Thousandstar

PANTHER
Granada Publishing

Panther Books
Granada Publishing Ltd
8 Grafton Street, London W1X 3LA

First published in Great Britain by Panther Books 1984

ISBN 0 586 05982 2

Printed and bound in Great Britain by
Collins, Glasgow

Set in Times

Prologue

She was lank and lithe and startlingly fair of feature for her kind, and as she ran her hair flung out in a blue splay. Her skin was blue, too, but light and almost translucently delicate. By Capellan standards she was a beauty.

'Jess!' she called, as she intercepted the blue man. 'What are you doing home?'

He grinned, his teeth bright against the blue lips. He was beardless and small, as like her in size and feature as it was possible for a male to be. 'I thought you'd never ask! It's a saw, of course.'

She kissed him with the barely platonic passion typical of this Solarian subculture, her teeth nipping warningly into his lip. 'Did you flip out from the training exercise? If they catch you—' She paused, her features hardening prettily. '*What* saw?'

He stepped back, ran one thumbnail along the translucent wrapping, and allowed it to fall open, exposing the machine. 'A genuine top-of-the-mill heavy-duty self-powered laser,' he announced proudly. 'Now we can hew our own timbers for the summer house. Bet we can carve the first ones this afternoon.'

'Jess,' she said, alarmed. 'You didn't—' But she knew from his aura that he suffered no abnormal guilt.

'Of course I didn't steal it,' he said, flashing a mock glare at her. 'I bought it outright. It's more legal that way. It's *ours*, Jess, all ours! Isn't it a beauty?'

'But Jess – we can't afford—'

'Girl, the trouble with you is you have no confidence,' he said with jubilant sternness. But there was something in his aura, an excitement that communicated itself to her via

5

their interaction of auras. 'Would I waste money?'

'Jess – you didn't remortgage the castle? You know we're on the verge of broke already. We can hardly pay our retainer, Flowers, or finesse the taxes! Besides, you need my countersignature to—'

'Remortgage, heavenhell!' he exclaimed. 'I paid off the old mortgage, O ye of little wit.' Even his aura was teasing her with its strange excitement.

'Come on. I can only chew so much joke in one swallow. What's the real story, Jess? Are the creditors on your tail?'

He settled into a serious expression, but still his aura belied it. 'Well, Jess, you have to void the safety latch, like this, so the thing will operate. Then you set it for the type of cutting you require, which we can skip because it's already set at the standard setting. Then you switch it on and—'

'Jess!' she exclaimed peremptorily. This time her aura gave his a sharp nudge.

'Jess,' he replied equably.

'Jess, pay attention to me!'

'Jessica, don't I always? What little I have to spare?' His eyes were blue mirrors of malicious innocence.

'The money, Jess – the money.'

'Now isn't that almost just like a woman,' he chided her. 'Here I have this superlative expensive laser saw, quite fit for royalty, and all she cares about is the morbid mundane detail of—'

'Jess, do you want me to start being difficult?'

He shied away with a look of horror he could not maintain, dissolving into laughter. 'Oh, no! Anything but that, Jess-ca! Anything you can do, I can do better, except that! Oh, I can't stand you when you're difficult. That's what the X chromosome does, all right; it is jam-packed with diffi—'

'That's not true!'

'Oh, it's true! Too too true! You are the most difficult creature in System Capella! You—'

6

'I was referring to the other thing, Jess. That I can do better than you.'

He glanced at her, seeing her vibrant in her petulance. 'That doesn't count, Jess. That's inherent in the sex. To be fair we'd have to survey my liaisons against yours, and compare partner-ratings. I'd bet I—'

'I was talking about the artistry,' she said, fending off the baiting. 'You can't make a decent holograph freehand.'

He held up his hands in the millennia-old Solarian gesture of surrender. 'Acquiescence, sis. *Two* things. Holograph and difficult. If I'd been the female aspect of the clone, I'd have them too, though.'

'If you'd been the female aspect, Jess, you wouldn't have squandered credit we don't have on a saw we can't afford, to build a summer house we'll never use because we'll be evicted for debt from the estate. Now out with it, and don't try to lie, because you know I can feel it in your aura.'

'That's the one thing about a cloned aura,' he complained. 'No decent secrets. Not until one clone abdicates his heritage and deviates too far to—'

'The money, Jess,' she prodded.

'Well, if you must pry, in your female fashion – it's the advance on the mission.'

'What mission? You're still in training!'

'Not any more. They needed an anonymous Solarian with intrigue expertise, and I needed a quick infusion of credit, so—'

'*Who* needed? For what? Where?'

'Thousandstar.'

She stared mutely at him.

'Segment Thousandstar,' he repeated, enjoying her amazement. 'You've heard of it? Farthest Segment of the Milky Way Galaxy, twenty thousand parsecs from here, give or take a few light seconds? All those non-human sapients crowded into—'

'I took the same geography courses you did. We have

7

just as many sapient species here in Segment Etamin. What about Thousandstar?'

'So the advance is twenty thousand units of Galactic credit, and a similar amount upon successful completion of the mission. This saw was only five thousand, and our old mortgage twelve thousand, so we have three thousand left—'

'I can handle the basic maths,' she said faintly. 'But that fee—'

'Well, I admit it's small, but—'

'Small!' she exploded. 'Will you get serious? It's a fortune! How could a nit like you, Jess-man—'

'But it's firm, Jess-girl. All I have to do is show. So I don't even need to complete the mission successfully, though of course I'll do that too. You won't have to go out selling your favours anymore.'

'I don't sell my—' She broke off, retrenching. 'Don't try to divert me with your spurious slights! Why would Segment Thousandstar advance twenty thousand Galactic units to an anonymous Solarian clone?'

'Hey!' he cried with mock affront. 'Don't you think I'm worth it, Jess?'

'You're worth a million, if you marry the right aristocratic clone girl and preserve the estate,' she said coldly. 'That's why I don't want your head on the royal execution block. You're no wild giant like Morrow who can get away with—'

'Ah, Morrow,' he said. 'What I wouldn't give for his muscle, money, and moxie, not to mention his cute wife—'

'Now stop fooling around and cough it out!'

He coughed it out: 'Jessica, I don't know. The mission's secret. But it's legal. It came through Etamin and Sol.'

'Through the Imperial System and the mother world,' she said softly. 'It *has* to be legitimate. Unless Andromeda's started hostaging again.'

'Impossible. Melody of Mintaka fixed that, remember?

8

For the past century there's been no hostaging; the host controls the body, no matter what the aura of the transferee may be, unless the host lets the visiting aura take over. Anyway, Andromeda's no threat; the Milky Way controls all Andromeda's Spheres.'

'True,' she said uncertainly. 'But it must be a dangerous mission. Really grotesque, to warrant such a fee.' She turned to him, and he felt the unrest in her aura. 'Jesse, you and I are closer than any two other people can be, except the same-sex clones, and sometimes I think we're actually closer than that, because we have been forced to concentrate on our similarity so constantly. If I lost you—'

He tamed his enjoyment momentarily, meeting her with equivalent candour. 'That's why I bought the saw, Jessica. I knew you'd go along. It's not a waste of credit; it will pay itself back within a year, slicing out all the boards and timbers we need. This is the break we've needed to put our family back into its aristocratic mode. The seed of Good Queen Bess will flourish again.'

'But the mission! All that credit for a secret job! Why is it secret, Jess? Because they know you'll die?'

'I asked about that. I have a cunning mind, remember; that's part of my training. Mortality expectation is five per cent. That's not bad, Jess. One out of twenty. So when I go on that mission, I have a ninety-five per cent chance of survival – probably ninety-eight per cent for someone as smart as me – and a hundred per cent chance of keeping the advance credit. So maybe the chance of successful completion is small – I don't know – but at least I'll be home again, and we don't need that matching payment. The advance alone will solve our economic problem. I'm willing to take that minuscule risk for the sake of our castle, our estate, our family line. Without that advance, we stand a thirty per cent chance of a foreclosure on the property. You know that. Royalty is no longer divine. We may derive from Queen Bess, but our family

9

power has been fading a thousand years, because we've become effete. System, Sphere, and Segment have waxed while we have waned. The universe does not need aristocracy anymore. Now at a single stroke I can restore our status – or at least give us a fair chance to halt the erosion. Isn't it worth the gamble?'

'I don't know,' she said, biting her lip so that it turned a darker blue. 'There's something funny about this deal. You didn't get this assignment through merit, did you?'

He did not bother to inflate his wounded pride. 'No, there are lots of qualified candidates. But two thirds of them wouldn't take a blind mission at any price, and of the remainder I was the only one with royal blood. Royalty has pride, more pride than money or sense; they know that. We won't let them down when the mission gets hard, because we are allergic to failure. It's bad for the image. So I was their best bet: a qualified, foolhardy royalist.'

'Foolhardy – there's the operative term. Jess, I don't like this at all!'

He laughed, but his aura belied him. 'Come on, let's make the first beam while we consider.'

She smiled agreement, troubled.

They took the saw to their mountain stand of purple pine. The old royal estate possessed some of the finest standing timber on the planet. Some of the pines dated from the time of Queen Bess, who as legend had it had taken jolly green Flint of Outworld as a lover, conceived by him, and settled his estate on the produce of that union. Regardless of the validity of this dubious historical claim, it was a fine estate. The castle still had the old dragon stalls and the equally impressive giant bed, where the green man was reputed to have performed so successfully. Unfortunately, that phenomenal two-hundred-intensity aura had never manifested in Flint's successors, and with the passing of the formal monarchy the proprietors had become virtual caretakers of the estate.

10

When the Second War of Energy burst upon the Cluster, a thousand Solarian years after the first, there had been no high-aura hero from this Capellan realm to save the Milky Way Galaxy. Instead Melody of Mintaka had come, an alien, unhuman creature transferred to a Solarian host. She had done the job, and she was indeed another distant descendant of Flint of Outworld via non-human line, but the lustre of Sphere Sol had dimmed, and System Capella had become a virtual backdust region.

That was part of what passed through the minds of the unique male–female clones Jess as they approached the stand of purple pine. To be an anonymous remnant of a once-proud System of a once-great Sphere – there was a certain dissatisfaction gnawing through the generations. The male wanted to achieve some sort of return to notoriety, if not to greatness, and the female, though more cautious about the means, desired a similar achievement.

Jess started the saw. The laser blade leaped out, a searing white rod terminating at a preset distance. 'Stand clear,' he said, but his sister-self needed no warning. She was afraid of that short, deadly beam.

He approached a tree. Not one of the millennia trunks, for those were monuments, but a fine century individual. Its bark was as blue as his skin, its needles deep purple. 'Where's the lean?' he enquired.

She surveyed it, walking round the trunk, her breasts accentuating as she craned her head back. She was highly conscious of her female attributes, because only here in the seclusion of the estate could she ever allow them to manifest. No one outside knew her for what she was. 'No lean,' she decided. 'It's a balanced tree.'

'I don't want a balanced tree! I want one that will fall exactly where I know it will fall!'

'Take another tree, then. One that suits your temperament.'

'Unbalanced . . . temperament,' he murmured. Then he

11

lifted the saw. 'I believe I'll trim off an excrescence or two here,' he said, making a playful feint at her bosom with the laser.

She scooted backwards 'You do, and I'll trim off a protuberance *there*,' she said, indicating his crotch. 'Your bovine girl friend wouldn't like that.'

He cocked his head. 'Which bovine?'

'That cow Bessy, of course.'

'Oh, *that* bovine.' He shrugged. 'How about your lecherous commoner buck, who thinks you're a chambermaid? Now *there's* a protuberance that needs trimming!'

'Don't be jealous. Nature grants to commoners' bodies—'

'What they lack in intellect,' he finished for her.

'You have a tree to fell.'

'Um.' He set his saw against the trunk just where the tree began to broaden into the root, and angled the laser blade slowly across the wood.

'It's not working,' the girl said, concerned.

'That's what you think, you dumb female,' he said with satisfaction. He angled his cut back without removing the beam from the tree. The bit of white visible between the saw and the tree turned red. 'Oops, I'm going too fast; the blade's dulling. Slowing, rather. It's molecule-thin; the visible bar is only to mark the place. Still, there's work in burning through solid wood; you have to cut slowly, give it time. There.' The beam had converted back to white.

'But there isn't any cut,' she said.

He ignored her, angling up. In a moment the beam emerged. The tree stood untouched. 'Now take out the wedge,' he told her.

'Sure.' Playing the game, she put her hands on the trunk where the imaginary wedge of wood had been sliced out, heaved with exaggerated effort – and fell over backwards as the wedge came loose.

Her brother-self chuckled. 'Now get your fat posterior off the grass and straighten your skirt; I'm not your protuberant commoner-friend. I'm going to drop the tree there.'

She looked at the wedge in her hands, then at the gap in the trunk. The edge of the cut wavered somewhat because of his unsteady control, and one section was ragged where he had pushed it too fast. That was why the wedge had not fallen out of its own accord. There was no doubt the laser had done it. She hoisted her slender derrière up. 'That's some machine!' she remarked with involuntary respect.

'That's what this mission means to us,' he said smugly. 'I've got three days' leave before I report; I want to get that summer house built.'

'In three days?' she asked incredulously. 'We can't even set the foundations in that time.'

'True, the saw can't do it all,' he said, reconsidering as he started to cut from the opposite side of the tree. 'You may have to put the finishing touches on it while I'm away. Give you something to do when you're not polishing your claws. The mission only lasts ten days or so. It's good payment for that time.'

'It certainly is,' she agreed, involuntarily glancing at her neat, short, unpolished nails. Her suspicion was reasserting itself. 'There has to be a catch.'

'So maybe it's an unpleasant mission,' he said, his eye on the progress of the cut. 'An obnoxious transfer host. A giant slug made of vomit or something. I can put up with it for ten days. And if the mission is successful, and I get the completion payment—' He glanced at her and the beam jerked, messing up his cut. 'We could afford a marriage and reproduction permit for one of us, nonclone. No more fooling around with sterile partners.'

'Yes . . .' she breathed. 'To be free of this ruse at last. To have meaningful sex, a family, security—'

'Recognition, status,' he added. 'Timber.'

'Timber?'

'That's what you say when the tree's falling.'

13

'Oh.' She skipped out of the way as the pine tilted grandly.

The crash was horrendous. Purple needles showered down, and a large branch shook loose and bounced nearby. The sound echoed and re-echoed from the near hills. The base of the trunk bucked off the stump and kicked back, as though trying to take one of them with it to destruction.

Brother and sister selves stood for a moment, half in awe of what they had wrought. Even a comparatively small tree like this had a lot of mass! A large one would shake the very mountain.

Jesse hefted the laser. 'Now for the beams,' he said, his voice calm but his aura animated.

'Beams? How many does that saw have?'

'Idiot! I meant the beams of wood. Measure off a ten-metre length, and I'll hew it now.'

'Doesn't it need to season?' she asked. 'Suppose it warps?'

'Don't you know *anything*, cell of my cell? Purple pine doesn't warp. It hardly even woofs. Or tweets. It merely hardens in place. That's why it's such valuable wood, that has to be protected by being included on grand old estates like ours. So that only selective cutting is done, to thin the groves, no commercial strip-cutting. We want to hew it now, while it's soft.'

'Oh.' She was of exactly the same intelligence as he, and had had the same education, but that particular fact had slipped by her. Sometimes they had substituted for each other during boring classes, so one could pick up sundry facts the other missed. She was beginning to diverge more obviously from her brother, and the mask of identical garb in public would not be effective much longer.

She brought out her measure, touched the little disc to the base of the trunk, walked along the tree until the readout indicated ten metres, then touched the trunk again. A red dot now marked the spot.

14

He trimmed the base smooth, then severed the trunk at the ten-metre mark. The log shifted and settled more comfortably into the spongy ground. Now he fiddled with a special control, adjusting the saw. 'Actually, I'm doing this for you. I'll have to marry another aristocratic clone; you'll get to pick a real person to family with.'

'Want to bet? There are more males of our generation than females. That's why they operated on me to turn me female, hedging the bet. I'll probably have to marry the clone, while you get to graze among the common herd.'

'There is that,' he agreed. 'I must admit, there are some commoners I wouldn't mind hitching to. Clonedom is seeming more sterile these days; so few of our kind have any real fire or ambition. They're mostly all socialites, forcing us to play that game too. Stand back, doll. This can be tricky.'

The laser beam shot out way beyond its prior length. He aligned it with the length of the log, then levered it slowly so that it made a burn in the bark from end to end. He moved the beam over and made a similar burn, a quarter of the way round. Then he readjusted the saw and used the short cutting beam to trim an edge lengthwise along one line. A meter on the saw showed him precisely what orientation to maintain to keep the cut correctly angled.

'You know, someday the other clones will have to find out about you,' he remarked as he worked. Jesse was never silent for very long. 'We can't keep it secret forever.'

She knew it. She had nightmares about premature, involuntary exposure. Yet she responded bravely enough: 'If you find an aristocratic spouse soon, we can. It would be nice to save this hedge for another generation, protecting our line. Once the other clones catch on, they'll all be doing it, and our line will have no advantage.'

He nodded soberly. With four cuts, he had a beam roughly square in cross section, ten metres long. The irregularities of his trimming only made it seem authentically hand-hewn. 'Where could we get a finer ridge-beam than that?' he asked rhetorically.

'Nowhere,' she answered, impressed.

'Still mad at me for buying the saw?'

'No, of course not.'

'Five thousand credits – you could buy a lot of silly perfume for that, to make commoners think you're sexy.'

'I'll take the saw.'

He grinned, pleased. 'Make that literal. You hew the next beam. Why should I do all the work?'

'And the castle mortgage paid off,' she said, liking the notion better. 'That's the first time our family's been solvent in a generation.'

'Still, considering the danger of the mission—' he teased.

'Oh, shut up!'

'Now you know how to turn it on and off, Jess. The saw, I mean. It's not heavy; just keep your arm steady and your dugs out of the way; don't let them dangle in the beam.'

'I don't dangle, *you* do!' But she accepted the saw, eager to try her skill. She had, of course, been raised in the male tradition, and there were aspects of it she rather enjoyed, such as hewing beams.

'I don't dangle when I'm with someone interesting.' He took the measuring disc and marked off another ten-metre section. 'Sever it here.'

She started towards him. 'The trunk, not me!' he protested, stepping back with his hands protectively in front of him.

She shrugged as if disappointed and set the saw at the mark. The laser moved into the wood. 'I can't even feel it!'

'Right. There's no recoil, no snag with laser. Just watch the beam, make sure it stays white. With this tool we can saw boards, shape columns, polish panels, drill holes – anything! I plan to cut wooden pegs to hold it together, along with notching. This saw has settings for carving out pegs, notches, and assorted bevels and curlicues; you just

16

have to programme it. We can build our whole house with this one saw!'

'You're right,' she said, no longer even attempting to be flip. 'We need this machine. It is worth the credit. You just be sure you report for that mission on time!'

'Precious little short of death itself could keep me away,' he assured her. 'And the Society of Hosts insurance would cover the advance, if I died before reporting, so even then you'd keep the money. But it's not just the money I'm doing it for; I'm tired of this dreary aristocratic life. I want real adventure for a change! I want to go out among the stars, travel to the farthest places, experience alien existence, see the universe!'

'Yes . . .' she breathed, envying him his coming adventure.

'You just make sure I wake up in time to report for transfer when—'

The log severed before she was aware of it. It dropped suddenly and rolled towards them. It was massive, half a metre thick at the cut: weight enough to crush a leg. Jessica screamed in temporary panic and swung the valuable saw out of the way, her finger locked on the trigger. Jesse grabbed for her, trying to draw her bodily out of harm's way.

The wildly shifting laser beam passed across his spine. His shirt fell open, cleanly cut, but for a moment there was no blood. He fell, his arms looped about her thighs.

The rolling log stopped short of his body, balked by the chance irregularity of the ground. Jessica, acting with numb relief, drew her finger from the trigger, turned off the saw, set it down carefully, and caught her brother under the arms as he slid slowly face first towards the turf. 'Oh, Jesse, are you hurt?'

But even as she spoke, she knew he was. His aura, which really merged with hers, was fluctuating wildly. The beam, set to cut wood, had touched him only briefly – not enough

17

to cut his body in half or even to cut his backbone, but sufficient to penetrate a centimetre or so. Elsewhere it would have made a nasty gash in the flesh; across his spine it was critical.

His body was paralysed, but he retained consciousness and speech. 'Jess—' he gasped as she rolled him over and tenderley brushed the dirt from his face. 'My aura – is it?'

'Jess, the beam cut into your spinal cord,' she said, horrified. 'Your aura is irregular.' She knew the extent if not the precise nature of the injury because the sympathetic response in her own aura touched her spine, lending a superficial numbness to her legs. His aura irregular? It was an understatement. 'I'll call an ambulance.' She fumbled for her communicator. The health wing would arrive in minutes.

'No, Jess!' he rasped. 'I may live – but hospital'd take weeks! I have only two days.'

'To hell with two days!' she cried, the tears overflowing. 'You can't go on that mission now! Even if you weren't badly injured, your aura would never pass. It reflects your physical condition. It has to be fully healthy to pass, you know that! I'll take care of you, I promise!'

'Kill me,' he said. 'Say it was part of the accident. Just pass the laser across my chest, slowly, so as to intersect the heart—'

'No!' she screamed. 'Jess, what are you saying?'

'The insurance – death benefit – only if I die, it covers—'

'*Jess!*'

'Jess, I can't renege on that mission. The advance would be forfeited, the insurance invalid, and we'd lose the whole estate and the family reputation. Have Flowers pick up the body; he'll cover for you. He's been in this business a long time, he's doctored family skeletons before, you can bet on it, and he's completely loyal to us. He'll do it. I'd rather die than—'

'Jess, I won't do it!' she cried. 'I know Flowers would

18

cover for us. I don't care. I love you, clone-brother! I don't care what—'

But he was unconscious; she knew by the change in his aura. He had fought for consciousness until his message was out, then let go.

She brought the communicator to her mouth – and paused, comprehending the position they were in. The first flush of emotion was phasing into the broader reality of their situation. She could save her brother's life – for what? For a remaining life of poverty and shame? He had spoken truly! He was a joker, but never a coward. He would prefer to die. Now, cleanly, painlessly, with a certain private honour, leaving her to carry on the reputation of the family and maintain the millennium-old estate. She knew this – for his aura was hers, his mind was hers, and she shared this preference. They were aristocrats! If she had been injured in such a way as to forfeit honour and fortune together, death would seem a welcome alternative.

She could do it. She had the nerve, bred into the royal line, and because she was royal, she would not be interrogated. Her word and the visible evidence would suffice. Flowers would employ his professional touch to make the case tight. She could kill her brother-self, and save the family honour and fortune. It was feasible.

Yet she did love him, as she loved herself. How could she face a world without him? Though he might later marry, and she also, with one being royal and the other becoming a commoner, they would always be closest to each other, clone-siblings.

She had to decide – now. Before his metabolism adapted to the injury, making a biochemical/aural analysis possible that would show the separate nature of her act. Now, this minute – or never.

Jessica picked up the saw and held it over Jesse's body. She knew the expedient course – yet her love opposed it with almost equal force. Was there no way out?

19

1

Alien Encounter

Heem of Highfalls emerged from the transfer chamber and followed the HydrO ahead of him towards the acclimatization wing. Another HydrO host rolled into the transfer chamber behind him. The operation had to move with precision; there were more than three hundred HydrOs to process as nearly simultaneously as possible.

Yet Heem moved without vigour, hardly perceiving his surroundings. A squirt of flavoured water struck him. 'Thirty-nine! Are you conscious?'

Heem yanked himself to a better semblance of awareness. 'Yes, yes,' he sprayed. 'Merely adapting to my transfer-guest.'

'Then get to your chamber. You have bypassed it.'

So he had. He was up to forty-two. Heem reversed course and moved to thirty-nine. He picked up the vapour taste of it and rolled into its aperture.

The chamber was small and comfortable. The air was fresh and neutral, with plenty of free hydrogen. 'You have three chronosprays before release,' the room informed him.

Heem collapsed. In his subconscious he dreamed the forbidden memory. He was a juvenile again, among his HydrO peers. In that secret time before he metamorphosed into adult status. He was rolling with his siblings in the beautiful ghetto of Highfalls, bouncing across the rock faces, through the chill rivulets, and around the huge soft domes of the trees. They were racing, their jets growing warm with the competitive effort.

Hoom was leading at the moment. He had the strongest torque jets and usually gained on direct-land terrain. Heem was second, closely followed by Hiim. Haam trailed; he had a clogged jet and it hampered his progress.

Heem had been gaining jet strength recently and had always had finesse in liquid. Today was especially good; his metabolism was functioning better than ever before. Now Hoom was tiring, becoming too warm; his conversion efficiency was declining slightly. Heem remained relatively cool, yet was putting out more water; he was gaining. The feeling of victory was growing.

Hoom, as leader, chose the route. Hoping to improve his position, he plunged into the highfalls itself.

It was an effective tactic. Heem plunged in after him, and suffered the retardation his cooler body was liable to. He lost position. But soon his liquid finesse helped him, enabling him to recover quickly, and he was gaining again. He caught up to Hoom, then passed him as they emerged from the water.

'Lout!' Hoom spurted. He fired a barrage of jets at Heem in an unsporting manoeuvre. Some of them were needlejets that stung. Heem, alert for such foul play, fired one needle back, scoring on Hoom's most proximate spout as Hoom's own jet faded.

'Cheat!' Hoom sprayed, enraged. He fired another barrage which Heem countered with another precise shot. Heem had the most accurate needles of them all.

Now the others caught up. 'No fighting, no fighting!' they protested.

'He needled me, trying to pass!' Hoom sprayed.

For a moment, the audacity of the lie overwhelmed Heem, and he was tasteless. Thus it seemed he offered no refutation, and that was tantamount to confession.

But Haam was cautious about such judgement. 'I did not taste the initiation of this exchange,' he sprayed. 'But it was Hoom, not Heem, who needlejetted me at the outset of this race, clogging my jet.'

Perceiving the shift of opinion, Hoom took the offensive again. 'What use in winning a race, anyway? We have raced

21

every day, now one winning, now another. How does it profit us? Which of you has the nerve to roll up to a real challenge?'

'Why roll to *any* challenge?' Hiim enquired reasonably. 'We have no needs we cannot accommodate passively. So long as there is air, we are comfortable.'

'*You* may be comfortable,' Hoom replied. '*I* want to know what lies beyond this valley. Are there others of our own kind, or are we alone?'

'Why not go, then, and report back to us?' Hiim asked him.

'I do not wish to go alone. It is a long, hard roll over the mountain range, perhaps dangerous. If we all go together—'

'I find difficulty and danger no suitable challenge,' Hiim sprayed. 'It seems foolish to me to risk my convenient life in such manner.'

But Heem found himself agreeing with Hoom. 'I do not entirely relish the roll up the mountain slope or the prospect of drastic shift in environment,' he sprayed. 'Yet my mind suffers dulling and tedium in the absence of challenge. I value my mind more than my convenience. Therefore I will undertake the roll up the mountain with Hoom.'

Hoom was uncommunicative, caught in the awkwardness of being supported by the party he had fouled. It was Haam who sprayed next. 'I too am curious about the wider environment, but disinclined to undertake the enormous effort of such a roll. I would go if I could ascertain an easier mode of travel.'

'Make it really easy,' Hiim scoffed. 'Ride a flatfloater.'

There was a general spray of mirth. The flatfloater was a monster whose biology was similar to their own. It drew its energy from the air, merging hydrogen with oxygen, with a constant residue of water. But its application differed. Instead of using jets of waste-water to roll itself over land or through the river, it used them to push itself up into the

22

air a small distance. This required a lot of energy; in fact the force of its jets was so strong, and the heat of its conversion so great, that a large proportion of its elimination was gaseous. Water expanded greatly when vaporized, so that the volume of exhaust was much larger than the volume of its intake. Hot water vapour blasted down from it, billowing out in disgusting clouds, condensing as it cooled, coating the surroundings. The sapient HydrOs stayed well clear of the flatfloaters!

Hoom, however, was foolhardy. 'Why not?' he demanded. 'The upper surface of the floater is cool enough, where the air intakes are. It indents towards the centre. We could ride safely there—'

It might just be possible! Their analytic minds fastened on this notion. But almost immediately objections developed. 'How would we guide it?' Haam asked.

'How would we get on it – or off it?' Heem added.

Hoom found himself under challenge to defend a notion he had not originated, for indeed if a flatfloater could be harnessed, it could surely take them anywhere rapidly – even over the mountain. If he could establish the feasibility of the flatfloater, he could make them all join the travelling. 'The floater is stupid. When it feels distress, it flees it. We could needle it on the side opposite the direction we wish it to go, and it would flee – carrying us along.'

They considered, realizing the possibility.

'And to board it,' Hoom sprayed excitedly, 'the floater descends to bathe itself, for it has no jets on its upper surface and the sun dehydrates it. Periodically it must immerse itself in water. We have only to lurk at its bath-region and roll aboard as it submerges. To deboard we must simply force it near a slope and roll off the higher side. Since the floater is always level, the drop to ground will be slight.'

They considered further, and it seemed feasible. Hoom

had surmounted the challenge of method; now they were under onus to implement it. Since none came up with a reason to refute this course of action, they found themselves committed.

Heem was excited but not fully hydrogenated by the notion. He wanted to explore, but feared the possible consequence. So he went along, as did the others. The physical race had become something else, and Hoom had retained the initiative.

Given the specific challenge, they set about meeting it without immediate emphasis on the long-range goal. They located the spoor of the flatfloater, in the form of taste lingering on vegetation and ground, diffuse but definite. They traced it in the direction of freshness, locating the floater's favourite haunts. It preferred open water, not too deep, with no large growths near enough to disrupt the takeoff. That made approach more difficult.

They decided to lie in wait underwater. It was more difficult to breathe in liquid, since it was in effect a bath of their own waste product, but there were tiny bubbles of gas in it that sufficed for slow metabolism, for a while. In flowing water it was possible to remain submerged indefinitely, for new bubbles were carried in to replace the used ones, and the non-hydrogenated water would be carried away. However, flowing water tended to be cool.

The advantages and disadvantages were mixed. Their ambient taste would be diminished by the reduced rate of metabolism necessitated by the limitation of hydrogen, and the surrounding water would dilute that taste, and the slow current would carry it away, until their precise location was virtually indistinguishable. The danger was that if the wait were too long, they could be cooled to the level of inadequate functioning. This had happened to a former peer; he had soaked himself in chill water to abate a fever, had slept and never awoken. He remained there now, functioning on the level of a beast, his sapience gone. It had

24

been a cruel lesson for the rest of them: one of many. Do not suffer your body to cool too far, lest the upkeep of your sapience deteriorate!

Heem remembered a time when thirty or more sapients had inhabited Highfalls; now only the four of them remained.

However, the season was warmer now, and the river was more comfortable. Heem wondered about that: what made the seasons change. The heat of the sun beat down throughout the year, yet in the cold season it came from a different angle and lacked force. Obviously the cold inhibited the sun, whose presence they knew of only by the heat of its direct radiation against their skins, or possibly the different course of the sun inhibited the season – but why was there a change? Heem had pondered this riddle many times, but come to no certain conclusion. The answer seemed to lie elsewhere than in this valley, perhaps across the mountain range. The more he considered the ramifications of this project, the more he liked it. Surely there was danger – but surely there was information, too. Since ignorance had caused most of the deaths of his peers, especially the massive early slaughter before the thirty he remembered had emerged from anonymity, knowledge was worth considerable risk.

They settled under the water at the site, hoping the monster would come soon. Heem, required to be still and communicative for an indefinite period in the proximity of potential danger, found his thoughts turning to fundamental speculations. Where had he and his siblings come from? How had they known how to intercommunicate? What was their destiny?

The third question had an obvious and ugly answer: they were destined to die. Most had succumbed already. Perhaps escape from the valley was their only hope of survival. Heem felt his own mortality, the incipience and inevitability of death. Was there any point in opposing it?

25

Why, then, *was* he opposing it?

But he rebounded from this line of thinking. He must be suffering the chill of the water, of immobility. He raised his metabolic level slightly, hoping the increased flavour diffusing about him would not be noticeable to his companions. Maybe they were doing the same.

Now he pursued the other questions. Communication? Somehow they had always known how to spray and jet and needle flavour at each other, and quickly learned to interpret the nuances of taste to obtain meaning. Certain flavours portended certain things, as was natural. Sweetness denoted affirmation, bitterness negation. From that point, the shades of taste flowed naturally to ever-greater definition. Why this was so seemed inherent in the nature of the species.

What was their origin? They had all appeared together in the valley, as nearly as he could ascertain. All had been physically small; he knew that because landmarks, boulders, and such things that had once seemed large now seemed small, and it seemed reasonable that it was the living things who had changed. All had been able to fend for themselves from the outset, lacking only the cautions of experience. Any could have saved themselves from any of the demises that had taken them, had they possessed Heem's present knowledge then. Surely they had come, innocently, from somewhere – but where? There was no answer; that was beyond the beginning.

There had to be an origin, he decided. Sapient creatures did not appear from nowhere. Otherwise more creatures of his kind would have appeared. This had not happened. So it seemed they had all been spontaneously generated in one single burst of creation. Or they had all been placed here, and left to their own survival. Heem found the latter alternative more convincing. That explained what had happened, but not why. Why would anyone or anything do this?

No matter how he reasoned it out, Heem could not roll up with an explanation he liked. Whatever had done this thing was evil. If he ever found opportunity to fight back—

The monster was coming! Heem felt the vibration in the water, separate from the vibration in the air, as the thing settled low. The massive jets blasted down into the water, initiating turbulence that was uncomfortably forceful. Only jets of phenomenal power could create reaction of this magnitude, and it was growing rapidly.

Heem was abruptly afraid. He had suppressed his nervousness before; now it burst out into uncontrolled random jetting. All his small pores opened, and the sphincter muscles of his body forced his reserves of water out. It was a panic reaction, accomplishing nothing except the depletion of his immediate motive fluid.

With an effort he controlled himself, and became aware of the diffusing taste of the exudates of his companions. They had wet down too, though that was anomalous here within the water. That reassured him considerably. Almost enough to make him want to roll on, on through this wild scheme.

The flatfloater was gliding in for its submergence much faster than any sapient creature could. Before Heem could formulate some objection, some reason to quit this project, the huge disc cut into the water and planed down. The turbulence was suddenly terrible. Bubbles swirled by in such profusion as to make froth of the water. Heem was rolled right out of his niche by the bubble current and wafted upwards a short distance. He drifted momentarily in the eddy, perceiving his companions in similar straits, before stabilizing. But he realized that this was fortunate, because otherwise he could have been stuck directly below the settling monster. Its weight would not be oppressive, buoyed by the water; but if it remained long, the four of them would have been trapped. The warmth of its gross body might keep them from cooling to the point of deterioration, which was good, but the low hydrogen of its elimination could stifle them.

The floater drifted to the bottom. The eddy drew Heem in towards the creature's surface, and this was another excellent roll. With minimal guidance, Heem was able to sink on to the upper surface of the disc. His companions did the same. They had in this surprisingly simple fashion achieved the first stage of their objective.

Yet the remainder hardly seemed promising. It was one thing to contemplate riding a floater, but quite another to do it. The many uncertainties of the venture loomed much larger now. How would they stay on, if the monster manoeuvred violently? Suppose it did not respond to their guidance?

The floater gave them little time to reflect. Its intakes were on the upper side, and though it lacked the acute perception of the sapients, it could hardly miss their presence in this case. Alarmed, it jetted upwards, its progress slanting because of the resistance of the water. The current across its surface became fierce, but at the same time the suction of its large intakes held them against it. They could not roll off – not while the floater's metabolism was active.

The flatfloater rose out of the water with a burst of meaningless spray. Sapients sprayed only for communication, emitting multiple fine jets of water flavoured with the chemical nuances that constituted meaning. It was an effective mode. If the neighbour to be addressed was too far distant for spray, a specific squirt could serve as well; in fact, such solitary jets were employed when the conversation was private. Once the residue flowed off the receiving skin, it lost its meaning in the welter of background contaminants, leaving news only that there had been communication. Thus public and private dialogues were matters of focus. Especially pointed or private messages were needled, as with insults during a fracas.

Heem had pondered whether a better system could exist, and concluded that this was unlikely. In fact, he suspected that intelligent dialogue would be almost impossible by any other means. The fact that none of the animals or plants had either sapience or precise communication mechanisms bolstered his view. Sapience and language and refined taste went together.

But such conjectures were out of place amidst violent action! Airborne, the floater was now fully aware of its burden, and did not seem to like it. Their four bodies had to be hampering its intake, though the majority of its pores remained uncovered. The monster cut its jets, then fired them all at once, bucking with horrible force.

Haam, nearest the rim, lost purchase and rolled off. Heem picked up the spray of Haam's despairing exclamation, for they were now high up. The fall would surely be fatal. The sapients of Highfalls were now abruptly reduced to three.

Again Heem experienced a wash of emotion, as though he had been doused with burning liquid. (This had happened once, when he ventured too near a source of hot water in the valley. Two companions had perished then, but his burns had been survivable. It had been just one more episode in his education.) Who had been responsible for Haam's demise? Not the floater, who only reacted to the unfamiliar burden on it. Not Hiim or Hoom or Heem himself, who only tried to get out of this dangerous valley. Who but the mysterious entity who had deserted them here!

The floater, under the impression it had dislodged its burden, smoothed its flight and settled nearer to land. Even with its great strength of jet, it could not maintain high elevation long. Its most effective travelling mode was close enough to the ground so that the backwash of its gaseous emission provided additional buoyancy. That was why they had not anticipated the kind of hazard Haam had experienced: fall from a height. What other surprises were coming?

There was a spray on Heem's skin, distorted by the velocity of air passage. 'Guidance,' the spray communicated, once he made it out. It bore Hoom's stigma.

Ah, yes. In the excitement of this adventure, he had forgotten that they planned to control the direction of motion of the monster. Could it actually be done?

After a brief exchange, they decided to let Hoom make the first try, since it had been his idea. Hoom flattened himself, overlapping more intake area of the floater, so that he was better anchored by suction, and let fly with what was calculated to be a painful needlejet.

The reaction was immediate and formidable. The floater took off exactly as they had surmised, but much more powerfully than anticipated. Hiim, caught unprepared, ripped free of the suction and dropped off the back. He did not even have time to make his despairing spray, or if he did, it was lost in the wind. Would he survive? It was possible, depending on the terrain he struck and his velocity of impact. Possible, but not likely. HydrOs had soft bodies, easily damaged by concussion. More than one of Heem's former siblings had destroyed themselves by rolling accidentally into rocks and splattering themselves across the landscape.

Now they were two. Heem and Hoom clung by staying flat against a broad section of suction. Soon the monster slowed, satisfied that it had escaped its threat. It was terribly stupid.

They relaxed slightly and surveyed the terrain. They were moving through the merged tastes of the exudates of hillside plants, and the trace reduction of atmospheric pressure verified the elevation. The mass of the moving floater compressed the air ahead of it, and waves of this compression reflected from the irregularities of the landscape. In short, they had an excellent vibration-perception

30

of the scene to buttress the typical taste of it.

Heem was sorry his friends had fallen off, but there was nothing he could do about it. He was all too likely to be the next. He did not know how he could get off the back of the monster safely – and after what had happened, he didn't want to. If he desisted now, all their effort and losses would have been in vain. He had to go on, to taste the other side of the mountain.

Hoom had come to a similar conclusion. 'We cannot guide this creature to any gentle halt,' he sprayed. 'We have to go on until it tires.'

Heem angled a moderately sharp jet into the hide of the floater. The monster veered, fleeing this new irritation. They had control, of a sort.

'Up, over the mountain,' Heem sprayed. 'We have to know – what lies beyond.'

Unwittingly responsive to their directives, the flatfloater jetted up the slope.

Heem broke from his memory-dream, sweating. His body was soaked with the fluid of his meaninglessly leaking jets. Why did he have to keep remembering? Not only was it illegal, it was quite awkward. He knew with a sick certainty that he would soon experience the continuation of that memory, and he hoped it wouldn't happen at a bad time.

Now he had a more immediate concern. Still semi-conscious in the acclimatization chamber, Heem reviewed his situation. He had been fleeing the confinement and danger of his home valley, there in his memory-dream; now he was still fleeing it, in a more complicated fashion. He was in trouble with the law/custom and had to get off-planet soon. The technological equivalent of a flatfloater was a spaceship; instead of escaping one valley, he had to escape one planet. Only through this specialized mission could he get a ship. So he had volunteered for host-duty, and qualified on the basis of his background, and entered the transfer chamber to receive his transfer aura—

And instead had received a staggering aural blow. Only sheer determination had carried him here before consciousness departed. What had happened?

He knew what had *not* happened. He had not received his transferee – and without that alien aura, he would be disqualified for the mission, and be planet-bound. That was doom.

He had wasted half his private orientation time, just recovering from the shock. He had never tasted news of a transfer failure like this before. Normally a transferee either arrived safely with the host, or it bounced, in which case the host felt nothing. The days of warring between transfer and host were over; Melody of Mintaka of far Segment Etamin had arranged that. Today the host-entity always had control. He could yield it to the transfer identity, but could take it back at will. The transferee could not knock him out. Therefore how could the act of transfer hit him like that?

Could it have been a function of his malady? Another aspect of the thing that had cost him his combat ability? He had been one of the leading combat specialists of his kind, owing to his superlatively sharp and accurate needles. He had become one of the few who could expect to overcome a healthy Squam in fair encounter. Normally a HydrO could beat an Erb, and a Squam could beat a Hydro, and an Erb could beat a Squam, making a vicious circle in this local eddy of the Segment. But exceptional individuals could break that circle, and Heem of Highfalls had been one. That was why he had qualified for this mission.

The mission was shrouded in secrecy, no faintest taste of its specific nature seeping out. But it was rumoured that it involved Planet Ggoff, in a neutral tract of Segmentary space. Fifty or more of the thousand species of Thousand-star might survive and reproduce on Ggoff without technological aids, but there were only three within

32

convenient access range, so those three were the obvious hosts: Erb, Squam, and HydrO.

Logic filled in much of the rest. There was something on Ggoff that virtually every species in the Segment desperately wanted, so by Segment custom more binding than war, a competition was being held. It might be a good Iridium mine, or a safe mutation-inducing chemical, or a superior and useful species of vegetation; protocol was the same. Competitions were the chief source of Segment entertainment and status, and the near presence of one caused waves of excitement to wash through local Systems. It had been Heem's fortune that a competition utilizing HydrO hosts had occurred at this time; without this avenue offplanet, he would have been sunk in a dire mire.

Of course he had fashioned much of this luck himself. He had remained in hiding while keeping constantly alert for any means of departure, and had made sure no news of his disability reached the administration files. He had waited to file for the competition until the last mini-chronospray, so that there would not be time for the Competition Index to assimilate his legal compromise before approving him.

'Time to proceed to mission orientation and transfer verification,' the chamber sprayed.

Already! That jolt had disrupted his time sense, too. Not only did he lack a transferee, he had no notion how he was going to proceed.

Only one thing was certain: he had to get into the competition. Because he had to have a spaceship. He could not roll offplanet by his own jets!

The competition participants were moving towards the indoctrination rendezvous. Heem rolled out of his chamber and joined the throng. The liquid of group motion was washing over the floor as each person jet-rolled forward, confusing individual identities. That was good; Heem did not wish to meet anyone who knew him.

But such confusion would not help him get through the

transfer recheck. There would be no anonymity there! The moment they discovered he had no transferee, he would be voided for the competition – and subject to the local law. He had to pass this mountain, lest he perish in the valley.

The passage debouched into an assembly chamber. The HydrO hosts spread out across it and occupied depressions in the floor keyed by impregnated taste. Heem found niche 39 and settled into place exactly like a legitimate host. He was fortunate that the indoctrination came before verification. Now he had a mini-spray more time to think. He had, in effect, to devise a way of riding the floater out of this valley, bypassing transferee verification.

The large ceiling public-spray system blasted on. The mechanically flavoured spume wafted down like the effusion of a flatfloater, raucous and barely intelligible.

Heem's immediate neighbour, number 38, jetted a semi-private groan at him: 'Why the rot can't they fix their churned-up nozzles? This is a pain in my skin!'

Heem jetted back a needle of agreement, but his mind was elsewhere. How could he pass the checkpoint without a transfer aura? He might finesse it, for the personality, claiming he was spraying for his visitor. But there could be no fooling the aura-pattern analysis of the machine.

'YOU WILL BE (UNINTELLIGIBLE) IN ORDER DURING THIS (UNINTELLIGIBLE) BRIEFING,' the froth proclaimed.

'Shall I fill in the blanks?' 38 enquired acidly. 'You will be dismembered in order during this disgusting briefing.'

Heem squirted a polite chuckle. HydrOs did not have members, so this was either a peculiarly obscene implication, or an image drawn from the mind of 38's transferee, who could indeed be a membered species. Regardless, the translation was clever.

Could Heem profit by the confusion engendered by the poor public spray? Unlikely; the machines didn't care about communication, just auras.

'The outline of the competition is this,' the public spray continued, abating its volume and gaining clarity in the process. There had been too much water in the spray, before. Machines normally became more intelligible as they flowed, cleaning out pockets of dead fluid and contamination. 'Nominal three hundred and thirty-three host-transfer sets of three physical species will proceed individually to spaceport where sixty-six single-entity space vessels await arrival of entrants.'

'Sixty-six!' 38 jetted. 'That's only enough for one in five of us!'

One in five. So this was to be a stages competition, with established elimination points. That made Heem's situation rougher yet. He had thought that all qualified HydrO entrants would receive spaceships, and would rendezvous at Planet Ggoff for the competition proper. But it seemed there was to be a contest for the ships themselves.

He could not afford the slightest delay in processing, for only the first entities to reach the ships would make the cut. Once he got offplanet, it wouldn't matter much if he didn't make the next cut; he would be on his own. Right now he had to move – fast. Somehow. He could not simply roll out early and go for the spaceport; they would have safeguards against that sort of thing.

'This start is being duplicated at the selected sites in colonies Squam and Erb,' the public spittle continued. 'The total number of ships is two hundred, fairly divided between the three hosts. Those who acquire ships will jet off for a planet preprogrammed in the guidance systems. The specific route can be modified marginally by the participants; some will arrive earlier than others. At the landing site there will be fifty single-entity tractors pro-grammed for the competition objective.'

'One in four!' 38 squirted. 'That reduces it to one in twenty, onsite.'

'They have to reduce it to one in a thousand before it

finishes,' Heem needled irritably. 'That's the object.'

'Swish, that's right,' 38 agreed, surprised.

But the public spray was still spuming. 'Onplanet, you will proceed as rapidly as possible to the site. The tractors will require one refuelling en route; fuel is available in limited quantity at selected stations. We anticipate that only ten tractors will achieve the objective, perhaps less, perhaps none.'

'Then the competition intensifies,' 38 needled.

'Why not let your transferee jet for a while?' Heem needled back. 'Let him stretch his limbs.'

That taste-faded his loquacious neighbour. None of the hosts were giving away the identities of their transferees. If it were known who represented what Star, a given contestant's liabilities could be fathomed, to his disadvantage. For example, the citizens of System Mebr were glassy, easily shattered in their natural state; they tended to shy away from rocky terrain, even when occupying hosts who were not shatterable, such as HydrOs. If Heem had to compete with a Mebr, he would try to force it into a canyon. But if he thought it was a Mebr, and went the rocky route, and it turned out to be a mineral-eating Tuvn, Heem would be the one at a disadvantage. Tuvns became highly excited by the presence of naked rock and put on their greatest energy in canyon situations. A competing HydrO could get himself splattered, crowding such a creature. So this competition would begin with the strategy of knowing one's rivals. And 38 had already given away part of the nature of his transferee.

Heem himself was secure in that sense. No one could fathom the liabities of his transferee – because he had none. That was the greatest liability of all.

'Swoon of Sweetswamp, report for verification,' a taste drifted through. Heem was irritated; private calls were supposed to dissipate without impinging on neighbouring sites. The public spray descended on all, but spot needles were strictly one-person efforts.

'Are there any questions?' the public spray enquired. Then, after a pause: 'We are in receipt of several questions, which we shall answer in order. First, what is the object of this competition? Answer: that information is classified. You will be informed when you are in flight to the target planet.'

Now Heem got a squirt from one side and a drift from the other: 'Probably hunting sapient flatfloaters in hostile wilderness.' 'Swoon of Sweetswamp, number 40, report for verification. Second jet.'

Why didn't Swoon of Sweetswamp answer? He was likely to find himself washed out of the contest before it even started. His transferee-Star wouldn't like that! 'Sweetswamp, roll your hulk over there!' Heem jetted at the errant neighbour.

There was no response. Heem was tempted to let Swoon wash out, but decided to give him one more chance. He jetted out of his niche and rolled the short distance across to nudge the inattentive HydrO – and found the spot empty.

No wonder Swoon hadn't answered his summons! Swoon was absent from his assigned place. Probably he had got confused and settled out of place, in niche or 400 instead of forty. That had been foolish. Of course a foolish HydrO would be a poor host, and would wash out of the competition rapidly, so perhaps it made no difference. Only one of the thousand would prevail, and the sooner the fools were eliminated, the better it would be for the real contenders.

Except that Heem himself, no fool, was just as likely to wash out now as was Swoon. Because there seemed to be no way to get past the transferee verification. How ironic that he, who for all they knew was the most able entrant-host, should be eliminated by a transfer malfunction. Had he been in Swoon's situation, he would not have squandered his chance like this!

'Swoon of Sweetswamp. Third jet. Report for verification, or forfeit.'

Suddenly Heem rolled rapidly from this region. He had a notion, a slim chance hardly worth tasting, but if it worked—

He rolled up to the nearest open verification alcove. 'Swoon of Sweetswamp reporting as summoned,' he squirted.

'Put your transferee on,' the alcove jetted impersonally.

'Transferee communicating,' Heem squirted after a pause. He made the squirt deliberately sloppy, as if an alien mind were operating it.

'State your home-Star, transferee.'

'I will not!' Heem squirted, almost missing the alcove receptor-surface in his supposed clumsiness. 'I will not give away my nature to your government. Use your programmed aura cross-check; that is all that is permitted.'

The beauty of it was that if the machine malfunctioned, Heem would be through verification. But if, as was far more likely, the machine showed that only a single aura occupied this body, it would be Swoon of Sweetswamp who was disqualified, not Heem of Highfalls. In this manner he could gamble and lose without paying the penalty. Of course, he would still have to figure out some other way to fool the machine, but he would worry about that in due course. Maybe they didn't really have aura readouts here; they might be depending on self-identification. So if he could pretend that—

'You are Heem of Highfalls,' the alcove jetted. 'What are you attempting?'

The taste of success dissipated. They had cross-checked his aura, and nabbed him. Now all he could do was ad lib. 'Swoon's name was called, and he was absent, so I tried to cover the taste for him so he would not be unfairly eliminated.'

'Swoon is a friend of yours?'

38

'Indubitably.' He could hardly afford the truth. 'Of course, we are competing against each other – that is, our transferees are – but here at the initial stage we are cooperating. You know how it is.' But he knew the machine would *not* know how it was.

'You are lying, Heem. You were not aware that Swoon is female.'

This was no machine jetting! The anonymous interviewer was entirely too clever, setting traps for him. But Heem fought it through: 'So I tried to get processed before my turn. My transferee wants to win this competition, for his Star.'

The alcove sprayed out a rude profusion of mirth. 'For *his* Star? Not likely!'

Something was wrong here. All the HydrOs were merely hosts for the representatives of the Thousand Stars. Why should his endorsement of the obvious be so humorous – unless the interviewer knew he had no transferee? Yet why continue this dialogue, in that case? They should just roll him out. So Heem waited without responding, knowing they had caught him – and that they had something else in mind. He knew there was heavy politicking in any Segment competition, and possibly he was about to get a taste of it here.

'You are aware that three species are serving as hosts for this engagement,' the alcove jetted. 'Roughly one third of the thousand are HydrO. All are good, healthy, apt specimens, approved by the Society of Hosts; there is no foolishness there. But there is one exception. No entity with a criminal record is permitted in a competition.'

Oh, they really had him!

'You, of course, are the exception,' the alcove continued. 'The law awaits you outside. You lack Society of Hosts approval. Your entire career betrays an unscrupulous and low-cunning personality. You possess a combat skill that is suspicious; you could not maintain it legally. You made application to enter this competition under false pretences. In summation, you are a disreputable entity.'

'You were aware of that when you admitted me?' Heem enquired, surprised.

'It was your primary recommendation.'

The wrongness magnified. 'I am not certain I comprehend your direction.'

'A little individual background, Heem. You are aware that there are approximately one thousand entrants to this competition, utilizing three host species, the Star of representation determined by the transfer entity.'

'I am aware,' Heem jetted nervously. Why were they repeating this basic information? Had they nulled his transfer deliberately, punishing him?

'But the three host species – what of their entrants?'

'Same applies,' Heem sprayed. 'Transfer in another entity of the same species, to be the representative. Two minds are still better than one, if their skills are complementary.'

'Or use the host as the representative, and transfer in an alien expert.'

Heem considered that. 'Could be quite a combination! If you transferred a renegade Squam into a dominant HydrO host, he'd be a potent competitor against both Squams and HydrOs.'

'Precisely. Odds against the success of that combination would decline from one in a thousand to one in one hundred or so, perhaps even lower, with the right combination.'

'Still, one chance in a hundred is a long one. Any one of the thousand could do as well merely by cheating a little.'

'Oh, there is no cheating in a Segment competition,' the interviewer squirted hastily. 'That would lead to voiding of any success achieved.'

'Could be hard to watch every detail, though,' Heem suggested, intrigued by the theoretical situation. 'This thing is basically a race, and I've been in enough local races to know that the winner is seldom completely clean.' He remembered how Hoom had needled him, back in the juvenile stage at Highfalls. His experience in subsequent life had shown him this was typical; the scrupulous seldom finished first.

'You are an excellent racer,' the interviewer jetted in an aside. 'This was salient in your profile.'

'Are you implying I am unclean?'

'The Competition Authority does not accept unclean individuals. We merely have need of a completely competent representative, with the strongest motive to succeed. Naturally we will tolerate no evidence of wrong-rolling, but since it would be an embarrassment to Star HydrO to have a winner with a soiled record, a pardon for your past activities has been filed. You are completely clean.'

Now Heem was catching on. 'You are entering *me* as the Star HydrO representative?'

'I thought that was understood. Surely you realized that your transferee is extra-Segment, though you covered that information beautifully.'

Extra-Segment? Heem set that aside for the moment. 'And if I happen not to overcome the odds—'

'It is possible that a clerical error would be uncovered, voiding your pardon, and you would again be subject to local System justice.'

The taste was coming through more clearly. 'And if I should, just by way of farfetched example, be caught employing unclean means in the competition—'

'The Competition Authority would deal with you in its own fashion. We certainly would not support such behaviour.'

So he had been admitted to the competition because of his record, and was expected to employ his nefarious skills to win for Star HydrO, without being caught. They had certainly given him an incentive: glory, honour, and a clean record if he won without fouling out; confinement or worse if he failed.

'I believe I comprehend the situation,' he jetted, subdued.

'We rather thought you would, Heem.'

'But a great deal depends on the transferee.' There seemed to be no reason now not to advise them of the failure; they would merely put him through the machine again and be sure the transfer took, this time.

'Do not underestimate your transferee,' the alcove jetted. 'He is a highly trained and motivated Solarian of Segment Etamin, apt at riddles and competitive strategy. We estimate that his presence will quadruple your chances for success. As you sit, you should have one chance in twenty-five to win – and perhaps you will be fortunate enough to improve on that.'

By cheating. Yes, he just might accomplish that; he did indeed know many little trick rolls of the trade that could not be readily exposed as illicit. 'There is just one problem—'

'We realize that it is difficult at first to come to terms with a completely alien mind, and the Solarians are as alien as any in the Galaxy,' the alcove jetted. 'By the same token taste, the strategy directed by this entity will be virtually incomprehensible to your Segment Thousandstar competitors. Learn to employ this alienness to your advantage, and—'

'Verification is complete except for those eliminated by default,' the public spray proclaimed. 'Prepare for onset of competition.'

'But for this first stage, your own expertise is best,' the alcove finished hurriedly. 'Now return to your niche for the onset of the competition. Do not fail us, and we shall not fail you.'

A pretty direct reminder! 'I'm trying to jet you that your alien Solarian transfer never—'

42

'If you miss the initial keying, you are unlikely to obtain a ship.'

Heem realized that an alien transferee would have little notion of local conventions, so would be no help in the first stage of competition. What could a Solarian of Etamin do in the Sphere of Star HydrO? He did not need the Solarian expert. Not to get offplanet. Once he had a spaceship, he wouldn't need the Solarian anyway. If he washed out of the competition, he could set down somewhere else, anywhere else but here, and they would never bother to extradite him. So what did he care if his transfer had failed? With no visiting mind to prod him, no inter-Segment involvement, he was on his own. That was the way he preferred it.

But he was dawdling, wasting invaluable time. Heem rolled swiftly back to his assigned niche. He should consider himself lucky that they had been so concerned with the cleverness of their hold over him that they had forgotten to verify his transferee aura. Maybe his attempt to borrow Swoon of Sweetswamp's identity had served him well, even in its failure. The anonymous interviewer had outsmarted himself. The authorities did not have a punishing hold on Heem; they had the illusion of a hold.

Heem reached his niche and settled in.

'Ascent is correct,' the public spray announced. 'Biim of Broadsea is granted the key to the sixth ship.'

There was a winner – evidently the sixth. Heem had missed five successful responses, in the little time he had delayed, and had no idea of the pattern that might be developing. That put him at a crucial disadvantage, lowering his chances of success. He could wash out right here, before ever getting started. The one thing he could not afford.

'So you are back,' his neighbour jetted. Not the communicative 38, who was now concentrating on the competition, but the one who had been absent before. Number 40, Swoon of Sweetswamp. The female he had

43

tried to impersonate, who had never answered her summons for verification.

'Descent is incorrect,' the public spray proclaimed. 'Maan of Makerain is disqualified.' There was a brief pause, then: 'Hard is incorrect. Soft is incorrect. Kreep of Kinglake and Toot of Tangspray are eliminated. Please depart promptly.'

So Ascent was a winner, but Descent and Soft were losers. Not enough information yet for him to form a notion of the pattern. He had to get a listing of the prior winners and losers so he could compete on an even basis.

'Swoon, would you provide me with a rehearsal of the prior—'

Her jet struck his skin before he finished. 'You stole my verification! Now I can't compete!'

'Bold is incorrect,' the public spray announced. 'Deeb of Deepocean is retired.'

'I did not steal your verification!' Heem protested.

'Yes you did!' she countered furiously, her jet warm with emotion. There was a special female flavour to her emissions that would have been quite interesting in another circumstance. 'Fuun informed me you had rolled for my summons.'

Fuun must be the loquacious 38 on the other side. Infernal loudsquirt! 'I merely tried to cover for you. But they fathomed my identity. Your qualification has not been compromised.' Yet if she had missed verification, she had been eliminated by default.

'Joy is incorrect,' the public spray wafted. 'Haav of Healthjuice is dismissed.'

'I don't believe you,' Swoon jetted, but there was a tinge of doubt. 'I was delayed by a malfunctioning door on my chamber, and only arrived here as the concepts commenced.'

'Then you are not at fault. Go to the verification alcove,' Heem urged. 'It is not yet too late.' He hoped. 'But first give me the data.'

'Dense is incorrect,' the spray announced. 'Poon of Puddlelove has washed out.'

She hesitated then decided. 'I will give you the data – after I qualify. So if you attempt to betray me again—'

Heem did not debate the point. 'Advise them Heem of Highfalls rolled you to them. Hurry.'

She rolled out with dispatch, for she was as eager as he to win a spaceship.

There was a pause. Six entrants had been eliminated in succession, so the others were getting more conservative. Once a contestant committed himself to a guess, he was either a winner or a loser; he had no second chance. It was evident that the odds against a right answer by pure guess were at least six to one, since that was the ratio of failures to successes he had noted so far. But the odds would be much better for a smart entity, or for a pair of entities (host and transferee working in tandem), and Heem did not care to gamble that so many others would wash out that any ships would be left over for easy taking. Even if there were ten ships remaining, and all entrants washed out except himself, he would still have to fathom the key before he got a ship. If he took a day to do it, he would be so far behind the other ships that he would never catch up before the race was over. So he had to fathom the pattern and get his ship early.

'Grief is incorrect,' the public spray sprayed. 'Fuun of Flowjet is finished.'

'May the monstrous amorphous Deity spray poison acid on us all!' 38 sprayed explosively, and there was a neighbourhood stir of shock at his obscenity. 'Joy was third, so I was sure the antonym had to be sixth.'

'But the concept at issue now is the seventh,' the HydrO behind Heem sprayed in a stage whisperjet.

'And the sixth was Ascent,' another sprayed. 'That was the antonym to none of the prior concepts.'

'Dry skin!' Fuun swore scatologically as he rolled away.

45

'I misremembered *and* misfigured! What a dehydrant am I!'

'On that, at least, he is correct,' another sprayed.

Nevertheless, it was valuable information for Heem. Now he knew that Joy had been third, and suspected that there had been at least one pair of antonyms among the others. Joy third, Ascent sixth. Descent had been wrong, so there could not be adjacent antonyms. Probably the key lay elsewhere. If only he had the full list!

'Brittle is correct,' the public spray came. 'Mees of Mistfog has Ship Seven.'

Ascent followed by Brittle. What did the two have in common? They were two entirely different types of concept. Heem's mind laboured vainly to spot something obvious. It couldn't be that successive concepts had to differ in nature, because then several of the guesses following Ascent would have been correct. Hard, Soft, Bold, Joy, Dense, Grief – three were descriptions of physical properties, three related to feelings or personality of living conscious entities. Brittle clearly fitted into the former category. Why, then, was Brittle correct, while Hard, Soft, and Dense were incorrect? And how had Mees of Mistfog fathomed the distinction? The guess had come after a fair pause, as though Mees had taken time to figure it out. What did Mees know that Heem didn't?

Obviously, the first correct and incorrect guesses: Mees knew them, Heem didn't. Heem had to have them, but did not want to betray his ignorance by enquiring of another contestant. Any of them might inform him incorrectly, so as to cause him to eliminate himself by a miscalculated guess, and perhaps make it easier for them. There was no rule against discussion and cooperation, but ultimately each entrant had to be for himself, and for his represented Star. No one could be trusted.

Where was Swoon of Sweetswamp? Could he trust her? He would have to! She obviously was not the brightest

46

HydrO extant, or she would not have got lost coming to her niche. He was sure it had been confusion, not door malfunction, that had delayed her. She would need help getting a good guess. He would give her the correct sequence occurring during her absence, and she would give him the correct original sequence. If he could crack the code for himself, he could do it for her too; two answers were as easy as one. If she gave him incorrect information, it would only wash them both out. So she could probably be trusted.

'Power is incorrect,' the spray announced. 'Sheev of Shadylake is out.'

This was awful! Heem, ordinarily apt at this sort of thing, could not get a jet on it. If he was too late getting the early sequence, too many others would solve the pattern before him.

'Justice is incorrect. Food is incorrect. Descent is incorrect,' the spray sprayed, following with the names of the unsuccessful entrants.

'Humour is correct,' the spray then came. 'Bloop of Blisswater has Ship Eight. Direction is correct; Poos of Peacepond has Ship Nine. Sour is correct; Zaas of Zoomjet has Ship Ten.'

Three in a row! Obviously one person had found the key, and given it to his friends, so that all three had won together. Much more of that and all the ships would go in a few big rolls! Yet these three would now find themselves racing against each other; their friendship would suffer rapid attrition. Since each host had a different transferee, representing a different Star, there could be no long-term collusion.

'Ocean is incorrect,' the spray announced. 'Season is incorrect. Hate is incorrect. Love is incorrect.'

Four more washouts in rapid order. That could be a group who had cooperated and lost. But the key remained opaque. With a sequence of ten winners and several times

47

that many losers, Heem should be able to determine the pattern. If only he had all the data!

There was another pause, a long one. Evidently the other contestants were as confused as Heem. That was good; that would give Swoon of Sweetswamp time to get verified and return to her niche. It was also bad; all the ships already acquired were zooming off to the rendezvous, becoming more and more difficult to catch.

Heem waited impatiently, making little restless jets that rolled him about within his niche, rotating his body in place. Baffled by the mystery of the pattern, his searching mind veered off, and he found himself remembering again. He had been in a kind of competition before, as mystifying as this one, and somewhat more final in its decisions. The competition of juvenile survival. He remembered how he and Hoom had ridden the back of the flatfloater as it jetted powerfully up the slope of the mountain range beside Highfalls. Their companions Haam and Hiim had fallen off, and now the two of them were the only sapients remaining in the valley. They had to know whether they were alone, or whether others like them existed elsewhere.

The flatfloater wavered, not liking the tremendous effort of the climb. Heem needled in on the lower edge of its disc, and it shot forward again, seeking to escape the irritation. Again Heem appreciated the stupidity of the monster, which made it so readily subject to manipulation.

Was it possible that the two sapients were also stupid, being manipulated by some power beyond their comprehension? Surely the valley of Highfalls had not been stocked with hundreds of their kind, most of whom would die at the outset, only to have them *all* die out eventually! Yet it had almost happened, and might happen yet.

With amazing swiftness, the taste of the top of the range approached. It was uncomfortably dry up here, and the air pressure was low, causing his body to fluff out. The ambient taste of vegetation was diffuse. Heem did not like

48

it, but was determined to go on. He knew now that they could not have made it by themselves; only the gross power of the floater sufficed. Even that would fail if they did not surmount the ridge soon, for the monster was tiring. It too was suffering from the rare air; fragments of its body were falling off, propelled by the uncontrolled expansion of its gases. Heem and Hoom were both working hard to keep it moving; soon even the sharpest needles would not be enough.

The flatfloater balked. Now all their prodding was vain; the monster's jets were exhausted, its body overheated to the point of shutdown. It crashed into the slope. Heem and Hoom rolled forward and off, jetting desperately to regain equilibrium and avoid a competing collision.

In due course Heem rolled to a stop, his body half-flattened against the tilt of the ground. The wind was cold against his skin, the taste strange. Perhaps it was some breed of swamp vegetation, fuzzed by distance.

Swamp? This draught was coming down the mountain. Was there swamp up there? Hardly! Where, then?

It had to be from the far side. A draught across the strange swamp, with its different flavour, up over the mountain ridge, down this side. If he rolled into the draught, he would find that swamp. All he had to do was keep rolling until he got there; the wind would guide him.

Beside him, Hoom was reviving. 'Do you survive, Heem?' he sprayed weakly.

'Yes,' Heem replied. 'We must go on.'

'We must go back! This diminished pressure is awful! The air is dry and cold.'

'Because we are near the top of the ridge! A little farther, and we will crest it. The flatfloater has done all it can; we must not throw away what it has given us.'

'I'm tired,' Hoom protested. 'I cannot climb anymore; I must roll down.'

'Then roll alone. I will cross the mountain.'

'But suppose you never return? I would be alone in the valley!'

'Yes,' Heem jetted forcefully, starting his roll uphill. He was bluffing; if Hoom did not come . . .

Reluctantly, Hoom joined him. Heem made a private jet of relief. He had not wanted to risk this venture alone, yet had not wanted to give it up so close to success. Now he had won; he had assumed the leadership, and Hoom would have to follow.

They forged up the slope. Abruptly the ground levelled, then angled down. They had crested the ridge! They had been virtually at the brink. What irony if they had given up when the flatfloater did!

There was a lesson in this, Heem thought. One must not give up an effort prematurely; success might be incipient, though it seemed otherwise.

What a relief to roll downhill! The slope was steep, forcing them to brakejet firmly, but progress was excellent.

'We made it!' Hoom sprayed jubilantly. 'We conquered!' He seemed to have forgotten his prior reticence. But that was the way Hoom was; his attention span was brief. He never brooded on the ultimate meaninglessness of things the way Heem did.

For example, Hoom was now happy to be rolling downhill. Heem was concerned with what they might encounter at the base of this slope. The valley of Highfalls had its perils, enough to eliminate all but two of possibly two hundred original HydrOs who had started there. Could this nameless new valley be any safer? Probably it was worse, for them, because they would not be familiar with its perils.

Yet this venture had to be made. Whatever the meaning of life might be, this exploration would help him to discover it.

The slope levelled, but the ground was too high yet for this to be the base. A variance in the mountain, after which the descent should resume.

Suddenly both of them blasted water violently forward, coming to a halt. There was something strange, alien, and horrible ahead. Both of them knew instantly it was an enemy. It exuded a taste of sheerest menace. They also knew they could not fight it; the thing was too horrible to oppose. Their only choice was to flee.

They tried. But progress up the steep slope was agonizingly slow. The thing rolled up behind them – no, even more horrible, it did not roll, its locomotion was part of its alien quality. It did not jet, it – it slithered. Heem had never imagined such a means of transport, but the faint, awful taste of this thing's presence evoked memories buried in his evolution. This creature – it had been the implacable foe of Heem's kind for an interminable time!

'Cease your struggle, HydrO prey,' the jet of the alien came. Even its communication was oddly sinister. There was a cold metallic flavour. The alien did not use jets for communication; Heem knew this too. Therefore this command was impossible – yet it had come.

Heem ignored it, naturally. He jetted so hard he practically flatfloated up the slope. Hoom was right beside him. Terror gave them strength.

'Cease, lest I destroy you,' the alien jetted.

Hoom had enough attention left to loft a hurried spray at Heem. 'How can it jet? It *has* no jets!'

'With my machine, HydrO prey!' the alien jetted. 'Last warning: desist or die.'

But Heem knew with the certainty of thousands of generations of his kind – it was amazing how self-realization came at a moment like this! – that there was no way to trust this alien. 'Divide!' he sprayed, warned by that instinct. He jetted at right angles to his former course and rolled to the side, separating from Hoom.

Even as he did so, there was an explosive spray from Hoom. 'Oh, it burns!' Then nothing – and Heem knew his friend was dead.

Heem dodged again, changing his angle of escape with his strongest jet. Then the alien's machinejet grazed him, just touching a small patch of his skin.

'Oh, it burns!' Heem sprayed and collapsed. It *did* burn, but his exclamation was more cunning than pain, a ploy of desperation. Let the alien assume he was dead; perhaps the killing shot would be withheld. It was his only chance.

He felt the slight vibration of the ground as the alien approached. It came to Heem first, its body emitting its faint but awful taste. It was difficult to fathom the nature of this dread creature, but as it came near the separate small indications of its mechanism evoked the instinctive memories in Heem's mind. The thing was long and slender, an undulating rope of flesh tapering into a rough point at either extreme. There was armour on it, mail formed from bone: the hardened tissue employed by some animals to stiffen and shield their anatomies. It moved by shoving its smooth, hard torso against irregularities in the ground, and sliding its dry scales past these irregularities. It was, Heem realized, a bit like rolling; instead of employing sensible jets of water to push its body around and forward, it employed natural objects. But it remained a horrifyingly alien mode of propulsion.

The thing slithered up to Heem, who dared not squirt even the tiniest jet. He knew, again by instinct, that he would only remain alive if this monster thought him already dead. He had to stay dead to stay alive!

The thing lurked beside him, a ghastly alien presence. Heem no longer had volition; even his hydrogen absorption was suspended. The monster unfolded three gross limbs, their nature shaped in Heem's mind by sound, ambient taste, and instinct memory. Pincers extended, three sturdy metallic claws, grasping Heem's vulnerable body, hauling one section of it into the air. Yet Heem did not react.

For a moment the monster held him there, pincers cutting cruelly into Heem's tender flesh. The taste-ambience was much stronger now, evoking a vivid picture of this creature's nature. The bone-plates were intricately overlapped and interlocked so as to be highly flexible and invulnerable to any needlejet. The appendages were sensitive to vibration in much the fashion Heem's own skin was, so the thing could – could – here another concept struggled and finally burst out: a discreet new sense. The thing could *hear*. Hearing was more than feeling, operating at a greater distance. The creature could perceive its environment by hearing rather than tasting; its scales were impervious to sapient communication – no, that was confusing.

The thing had no jets, yet it had jetted. Instead it had a machine, which Heem now realized was a construct of inanimate substance that squirted intelligible jets. Thus the monster could talk despite its lack of natural means. By putting acid in that machine, it could burn and kill. Heem's skin still hurt fiercely from that glancing jet.

The monster opened its pincers, letting Heem drop. It slithered across to locate Hoom. Vibration commenced, and a terrible taste drifted across. The awful exudate of fresh wounds in HydrO flesh.

The thing was cutting up Hoom's body with its pincers! Hoom's natural juices were squirting into the air, spreading the horrible taste of death. By vibration and taste, Heem was treated to the most terrible experience of his career. The monster, not satisfied with killing his friend, was now destroying the body!

The utter alienness of this action made Heem's jet apertures lose control, and some of his reserve water leaked out. Still he could do nothing, not even move.

Efficiently, the monster reduced Hoom's body to juicy pieces. Then the most sickening thing of all occurred. The thing extruded its own internal membrane and spread it over Hoom's pieces. Heem tasted the vile acids; their vapours burned his skin anew. A poison jet was bad enough, but this complete inundation was appalling. What

53

possible purpose could there be in it? Nothing in his experience accounted for anything like this. His instinct-memory offered no clue; whatever it was was too horrible even to comprehend.

Heem's discomfort was growing. He had to breathe or he would perish anyway. Cautiously he took in air, circulating the molecules of it through his system. Energy was harvested, and water flowed, restoring his power. But what good did this do him? The alien could shoot him down again with that mechanical jet. Heem stayed still.

The ghastly process of demolition continued. Heem found himself becoming inured to it; it was impossible to maintain a condition of total horror indefinitely. Hoom was dead; he had accepted that, and with the flow of energy through his system he was better able to tolerate it. The experience and memory were awful and would remain so, but Heem could at least function. He had, after all, tasted the deaths of his companions many times before, from many different causes.

Suddenly he realized that the alien was temporarily restricted. How could it move rapidly, while its insides were outside? Perhaps it could still use its weapon, but it could not pursue a rolling object.

To wait here was to risk getting cut up and destroyed in the manner Hoom had been. There was really no choice. The alien had thought Heem dead, since it lacked proper taste; when Heem remained limp, he had been set aside while the other victim was verified. The alien was not omniscient; it had to check things physically. So Heem had fooled it – and now might escape it.

Heem blasted out his jets, initiating a violent roll down the slope. If the acid did not strike him in the first moment, he should escape it entirely. And – it did not strike. He had fooled the enemy and won his freedom.

Now he was rolling down the steep incline, much faster than was comfortable or safe, yet he dared not brake.

Better the risk of getting smashed against a rock, than of waiting for an acid bath!)

But as he became assured of escape, his concern about his high-velocity roll grew. He had to slow, but his momentum was such that his jets seemed to have no effect.

Still the slope catapulted him down. Heem bounced, his skin abrading. A welter of tastes impinged on his awareness: animals, plants, minerals, not-quite familiar. The tastes of this strange valley, only a little different from Highfalls, yet remarkable because it was the first foreign valley he had known. A region he could live in, if he could only enter it safely.

He tried again, without effect. The slope was simply too steep! Now he tasted the spume of broken water. There was a river here, rocky, with falls, like that in his own valley; he would smash into it and die, for water could not sufficiently cushion his present plunge.

Heem jetted with all his strength to one side. His plummet veered, and he rolled on a slant down the mountain. Now at last he could gain a little purchase. He veered further, beginning to catch the ground; in a moment he would be rolling back uphill, and gravity would help stay his motion. Why hadn't he thought of this before? He slowed, curved—

And dropped off another ledge, one that ran parallel to his original line of descent. He jetted wildly in all directions, accomplishing nothing, and splashed into deep water.

Dizzy, exhausted, he struggled to the surface – and could not maintain the elevation. Slowly he sank down into the depths, losing all control. There was hydrogen here, plenty of it, but he lacked the energy to process it properly at this depth. He was in danger of drowning.

Then something bumped him. Dazedly he tasted its ambience – and discovered the stigma of another of his kind. But Hoom was the one who remained, and Hoom was dead!

The strange HydrO shoved him out of the water. Heem cooperated feebly. There was something very strange about this person. It was a stranger, certainly, probably a HydrO of this valley. But also—

As they emerged from the water, Heem realized what it was. His rescuer was female – the first Heem had ever encountered. Suddenly a new universe had opened to him.

2

Triple Disaster

'Wake, Heem,' the female jetted peremptorily.

Heem snapped alert. It was not the female of his memory, but Swoon of Sweetswamp of nowtime. 'You qualified?' he jetted anxiously.

'I did. You squirted truth. When I invoked your name, they removed me from forfeit and verified me instantly.'

'You took long enough to return,' Heem jetted irritably.

'How would you know? You were unconscious.'

'Pain is incorrect,' the public spray sprayed. 'Zuum of Zestcloud is out. Plan is incorrect. Baas of Basewater is through.'

'Give me that data,' he sprayed.

'Three is incorrect,' the public spray announced.

'Very well,' Swoon agreed. 'Here is the list of correct entries. Hard, Soft, Joy, Dense, Tedium, Ascent, Brittle, Humour, Direction, Sour.'

'Diffuse is correct,' the public spray announced. 'Diis of Delightfog possesses Ship Eleven.' There was a spray of sheer jubilation nearby as Diis vented his joy.

Heem considered the elements of the puzzle, at last prepared with complete information – but was distracted by another announced wrong guess. It was hard to concentrate on the growing list while keeping up with all the wrong guesses, yet he knew he could not afford to ignore those errors. 'Swoon, we have reconciled our difference of the moment,' he jetted. 'But we both have lost time. Suppose we cooperate further?'

'This is sensible,' she agreed. 'For this stage of the competition only.'

'Agreed. We work together to fathom the key, then

derive two answers. Once we have our ships, our deal is over.'

'Agreed,' she jetted. 'Are you apt at puzzles?'

'I am. But I need a ready recall mechanism for the rejects.'

'I have an excellent memory. That makes me an apt space pilot, but a poor riddler. You cogitate; I will recall.'

Heem rolled into it. Obviously there was a pattern of concepts, no two of which repeated. Hard, followed by Soft – two extremes of physical properties. Then a shift to a new variety of concept, Joy, followed by – Dense? Why not Sadness, or Grief, or Misery? If one pair of extremes was correct, why not another?

Maybe no one had thought to guess the opposite of Joy, so a new concept had been introduced instead. He could check that now. 'Swoon, what were the error-guesses for Ship Four?' He hoped she was correct about her excellent memory.

'Sorrow, Grief, Pleasure,' she jetted immediately.

She did indeed have a good memory! It probably did help her in piloting, for there were many details of fuel economy, energy absorption, and trajectory that were greatly facilitated by ready recall. Heem's own piloting was excellent, but he depended on experience and intelligent exploitation of momentary realities, rather than on his merely ordinary memory. He could do with less memory yet, since the illegal juvenile recollections were a constant liability for him.

But he could not afford the liability of that distraction now! His theory had just been disproven. Either Sorrow or Grief should have sufficed, but both had been rejected.

Could it be a number sequence, with concept irrelevant? Every fourth guess was accepted as correct, after three rejections? That would neatly eliminate three quarters of the contestants, guaranteeing that a sufficient number would remain to fill the available ships. A very simple

58

formula – but there was no requirement of complexity here. Any entity who caught on could win his ship, regardless.

'What were the errors for Ship Three?' he jetted.

'Fear is correct for Ship Twelve,' the public spray announced. Annoyed, Heem blotted out the rest; he needed to fathom the pattern of the early answers, then verify it with the subsequent ones that Swoon would retain for him.

'Fuzzy, Brittle, Bold,' Swoon replied.

Three errors. Good. He already knew there had been three for Ship Four. 'What errors for Ship Five?'

'Diffuse, Hard, Soft.'

Three more! Hard and Soft had been specific repeats, automatically void. But they counted as errors, setting up the next.

'Errors for Ship Six?'

'Joy, Hard, Soft, Thick.'

Four errors. There went that theory! Unless it were progressive, the number growing as the game continued. 'How many for Ship Two?'

'None,' she jetted. 'The first two guesses were correct.'

So there had been zero errors, zero errors, three, three, three, four – not hopeful. 'Errors for Ship Seven?'

'Think, Bold, Descent, Hard, Soft, Joy, Grief.'

She had certainly been paying attention! Six errors, including three repeats of prior winners. The stupid guessers kept trying those repeats, not catching on. But soon the stupid ones would be eliminated, and the repeats would stop. Except that *any* guess before the assigned number would be wrong, so it made no difference. But how did six errors fit the pattern? This was not an even progression. Was it that the wrong guesses had to match or outnumber the prior totals? Then why had six guesses occurred, when four or five should have sufficed? Also, at that rate, all the contestants would be eliminated before all the ships were taken. And—

'They are making more correct guesses now,' Swoon

advised him worriedly. 'Fifteen ships have been taken. Sixteen.'

'I'm rolling on it!' Heem needled back, then picked up his thought. He had just found two overwhelming flaws in the error-count theory. He had himself tasted a run of several correct guesses in succession, so he should have known from the outset that wasn't it. And even had that not been the case, that system would not work. As soon as enough contestants caught on to it, no one would volunteer the wrong guesses. The competition would roll to a halt, as all waited for others to eliminate themselves. There *had* to be some way to have many successive correct guesses.

'Five more correct ones,' Swoon jetted. 'Too many are catching on; haven't you solved it yet? They'll roll out of ships!'

Heem suppressed an irate blast. 'Two thirds of the ships remain.' But he was worried. Too many other contestants, able to work on the problem with full information from the outset, were fathoming the pattern and gaining their ships. Twenty more ships might be taken suddenly.

Back to concepts: the identical ones did not repeat, but what about variants? Hard and Soft were physical properties; so was Dense. But the sequence was Hard-Soft-Joy-Dense. If Dense was right, why had another physical property, Brittle, been ruled wrong, while Joy had been accepted in its place? Followed by Tedium-Ascent-Brittle. And Brittle had been rejected before. How was it that an invalid concept had become valid?

The key could not be in the number of rejections or in the particular concepts. It had to be in the order of the concepts, so that any concept became wrong when out of place. Now what was that order?

'Seven more ships!' Swoon jetted despairingly.

- Heem washed her out of his perception, along with the public spray's pronouncements. He was beginning to get it; all he needed was uninterrupted thought. First, he had to

60

analyse and classify the concepts. Then he had to formulate a theory of progression. Then he should verify it by predicting to himself the nature of several forthcoming correct guesses. Finally he had to make his own guess – before the supply of ships was exhausted.

He worked it out, calling on the increasingly nervous Swoon for data on occasion. There were seven or eight categories of concept: physical Properties, such as Hard, Soft, Dense, Brittle, and Diffuse; Sentient Feelings, such as Joy, Tedium, Humour, Fear, and Courage; Special Motion such as Direction, Aslant, Plunge, Rotation, and Arrival; Taste Sensation, such as Sour, Sweet, Pungent, Savoury, and Insipid; Fluid Matter, such as Rain, Sea, Moist, Dry (i.e., absence of fluid), and Liquid; Number, such as One, Two, Three, Four, and Five; Sapient Qualities, such as Wisdom, Stupidity, Sanity, and Craziness; and several stray concepts that could not yet be classified with assurance because there were too many examples of each. Concept categories tended to merge at the edges, as did tastes when the fluids bearing them mixed.

Now the order: the first two were Physical Properties, the third a Sentient Feeling, the fourth another Physical Property, the fifth another Feeling, the sixth a Direction, the Seventh another Physical Property. Did he have a pattern here? It was hard to tell.

Analyse it mathematically, he thought. *Let the first class of concepts be A, the second B, the third C. Use exponents to indicate repeat concepts.*

Heem paused. Had he really thought that? That was not the way his mind ordinarily worked! He knew of the symbol-conventions of Galactic notation – A, B, C – but did not *think* in them. This pressure was having a strange effect on him. Nevertheless, it was a good thought.

He made a mental list of the successful concepts, classifying each as a mathematical notation. Taste A, taste B, taste C, and so on, eliminating for the moment the actual concepts so that the pattern, unobscured by meaning, could emerge.

That's it exactly.

There he was, tasting to himself again, encouraging himself. Perhaps this atypical mannerism stemmed from the lingering disorientation of his failed transfer-hosting. He hoped it would not interfere with his performance.

Onward: Hard-Soft-Joy-Dense-Tedium became A-A-B-A-B. He did not bother with the exponents after all; $A-A^1-B-A^2-B^1$ seemed to be superfluous refinement, so far. He could taste the pattern quite well without it.

Now what about the next five concepts? Would they be a repeat of the initial sequence, or a variant, or a continuation of a developing sequence? No time to conjecture; he would have to translate the raw data directly into the format and see. The concepts were Ascent-Brittle-Humour-Direction-Sour. Categories C-A-B-C-D. No repeat of the first five-concept pattern.

Well, there was no reason the sequence should be in fives; that was just for his convenience in organizing. Consider them all together: AABABCABCD.

Suddenly a repeating subsequence leaped out at him: ABC-ABC. Preceded by AAB, followed by D. What sense could be made of that?

It was pointless to struggle with it when so much more data was available. He had Swoon jet him the next ten concepts, and translated them into taste categories with increasing proficiency. Diffuse-A, Fear-B, Plunge-C, Sweet-D, Rain-E, Elastic-A, Courage-B, Rotation-C, Pungent-D, Sea-E. And there it was, beautifully, stupidly simple: a concept progression!

Reverifying, he worked it out. A-AB-ABC-ABCD-ABCDE-ABCDE. The next one, the twenty-first concept had to be F – a new category. A Sapient Process, or a Number, or something else – anything but a repeat category.

'Give me the concept for Ship Twenty-one,' he jetted.

'Nine,' Swoon answered promptly.

Victory! The category of Number, new to the progression. 'Now feed me the remaining ships, slowly,' he jetted.

'Rare,' she jetted back, and he translated that to A. 'Caution.' He rendered that B. As she continued, he hardly perceived the specific concepts, so readily did they become taste-designates. C-D-E-F-G, and then a new sequence in the progression: ABCDEFGH. And another: ABCD—

'Where's the next?' he needled irritably.

'That's it' Swoon jetted. 'Forty ships taken! Have you solved it?' Anxiety was beginning to blur her communication, intruding irrelevant tastes.

'Yes. The next one will be an E concept, followed by—'

'What?' Her jet was pure confusion.

Oops – he had squirted her with his notational symbols. 'A concept relating to Fluid Matter, that has not been used before, like—'

'Liquid is correct,' the public spray sprayed.

'You've got it!' Swoon jetted jubilantly.

'I just lost it,' he responded. 'I didn't make that formal guess; another HydrO did, and he got the ship. The others are catching on rapidly.'

'Five is correct,' the spray announced. 'Stupidity is correct. Victory is correct.'

'There went F, G, and H,' Heem jetted in alarm. 'We've got to grab our own ships before the entire next sequence goes!'

'Yes!' Swoon agreed. 'Give me a concept!'

'It has to be a new category. Maybe an Abstract Relation, like Strength—'

'Virtue is correct,' the public spray came.

'That too; that's category I,' Heem jetted. 'The next eight will be easy.'

'I will settle for the next one,' Swoon jetted.

'A Physical Property, but not one that's been used before.'

'How about Light, the opposite of Heavy? Heavy has been used, but not Light.'

'That should roll it,' he agreed.

'If this is wrong—' She squirted with needlesome force into her niche-receptor. There was a pause.

'Light is correct,' the public spray sprayed. 'Swoon of Sweetswamp has won Ship Forty-six.

Swoon practically melted. 'Thank you, Heem, thank you! I will repay you for this! Catch up to me at the target planet—'

But Heem had little faith in such gratitude. 'Only one can win the competition,' he reminded her.

'The competition is not yet over. Perhaps there will be occasion to cooperate again.' She doused him with a jet of intensely erotic suggestion and rolled out of her niche. She was off to collect her key and her ship.

Heem took a moment to reorient. Swoon might not be the cleverest concepts-riddle manipulator, but she certainly had sex appeal!

He was now free to win his own ship. That should be no problem. The next concept should be B—

'Humility is correct,' the public spray announced. 'Arrival is correct.'

They were going rapidly! Forty-eight ships out of sixty-six total. The next would be—

'Rich is correct. Czeep of Czealake has Ship Forty-nine.'

He had better figure ahead several ships, so as to be ready when his chance came up. Right now he was guessing correctly, but losing out to others who were responding more quickly. He would try three ships ahead. Rich had been a D concept; E-F-G – he needed a G. G was— he paused, ransacking his memory – G was Intellectual Faculties, like Wisdom and Stupidity. Had these specific concepts been used? Probably. So he had to take something different like Eccentricity. That had an original feel. Eccentricity – his ticket to space!

'Stream is correct.' There were now very few wrong

64

guesses; only those who knew they had fathomed the pattern were expressing themselves. The ships were going swiftly. 'Six is correct.'

Now it was up to G – his turn. Heem started his jet—

And balked. His jet clogged, the fluid dribbling down his skin meaninglessly. What had happened? It wasn't like him to clog in the crisis!

It's a repeat, he thought suddenly. *A void response!*

'Sanity is correct,' the public spray came. 'Prosperity is correct.'

A repeat! Quite possible, for he had hardly assimilated the concepts themselves. He had translated them to letter-tastes automatically, depending on Swoon of Sweetswamp to recall the specifics – and now she was gone. He could not trust his memory on *any* of the repeat concepts!

'Vice is correct. Knyfh is correct.'

Two more ships gone – the fifty-fourth and fifty-fifth. Only eleven left – and though he had fathomed the pattern, his memory was suspect! He had perhaps two chances in three of choosing correctly on any single one – but he hardly wanted to stake his freedom on those odds! He wanted to be *certain*. What was he to do now?

'Firm is correct. Maat of Mainstream wins Ship Fifty-six.'

The fifty-fifth concept had been Knyfh – evidently the new category J, Cluster Geography. Segment Knyfh had been at the heart of the Milky Way Galaxy defence, during the Second War of Energy. Probably the next J concept could be any of the other Galactic Segments – Quval, Etamin, LoDo, Weew, even Thousandstar itself. But this was too obvious; a number of contestants would fathom it, and be waiting for J to roll around again, and it would be pure chance for him to get his answer in first. He could not jet his answer in one moment beforetime; an answer out of place was a wrong answer.

'Excitement is correct. Departure is correct. Spicy is correct.'

Three more ships gone – and Heem could have taken any of them, had he dared risk a repetition. He still could not risk it! According to his understanding of the pattern, the sixty-sixth ship would represent a completely new concept. While the others were jetting over the second J concept, he should needle in with the K concept.

The problem was that K, sixty-six, was the last ship available to a HydrO host. If he lost that one, he lost everything.

'Exhilaration is incorrect. Seven is incorrect.' Two bad guesses. What was required was an E concept, relating to Water, while these related to Emotion and Number – B and F. Other contestants were getting nervous, afraid they would lose out by failing even to try for the remaining ships in time. Well, good, the more fools who washed out, the fewer to interfere with his own guess at the end.

Heem was abruptly tempted to take his chance on this next ship. Had Ocean been used? Lake? Sea?

'Lake is correct,' the public spray proclaimed. 'Soop of Soulwet has won Ship Sixty.'

Six ships to go! He could have won Ship Sixty if he had only jetted Lake. But supposing he had jetted Sea, and it turned out to be a repeat? In fact, he was almost sure now that Sea had been used, back in the first or second E. He had to stick to his decision: a completely new concept-category for Ship Sixty-six. That remained his last and best chance.

'Six is incorrect. Seven is correct.'

Someone had forgotten and reused a number – as Heem might have done. The next guesser had quickly rectified the situation, and got the ship. The remaining contestants were under pressure, as Heem himself was; they were making stupid mistakes. But that was their problem; he had to be concerned with his own. What was a completely new concept-category?

'Eight is incorrect. Crazy is correct. Success is correct.'

66

There went Ships Sixty-two and Sixty-three. Three ships left – and Heem's mind was blank. Where was his new category? He had to have it now!

'Justice is correct. Potency is incorrect.'

Curses! Two ships left – and he could not force his stalled mind to come up with the category! Should he take his roll at the next-to-last, since no one had—

'Etamin is correct. Jool of Jeweluster has Ship Sixty-five.'

Now! Now! Or forever lost! Yet he could not—

Idiot! It's Potence!

But Potence was a repeat; he had tasted it used!

No! Use it now!

'Novagleam is incorrect.'

Potence. Now!

Confused, Heem yielded. Better to wash out on a bad guess than to wash out without even trying. But even as he jetted, he knew others were doing the same. All through the chamber, needles were being fired.

With despairing certainty he tasted the concluding public spray. A group of others had jetted before he had! One of them was sure to have the answer.

'Frustration is incorrect. Jubilation is incorrect. Spray is incorrect. Thousandstar is incorrect. Ten is incorrect. Sickness is incorrect. Sand is incorrect. Potence is correct. Heem of Highfalls has won the final ship. All others are disqualified.'

Numb, Heem rested in place. *Potence was not a repeat; it was an advance guess*, the taste in his mind jetted. *Out of place, therefore wrong – before.*

Hardly believing it, Heem lurched out of his niche and rolled to pick up the key to Ship Sixty-six.

The key was a simple yet unguessable taste-code that would admit him to Ship Sixty-six and no other. Heem rolled rapidly out to it, jetted the key, and rolled up the ramp that

67

opened out to him. He entered the ship, squeezed into the control chamber, and settled into the acceleration cup. No one but a HydrO could use a HydrO ship; the bodies of other sapients differed too grossly. He jetted the TAKE-OFF button. The ship's acceleration panels closed in about him, sealing the chamber; water flooded the compartment, and the huge gaseous jets blasted at the ground. Like a flatfloater, the ship hurled itself into the sky.

Heem could do nothing for the moment. The ship would remain on automatic pilot until it achieved escape velocity; only then would the controls be returned to the passenger. Initial acceleration was always a compression; fortunately the HydrO physique, when properly supported, was ideally suited to it. Only a creature who could survive in fluid could accelerate rapidly; other forms were severely handicapped, lacking the ability to use hydraulic support for living tissues. Yet somehow many other species had achieved space.

That thought put Heem into a muse: how had his kind really come to space? The HydrO species could hardly have evolved for it – on the surface of a planet. Yet this almost perfect adaptation to the conditions of space could hardly be coincidental.

No, of course it was not coincidental! The awareness of outer space had not come easily to the HydrO kind, because the radiation of stars was not directly perceivable to HydrO senses. A star could not be tasted; it had no characteristic vapour, no vibration; it could not be touched. The home-Star, HydrO, was perceived through its caloric ambience; it heated the land and air by day. This, of course, had been the key, though Heem had spent his juvenile state on a colony world, and had never tasted the environs of Star HydrO itself. If a thing that was too far away to be touched made the difference between comfort and discomfort, that thing was important enough to be studied. Suppose Star HydrO were to depart or fade? It had been necessary for Heem's ancestors to roll into a situation where this could not happen.

So those ancestors had studied Star HydrO, and discovered marvellous qualities in it. Generations were lost in the pursuit of this knowledge, but in time the conceptual framework was secure. Star HydrO not only related to day and night (i.e., the alternating periods of warmth and cool), it bore on the seasons of the year, and the larger cycles of climate. The perfection of this comprehension was fraught with error, but at the end of that long roll, the nature of the modern universe had become quite clearly flavoured.

The HydrOs had realized that there had to be other life in the universe, just as there are other Stars. Nothing appeared alone; like juveniles in a valley, there were always one or two hundred. Indeed, there were ancient ruins within System HydrO, unmistakable remnants of the onetime presence of a highly technological alien species. On a planet orbiting another star (a star was a great radiating ball of gas; a Star was a star with an associated sapient life-form) within Sphere HydrO were the remnants of an entire life-ecology, once flourishing but now completely obliterated. Painstaking analysis of the traces indicated that the aliens had utilized other perceptions than taste. They seemed to have been able to perceive directly the reflected radiation of the stars. Since such radiation, according to HydrO research, propagated directly and rapidly – far more so than the vapours and currents of taste – this had enabled the aliens to react much more swiftly to stellar phenomena. In fact, this ability might be a formidable asset to spacefaring creatures, and might even be of use on the surface of planets. So the HydrOs had developed machines to perceive this radiation, and translated it to the molecules of taste, coding it much as Heem had coded the concepts of the contest. This had led to an enormous increase in astronomical information.

'I can't see!' he thought despairingly.

What? Of course he couldn't see; that was the term for the direct perception of radiation of certain wavelengths, that only machines and aliens seemed to have, as though to compensate them for their inadequate resources of taste. No HydrOs could duplicate the feat, had they desired to; the instruments were quite satisfactory to make the effects of radiation comprehensible. If he were ever deprived of his sense of taste, he would have reason to despair; but why bemoan the lack of an alien perception?

'I'm blind!' he thought again.

Blind: a manufactured term relating to that deficiency of radiation perception. It might, in a crude manner, resemble tastelessness – at least to a species so foolish as to depend on radiation perception for primary awareness. Such loss might be very disturbing. But not to Heem, who had never had such ability, and never desired it.

Maybe this was some anomaly of his thinking, spawned by the pressure of acceleration. Heem had been to space before without any problem like this, but it was possible that his secret incapacity touched this too. Was he suffering a lapse of sanity?

'I can feel, I can taste,' he sprayed, though his spray could hardly be effective in this water ambience of acceleration. He remembered waiting for the flatfloater, long ago as a juvenile, and feeling a similar restriction. 'That is all I require.'

'Not you, idiot! *I'm* the one who's blind!'

Was he jetting to himself? He had always been full of thoughts, but seldom tried to spray them to himself, before.

'I never realized it would be like this! No eyes, no ears – I'm locked in a dark and silent cell. I'm going crazy!'

'So I *am* jetting to myself,' Heem jetted, answering himself in the same fashion. 'If I am losing my sanity, as I suspect, at least I am doing it in space instead of in confinement.' Technically there was nothing quite so confining as space travel; no claustrophobic creature could pilot a spaceship. But beyond that close and pressured metal lay the glorious vastness of space, the ultimate in unconfinement. 'But why am I so concerned about – what were those organs of radiation?'

'Eyes! Ears! To see and hear. How can you stand it, blind and deaf, without even hands?'

'Hands! The only creature I have encountered with such awful appendages is—'

'*All* sapient creatures have hands! Or opposed thumbs, or the equivalent. So they can handle tools, build buildings, operate machines, so they can develop Cluster-level technology.'

'This is not my thinking!' Heem jetted violently. 'I may be losing my taste perspective, but not my common sense. HydrOs have no hands, yet we are among the most technologically advanced species of Segment Thousandstar. Here I am, piloting a HydrO – spaceship – no-handed.'

'Of course it's not your thinking. It's mine. I never thought it would be like this!'

The taste of comprehension flooded across his surface. 'The transferee! It arrived after all!'

'It – I mean I – arrived almost dead. I'm hardly conscious now. I'm operating solely on temporary nerve; in a few hours, if I'm not out of this nightmare, I'll collapse entirely. I can operate on nerve for a little while; I can endure anything so long as I know it's temporary. But once my strength gives out—'

'That's why I was not disqualified by the Competition Authority! I had another aura!'

'That's the way transfer works, isn't it? What did you expect?'

'I expected a visiting personality. I received a near-knockout blow.'

'Me too,' the transferee jetted. Except that it really was not a jet. It was an internal communication most resembling a thought.

71

'You're – the Solarian? Trained in intrigue?'

'Have you had transferees before? Is it always like this?'

'I have not hosted before. But none of the other hosts seemed to have trouble. I thought I had received no aura. But you have not answered: are you the Solarian?'

'I am Solarian.' There was a complex wash of thought and feeling, indecipherable.

'Control your reactions!' Heem needled. 'When you think a dozen alien thoughts at once, I cannot decipher any of them!'

'Well, at least I have some privacy.'

'You weren't transferred to my body for privacy! We have a competition to win!'

'Well, yes, I know about that. And I've been helping, I think.'

'Helping! By knocking me out just before the opening challenge?'

'Knocking *you* out!' the alien responded indignantly. 'I barely fought back to partial consciousness in time to solve the concept-pattern – and the effort made me lose consciousness again. The horror of blindness—'

'*You* solved the pattern? *I* analysed it, and—'

'And tried to disqualify yourself with a repeat, then balked at the final concept as though you had a death wish. *I* don't have a death wish! I had to jam the winning concept through your stalled alien brain, or whatever it is. *Do* you have a brain?'

It was a serious question. 'If by that you mean an organizing intelligence, I do. It is diffused through my body, relating to every aspect, as it should. Are Solarians differently organized?'

'We certainly are! We have a head, with most of our specialized organs of external perception there, next to the brain, up where they can be used most effectively.'

'Up? You have a – a permanent upper side to your body?'

'Of course we do! Don't you?'

'Of course not. How could anyone roll, if one side had to be always up?'

'Who would *want* to roll? Oh, don't answer that! What are you doing serving as host, if you don't know the nature of your transferee?'

'What are you doing transferring, not knowing you were entering a sightless host?'

'Touché,' the creature agreed. 'But I asked first.'

'The identities of the transferees were kept secret, so that no favouritism could be applied. I was not aware that I was to be the HydrO representative, until the presentation. All I know of Solarians is that they are a wild, undisciplined species, given to low-cunning plotting and warfare.' He paused. 'No offence intended to you, Transferee.'

The Solarian's burgeoning anger converted to mirth. 'No offence, slugball! It is an apt synopsis.'

'We shall be some time in initial manoeuvres. We must acquaint each other with ourselves, so that we can integrate properly for the competition. The other competitors had time back onplanet to do this, but we are late. When the ship achieves escape velocity and a stable trajectory, it will acquaint us with the location of the target planet and the nature of the quest. Then we shall be very busy, for we are the last ship to take off. We shall have to pilot with consummate skill so as to pass three quarters of the other ships and gain a tractor on the planetary surface.'

'We? I know nothing of spaceship piloting!'

Heem had feared that. 'Then we must come to an understanding before then, so that I will not be distracted. I am an excellent pilot, but there will be a considerable challenge.'

'Yes.' The alien paused. 'There is something you should know, and something I must know.'

'Make your statement and query efficiently, then.'

'I – am an imposter. I'm not qualified for this mission.'

73

'Impossible. You were transferred. That could not be a mistake. Segment Etamin would not cheat in a matter like this.'

'I – the real transferee was unable to perform. So I – substituted.'

'Impossible,' Heem repeated. 'They don't accept unqualified substitutes.'

'They did not know. I used the identity of the proper person.'

'The machine would not have transferred your aura. There is no way to deceive an aura verification. I should know; I was trying to do it myself, not long ago.'

'My aura is – very similar to his. The machine couldn't tell the difference.'

'Something's rolling very strangely here. Solarians may be backward, but not *that* clumsy. Obviously you are the entity selected and sent; it could hardly be otherwise, considering the verifications applied at your end and this end. Unless you are a construct of my tortured imagination. Is that what you are jetting? That you are not real?'

'I am real. I am Solarian. I am a transferee. But I am not the one trained for this mission. Not the one who was supposed to be sent here. I'm sorry.'

Heem pondered, becoming intrigued. 'Now I can appreciate why I might choose to imagine that I had a transferee; it might give me valuable confidence to proceed with this mission. I can taste why such an invented visitor would try to convince me of his authenticity; the ruse would not be effective if I did not believe. But I cannot perceive why such an invention would attempt to discredit himself. That would only subvert—'

'Himself?'

'Yes, himself. I am not questioning your validity, *you* are. By insisting on an obvious flaw in your story. So—'

'Oh, figure of speech. Male-person singular, standard convention.'

Heem let that roll by. The transferee was attempting to divert him with quibbles, while the significant matter receded. He picked up the taste again. 'So I doubt you are from my imagination; my mind is too logical to account for you. That means you must be real.'

'What do you mean, too logical for me? I am every bit as logical as you are!'

'That is what we are in the process of ascertaining. I accept you as real, but your logic is suspect. You claim that you deceived an undeceivable machine.'

'I did deceive it!'

'Are you not aware that no two auras are alike, and that the machines type the auras infallibly? Otherwise they could not transfer them.'

'Yes, of course I'm aware. But this is a special case.'

'It would have to be extraordinarily special.'

'It is.'

'In fact, you would have to be identical to the original subject. Which means—'

'Not me personally. My aura – that is what is identical.'

Heem did a mental roll of equilibrium. 'No two auras are identical. Each aura differs precisely as the entity with which it is associated differs. That is why the entity can be recreated in a foreign host, because the truest identity lies in the aura, not the body. You claim you are not the original subject. You also claim your aura, the source of your identity, is—?'

'Yes. That is the unique aspect.'

'And you also claim to be logical?'

'I am a clone!' the Solarian exploded in a taste overload.

This rolled Heem back somewhat. 'A clone! A person identical to another, fashioned from the same genetic pattern. A split personality. I suppose that could work, theoretically.'

'And in practice.'

'You claim you are cloned from an adult Solarian?'

'No, cloned at conception. We were born as siblings.'

'But the aura is changed by experience. By the time you metamorphosed, you would be too far apart to fool the machine.'

'We were raised together, sharing all things. Our auras constantly interacted, evening out any developing distinctions. We were not identical – far from it! – but machines aren't geared for clones.'

'Yet you lack the training and abilities of your clone-brother? I find it hard to believe that you could be close enough to fool the machine, without being close enough to do the job.'

'I possess the same potential, but not the specific training, much of which was very recent. I don't think the machine was looking for differences in the area where those differences existed. But it may have interfered with the actual transfer.'

'So that you arrived slightly out of phase, and knocked us both out!' Heem jetted, comprehending.

'I'm sorry.'

'You're sorry! You almost wiped me out of the competition!'

'I really had no choice. My clone-brother had accepted the commission, spent the credit, then when he got hurt—'

'You rolled in to cover his error – at least until the technical situation was met.'

'I realize this is unfair to you. But we were desperate. Our whole way of life – my alternative was to kill my brother, to abate his commitment without prejudice—'

'I comprehend.'

'So if you want to be angry—'

'Solarian, I would have done the same in your situation. My own sibling died, enabling me to survive, but my demise would not have helped him.'

'You are not enraged?'

'I am here on false pretences myself. I had to get

offplanet in a hurry, so I took the only route available. The competition – though I knew I did not qualify.'

The transferee was amazed. 'You did the same thing I did!'

'I did. So I can hardly blame you for that. You seem to be my type of personality, even though your body may differ drastically from mine.' He reflected on that, remembering the various hints the Solarian had jetted about those differences. 'I really do not know what the physical form of a Solarian is.'

'Not like the HydrO form, I assure you! We have muscle and bone, and carry our heads high, and have arms and legs and hands and eyes and ears—'

'Awful!' Heem sprayed. 'You taste almost like a—' He hesitated, not wanting to produce the repulsive concept.

'Like what?' the alien demanded. 'I noted that note of revulsion. Like pickled sewage sludge – awful taste!'

'How do Solarians derive their life-energy?' Heem temporized.

'We eat food, of course, like any other creature.'

'Not HydrOs. Not the Erbs. Not a hundred other Segment species.'

'HydrOs don't eat?' the alien jetted incredulously.

'We absorb hydrogen and oxygen from the atmosphere and combine them, with release of energy, on a controlled basis. That fuels our metabolism, and the residue is OH_2.'

'Water, you mean? H_2O? Your waste product is water?'

'Hardly a waste. We use it for propulsion, combat, communication, manipulation of objects, perception, cushioning of impact – at this very moment we are cushioned by—'

'Flavoured water for speech!' the alien sprayed, amazed. 'I never would have thought it possible!'

'Not only possible, but practical. For communication and life-style. HydrOs can exist and function on any planet where a suitable atmosphere and temperature exists.'

'But I thought it took more energy to separate the oxygen and hydrogen in water than could be obtained rejoining them.'

'We don't separate them from water. We draw the elements we need from the air, using enzymes to process them efficiently. It is by far the readiest source of energy, and the trace impurities we utilize to build body mass.'

'I guess it works. You're here; that proves it. Maybe your atmosphere is different from ours.'

'Perhaps. Hydrogen is very common in the Cluster, but I can't vouch for strange systems like Sol. We HydrOs are the elite of the Segment Thousandstar sapients, in contrast to—'

'You're hiding something! I can feel it in your system.'

'In contrast to the eating species,' Heem continued unwillingly. 'Who are our natural enemies.'

There was a period of tastelessness. 'You mean it?'

'I mean your kind as you describe it – the eyes, ears, appendages, eating orifices, and other allied organs – most nearly resemble the species we know as the Squams. They lack the eyes, but apart from that—'

'Oh, I caught that awful emotion! You really do hate the Squams. Not only as a species. Personally!'

'I have reason,' Heem sprayed.

'You must have. I can feel the taste burning through your whole body. But I don't even know what a Squam is ! Why don't you show me a mental picture?'

'A what?'

'A picture. An image, so I can see—' She rolled to a halt. 'Oh, I understand. You don't have eyes. You don't even think in terms of sight. You only know of that sense through the contacts your species has had with other Galactic creatures. You *can't* make a picture!'

'I can make a taste pattern,' Heem offered.

'Very well. Try that. I am very good at analysing patterns. We call it art. I work in holographs, in three-

78

dimensional art. Art is a property centred in the right hemisphere of the brain, complementing the logic of the left.'

'Hemispheres? Your brain is in several parts?'

'Never mind that now. Just make the pattern.'

Heem projected the taste of the dread Squam as it fed on his sibling-juvenile Hoom. The pattern of horror still revolted him – and that was the origin of both his success and his failure, as an adult.

'I'm suffocating,' the alien sprayed. 'It's horrible! But I still can't *see* it!'

They had a problem of communication. The Solarian seemed not to comprehend something unless he could visualize it, while Heem had only taste to offer. They discussed the matter, going over the Squam memory in detail, and finally the Solarian began to comprehend. 'I'm forming a mental picture now. It's not a direct translation of your memory, but more of a reconstruction from what I am grasping intellectually. That monster is not at all like me. It's a snake – a snake with arms, and no real head. I have legs, while it doesn't, and I don't spew out my stomach – Heem, if you could see me, you'd see how little I resemble your Squam.'

'Project a taste-pattern of your physical self,' Heem jetted amenably.

The alien tried, but all that came through was a mélange of peripheral flavours. The alien had no more mind for taste than Heem had for sight. 'It's lucky we can even communicate,' the Solarian jetted at last.

'Meaning transmission is a separate function, integral to all sapients,' Heem jetted. 'Transferees never have language problems. I am not certain why we are having *any* communicatory problems; it is my understanding that even creatures with grossly differing life-styles and modes of perception normally mesh perfectly in transfer. Your impersonation of the original Solarian schedule for this

79

mission may account for it.'

'It may,' the Solarian agreed. 'There is something else, however.'

'You are full of little surprise rolls! First you are unqualified, then you resemble my worst enemy. What now?'

'You – does your kind have sexes? Male and female?'

'Yes, we are a bisexual species.'

'And you – you are of which sex?'

'Male, naturally.'

'That – is what I was afraid of.'

'Afraid? Did you crave to have a neuter host?'

'No. You see, I am female.'

'Impossible!' Heem exploded. 'Cross-sexual transfers do not occur. It must be a confusion of nomenclature.'

'Cross-sexual transfers are not *supposed* to happen,' she jetted. Actually, she was probably sounding or lighting, but he perceived it as jetting. 'They even use transfer as a definition of sex, in questionable cases. As when an individual of a species changes back and forth at different stages of life, now male, now female, like the Mintakans. If a given aura arrives in a male host, it's male.'

'Agreed. Therefore, what you term female must in fact be male.'

'Do males bear offspring, among your kind?'

'No. Females do that.'

'I – do that.'

'You claimed you were a clone of a male!'

'I am. One detail was changed, after the cloning.'

'Some detail! You could not consider yourself the same person, after that!'

'I had little choice in the matter, since it happened when conception was only hours past.'

Heem ignored her strange time-unit. 'You would have grown completely apart from your other half!'

'No. We were raised as siblings, as I said before. We were

80

treated identically. I was called male, so there would not be any fuss – but Jesse and I knew, always. When we matured, we lived apart from our peers, and anonymous to our neighbours. Which was not hard to arrange, since we were of the royalty. Our auras changed together, constantly interacting. Really a single aura with two bodies.'

There was an uncomfortable pause. 'The transfer should not have taken,' Heem jetted at last. 'You should have arrived in a female host, or bounced.'

'That's what I assumed would happen. If the transfer took, I would occupy a female host, or at least a neuter one, of Segment Thousandstar, and my brother's onus would have been abated. He had only to report for transfer; no more was guaranteed. If I bounced, then it would signify that the Thousandstar host had not been adequate, and the advance payment would forfeit to Jesse. I expected to bounce – and thereby save our family fortune without actually undertaking a mission for which I was not qualified.'

'They will know – the Society of Hosts will know that your body is female, when they exercise it.'

'We prepared, just in case. Our old estate retainer, Flowers, was to take the body home for care, so no one else saw it. Lucky thing we set that up, I suppose!'

'But the fact that transfer did occur – to a male host! This can not be explained.'

'It seems unique, certainly. My arrival was painful to us both; I must have come close to bouncing, but didn't quite make it. I still feel the effect; your system is basically hostile to my aura. I think the clone-factor must have made the difference. My aura was close enough to fool the machine, so it sent me through as a male, and your system had to accept me as a male even though I was not. *Am* not! Since the original entity, before cloning, was male, I could be considered as a male with an added X chromosome. Really, Jesse's aura is awfully close to mine. In the circumstances—'

81

'Your logic is female. It must be so,' Heem jetted limply. 'That would account for the initial unconsciousness we both suffered, and for the trouble we now have communicating. It is not that you are alien; it is that you are female, and therefore the most alien creature of all. Your mind does not operate in comprehensible fashion.'

'In the circumstances, I'm disinclined to argue. I have brought three disasters upon you, and I don't know how to mitigate any of them.'

Heem rolled those disasters around in his mind. First, an unqualified individual, thereby serving as a liability instead of an asset, when he desperately needed an asset. Second, a creature of an anathema-species: one that consumed food. Third, a female. Three things in ascending order of mischief.

Yet was he blameless? He too was unqualified for this competition, and to her *he* was the anathema alien without the organs of perception she required, and she had no more desire to occupy a male host than he had to have a female transferee.

'That's kind of you to think that, but—'

'I wonder.' Heem jetted slowly. 'I had a desperate need to get into space, and I knew I needed a transferee. I must have encompassed any aura that came, overriding the natural cautions of my system. It could be as much my fault as yours.'

'I do prefer your logic to mine,' she admitted.

'And you did accomplish what I required,' he continued. 'They must have verified my aura and yours, and approved me for the competition while I was still trying to devise a scheme to slip through without a transferee. So I made it to space after all. But now—'

''Now my presence is hampering you,' she said. He now found it easier to stop attributing her communication to jets; she simply did not jet or spray, even in her mind. She spoke. She seemed to become more intelligible as he accepted this alien reality.

82

'I really had little hope of winning the competition anyway. I am satisfied to be offplanet, with or without a transfer aura. But I do not know how you will return to your natural body if we leave the competition.'

'I *have* to return!' she cried. 'I couldn't stand to be blind and deaf all my life!'

'To do that, we will have to win the competition. That will not be easy.'

'But only one person can win. Don't all the transferees get to go home, after it is over?'

'They should. But I personally do not dare return to my home-planet for the retransfer of my visitor. *You* would go home – but I would be perpetually confined. I joined the competition to get away from that fate.'

'But if we win the competition—'

'Then I will return as a hero, my criminal record pardoned. They have given me a considerable incentive.'

'Then it's decided. We both have incentives. We win the competition!'

'Solarian—'

'Jessica. That's my name.'

'Jessica Solarian – this competition may be more hazardous than you appreciate. We could both perish.'

'I understood it was a low-risk mission!'

'It is supposed to be. But I have had news of prior competitions. If the objective is important, the participants get highly competitive. A certain amount of intrigue, even violence occurs. It is not supposed to, but it does.'

'Oh,' she said faintly. 'But maybe this objective is not so important.'

'Perhaps. We shall soon know. The ship is stabilizing; we have almost achieved escape velocity.'

'Um,' she agreed nervously. 'So we may face real action. Look, Heem, we should get to know each other, so we know how to integrate. It could make a big difference.

83

Exchange memories, compare notes, values—'

He had had enough of this. 'No!' he jetted. 'Go away!'

'I can't go away. You know that. I'm stuck here in your body until we get to an aura transfer machine, besides which, I genuinely want to help. I feel responsible—'

'I don't want your help!'

'Well, my help has been forced on you. You shouldn't have signed up for this mission, if you really didn't want—'

Heem needled an intense negation at her.

'Hey! That hurt!' she protested.

'Then be tasteless. Silent. I don't want to be aware of your presence when I begin piloting this ship.'

'Well, you needed my help before, and I think you'll need it again. Since my own welfare is tied up in this just as much as yours—'

Heem, furious at her persistence, needled angry loathing at her.

Jessica bounced it back at him. The impulse washed through his mind, disgusting him.

'See, I can do it too!' she said. 'I can make your mind just as miserable as you make mine. And I *will*, if I have to. But I don't want to have to.'

'What *do* you want?' Heem demanded. A part of him wondered why he had turned so negative, and another part of him did not want the answer.

'Just to get to know you. So I know what I'm involved in. *Really* know, instead of just that you're—'

'No!'

'Now look, Heem. You're being unreasonable. What do you have against me? Maybe I can alleviate it.'

Heem formulated a savage needlejet, thought better of it, and sprayed irately, 'You're alien! I don't want you poking into my mind.'

'I think we've been over that, Heem. What either of us wants in that respect is pretty well irrelevant. You knew there'd be an alien transferee—'

'Not a female one!'

'Oh, now we have it, do we? It isn't just the shock of encountering a female where you didn't expect one. You're a male chauvinist!'

'Females are all right in their place.'

'And what is that place? In the steaming kitchen, the nursery, the laundry room—'

Heem interrupted her with a spray of pure incomprehension. 'What is a kitchen? A nursery? A laundry?'

'Oh, my. Maybe I'd better find out more about your females! Let's start with the basic common ground. Your females do bear children, don't they, so—'

'They do produce litters.' But he did not want to discuss that aspect. It was a private female thing about which he knew no details. 'What is this kitchen your females belong in? This laundry?'

'They *don't* belong in – oh, never mind. It's where we fix our meals and clean our clothing.'

'Meals? Clothing?'

'You know. We just covered that. Food, to eat, and—'

'You are not revolted?'

'Let's leave the ramifications for later. What do you really have against females?'

'I do not—'

'Yes you do. You are against me not because I'm alien but because I'm female. I mean to get to the root of this. Why don't you want to associate with a female?'

'Because you invade my privacy! There are thoughts that are not meant to be known to your kind.'

'Thoughts? It's not as if I were parading nude in public! I—'

'Nude?'

'Without clothing. Exposed.'

'We wear no such encumbrance. Our bodies are always exposed. Why should any creature *not* be exposed?'

'Well, we Solarians do have some exposure. I meant in a

85

sexual connection. Copulating in public, that sort of thing.'

'What is private about copulation?'

'Oh, my! I think I see the problem. To Solarians, sexual activity is generally private – even the necessary organs are called privates – while thoughts may be disseminated freely to an audience of millions. To you HydrOs, I gather—'

'Thoughts are private!' Heem sprayed, shocked. 'Among comprehending males, thoughts may on occasion be broadcast. But never in mixed company!'

'And I, as a female able to read many of your thoughts – I guess that has a certain effect on you, as it would on me if I were thrown naked into the men's room at a busy hour.'

'I do not comprehend your analogy, but your emotion seems equivalent.'

'Uh, yes. And I must admit your view makes about as much sense as mine. Bodies are not obscene, really; it's only the mind that makes them so. I'd hate to have my thoughts advertised at certain times.'

'You do not object to a male fathoming your most private thoughts?' Heem found the notion incredible.

'Well, you're alien. Your metabolism is completely different from mine. I wouldn't object to walking naked before a dog or a horse or a dragon of either sex; they're different creatures. But the cynosure of my own kind would be devastating. Now you – you're alien, but you're also sapient. That makes it hard to judge. But I think you would hardly care about my human attributes, so it wouldn't matter if you saw them. If you could see.'

Heem pondered that. She only minded being perceived by those who comprehended what they saw? She was certainly alien! Yet her rationale made a certain devious sense. She was so far removed from him that she had little comprehension of his concerns. What relevance, then, did her sex have? He began to feel easier.

In a moment the fluid cushion of the acceleration compartment drained, and Heem found himself in near-free-fall, in control of the ship. He jetted the Mission button.

'Welcome to the competition,' the ship's nozzle sprayed. 'The target planet is Eccentric, in this System. The three host species are HydrO, Erb and Squam.'

'Eccentric!' Heem exploded. 'I anticipated Ggoff!'

'I am not familiar with your local geography,' Jessica said. 'I presume this is System HydrO, so Planet Eccentric must be fairly close to your home-world. But where is Ggoff?'

'This is not System HydrO!' Heem corrected her. 'This is the colony System of Holestar, shared by three species. My home-world is Impasse. Ggoff is in System Erb, adjacent to us.'

'I'm getting confused already!'

'Ggoff really is as close to us as to the Erbs; closer, considering that we have a better established sub-Sphere here. Ggoff is habitable by both Erbs and HydrOs, so—'

'Since we're not going to Ggoff, stop confusing me with irrelevancies. What about Eccentric?'

'Eccentric is quite a different roll.'

'The objective is an Ancient site,' the ship's spray continued after its reasonable pause. 'Suspected of being in operable condition.'

'An operative Ancient site!' Jessica exclaimed. 'That's the most important thing there is!' Then she realized: 'Which means this is going to be the most savagely contested competition of the century . . .'

'Agreed,' Heem jetted glumly. 'There will be murder.'

'We had better get moving right away, then.'

'No. I mean to roll along sedately at the end of the line, vying with no one for position.'

'I don't understand.'

'This ship is last among the HydrOs in a race that is guaranteed to be savage. I cannot win the race; therefore I must secure my own survival. I can do this best by

87

conserving fuel, proceeding to Planet Eccentric, landing in a wilderness region – which is not hard to do, since it is a wilderness planet – and preparing to survive the winter. If I retain sufficient fuel, I may be able to use the ship to expedite my construction.'

Her reaction was oddly constrained. 'You are aware that this means my death? I cannot survive indefinitely in an alien host.'

'I am aware. But since I can save you only by winning the competition, and I cannot win, I must at least save myself.'

There was a pause. Then: 'If you are proceeding to Eccentric anyway, why can't you race there? You might do well enough to make the next cut, and get a tractor. If not, you'd still be on the planet.'

'And under the control of the Competition Authority, who would return me to my own planet. Had the destination been Ggoff, which is further distant, I might have had play to travel there fast enough; I have been there before. But the route to Eccentric is so restricted it must be buoyed, and I cannot gain sufficiently. I will arrive too late, so prefer to make it later yet, to avoid the Competition Authority.'

'Oh.' She considered some more. 'You mentioned a hard winter on Eccentric. Are there colonists there who might help you? I mean, you wouldn't have to go home? You could volunteer to be a settler—'

'No. No colonists. The winter is too difficult.'

'Then why would you want to suffer that winter alone?'

'It is preferable to what awaits me on Impasse, and winter is some time distant. At least I will have the long summer free.'

'Followed by the long winter.'

'Short winter. Short but intense.'

'I don't understand. Winter doesn't come to an entire planet; when it is winter in one hemisphere, it will be summer in the other. So you could travel—'

'Winter comes all over the planet, simultaneously.'

'That doesn't – does Eccentric have an orbit that is – oh, of course! Eccentric! Like a comet or planetoid. With a short, hot summer during the near approach to the sun, and – but you said a short winter.'

'This is a double system,' Heem explained wearily. 'Holestar. One Star and one Hole. Eccentric orbits—'

'One hole?' she enquired, perplexed.

'So designated. A collapsed star so dense that light cannot escape from it.'

'Oh, yes – what we call a black hole. I wouldn't want to get near one of those!'

'Eccentric is near one. It orbits both Star and Hole, and periodically the Hole eclipses the Star. Then—'

'Then all light is trapped by the hole! That would be one hell of a shadow!'

'A distasteful winter,' Heem agreed.

'What about Planet Impasse? Winter should be just as—'

'No. Impasse orbits the binary at an angle. It is never eclipsed by the Hole, so its winters are normal.'

'Two different orbital planes,' Jessica murmured. 'A star and a black hole. This is some system!'

'Correct. Eccentric is currently on the far side of the binary. The ships must skirt the Hole to reach it. Hence the buoys marking the most direct course that remains safe. The wise pilot will not stray far from the marked channel; he would either lose position or fall into the power of the Hole.'

'Yes, I can appreciate the need for caution,' she agreed. 'I suppose technically an orbit about a black hole is no more hazardous than one about a normal star. But emotionally it's horrifying!'

'Not to me,' Heem jetted, relaxing. 'I find it rather intriguing. I would be interested to explore within the range of no return except—'

'Damn it, I don't want to die blind!' she screamed

suddenly, jarring his nerves. 'You've got to win that competition!'

'Why should I roll away my chance for life, in a futile effort to promote yours?' Heem needled irritably. 'You're nothing but a Squam in alien guise.'

'I'm *not* a Squam. I'm a human being!'

'As I described. A female alien food-eating—'

'Oh, so that's it again! You just can't stand the thought of an objective female intellect in your sordid masculine brainless brain!'

This was useless, but he continued. 'Females just don't belong in sapient minds.'

'Sapients don't belong in male minds!'

'Flavour it as you wish. You do not belong in my mind.'

'That's what I'm saying! I'm desperate to get *out* of your roly-poly mind before I go crazy!'

'You are already half there.'

'Well, I'm not going crazy alone! If you don't at least try to get me transferred home, I'm taking you with me wherever I do go. Right into insanity if need be. See how you like that!'

'If you would rather be crazed than dead, roll on.'

'I'm liable to get difficult. I'm very good at that, Heem.'

'Be as difficult as you want. I control my body.'

'Fair warning: I'll scream.'

'I don't even know what a scream is.'

Jessica screamed. Her sound was transformed to his perception of taste, and it was horrendous. The savage impulses scoured their paths along his nerves. Her terror became indistinguishable from his own emotion; he suffered increasing apprehension and fear, though he knew there was no proper basis for such emotions. Her scream compelled them.

She really *could* roll him with her! Because she was inside his mind; he could not close her out. Soon he would be as demented as she.

'Mute your taste!' he sprayed violently. 'I will try the competition!'

The scream-taste abated instantly. 'How very sweet of you, Heem.'

She resembled a Squam, all right.

3

Space Race

Heem activated the space-taste spray. The flavour of System Holestar was emitted by the machine. There was the fleet of ships strung out ahead; his own was the last. There to the side was—

'I don't understand!' Jessica cried, disrupting his perception. 'What do all those tastes mean? If only I could *see*!'

She was really rolled up about her lost perception! 'Why don't you just try tasting?' Heem enquired, irritated. 'It is really quite sufficient.'

'My system is not oriented on taste,' she retorted. 'Except when I eat—'

'Ugh!' Heem spat, repulsed.

'Well, if you find it hard to think of eating, I find it just as hard to see by tasting. I naturally associate taste with eating.'

'Taste is civilized! Eating is – eating!' He could think of no worse insult than the term itself.

'Eating is fun, if you just had an open mind about it.'

'Never!' How like a Squam she was! 'Then why don't you go dream of eating or whatever other abomination pleases you, and let me concentrate on the position of the ships of the fleets? *I* can do it very well by taste.'

'Because my life is at stake! If you don't win this competition, my aura will fade and fade until it is gone, and I'll be dead. *I don't want to die blind!*' Her emotion, verging on another scream, threatened to overwhelm his equilibrium again. She was correct: she was very good at being difficult.

'I am willing to make the attempt to win the contest. But

two hundred entrants remain, of which I am at or near the end. Chances are not at this moment good.'

'Well, if I could see, I could help.'

Heem doubted that, but thought it better to placate this temperamental alien if he could. She really was no more guilty in the arrangement of this situation than he was, and he did not want her demise on his conscience. Also, she was raising an intolerable taste in his mind. 'Perhaps we could manage to translate the taste into sight. The data are similar – the ship's sensors actually utilize radiation, which they translate into taste. In interplanetary space, radiation is superior to taste for transmission of information.'

She fixed on that eagerly. 'Yes, maybe it could be done. After all, the human eye merely translates light into patterns of nerve impulses for the brain to interpret; it is really the brain that makes the comprehensive image. Just as your brain does for taste. It isn't taste that has meaning for you, it is the pattern that it dictates in your brain. So if we interpret your signals in terms of sight rather than taste—'

'It seems worth an attempt. But at the moment we have a race to roll.'

'A race to *run*!' she cried.

'As of what occasion do spaceships *run*? That mode is ungainly enough when executed by the species that do it, but no spaceship has legs, or ground to apply them to.'

'No space ship rolls, either! Not the way you mean. You need ground to roll on, to.'

'If we exhaust our time debating cultural figures of taste—'

'Figures of *speech*!'

'We shall never have a chance to compete in this competition.'

She pondered momentarily. 'You do make obnoxious sense. All right, operate your spaceship. For now. But tell me what's happening.'

It was a fair compromise. Heem reactivated the space-taste. 'There are three fleets comprising the roster of this competition. They—'

'Three fleets?'

'The sixty-six ships of the HydrOs, sixty-six of the Erbs, and sixty-seven of the Squams,' Heem explained, irritated again. 'This is a three-host mission.'

'Oh, I suppose that makes sense. A variety of hosts offers more – variety. But why didn't we see any of the others before? They can't have come from different planets; that would take years at sublight velocities.'

'No, many of the Stars of Thousandstar are closely set. Separated by a quarter parsec or less. Ggoff could be reached in several macro-chronosprays—'

'I can't make head or tail of your units of time.'

'There are several other planets in System Holestar, and they are only – I do have some notion of your time-scale – only light hours distant. But you are correct; these fleets all derive from Planet Impasse.'

'Three totally different sapient species couldn't have evolved on a single planet!'

'They did not. This is a colony system, occupied by three Stars under terms arranged millennia ago. The Erbs have the tropic region, where there is the strongest starlight; we HydrOs have the temperate zone, and the Squams have the polar regions. We are all able to survive similar climate and atmosphere, but prefer what we have chosen.'

'Three technologically sapient species sharing a planet? Whatever for?'

'It dates from the years of Sphere formation. The planet was within the expansion area of all three, habitable by all three. Warfare threatened, for this was before Segment Thousandstar was firm. Yet war between Stars would have been disastrous; it would have weakened us all, allowing other Spheres to surpass us. We desired neither to fight nor to yield a valuable planet and system. It was an impasse.'

'There's its name! Impasse!'

'Rolled on. So the compromise came, and war was averted. But it put the three species into direct physical contact with each other, rather than merely transfer-contact – and we did not get along well. The planetary boundaries have been freely violated, and there have been periodic outbreaks of localized war. The impasse has remained for many centuries, and we have come to know our companion-species rather well, but it has not brought amity.'

'So now your three species are the focus of a Segment competition for a prize of Cluster significance,' Jessica said.

'Yes. It will come to personal combat at the Ancient site. The HydrO authority knew this, and this is the reason they selected me to represent the home species.'

'You are good at combat?'

'So they believe.'

'Why would they believe it if it were not so?'

'That becomes complex to explain. We had better get in the race at this time.'

'You can be the most infuriating creature! Every time something interesting comes up, you get interested in the race.'

'There will be occasion to review matters of interest. Now we are perhaps last of two hundred ships, and must pass a hundred and fifty of them before we reach Eccentric.'

'A hundred and ninety-nine ships.'

'What?'

'You said there are sixty-six HydrOs, sixty-six Erbs, and sixty-seven Squams. That's a total of one hundred and ninety-nine, not two hundred.'

'Will you stop quibbling while I'm trying to race? I should have jetted sixty-seven Erb ships.'

'Well, maybe I can still help, somehow. How do you do

95

this race? I mean, are there special tricks, or what?'

'A million. But most of the others in the race are well aware of them. You can be sure every transferee is a good pilot.'

'Then how can we gain on them? How can we pass one hundred and forty-nine competent pilots piloting ships identical to ours?'

'There are ways,' he assured her. 'But not all of them are strictly ethical.'

'Which is another reason they selected you,' she said. 'They expect you to come out ahead without getting caught in any infractions.'

'Correct. This is what I propose to do, since you compel me to compete in an unwinnable race.'

'But that's cheating! I won't countenance that!'

'They expect you, as a typical Solarian, to apply the notorious cunning of your kind to the same flavour.'

'Are you implying that Solarians are unethical?' she demanded, stamping one of her imaginary feet. Heem was intrigued by the concept.

'*Are* they ethical?'

She hesitated. 'Some are. *I* am.'

'You consider it ethical to impersonate another individual, assuming a mission for which you are not qualified, for the sake of—'

'Enough!' she cried. 'I withdraw the claim.'

'Like a Squam, you slither away when challenged to justify your—'

'We have a race to run!' she cried.

'Precisely. I would think the most ethical thing you could do would be to make every effort to complete the mission you undertook.'

She was silent, and he proceeded to his business. He set the ship on the ideal course, as marked by space buoys that the ship's sensors read. He angled his canopy for maximum absorption of radiation from the Star. And he waited.

The space-taste indicated one column of ships rising from the equatorial zone of Planet Impasse, the individual craft strung out like floatpods along a succulent vine. These were the Erbs. Their vessels opened like flowers towards the Star, gathering extra energy. Another column extended from near the north polar region, its members strewn into a serpentine array: the Squams. The third was the HydrOs, from the temperate latitude, Heem's own ship trailing.

'Why aren't you accelerating?' Jessica demanded. 'We're way behind; if we don't even try to catch up—'

'Taste those two other columns; they will converge on us shortly, seeking the ideal channel.'

'All the more reason to hurry!' she cried. 'Can't this ship go any faster? We can take more than one g, can't we?'

'We have a limited amount of fuel,' Heem explained patiently. 'If we squander it with foolish acceleration, we will roll out prematurely.'

'But how can we ever *race*, then? If only the first fifty have a chance for the tractors—'

'The race began with the concept-pattern riddle. The first to gain their ships won a decided advantage. But it is possible to make up in this roll of the race what we lost in the prior one. Careful management is the key along with a little bit of luck.'

'You're planning something sneaky,' she said accusingly. 'I'm getting to know you, Heem. You have a disreputable masculine mind.'

'If you prefer that I give up the race—'

'No!'

Heem made a mental flavour of mirth. He was learning how to manage his transferee, alien though she might be.

'That's what you think,' she muttered irately. 'If it weren't a matter of life and death—'

Heem accelerated slightly, concentrating on the flavour of the spaceship pattern. A bunch was forming near the head of the line, as foolish pilots vied with each other for the lead. All ships were accelerating at close to one gravity – one Planet Impasse gravity, he clarified before the alien could interact a remark – obviating the need for rotation; it was a fuel-inefficient way to travel, but only a ship in full free-fall could be truly efficient, and free-fall was not much good for a race. But those pilots who jumped the acceleration rate were consuming fuel too rapidly in proportion to their gain in velocity; they could exhaust their tanks before the target planet was reached. Those who conserved too much fuel would finish too far back. It was a delicate judgement, and the pilots who were most apt at rolling this line would gain position.

'I'm picking up some of that,' Jessica said. 'Your conscious thoughts are open to me, as I suppose mine are to you. But the background remains opaque. If the most efficient mode, all things considered, is a straight-line acceleration and deceleration, and all ships have the same mass and fuel, how can anyone hope to gain position? Skill in making the judgement between velocity and fuel economy is fine, but that can only make a marginal difference, and we need a gross difference. How can we *gain*? If we use extra fuel, we'll run out; if we don't, we'll lose the race! So why should we even try to do anything special?'

Heem, concentrating on the pattern of ships, did not respond to her reiteration of the problem. He was studying the flux developing in the line ahead, shrewdly judging at what point a wrinkle would manifest.

'But I suppose that's exactly what a lot of pilots will think,' Jessica continued. 'So they *won't* try, especially the ones up front, assuming their place is secure. So if someone behind has a smart idea, like shooting ahead and messing up a leading ship, so maybe a friend can pass them both up and . . .'

Heem upped his acceleration a trifle more.

'Aren't you wasting fuel?' Jessica demanded. 'You're

edging up past one g and closing on the next ship ahead.'

Still he did not answer. He nudged the ship to the side of the buoyed route, using more fuel. His velocity was now substantially greater than that of the several ships immediately ahead of him, but he was somewhat outside the ideal route.

'This is crazy!' Jessica cried. 'I can pick up a vague picture from your comprehension. You are deliberately putting this ship into a bad position. Too fast, too soon, and out-of-channel. If you were the leader, you'd be throwing away your chances; as it is—'

The line of ships rippled. A clot developed near the end. Suddenly three ships were flying side by side, forming a triangle, almost touching hulls, blocking the main channel. Four more ships closed in on them, becoming part of the jam. The taste-blips that were the reproductions of these ships wavered and blurred as they came too close together; their pilots jetted desperately to avoid near collision. Several tried to accelerate out of the clot; others tried to decelerate.

'A traffic jam!' Jessica exclaimed, finally seeing it. 'We have those in System Capella, when too many groundcars try to navigate an intersection.'

Heem needled the control buttons. The ship surged forward, increasing its acceleration to 1.5 g, and shot past the jam. Three, four, five, six ships fell behind. Then Heem eased back to a single g and angled smoothly into the main channel.

'Very nice manoeuvre,' Jessica said. 'You bypassed the jam and passed six ships for the price of one, and probably wasted no more fuel in getting ahead than any of them did in getting behind. Perfect timing! But how did you know the jam was coming? You were creeping up on it before it ever happened.'

'Flow dynamics,' Heem replied. 'Though each ship is separately piloted, the channel for maximum efficiency is

99

extremely narrow, so the ships are forced into a column. They are thus subject to the flows of channelization. I happen to have a talent for analysing such flows.'

'I can see that,' Jessica agreed. 'My own talent is art, but it is really more static. Once you completed your manoeuvre, I could appreciate the precision and beauty of it, but I could not have executed it myself. But will there be enough jamming for you to pass another hundred and forty-four ships?'

'Doubtful. The smart ones will stay out of clots and pull ahead; I cannot gain on them unless they foul each other up.'

'I was pessimistic a while ago,' she said. 'Now I have hope. You have real skill, Heem.'

Heem suppressed a wash of pleasure. What did he care what this alien thought? 'That is why they selected me. I have a skill in piloting and in combat – skills unusual in my species.'

He perceived another clot-incipience, and positioned his ship accordingly. This time he found a channel through the middle of the jam and blasted through with precise timing. Eight more ships were passed.

'Beautiful, absolutely beautiful!' Jessica exclaimed. 'But suddenly I feel dizzy! What is happening?'

'We got a taste of jet exhaust,' Heem explained. 'The backlash of each ship is flavoured with chemical wastes, and the velocity of those gases also affects our own propulsion. It is unpleasant to be directly in the exhaust of another ship. The effect dissipates rapidly with distance, however, as the exhaust fans out and soon departs the main channel. Otherwise it would be difficult to maintain a column in space.'

'Yes,' she agreed. 'No doubt tempers get short when the ships get too crowded.'

'Tastes become volatile,' Heem jetted. 'This causes errors. Errors lead to clots that should not otherwise occur.

100

There is an error now.' He made a mental tasteblip to indicate the location.

One of the ships they had passed was accelerating at a good three gravities, rapidly overhauling the others. 'Roll out of my way, you sours!' the ship's spacespray sprayed.

'I didn't know the ships could communicate with each other!' Jessica remarked, surprised.

'Of course they can; this is mandatory in space. These vessels are normally employed for courier duty, and on occasion get disabled or shy of fuel. They must be able to spray interplanetary distances. But this requires energy, so few are spraying during this race.'

The speeding ship came up behind Heem's. 'Move it, H-sixty-six!' its pilot sprayed with the flavour of acute annoyance.

Heem obligingly jetted slightly to the side, giving the ship clearance. 'I move it, H-sixty.'

'Why did you let that oaf through?' Jessica demanded. 'That was Soop of Soulwet, who took the ship you were about to guess. You should have given him a good taste of exhaust! Isn't it his job to manoeuvre around the ships he passes, instead of making *them* waste fuel for his benefit?'

'True. But he will gain us much more ahead,' Heem assured her. 'Taste.'

'All right, I'll watch. But it seems crazy to me, and it galls me to let that particular nut through unscathed.'

The speeding ship closed the gap on the two ships ahead. The spot-flavours identified these as H-54 and H-55: Vice and Knyfh in his memory, for the concepts that had won them. Heem ordinarily did not have that precise a memory, but he had put extraordinary concentration into his pattern-analysis effort in the later stages. These two ships had been taken almost together, and now were travelling together: probably a cooperating pair. That could mean trouble for a third party.

Indeed it did. H-54 and H-55 did not follow Heem's

polite example; they held firm in their places, effectively blocking the channel.

The irate H-60 was moving too fast to swerve around them in the room he had. Manoeuvres that could be readily accomplished at low velocity became more difficult at higher velocities; this was one of the variables it was easy for an inexperienced pilot to forget – until too late. H-60 did not even try to dodge around; he shot right between the two. The aperture was so narrow that the three blips merged on the space-taste as a single mass . . .

And fissioned in an awkward explosion. One ship shot forward, one backward, and the third skewed to the side.

Smoothly Heem veered, for he had room to manoeuvre. The backward-jetting ship, H-55, shot past, creating an eddy current that shook Heem's vessel. 'What happened?' Jessica cried.

Heem veered again, to avoid the sidewise ship, H-54, then accelerated fiercely. 'When two ships pass too close to each other under acceleration, their cone-wakes interact. That speeding H-sixty abruptly put three ships together within strong interaction range, since the other two were already at minimum safe separation. That, coupled with a fair velocity differential, fouled up all three drives. One cut out entirely.'

'The one going to the side,' she said.

'No. That one remains under normal acceleration; it merely drifts to the side from the lateral confusion. Probably its pilot is unconscious, unable to correct course.'

'But the other two are both accelerating, one forward, one back. The one going back is gaining speed—'

'The one going back has lost its drive. Thus it is drifting at constant velocity, directly on course. The rest of us are all accelerating at one g, leaving it behind more rapidly with every passing moment.'

'Oh – I see. Of course you're right. I keep forgetting that we're constantly speeding up, not just travelling.'

'It is an easy thing to confuse, for one unfamiliar with space,' Heem jetted charitably. He still felt the ebb-wash of pleasure from her prior compliment.

He received another dose. 'I can certainly see why they wanted you for this mission. You're really expert!'

'Yes. But I deceived them nevertheless. I can pilot a ship as well as I ever could, but I can no longer defeat a Squam in single combat.'

'If you could do it before, you can do it now, can't you?'

Heem did not respond. The driverless ship was disrupting the column behind, but he was more concerned with the column ahead. The speeder, H-60, had survived the encounter with the other two ships, and had not improved his manner. 'Roll out, noxious!' H-60 sprayed on the spacespray as he charged into the rear of a tight line. Several ships tried to, realizing that it was better to give way, as Heem had, than to suffer rear collision. H-60 was crazy, but dangerous. But they, too, had been tasting ahead rather than behind, and perceived the speeder too late. H-60 shot up the line, extremely close.

The effect was disastrous. Ships were jerked out of their courses, drifting from the channel in all directions. Some lost power and fell back. One meandered erratically, as though its pilot were crazed. Two retained control – but were angry. They were H-45 and H-41. 'Let's put that monster away!' H-45 sprayed.

'They are all fools,' Heem jetted privately to Jessica. 'They are not reacting as they would on land. They can only put themselves away.'

The two ships accelerated, jumping to three g. Slowly they abated their rate of loss and began gaining on the speeder. But now other ships were being disturbed, and at three g the pilots were under heightened stress, and suffered diminished responsiveness. They cruised too close to the other ships, and angled out of the channel, while H-60 zoomed on ahead.

Heem, analysing the pattern of disarray, jetted carefully forward at one and a quarter g, threading safely through the clutter. He managed to pass seven more ships before another pilot tasted his technique.

'Where are you rolling, Sixty-six?' the other HydrO demanded, accelerating to cut him off. It was H-49.

'That's Czeep of Czealake,' Jessica commented. She seemed to have a good memory; maybe that had enhanced Heem's own memory.

Heem deftly manoeuvred his ship to place it behind a third ship, H-46. H-49 swerved to follow him.

'H-Forty-six – that's Swoon of Sweetswamp!' Jessica said. 'But she doesn't know us, because she was gone before we got our ship.'

'Let her remain in ignorance; we are not cooperating anymore,' Heem jetted to Jessica. 'Must avoid rolling into a clot.'

'Yes, indeed,' she agreed. 'These column-dynamics are getting fierce.'

But H-49 was determined. The ship jetted forward and across, seeking to bathe Heem's ship in its exhaust. Heem avoided it adroitly, but this was costing him fuel. Even though he used less fuel than 49 did, he could not win the race by getting caught in this sort of thing.

He was saved by the first speeder, H-60. The foolish pilot finally crashed into another ship that was unable to move aside in time. The resulting confusion disrupted the entire line, sending so many ships into erratic manoeuvres that there was no point in individual competition. Heem's full attention was taken up by the sudden challenge of merely staying clear of the mess.

'Look at H-Forty-six go,' Jessica exclaimed. 'Swoon can really pilot, when she sees her chance.'

Heem ignored that. Ships Sixty and Forty-nine were derelicts, coursing back along the line without power, their relative velocity seeming to grow as they went. The ships

104

coming up on them jetted violently out of the way, their pilots panicking. They should have made minor course corrections to allow the derelicts to slide by, as Heem was doing. Now Heem had to correct for the motions of the reacting ships, and since he was close to the centre column, this was difficult. They tended to fling out randomly, posing a hazard to traffic.

But he was not so preoccupied that he neglected to take advantage of his opportunities to pass a few more ships. By the time the column firmed, he was forty-fifth in the line of HydrOs. Swoon of Sweetswamp was far ahead. Unfortunately, there were two other columns to contend with, and now they were converging.

Heem analysed the pattern of convergence. There was promise there. The ships had to form a single column for maximum efficiency, and were vying for position as they merged. 'What has rolled before was the polite preparation,' Heem jetted. 'Now the real competition begins.'

'You've done very well so far,' Jessica commented. 'With all this new confusion, you should be able to do better yet.'

'I've been competing with the less intelligent entries of my own species. Now I'm rolling up against the smarter ones towards the front of the line – and the smarter ones of two other species. This will not be quite so much fun.'

'I have confidence in you.'

'Your confidence is desperation. I am an excellent pilot, and in an even race I could probably prevail, though it is evident that some expert pilots have been transferred in. Swoon of Sweetswamp, in H-Forty-six, must have been the top pilot of the Star she represents; she was biding her time, waiting for disruption, before showing her expertise. There are others like that. Starting where I did, it will take a great deal more than confidence to make sufficient progress.'

Jessica made a mental shrug – a distinctly odd experience for Heem. She was retaining her confidence.

Now that he was committed to the race, Heem intended

to put his best effort into it. He had not boasted idly about his skill; in a fundamental sense he lived for space. All HydrOs had evolved for this destiny: to travel between planets. All HydrOs hoped to pilgrimage in space before they achieved the second metamorphosis.

'Metamorphosis?' Jessica enquired.

'Get out of my mind!' Heem needled.

'I wish I could. Your body is a horror to me!'

Heem concentrated his taste on the race. His ship was coming up to the mergence of the three columns. 'The sensible procedure is to give way to the Erb and Squam ships that intersect our route,' he jetted. 'Unfortunately this will cause our position to suffer, and we will have no chance to make the cut.'

'So the only safe course is unreasonable?'

'No. The safe and reasonable course is not to race.'

'Do you want me to scream again?' she enquired sweetly.

'The only thing worse than a Squam is a female Squam.' Heem needled the controls, and the ship angled forward responsively, seeking an opening in the threatening clot.

'Better than a blind male blob!' she retorted, but he had already forgotten what she was responding to.

The blips were taste-coded to show species as well as number. Heem experienced involuntary constriction of his jet-apertures as he identified the Squam ships. He did not like Squams, even in the form of spaceships. Jessica's resemblance to a Squam constituted a significant portion of his objection to her. He knew, intellectually, that she was an alien of quite another type, but the fact that her natural body had eyes and hands and consumed physical substance – appalling! And to be, in addition—

'Your thought processes are about as subtle as a clout on the head.'

'I don't have a head.'

'Which is part of your problem.'

The mergence of columns loomed. Heem knew that once

106

he got locked into the enlarged column, he would have little opportunity to move up without prohibitive waste of fuel. Yet to break out of the buoyed route would also cost too much.

'There has got to be some way!' Jessica cried.

'There is, but not a way you will like.'

'To hell with what I like! Try me and see. Anything's better than – this!'

'I take you at your taste,' Heem jetted, and cut into the heart of the massing pattern. The taste-blips of the competition suddenly surrounded his ship.

'I think I'm going to regret opening my big mouth,' Jessica said. But then she was distracted by the blip pattern. 'Oh, they're so close, so close! I think I'm beginning – beginning to see them, a little. The merest suggestion. Focus the image, so I can—'

Heem concentrated, not entirely to please the alien. For the kind of manoeuvring he contemplated, he needed to have acute spatial awareness. If she wanted to think of that as an 'image' she was welcome. Maybe it would keep her from pestering him so much.

'Oh, it is beginning to shape. Like a surrealist dream, not quite clear but significant – I have to connect my sight awareness to your taste inputs – tricky, but with my mind's eye—'

Heem ignored her. He had a race to roll! The mergence of the three columns caused Squam and Erb ships to close in about him, vying for position. The blips were now so close to his own ship that they were merging on his space-taste. Heem experienced the mounting tension of competition; he liked this! To be in space, manoeuvring against others in space – here was the essence of living!

'The essence of masculine foolishness,' Jessica said sourly. But again, she was distracted by what she perceived. 'The Erb ships – they are like opening flowers – only they're flying sidewise!'

107

'Their energy-receptors orient on the Star, of course,' Heem needled. 'They need to augment their energy as much as possible, to make the artificial power last. It can readily make the difference between victory and defeat.'

'Oh, of course. You've kept us in the sun right along, haven't you!'

Idiot comment! Heem angled to put a hooded Squam blip, S-47, in shadow.

'And the Squam ships are like cobras!' Jessica continued blithely. 'Oh, you may not know about them, Heem. They're original Solarian reptiles – here, I'll project a picture.' She formed a composite taste that did vaguely resemble a Squam.

The Squam ship reacted angrily to the shade. It twitched out of the way, trying to get around Heem to cut off *his* Star radiation. But the Squam misjudged Heem's acceleration and missed. Heem made a flavour of satisfaction: the Squam had expended more energy in the attempted retribution than it ever could have gained in Star radiation. It would exhaust its fuel that much sooner.

Actually, there was little to be gained by interfering with ships here at the merger. Few if any of them would be in contention for the lead, and if he allowed himself to remain at this stage of the column he would fail to make the next cut. He had to pass these, get into the first fifty, and do it without consuming too much fuel or gaining too much velocity.

'Too *much* velocity?' Jessica enquired. She had a way of accenting her concepts that annoyed him. 'Don't you *want* to go fast?'

'Not so fast that I cannot decelerate on target,' Heem jetted gruffly. 'Accelerating is only half the job.'

'Oh, I see! Yes, of course! I'm used to land, to the planetary surface, where you will always coast to a stop if you stop pushing. But in space, with the conservation of angular momentum—'

'No. This is a powered trajectory, not an orbit.'

'Anyway, you can't stop unless you decelerate, so you must save half your fuel, or – Heem, what happens if you miscalculate?'

'We may have occasion to taste that before the race is done.'

She moved away from that aspect. 'The picture is coming in better, now! All the ships – it's like watching a holograph through a fog, but I'm really beginning to see! Oh, Heem, this makes it so much better! I don't feel so blind anymore!'

Heem intercepted the Star radiation of another ship, this one an Erb, E-38. He was accelerating marginally faster than the ships of the main column, but was outside the ideal channel. His freedom of travel counterbalanced his loss of the best route, so the only way he could gain was by shading the others. This was hardly enough by itself to enable him to win – but he had a strategy in mind.

The Erb, like the Squam, reacted angrily, trying to get out of the shadow. Heem manoeuvred to keep it shaded. Erbs, more than most creatures, were extremely sensitive to radiation, as it was their main source of body energy. Heem had counted on that. The longer he shaded E-38, the more irritated the Erb would become.

'Now there's all kinds of things wrong with that!' Jessica protested. 'First, why upset the Erb when you can't gain anything for yourself? All you can do is invite retribution that will cost you both energy. Second, the light-energy involved is small, and the Erb knows that. The Erb can see, after all, just as I can in my own body; it knows exactly how much light is worth. It won't do anything foolish just because you shade it.'

'We shall taste,' Heem jetted, feeling the thrill of incipient challenge.

'All right. I'll watch. But I don't see what you hope to accomplish.'

E-38 suddenly veered, trying to leap out of the shadow.

In the process it moved into the path of a HydrO ship just overtaking it. The HydrO ship veered. 'Get your mass out of my way, E-Thirty-eight,' the HydrO sprayed.

The ships were so congested here that the erratic motions of the two were now interfering with several others. 'Keep a straight course, fools!' S-47 sprayed.

'Do Squams spray too?' Jessica asked. 'I thought you said they used sound.'

'They do. The three-species communication grid renders their barbaric noise into intelligible taste. The same is true for the radiation emitted by the Erbs. HydrO taste is changed into their noise and radiation in their ships, too. No doubt the tractors on the surface of Eccentric will have a similar system.

She subsided, and he concentrated on the race. The disruption he had started had spread along a fair segment of the column. Ships were jerking in and out, and there was a medley of three-species cursing on the taste net. Heem remained safely out of it.

Suddenly he angled in just ahead of the mêlée, boosting his acceleration. 'Look what I did to you, you idiot pilots!' he sprayed into space. 'Not one of you has the wit to run a true course!'

'What are you doing!' Jessica cried, horrified. 'You're stirring up a hornets' nest! They'll group against you and wipe you out!'

'That's HydrO-Sixty-six,' a Squam exclaimed. 'He started this!'

There was a smear of responses. Soon a minor fleet of irate ships came after Heem.

Heem positioned himself in the centre of the buoyed channel. 'You imposters can't even catch me! What do you think you're trying to do? Turn about and go home before you get lost in space!'

'This is absolutely crazy!' Jessica cried. 'They'll kill us!'

'Lost in space!' a HydrO sprayed indignantly. 'We'll lose *you* in space, foulspray!'

110

'They have nothing to lose,' Jessica said. 'They know they're too far back to win. They need a scapegoat. They'll use up their fuel going after you, instead!'

'So they will,' Heem agreed. 'I did advise you that you would not enjoy this aspect of the race.'

'You sure did,' she agreed glumly.

A Squam ship shot out of the pack, accelerating at several gravities to catch Heem. But as it came near, Heem angled his drive-jet to give it an unhealthy taste of exhaust. 'Eat *that*, fool!' he sprayed.

'A foul! A foul!' another Squam cried as the first Squam lost power and fell back through the column. 'Did you perceive that? H-Sixty-six deliberately exhausted that ship!'

'What?' Heem enquired with mock innocence. 'I merely adjusted course to avoid collision. Nothing other than that can be proved.'

'Ooooh!' Jessica cried, half angry, half applauding.

'This is foul!' the Squam exclaimed.

'*Squams* are foul!' Heem sprayed. 'What else except the foulest would eat animal tissue and excrete compost?'

'A Solarian would!' Jessica objected.

'H-Sixty-six has a good roll on that,' a HydrO sprayed. 'Squams *are* basically disgusting.'

'Look who's squirting!' another Squam retorted. 'Any creature who slimes continuously and rolls about like a loose rock—'

'The truth is obvious,' an Erb glinted. 'Both Squams and HydrOs are disgusting.'

'Especially incompetent ones like all of you,' Heem sprayed.

'First we must dispatch this troubler,' S-52 said. 'Then we can debate aesthetics.'

'You could not dispatch a dead plant, Squam!' Heem sprayed.

'Why do you keep antagonizing them?' Jessica demanded.

111

'Do you have a death wish? You're starting a race riot!'

'Angry creatures are not sensible creatures,' Heem explained.

'That is my point! They will destroy us!'

Two more ships shot out of the mass at high acceleration. They drew up parallel to Heem, then angled across. They were S-44 and E-49. 'We'll knock you out of space, H-Sixty-six!' the Squam cried.

Heem juggled his ship precisely. The two attackers missed, closed on each other, and rebounded apart, out of control.

'What happened?' Jessica demanded. 'They didn't crash, they didn't foul up on their own exhausts; they bounced apart without touching!'

'Each ship has a repulser shield to ward off meteorites and prevent collisions. This is necessary and standard with narrow-channel interplanetary traffic. None of these ships will crash into each other.'

She sighed. 'These little details you assume I already know! But they – something happened to them, more than just bouncing.'

'The repulsers can be harsh, especially when the effect is unanticipated. Those two pilots are probably unconscious.'

'So you knocked out two more rivals who were already behind us! What does it gain you?'

'The pattern will emerge.' Heem turned his attention to the other ships again. 'Real amateurs!' he sprayed derisively. 'Unfit to clutter space.'

There was a confusion of tastes, sounds, and glints on the communication net. Then six ships were accelerating rapidly towards Heem's ship. 'Close him in,' S-51 directed. 'Do not let him escape again!'

'Now you've done it!' Jessica said. 'You are positively suicidal! Just like a male!'

'A number of these competitors are female,' Heem remarked. He noted the ominous convergence of ships, but

112

did not attempt evasive action.

'You want to accelerate?' the Squam demanded. 'We shall provide you acceleration!' The six ships formed a tight ring around Heem's ship, battering him with their massed repulser fields.

'What are they doing?' Jessica cried, alarmed.

'They're giving us a ride.'

'A ride? That doesn't make sense!'

The six ships jumped their acceleration. Heem's ship, shoved violently by the repulsers, leaped forward, pinned within their cone. The acceleration climbed to three g, then four g, then five g.

The other ships of the column got hastily out of the way and fell behind.

Then the ring of ships contracted. The pressure became intense. 'They're crushing us to death!' Jessica cried.

'That is the intent,' Heem responded. 'They are using the positioned repulsers to compact us, to put us under such pressure that we cannot resist what they will do next.'

'Do next? There's worse coming?'

'They will hurl us out of the column, into the Star or the Hole. With luck, we will not recover in time to jet out of that well – or if we do, we will lack sufficient fuel to make it safely to planetfall. In any event, we will be out of the race.'

'Can't we do anything?'

'Have no concern. I flavoured the text on space manoeuvres.'

'You flavoured – oh, you mean you wrote the book on dirty tactics! Well, I certainly hope you know what you're doing. All I can see is that your insults are getting us further behind and deeper into trouble.'

Heem jetted a complex pattern on the button controls. Water swished into the compartment.

'But this is the acceleration protection!' Jessica cried. 'For takeoff and landing, when you have to withstand up to ten gravities—' She broke off her thought, reconsidering.

113

'Oh – to withstand the repulser pressure. How clever. But then you can't manoeuvre the ship; it's on automatic.'

'I have just preprogrammed the ship to cut the main drive and stabilize with the side jets after acceleration. After that it will return to pilot-control phase.'

'But that won't stop them from hurling us out of the channel!'

'Their operation is based on the assumption that I will maintain normal acceleration, or raise it up several gravities in a vain attempt to escape them. The reactions of a pilotless, driveless ship are quite different.'

'Quite helpless, it seems to me!'

The pressure exerted by the six ships continued, but now Heem hardly felt it. The fluid of the ship held him cushioned. The drive cut off abruptly, releasing his body from gravity. There was a jolt as the six ships took up the slack, shoving his ship forward with the same acceleration.

'What's happening?' Jessica demanded. 'I was just beginning to see, but now there is no input. Just the blankness of suspension.'

'They are boosting us forward at about three gravities,' Heem explained, basing his judgement on experience as he felt the diminished impact of the thrust. 'They aren't skilled enough to coordinate the package for a turn, so they're trusting to random imbalances in thrust to cause us to veer out of the channel. But my ship is stable and precisely on course, so we are progressing due forward. They think that my cutting off the main thrust means that I have lost control; now they are shoving a derelict.'

'*Aren't* they?'

The extreme impetus continued for some time, then ceased with a jerk. 'Now they have turned us loose. They are probably almost out of fuel themselves; pushing a spaceship is immensely wasteful.' The liquid drained, freeing him for action. Heem activated the space-taste. 'Taste where we are now!' he jetted jubilantly, picking up the pattern of blips.

114

Jessica looked. 'We're halfway up the line!'

Heem cut in the main jet. 'And we have saved a fair margin of fuel. We can now accelerate at a slightly greater rate without exhausting our available supply.'

'But that means those six ships really helped us, while using up their own reserves!'

'As I jetted before: they are fools. Had they boosted one of their own number similarly, they could have vaulted him back into contention. But they allowed my impertinence to befuddle their rational processes.'

'They certainly did! Imagine allowing the quest for short-term vengeance to ruin your own chances! I would not have believed it possible.' She paused. 'No, it is possible. My own people are like that. Through history deeds are done that should not be, in the name of vengeance, while positive and necessary things are left undone. Billions for defence and not one cent for improvement. But it's still a ridiculous way to operate!'

Heem found he agreed intellectually, but not emotionally. He had been motivated to avenge what Slitherfear Squam had done, and this had profoundly influenced his entire life. He could not claim this was wrong; there needed to be justice, and without retribution there would be no justice.

'Oh, I don't agree with that!' Jessica protested.

'You hardly need to.' Heem angled back into the line so that his blip would not be so obvious to the others. There had been no reaction from the six ships who had boosted him; they had realized that they had been outmanoeuvred the moment his main jet came back on, and they were not eager to advertise the manner in which they had been fooled.

Heem, accelerating at a steady 1.1 g, was passing ships steadily now. Here in the midsection of the column they were strung out more evenly, and less given to direct rivalries. In short, they were more intelligent, disciplined

115

competitors, which was one reason they were here, making a fair roll for it.

It was a long, steady movement. Heem, tired, slept. Jessica, deprived of Heem's sensory input, slept also.

Heem, like most sapients, dreamed. Dreaming was a kind of sifting and tagging of recent experiences, identifying the important ones in key respects so they could be cross-referenced and filed safely in memory. Often Heem's dreams were unpleasant, for his life had not been generally satisfactory to him. Quite a number of his dreams were of the illegal variety. This time, however, his sleep imaginings were strange and pleasant.

He found himself riding a docile flatfloater, one that obeyed his every needlejet without quarrel. But he did not needle it; he let it take its initiative. Together they sailed over slopes and ridges, slid down into a river valley, and across the river. The scenery was delicious, with the vegetation spraying gentle wafts of delicate flavour in waves. He was back in his juvenile phase, happy, careless of the future. His juvenile siblings were with him here in the valley of Highfalls.

'Make it go faster, Jess!' his companion jetted.

'It's already at its cruising velocity, Jess. It can't safely accelerate.'

'Cruising velocity? Dragons have no cruising velocity! They just accelerate till they can't go any faster!'

'Well, that's how fast I want to go, clone-brother!'

Clone-brother? *This is not my dream!* Heem needled internally. But he did not wake. His dream shifted into another reality. He was rolling desperately towards freedom in the recurrent nightmare re-enactment of his escape from captivity. Yet the deepest element of that experience was not the physical escape, for that had succeeded. It was the emotional escape that had failed.

He rolled up to a safecage and needled his signature-flavour into its lock. Its mechanism took a moment to

116

absorb this. Then the lock released and the gate fell open. Heem rolled in, and his weight caused the gate to counterbalance, sliding back into position and relocking.

Now he was safe for the night. The cage was designed to keep Squams out; Erbs of course were no threat. He could rest and sleep, letting his guard relax. Of course the lock now had his flavour, and that would alert the authorities to his location, but the flavour-credits were collected only once a day, and by the time his flavour was fed into the credit computer, he would be gone. His credit was good; it was his citizen's status that was invalid.

Now for a good evening meal. He punched the food display, summoning a pseudosteak and sparkledrink, grey-flavoured. He picked up the drink—

Eating? In absolute shock and revulsion Heem voided all his jet-reserves. The ship, responsive to random commands resulting from this explosion, damped its main drive and veered. Suddenly he was in free-fall and fully awake.

He reacted with experienced proficiency, quickly restoring the drive and stabilizing the ship. Then he turned inwards. 'Solarian, that was your dream, was it not?'

'Yes – at the end. I'm sorry – I did not realize—'

'It is not bad enough that your female alien presence intrudes on my mind, but to have your Squam-begotten dreams polluting my sleep – eating! You make my imagination unclean!'

'I see that. I'm sorry. But I do not control my dreams.'

Heem's attention was already on the column of ships. It had thinned out; now all the ships were single file and well spaced. 'We are rolling to the midpoint; now we shall discover how we situate.'

Translating his taste, Jessica looked at the scene. 'We slept longer than I supposed! We're halfway there already?'

'The time sense is distorted under constant acceleration. We have been half a day in space, and now approach a velocity of one thirty-fifth light speed.'

117

'Half a day? Twelve hours?'

'As I recall the Solarian scale, correct. If a day on your home-planet is similar to a day on mine—'

'I – I can't tell, but from your feeling about it, it *feels* the same. Let's assume a day is a day the Galaxy over, and go from there.'

'We accelerate for half a day, and decelerate for half a day, our full course between planets being about one seventy-second of a light day.'

'I – see,' she said uncertainly. 'We accelerate to only a fraction of light speed, so it takes us much more time to travel the distance light does. I think your planets must be about as far from their primary as ours, and ours are only a few light minutes from—'

'Your distances are irrelevant,' Heem needled in impatiently. 'The moment of truth is upon us.'

'But the course is only half run. You said—'

'It is not yet half rolled. There will be a period of free-fall; ships who do not utilize this will be short of fuel. But it is the point at which approximately half our fuel has been expended. We can gain on the other ships only if we have more fuel. The initial bunching and column-merging is done, and the fools have been eliminated. From this point on, only power and margin suffice.'

'Oh, yes, I see that. But we're well up in the line, now, aren't we? We don't need to win at this stage; all we have to do is finish in the top fifty.'

'Yes. Therefore we now assess ships to determine our place. This is most accurately done at the moment of turnabout, for only then do the other ships betray their situation. They must turn on schedule.'

'Suppose they don't? I mean, suppose they coast a little longer at top speed, then brake more suddenly at the end, gaining a few places?'

'Some will try that, especially if they are just behind the

fifty-cut position. But if they cannot decelerate to landing velocity—'

'Crash,' she said. 'That's a risky game.'

'Extremely. Most will roll it safely, not endangering their lives for the gain of one or two places.' He needled the buttons, establishing a composite flavour for the ships of the column ahead and behind. He wanted every one of them in mind, for this critical survey.

'I see the ships!' she exclaimed. 'It's almost like having eyes now! But why are you surveying the ones behind us also? We don't have to worry about them, do we?'

'We do not yet know who is ahead and behind,' he explained. 'Their present position in space is deceptive. Some have too much velocity; they will not finish.'

'Oh, I begin to understand. If they're too fast at the turnover, they can't decelerate in time to land. I mean, they might decelerate to landing velocity, but only some distance beyond the planet, which would be no good. They won't really crash, will they?'

'They should signal for a fuel recharge – after the cut has been made. They will not crash, but they will be out of the race.'

Heem and Jessica spotted the ships. Heem used the ship's computer to calculate the velocity of each vessel as it turned over, while Jessica kept track of the leaders. It turned out that ten of the apparent leaders were over-velocity and were unlikely to finish; but fifteen ships behind Heem's own turned about on a schedule that would normally put them in the first fifty. Some of these might be within-velocity, but actually be scant on fuel – but others might be below-velocity and have reserves of fuel, enabling them to gain at the end. Strategies varied, and it was necessary to make educated guesses. There could be a lot of shifting of places at the end of the race, as all velocities were reduced.

The best finish Heem could reasonably hope for was sixty-one. That represented an excellent gain, from his start at or near two hundred – but not quite enough.

'But if you do some more clever manoeuvring, antagonize a few more pilots—' Jessica said.

'I might gain four, five, possibly even six places, no more,' Heem jetted. 'We are not competing against fools and amateurs now; these are natural spacers like myself. They will not react, they will not be deceived; they know they have the advantage, and they will maintain it. I used up my surplus fuel getting to this stage; this is my maximum position. To push beyond this place in the column would be to disqualify myself for inadequate fuel, or to crash.' He needled the buttons, and the ship abruptly changed course without turning about.

'Is something wrong?' Jessica enquired worriedly. 'The ship doesn't seem to have reversed. It's still accelerating forward, angling out of the column.'

'The ship is responsive. It is on course for my destination.'

'But there is no habitable planet in that direction, is there?'

'Correct. And if there were, I would not have the fuel to make a safe landing, after correcting for a non-buoyed and therefore inefficient course.'

'Then where are you going?' Her alarm was burgeoning, anticipating his answer.

'Into the Hole.'

4

Holestar Abyss

She did not taste very much different than a male, in general flavour. But the distinction was instantly manifest. Every jet she made possessed the female attribute, clear only to another HydrO but extremely significant *to* that HydrO. Heem had never before encountered a female of his species, but from the outset he had not the slightest doubt of her nature.

'Who are you, who preserves me from demise?' Heem enquired as he recovered his equilibrium.

'I am Moon of Morningmist,' she responded with a jet so diffident he hardly felt it. She, too, was acutely aware of the presence of the alternate sex.

'I am Heem of Highfalls.' He paused, absorbing further impressions of her, and discovered an urge he had not felt before. 'You are the first female I have encountered in my life. Shall we indulge in sexual play?'

'Of course,' she agreed.

'Is this valley otherwise occupied?' He was not certain why he enquired, but knew it was important.

'Four of my sister-siblings remain.'

Therefore he knew that there would be no reproduction. He needled a splash of the purest lust at her, the product of a lifetime of innocent abstinence, but did not include the key flavour of his signature. She responded with a passionate spray that soaked him with her essence. The result was a pleasure so novel and intense that he gave himself up to it entirely. He knew that Moon was reacting similarly.

'You just met her, and you copulated?'

Had Heem needled that question to himself? Mentally he

answered it. As a juvenile he had no reservations about pleasure, and sexual gratification was the most available and harmless of pleasures. It was practised as a routine courtesy whenever male and female HydrOs associated with each other on an individual or group basis. As an adult he discovered that many other sapient Cluster species regarded sex in another flavour. But alien ways were alien ways; why any creatures should choose to restrict something as natural and necessary as this was not a thing he needed to make the effort to understand. Alien species had a number of strange and appalling attitudes, such as eating or—

'Doesn't that leave offspring littering the landscape?' the internal needle came quickly.

Natually not! Sexual interplay was a prerequisite for procreation, but not identical to it. Reproduction occurred only when the male included his unique signature in the needlejet and when the female accepted that flavour. Neither would do this unless the habitat were suitable. Reproduction, unlike copulation, was a serious matter.

'I suppose it really is the same with us,' the mental jet continued. 'We invoke contraceptive measures so that we can indulge in similar play without conceiving offspring. Nevertheless, we do have a certain discretion about the choice of partners for such intimacies. Sex, to us, is not a casual matter, even without procreation.'

Heem ignored the alien taste and continued his forbidden memory-dream. After sating himself pleasantly with Moon, he rolled with her on a tour of the valley of Morningmist. It resembled Highfalls, but lacked the great central river; instead small streams fed into a good-sized lake, from which mildly flavoured vapours rose in the early section of each day. Heem soon became acclimatized to the variant tastes of this region, which were not far distinct from those of his own valley.

The sapient inhabitants of Morningmist were female, as

122

only one sex was littered in any one site. Heem met them singly and needled each courteously with lust, and each responded with a spray of gratification more passionate than his own gesture. This was natural, for he was recently sated while they were not. In due course all rolled together beside the lake and Heem, with a special effort, sprayed all five simultaneously with passion. They needled him back, all together, and his pleasure was so strong that he rolled into the water and sank to the bottom. They shoved him back to land cheerily. It had been a wonderful occasion.

'Simultaneous group sex with five females?' the interfering thought came. 'This is beyond the capacity, if not the aspiration, of our males.'

It would have been embarrassing had it been beyond the capacity of Heem, for the females of Morningmist were all deserving. It would have been a shame to exclude any from the polite welcome.

'Some polite welcome!' the private needle came.

While they toured the valley, he jetted conversationally with them, learning about their situation. It was similar to his own. They too had been seeded in their valley and left to develop independently; they too had suffered crucial attrition from hundreds to the present five. In crossing the mountain range he had learned only that the next valley was different in detail, not nature. He had not solved the mystery of his existence.

'What of your valley?' Moon jetted delicately after they had satisfied themselves with another copulation and settled for the night in her cave. 'How did you travel to ours?'

'Two of us rode a flatfloater up the mountain slope,' he jetted back. 'The floater lost propulsion near the apex, and we managed to roll on over the top. My sibling was slain by an alien monster. I am the last survivor of my valley, I believe.'

'Slitherfear!' she sprayed with horror. 'The nemesis

that—' She nerved herself for the foul taste. 'That eats.'

'You know of him? We did not know his name.'

'He has no name we can conceive. He is a dread Squam, predator on our species. We named him for his attributes. He has been preying on our number since he appeared recently in our valley. Every several days he destroys another sister, most horrendously.'

'We tried to escape him, but he was too strong for us. He had a thing he called a machine that jetted burning fluid. He killed my sibling Hoom and – did something horrible.'

'Yes,' she sprayed. 'We try to hide, but somehow the alien finds us, and consumes us. It is invulnerable to needles; we cannot oppose it or escape it.'

'I know.' The horror of Morningmist was worse than that of Highfalls. 'I escaped only by pretending to be dead, while it consumed my companion.'

They were tasteless for a time, unwilling to dwell further on the horror. Then Moon enquired with a diffident jet, 'Did you spray that Highfalls is vacant?'

'I believe it is. Only four of us survived before we boarded the flatfloater; then Haam fell from a height and Hiim fell when the floater moved away at sudden speed. Hiim may have survived, but this is unlikely.'

She emitted a cute spray of revelation. 'A vacant valley, with no Squam menace, is suitable for a litter of HydrOs!'

Heem realized that it was; his instinct told him so. Secure, sapient-devoid places existed only to be seeded with sapients. Part of the riddle of his own origins had been answered. 'But should Hiim survive—'

'We must go there and verify this. He might have survived the fall but be injured, then roll victim to a predator. Then we would seed the empty valley and depart. It is the HydrO way.'

Heem recognized the validity of her point, but remained reluctant. 'The mountain is high and steep, too difficult for us to cross.'

'We could harness a flatfloater, as you and your siblings did.'

'Half of us died in the effort – and another died on the mountain.'

'Yes, it is dangerous. But we must do it.'

She was correct; HydrO instinct required this effort. Still, he balked. 'No. I will not do it.'

Genuinely perplexed, she sprayed her gentle query, tinged with her sex appeal. For the first time, Heem appreciated the subtle power the female could exert. He felt cruel and guilty, opposing her. 'Why not, Heem? Are you ill, or of suspect stock?'

'I am not physically ill,' he jetted, working his rationale out as much for himself as for her. 'I have no reason to question my stock; my siblings perished from external causes, not from any internal malaise. But I have experienced the horrors of growing up among peers. Of two hundred or more, I alone remain. All the others fell horribly to predators or accidents – because there was no adult sapient to care for them. I have always hated the power that placed us in that situation, and now I cannot do the same thing to my own offspring.'

'But it is the HydrO way!' she jetted back, working out her own rationale. 'Any couple who discovers a suitable and vacant place must repopulate—'

'No!' he needled so sharply that she made a little spray of pain. 'I will not contribute to such an infernal system!'

'It is – it is natural selection. You survived in the valley of Highfalls because you were – were the fittest in the region,' she insisted, her jets overlapping each other. 'And I – I am among the fittest also, for I am among the few remaining sisters of Morningmist.'

'I survived because I was lucky. I have no special merit.' Yet he remembered occasions when he had avoided some threat that others had fallen prey to, because he had been more intelligent. And his needles had always been among

125

the most accurate. Luck could not account for all of it. 'And I refuse to believe that it has to be this way – the ignorant generating new litters of the helpless, never staying to help, to teach—' He damped his jet, thinking of another aspect. 'Why could we not remain in Highfalls, to instruct—'

'That is not the HydrO way!' she sprayed, shocked.

So it was an impasse. 'We will jet on this another time,' she jetted, meaning that she would be trying again to change his mind. They settled down to sleep, irreconciled.

Heem woke to the alarm of the ship. A quick savouring of the composite flavour assured him that he was on course. *His* course. The ship, naturally, assumed he was unintentionally drifting into danger.

'H-Sixty-six, are you in control?' It was H-46 on the taste net. Swoon of Sweetswamp, the female he had helped get her ship. The one with sex-appeal flavour like no one since Moon of Morningmist. He regretted he would never have occasion to roll Swoon up on her offer of further co-operation; it would almost certainly have been fun.

'I am in control, H-Forty-six,' he responded. It was nice of her to express concern for him. She knew his identity because of his prior antics in the column; she would have tasted all the intership signals. But they were competitors now, and she had turned out to be a superlative pilot. 'Congratulations on advancing into the first fifty. You made the cut; I did not. I wish you further success.'

'Just don't drift too far towards the Hole before the Competition Authority rescues you,' Swoon jetted. 'We may yet meet again, after this is over.'

It was a strongly flavoured reminder. She remained grateful. But Heem did not answer, for he knew he would never be able to indulge himself of that offer.

The ship was angling towards the Hole. The turnover point of the race was at the closest buoyed approach to the primary pair, since the destination planet was at the moment across the System from Impasse. Acceleration had been aided by the fall towards the primary, and deceleration would be aided by the climb away from it. But it was not safe to pass too close, for within a certain radius the well of the Hole became total: not even radiation could escape.

Now, suddenly, the Hole seemed much more powerfully flavoured. Growingly huge yet tasteless, it loomed upon the ship: the region of No Return. Though Heem's ship was now in free-fall, it was accelerating – towards the abyss.

The alien transferee within him took one translated look and retreated in numb horror to her own nightmare. Heem found himself drawn into it, as it were into an internal Hole.

Cloning was done to safeguard the ancient and dwindling lineages of the aristocracy of System Capella. It was not that these few scions were more subject to premature demise, but rather that when such demise occurred the consequences were more formidable. With cloning, there was always a replacement with full status.

The problem was that in the absence of demise, there was a duplicate heir. The purpose in preserving these lives was not to subdivide the estates. Therefore the clones who married were permitted only one offspring. That infant was cloned well before infancy. After that, both parents were sterilized. The line continued – rigidly. Since only the clones who married other clones could carry the inheritance, the great old estates did not stray from the original bloodlines. They shuttled back and forth within the aristocracy. The names might change, but not the blood.

Sometimes only one clone married legitimately, releasing the other to take a commoner-spouse. Any taint of commoner blood negated the heritage; no issue of that union could inherit. Yet it was mooted that those 'adulterous' marriages were often the happiest. Clones knew each other too well for there to be many attractive mysteries.

127

There was an occasional hitch in the process. In the current generation there were too many males. The sex of the offspring could be controlled, but some didn't bother until an imbalance occurred; then the ratio shifted to compensate. But there could be one or two left over – of either sex. If there were too many females, it was not serious, since the estate merged with that of the male, and the clone of a male could not marry adulterously while any female estate remained unattached. But in this case all the females would be taken, while some male or males would have to marry adulterously – thereby forfeiting their estates. That was very bad.

The progenitor of Jess had anticipated such a bind. He desired to retain the estate within his own named family, as it was the choicest (though not the richest) estate of them all: the original palace of Good Queen Bess. But to sire a male offspring was to risk losing both name and blood. Thus the progenitor hedged his bet by producing a male heir, with a female clone. If the male could not find a clone-mate, the female would assume the office and merge with another estate. There would be no forfeit.

It was an extremely neat device, but there were certain practical problems. The female split was secret, for too early a revelation could cause other families to produce similarly split clones, complicating or nullifying the advantage. Both clones were listed as male, and both adopted the dress and manner of males. In private it was otherwise, and among commoners Jessica could adopt a pseudonym and be fully female. This was encouraged, for if she ever had to assume the burden of the blood, she would need to be a fully conversant woman, desirable as such and able to perform. But when among cloned aristocracy, she was always male.

This became awkward at times, especially as Jess grew to maturity. Jesse and Jessica were both on the sterility diet, of course; only in marriage could the counteractant be prescribed. But she was expected to play the role of a male in the clone society. She had to defer to females with mock archaic gallantry, and run her eyes over the girls' covert spots with evident lust, and pinch their haunches just as her brother did – *because* he did. Because to fail in the male mannerism was to betray her nature prematurely, perhaps hampering her brother's chance to make a suitable marriage.

'You are a female – yet you acted in the manner of a male?'

'I *had* to! At first it was a game, but when I grew older I hated it, yet I still had to do it.' She found herself reacting to the scepticism in the theoretical question.

'Yet it was only a matter of role – a part in a drama, of no private consequence. You would inevitably mate as a female, with a male opposite, when that occasion came. No cause for distress.'

Was she baiting herself? No cause for distress! 'Here's how it was!' she snapped back, and opened a long-suppressed memory of herself at fifteen. She and her half attended a clone ball put on by Cyrus and Cyron, aged sixteen. It was titled Cyclone, naturally, and had a storm motif.

Jesse and Jessica travelled together, as was the fashion for clones, in a closed dragon-drawn coach. Closed to conceal their doubled nature from the prying gaze of commoners; dragon-drawn to show their aristocratic heritage and affluence. A modern float-car would have been more comfortable, much faster, and less expensive, but Jessica had to admit the rented dragon had more class. The coach was of one-way foam fibre, insulating and reflective externally, pervious internally, so that they could see without being seen.

The landscape was lovely. This was part of the Nature Reserve that had been set aside a millennium ago when the rising population of System Capella had threatened to spoil the planet. The huge old estates suffused the region, and the aristocracy maintained the native wilderness as part of their system. No one hunted here, or mined or built cities – no one except the clones themselves, whose damage was minimal. Thus the mountains were largely unspoiled, the trees enormous, the rivers clean. Jessica touched a section of the coach wall, dilating it with the fingers of her hand so that a fresh gust of air came through to caress her face. That breeze was redolent of pinesap and Capellabloom, and for a moment she closed her eyes and let it transport her. Here, forever, swaying on the suspension of the coach, breathing sap and bloom . . .

Then they rounded a turn, and she almost fell into her brother, embarrassingly. Her eyes snapped open, and she spied the head of the dragon, normally hidden beyond the mass of its body. Its breath was jetting up and back, forming diffuse vapour-cloudlets that were dispersed by the beat of its vestigial wings. The dragon was not really a magical creature, of course; it was a native animal that happened to resemble a creature of Solarian folklore, so naturally it had assumed the appropriate name.

Yet perhaps, she thought, reconsidering, there *was* magic in it, for it was largely the mystique of the dragon that had created this pastoral reserve. Dragons required large foraging grounds; to intrude on this space with too much civilization would have been to destroy the unique creatures. Man had already committed genocide too many times, inadvertently; there had to be a halt. Star Capella was the fabled Eye of the Charioteer – and what was a chariot without a dragon to draw it? So it was a mark of System pride that the dragons flourished, and to ensure that, it had become necessary to preserve a major portion of the planet's original ecology. That was magic seldom seen in Sphere Sol!

Now the site of Cyclone came into view, one of the fine old castles, dating from the age of Queen Bess. It had been decked out garishly with tattered stormwarning flags, as though the eye of a hurricane had passed and left its mark. The embrasures were crossed by crudely nailed boards, mock protection for nonexistent glass.

'Cy and Cy have already had their ball,' Jesse muttered. 'Beyond a certain point, a motif becomes inane.'

Jessica agreed, as was her wont; she was as close to her half as it was possible for another person to be. She should have been identical, but for that matter of sex, and that was really the gift (curse?) of the laboratory. Genetic surgery, adding one X chromosome – that sort of thing had not been possible until recently, and was no simple procedure today. The waning fortune of this estate had been further impoverished to finance that operation.

Knowing she had to compensate for the sex-change, she had tried very hard to emulate her brother, and so was in certain respects closer to him than normal male-male or female-female clones were to their respective halves. As it was, she was less enthusiastic about this party than her male half was. This was not merely because she was female, but because she was anonymously so. She could not let herself go; she had to guard her every reaction, lest she betray the secret of this cloning.

She was used to this, of course. She had played this role from infancy. She could emulate her half's mannerisms with such precision that not even other clones could tell them apart. But most of that experience had been before the onset of sexual maturity.

Now Jesse and Jessica were past puberty, and the secret had become enormously more challenging to keep. She was slightly shorter than he, now, though for a time she had been taller; special elevated shoes made up for that. She had developed breasts, now, and other distinctly distaff attributes, as that X chromosome did its relentless work. Jesse had playfully complimented her more than once in this connection. 'Now I know how great I look in femme,' he told her. 'But if I were you, which I almost am, I'd strap my udders down with a belt and put a bra on my glutes . . .' She had hit him with a pillow, of course; that was protocol.

They had had to move to specially designed clothing to retain their symmetry of appearance. She wore a body-sock girdle to flatten her breasts into a male-type chest; he wore padding to amplify his hips and buttocks. Now they both resembled a slightly overweight male, and neither liked this – but the secret had to be preserved until the pairing of clones was far enough along. If he failed to come to terms with a female, she would have to do so with a male. If they revealed this option prematurely, the other clones might force a clone-marriage on her, preventing him from carrying the estate name to his heir. Jessica wanted him to succeed; she liked none of the male clones available. She actually preferred more mature men, but the older clones were all committed. Thus she felt her best course was to retire into anonymity with some handsome commoner.

The dragon steamed into the terminal and stopped. Attendants took over, leading it to pasture after the passengers disembarked. Dragons were omnivorous, preferring to chase down the fat monster caterpillars that stood the height of a man, but also grazing on the plentiful pine needles. They preferred the needles fallen, and aged somewhat, so the dragons never harmed the trees. Their teeth were phenomenal, for there was enormous difference between the soft flesh of caterpillars and the toughness of dried pine needles. It seemed the dragons had evolved as herbivores, but developed cutting teeth for combat purposes, then discovered that those specialized teeth could be adapted for masticating meat.

'Snap to, Half,' Jesse said brightly. A necessary caution; she was becoming moody and introspective these days, while he retained his surface awareness. Was this a sexual difference, or did it derive from her natural distaste for her masquerade?

The entrance passage was decorated with artfully placed

fallen timbers and floodwater stains. There was even an alluvial delta at one end. Then they had to climb through the wreckage of a ship to enter the main chamber.

Jesse paused just before taking the final step. He grasped a splintered pole and used it to poke up into the ceiling. A plastic bucket of water tipped down, splashing on the floor. 'Saw the stain from the last splash,' he remarked wisely, completing his entrance, and got soaked by the second bucket of water.

Jessica then stepped out. She had noted the splash too – such things were ubiquitous at clone balls – but still had residual caution. A soaking could have interfered with her camouflage clothing. Now, unfortunately, they were readily distinguishable: Jess-wet from Jess-dry. That could be awkward.

There was a stiff breeze inside, consistent with the motif. Jesse shivered as his clothing evaporated, and hurried to the refreshment alcove for a mildly intoxicating Cyclomate beverage. Jessica had to accompany him and take one also, but she imbibed it far more cautiously. It was considered humorous to spike these drinks with hallucinogens or aphrodisiacs. She still felt nervous, afraid someone would see her flattened breasts sneaking some stray bulge through her masculine shirt.

As Jesse consumed his drink he became more sociable. Jessica grew more alarmed in corresponding proportion. Her situation forced her to be less and less like him, so that she could *seem* more and more like him. If he got careless, talked too much—

They circulated, chatting with other clones. The older ones were married, each member accompanying his/her spouse; the child-level ones, already bored with the introductions, were playing noisy team-tag in the basement. Jesse and Jessica were among the select minority of adolescents; in self-defence they tended to associate with these.

'Hey, Jess! Where were you, Screwball?' a husky male bawled, clapping Jessica jarringly on the back. Her drink slopped on to the floor: no loss. Her fear was growing, as she noted her brother's unconscious fidgeting, that the juice really *had* been spiked.

'We were indisposed, Jules,' she responded. Actually they had skipped the Scrub-clones' party, titled Screwball, because of the maturation problem. But too many skips would become suspicious, and the last thing they wanted was suspicion. Theoretically all the unmarried clones of any age were eagerly mixing, trying to line up the best marital alliances early. It was a bit like musical chairs, with the 'music' – i.e. intense social and sexual interplay – continuous, and the competitors eager to be the first to drop out by pairing off. The ones who played too long, or not enough, might not make their necessary connections. So the Jess-clones had had to make Cyclone, ready or not. Jesse was all too ready; Jessica was not.

Jules leaned down confidentially. 'You missed some real screwing, Jess! But you can make it up this time, eh?' And he aimed another devastating smash at her back. She ducked neatly to avoid it, dinking him in the stomach with three stiffened fingers. He thought his pun about 'making it up' was terribly clever; she thought it proved him a bore.

'Eh,' she agreed, emulating Jesse.

Privately, she was disgusted. Sex was not only fairly open, it was expected. How else, the theory went, could the clones find suitable partners for marriage? Jesse was quite interested in the subject now; he hardly needed the stimulation of an aphrodisiac drink to get him going. Jessica, even had she been overtly female, would have preferred to wait. It was inherent in the Solarian species, she decided; it was the male's prerogative to seed whatever furrow he could find, and to do that all he needed was a wandering nature and a ready tool. It was the female's duty to bear and raise the young; for that she needed to stay at

134

home and work. So the male craved sexual expression constantly, lest his tool sag from neglect, while the female could take it or leave it, as befitted the situation. She hoped the situation never befitted a marriage with Jules; she couldn't stand him.

A well-developed pair sashayed up. 'Jess! We've been looking for you!'

'And we for you, Bessy!' Jesse responded, his eyes ogling the left Bess with more than mock appreciation Jessica hurled another mental curse at that drink. The Bess clones took pride in their purported resemblance to their name-sake ancestor, Good Queen Bess; possibly this was valid, assuming the Queen had been voluptuous and stupid.

Jessica, her annoyance verging on wrath, painted an ogle similar to her brother's on her own face. The Bessies were only a few months older than the Jesses, but their female attributes had manifested explosively. *They* would never be able to pass for males!

The Bessies took a deep tandem breath, causing their four mammaries to overflow their costumes dangerously. 'Shall we try it out?' And they winked in broad unison, though that was hardly necessary.

Jessica wondered: what was it that she had been thinking about the woman's role? The Bessies were coming on with disgusting directness. And Jesse, damn him, was raptly interested! She nudged him warningly with her elbow, but he was so absorbed by the quadruple revelation that he ignored her. He was male, therefore he chose a woman by shape, not intellect or personality. By shape! How foolish was it possible to get?

The Bessies took firm hold of the Jesses and propelled them towards the private rooms. Jessica could not resist effectively, since Jesse was eager enough to go. But the thing was impossible!

'What is impossible? Sexual play is natural.'

'Not between females!' Jessica retorted.

135

'Beg pardon?' Bessy enquired, already half disrobed. Jesse and the other Bessy had vanished to the adjacent chamber.

Even had it not been impossible, it would have been undesirable. Bessy was a cow, huge of haunch and udder (exactly as Jesse liked to pretend his sister was; she was definitely not!), scant of intellect, basic of instinct. At least Jesse should have evinced some taste in bovines!

Shape. It was so damned stupid! As well to judge a drink by the contour of its container.

'Yes. Taste is the only criterion—'

'Oh, shut up!' she snapped.

'But I wasn't speaking,' Bessy protested, hurt.

'Uh, I mean shut off the light.' Jessica lurched to wave her hand across the illumination control, and the light faded.

'Oh, in the dark,' Bessy cried. 'How quaint!'

'Yes. It's the newest fashion,' Jessica said. 'Give me a moment to get ready.' She moved silently to the door between rooms. It was a privacy curtain, fortunately: opaque, but of no substance. She stepped through.

And was momentarily blinded by the light. Jesse, unclothed, was just rising from his willing conquest. That drink had given him jet propulsion!

'Your kind employs jets?'

'In a manner of speaking,' she answered, this time silently. 'The man's role – oh, never mind!'

'And the female remains to care for the offspring. This is a desirable procedure.'

'That depends.' Jessica closed out the nagging thoughts and returned to her dream, though it horrified her.

Bessy's eyes were closed, her body open. Jessica suppressed another surge of revulsion. She understood, to a certain extent, the male imperative; sex was an inherent hunger that he sought to gratify. But this type of female, who surely had no similar incentive – why was *she* so eager

136

for it? It had to be a perverse pride of conquest: she bolstered her undeserving ego by proving that men found her desirable. But she *wasn't* desirable; she was a great mass of incipiently sagging flesh. A sow.

Jesse spied Jessica, his brows lifting questioningly, but almost immediately he understood. The abatement of his lust allowed his mind to function again, making him aware of her predicament. He rose from Bessy, gestured Jessica to take his place, picked up his clothes and tiptoed through the curtain to join the other Bessy. How he would perform there Jessica could not say; presumably he would stall until he was able to rise again to the occasion. Served him right.

Jessica sat beside Bessy, afraid to arouse suspicion by turning off this light. She took her clothing partly off, to look as if it had been hastily donned, and waited.

Bessy stirred, eyes still closed. 'Am I a good lay, Jess?'

Jessica experienced the mental image of a monstrous laser beam destroying the whole castle. But her voice was controlled, artificially sincere. 'As good as any I've had,' she replied, biting her lip. Another wash of furious frustration and jealousy suffused her – and the very existence of *that* reaction made her more angry yet. No, she didn't want to be like Bessy – did she? 'How am I as a stud?'

'Oh, the best, the best! Sort of quick, though.' Bessy opened her eyes. 'How did you get dressed so soon?'

'Part of the art,' Jessica said with assumed smugness. 'If you'd kept your eyes closed another moment, I'd have tucked in my shirt before you ever noticed.' She did so now.

'Some trick! You dress almost as fast as you perform,' Bessy stretched languorously. 'If you were to marry me, it would be like this every day. More often if you wanted.'

Age fifteen, so hot to get married to a clone! The artifice was so obvious it was painful. 'If I were to marry you, I couldn't have it with all the other girls anymore,' Jessica

137

said with simulated regret. When she got home, she intended to wash her mouth out with detergent.

Bessy sighed. Her wit was not sufficient to cope with that rejoinder. Her expertise hardly extended beyond disrobing and spreading her legs. She closed her eyes again. 'Stroke me again, Jess, as you did before.'

Jessica gritted her teeth. How far did she have to carry this infernal charade? She knew where her half would have stroked this bovine. He would have milked her.

Jessica closed her fist, aiming it – no. This was a temptation to which she could not afford to yield, lest she betray her affinity. For Jessica was really another female mammal.

She put out her hand. In her imagination it held a butcher's knife. *Let me carve you, cowpig! From here a fine juicy steak; from there a fat roast . . .*

'Oh, Jess, you really know how to do it,' Bessy said.

Jessica wrenched her eyes open from the nightmare – and found she had no eyes. She screamed – and had no voice. She had only touch and taste – mainly the latter.

'Will you stop it? Heem demanded. 'You are burning out my nerves!'

The horror subsided slowly. 'I was dreaming, reliving—'

'I perceived, sharing your horror. Impersonating the alternate sex – I comprehend how revolting that would be, though it surely prepared you for your cross-sexual transfer. But to imagine carving eating-chunks from the flesh of a sapient—'

'Bessy was not *very* sapient.'

'But the most remarkable thing – I almost thought I could see.'

'Of course you can see – when you're snooping on my dream! Because my mind is oriented on seeing and hearing, and the impulses translate.'

'Horrible,' Heem jetted.

'You, blind and deaf, talk of horror? You, who diverted

this ship into—' But she did not voice the concept.

'You are aware of my rationale,' he reminded her. 'Better to die cleanly and honourably in space, than in confinement.'

'What could be more comforting than a black hole?' The scream was forming again, causing him to wince internally. She had a considerable weapon, there!

'A thorough and honourable death is not confining,' he informed her. 'It is an excellent liberation from an intolerable situation.'

They oriented their attention on the Hole ahead. The Hole itself was blank to the ship's instrumentation, because it was what it was; but there were considerable phenomena at its fringe that were perceptible.

'I don't resign myself to this at all, you know,' Jessica said tersely, and indeed there was an undercurrent of purpose in her being that was alarming in its strength. 'There has to be some escape. If only I could *see* it!' She considered in her brief, Solarian, feminine way. 'Heem, you have to develop sight. That's all there is to it. I absolutely refuse to die blind. I want to see what I'm getting into.'

'I am having difficulty making you understand that I have no perception of sight. In this competition, only Erbs see. Squams hear and HydrOs taste.'

'Well, Solarians see, hear, *and* taste. And feel. We have senses bristling out all over! And right now I want to see.'

'It is impossible!'

'I'll scream!'

The ultimate argument! 'There are some things, like sexual identity and fundamental perception, that simply cannot be changed. You may scream the nerves right out of my body, but you can't make me see. Why not at least permit us to die in dignity?'

She assumed a pose of reasonableness, but that chill current remained beneath. 'It is possible to alter sexual identity, because I am an example. It should be possible to

139

adapt the informational channels and impulses to a new configuration. The brain does it. All it needs is discipline. If you work with me, I should be able to see – and so should you. We're doing it already some in our dreams. If we work at it—'

'No!'

'Oh, come on now, Heem! I'm not trying to pry into your doubtless guilty secrets. I don't *care* about your secrets. What difference do they make, if we are about to die? You want to die in space; I want to die with sight. Because I'm an artist at heart, visually oriented. The least you can do is try to learn to see.'

Heem did not follow all her alien logic, but there seemed to be some sense there. 'I will try to see,' he sprayed with resignation. Obviously she would not allow him to die in peace if he did not make this effort.

'Good. Let's start with that – that thing out there. The main ball of it can't be seen or perceived at all, directly, because it is what it is, by definition unperceivable. But around the edge – what is there?'

Heem tasted the impulses the ship fetched in. He tried to suppress his taste sensation, allowing information to remain just that: information without perception. An increasing bulk of it was non-information, as the Hole made its massive non-presence felt.

Around the fringe of that vast blackness were lesser phenomena. Matter was being drawn from the Star to spiral into the Hole. It was a gradual process, for only the substance erupted from solar flares escaped the Star's own gravitational well – to be captured by the smaller but deeper well of the Hole. Ribbons of gas formed concentric rings about it, admixed with meteoric rock and other debris. The radius of no-return was much larger for solid matter than for gas, and smaller for energy. They were now at the fringe of the solid limit for chemical propulsion; a really powerful jet-drive might enable H-66 to break free.

But that was not what they had. They had barely enough fuel left to decelerate for a planetary landing, academic as that had become.

And – Heem almost began to see it. He knew he was merely picking up the feedback from Jessica's effort of imagination, but she *did* know how to see, which was something no HydrO knew, and she did have a fine, focusing mind. When not distracting herself with pointless jealousy of more lushly fleshed females of her kind.

'I heard that!'

'You were snooping.'

'Oh, I suppose I can't deny all the Bessies of this galaxy their right to use what little they have to better their situation. It's just that I wish other things counted for more.'

'Flavour counts for more.'

'Go to hell.'

She was determined to expire in her own style, though what he grasped of her image of hell was not far removed from the Hole they were entering. She wanted to distract herself from the reality of death. That was something Heem should be doing too; his weakness was—

A planetoid loomed near, its rocky surface cratered and ragged. The light of Holestar reflected from it, making it sparkle. There must be reflective minerals—

Shock ran through him. *He had seen it!* He had seen glints of brightness, rather than tasting nodules of flavour. He – no, of course he hadn't. He had no—

'Oh, now you've spoiled it!' Jessica cried. 'Just when it was coming clear!'

So he had. 'Seeing – it just is not natural,' Heem sprayed apologetically.

'Maybe not to *you*. Why don't you just tune out for an hour or so while I play with it? I promise I'll wake you in plenty of time for your demise.' Now there was a brittleness to her cleverness. She was angry about dying.

'I shall,' he agreed. And relaxed into memory. These recollections might be forbidden and unsocial and illegal – but what did such things matter now?

Moon of Morningmist woke him with a fine-spraycaress that proceeded quickly to further copulation. She tasted wonderful. Then they rolled out to interact again with her siblings, Miin, Maan, Muun, and Meen. Heem, fresher this morning than he had been on the prior day, doused them all with a splendid sex spray, and they needled him back delightedly. There was no joy in life to match that of such a welcome!

They toured the further aspects of the valley of Morningmist, paying special attention to the swamp that degenerated from the nether end of the lake. There were flatfloaters in it, big, healthy ones, that took easy jaunts over the surface of the water, swamp, and land.

'Heem came over the mountain on a flatfloater,' Moon sprayed proudly. She had a proprietary attachment to him, for he had encountered her first, and he chose to copulate with her for pleasure rather than mere politeness. 'The creatures can be guided by jets. We can do it too, with courage—'

'My brothers died!' Heem interjected. She was spraying as though she had entirely forgotten their dialogue of the night.

'Females do that,' a thought needled him. 'Be assured she has not forgotten a thing.'

'Therefore your valley of Highfalls is empty, and requires seeding,' Moon concluded firmly, demonstrating the accuracy of his thought-warning.

'No! We are not sure of that!' But they were not convinced; he could taste it even without their sprays of demurral. 'And – I am afraid to risk my life on another flatfloater.' That was a half-truth, but it would have to do.

'Yes, there is fear,' Moon agreed.

They continued the tour of Morningmist, visiting its pleasant seclusions, playing challenging games, comparing personal histories. It was very like his prior life, with the added dimension of sexuality. Heem enjoyed it greatly. In fact, tasting back later, he was to conclude that this was the happiest of his forbidden memories.

Yet after the first full day he began to wonder: was this all there was to life? Residing in one valley or another, sporting, while things like Slitherfear Squam consumed them one by one? Where was the meaning in that?

Maybe he was wrong about repopulation. If he were to procreate, seeding his valley of Highfalls, then stay to protect and guide his offspring – he knew Moon would not agree to that, for she had already jetted that it was not the HydrO way, but if he deceived her into thinking that he was departing the valley, then secretly returned—

No. Deception was not his way. He had to convince her, or not seed the valley at all.

'That is an honourable sentiment, Heem.

There went his thought again. Still, the impasse remained. Suppose Moon could not be convinced? He found himself yielding, preparing to follow the HydrO way. It was better than being idle.

Next day they came across the remains of Miin. Slitherfear had descended to the valley floor and caught her as she slept. The Squam had not been hungry enough to consume her entirely, so had left half of her lying in her burrow. That was how they knew what had happened. Usually members of their number had just distasted, with no indication of the manner of their demise.

They rolled rocks to block up Miin's burrow, sealing her in. Her body would decompose into its components in the natural way. It was all they could do for her. They sprayed about the nice things she had done in life, the sweet thoughts she had jetted, how pleasant she had been to associate with, and their grief at her loss. Then they tried to

143

forget her. After all, almost two hundred of her sisters had died before her; it was hard to keep track of them all, or to feel prolonged sorrow for each individual.

Heem's resolve hardened. *This* was what unsupervised seeding meant! Never would he contribute to this dread cycle!

Moon importuned him between and during copulations. 'If not with me, with one of my sisters,' she pleaded. 'With Maan, maybe. Ride a flatfloater over the mountain. There is an even slope we can indicate for you, making an easier crossing. We could all go, and at least look.'

Grudgingly, he agreed. It was difficult to jet no to a female in the throes of copulation.

'Uh-huh.'

They scouted the swamp, and located a suitable floater, and made arrangements to get aboard it. Heem's prior experience would help them do it correctly. The important thing was not to get careless; they would have to spread themselves across as many of its intakes as possible, so that its suction held them secure. Its reduced efficiency, because those covered intakes were inoperative, would also help them to stay on – in sudden bursts of motion like those that had wiped out two of Heem's brothers.

Then Maan was discovered, a quarter consumed. Slither-fear, again.

'I am coming to understand your intense aversion to eating.'

'We have the wrong priority!' Heem needled the others. 'First we must deal with the Squam enemy, then go exploring. No seeding is worthwhile if it is only to be prey to the Squam, as your siblings have been.'

But the females were afraid. They sealed in Maan with ceremonial sorrow, and resumed work on the flatfloater. Heem, Meen, Muun, and Moon hid under the water in the place the monster most often rested, ready to board it.

Experience did help. Heem knew exactly how to prod the

monster to keep it from bolting. Their ride was successful. They cruised around the valley, then guided it back to the water and rolled off. Success!

Next day they did it again with another flatfloater. The females learned to control it. It was fairly easy, once the trick was mastered.

'Now we have transportation over the mountain,' Moon sprayed. 'We can verify that Highfalls is vacant.'

Whereupon they would renew the cycle of innocence and grief. 'We are dealing with Slitherfear first,' he reminded them. He sprayed them with erotic flavour: he had learned how to make a convincing argument!

'But we only have to verify it! Maybe your brother Hiim is alive.'

'Then there is no present point in going to Highfalls; it remains occupied.'

'No, one of us could join Hiim, and seed that valley,' Muun sprayed. 'It is the HydrO way.'

'How do any of us really know the HydrO way?' he needled back. 'We have never encountered any other HydrOs!'

'It is inherent,' Moon replied. 'We *know* what is fit.'

It was hard to argue against absolute knowledge, but he tried. 'You call it fit – to subject another litter to the suffering we have had?'

'It is the HydrO way.'

'Then maybe the HydrO way is wrong!'

For that blasphemy they had no answer except shock.

'Maybe,' Moon sprayed at last, 'we should deal with Slitherfear first. Then the valley will be safe for our kind.'

Heem refrained from reminding her that this was exactly the case he had been arguing.

'You're getting smarter, Heem.'

But of course after the Squam was gone, Heem would be committed to the seeding. He had won only a partial victory.

All three females were terrified, and Heem himself was afraid, but they did go after the dread Squam. Each rode on a flatfloater. Their plan was to crash the flatfloaters into the Squam, crushing him again and again until he expired.

'That's simplistic. I don't trust it.'

But Heem kept his private doubts tasteless from his companions, lest they lose nerve entirely. Taming the floaters had been easier than anticipated; maybe killing Slitherfear would be the same.

It was not hard to locate the Squam. Never before had they actually looked for him, and he had no fear of them, therefore no reason to hide. They found him by a cave in the slope of the mountain, doing something with a structure made of metal. There was a strange taste in the air not merely of the metal; it was a little like burning, yet of no fire they knew.

They charged in on their mounts, going for the freshest taste. Heem felt a cold fear of the monster. Yet that fear was what had brought him here; better to attack in a group than to wait for Slitherfear to murder them singly.

The Squam stood still for a moment, as if not believing what was happening. Then it fired out its mechanical spray. 'Shy off, or I destroy!'

Heem suffered an acute memory of his brother Hoom, shot down at a distance by this alien. Rage suffused him, almost abolishing his reasonable fear. He needled his floater, directing it straight at the Squam.

Heat struck him. This was no spray; it was like concentrated Star-energy! Heem experienced the taste of his own burning flesh – not acid-burning this time, but fire-burning. His floater swerved, dropped, and crashed into the ground, and Heem rolled violently and helplessly forward. That new weapon was potent!

He tasted Moon and Meen and Muun gliding past him, orienting on the monster. Then he fetched up against the entrance to the cave and lay stunned. His skin was flaming

146

with pain on the side that had been struck.

The attack was being carried forward without him. Heem felt a surge of pleasure in the courage of these females, for he knew how frightened they were. The three swooped their beasts at Slitherfear. The Squam's weapon flashed—

Flashed?

Radiated. He felt the slight additional heat from its operation, and then the shudder in the ground as another flatfloater fell.

Then came the awful taste of death and it bore the flavour of Moon of Morningmist. The Squam's terrible weapon had destroyed her.

Meen's mount bolted. Heem picked up the lingering traces of its explosive jet, and knew she had lost control. Only Muun remained to attack the Squam.

Muun crashed in, almost striking Slitherfear. But the creature dropped low to the ground, letting the floater pass over, then fired the weapon again. The taste of scorching flesh drifted out; then that floater was gone from perception range. Was Muun alive or dead?

Heem was now alone with the dread Squam. But Slitherfear was not paying attention to him. Laboriously, Heem rolled into the cave, trying to hide, his burned skin hurting and leaking.

There was machinery inside the cave. Heem had no notion what it was for or how it operated, but it was all associated with Slitherfear, and therefore was cold and hideous.

Somehow the Squam used this equipment, as the HydrOs had learned to use the flatfloaters. Therefore, destroying this machinery might be like shooting down a floater. If he only had some way—

Heem fought back the pain of his burn. His jet-pores remained functional, and his internal system was strong; his injury was after all superficial. He could do something—

147

if he could only figure out what. Before Slitherfear returned to his cave, forcing Heem to fight for his life.

Heem jetted softly, rolling slowly, exploring the situation with the caution of fear and ignorance. He knew so little about this stuff. Would a sharp needlejet in the right place have an effect? Or would it be better simply to push an item over?

Experimentally he needled a crevice. Nothing happened.

He rolled to the side, found another crevice, and needled again. Still nothing. There were irregularities all round the machine, but its cold metal was like the Squam's overlapping scales, proof against mere jets of water.

Then another taste wafted in to him. He recognized it instantly, from his prior experience with the Squam, when Hoom died. *Slitherfear was eating.*

And the only body the monster had to eat was Moon of Morningmist.

Heem forgot his physical pain. He jetted forward with such force that he crashed into the machine and knocked it over. It crashed on the ground, emitting sparks of energy. But Heem was beyond it, caroming towards the Squam, heedless of any consequence.

Slitherfear had extruded his stomach to consume Moon. He could not react with his usual speed. Heem rolled in, oriented, and struck with his sharpest, hottest needle, right at that extruded tissue. There were no scales to protect this ˌrgan! Again and again he lanced into that vulnerable material, holing it, cooking it, cutting it to pieces.

Then, before the dread Squam could recover, Heem rolled away. Slitherfear was not dead, only injured, as Heem was. The weapon jetted its disaster at Heem, scored only peripherally. It must be hard, Heem thought with a certain grim satisfaction, to concentrate on a fleeing target when one's innards have been shredded.

So he escaped. He rolled into the swamp, letting the water cool his burns. He was fortunate; they were not serious. They would heal.

A day later Meen found him. 'I am sorry, Heem,' she jetted. 'I tried to turn the flatfloater, but—'

'I know. The thing bolted. At least it carried you out of danger.'

'I feared you were dead. I tasted your fall—'

'My floater took the brunt. I was only burned and stunned.'

'My sister Moon—'

'Dead. I attacked Slitherfear while he was eating her. I did not kill him, but he will not eat soon again. Muun was also hit; what became of her?'

'I found her body this morning. The burn was too much; she rolled off her floater and died.'

What devastation, from that brief encounter! The Squam had killed two, injured one, and driven away the floater of the last. How could they kill it?

Meen suffered grief for her sisters. But soon the deeper implication came to her. 'The valley of Morningmist is now vacant,' she sprayed. 'We must seed it.'

Not again! 'I will not seed after the misery I experienced in these two valleys,' Heem needled. 'My siblings dead, yours also—'

'But it is the HydrO way!'

'It is not *my* way. I have another mission: to abate the menace of the Squam, the evil thing who slew my brother, your sisters, and my love.'

'We tried to kill Slitherfear – and lost all but us two. He is too strong for us.'

Probably true. Yet Heem could not give up. 'I shall find out how to kill him. Maybe he will die from the injury I did him. If not, I will find another way.'

'But first we must seed the valley!' Meen was as single-minded about this as Moon had been.

'No! Not now, not ever!'

'Then I must go over the mountain into Highfalls.

149

Perhaps your brother survives, and he and I can seed that valley.' And she rolled away to find her flatfloater.

She did not return, somewhat to Heem's relief. Had he seeded with anyone, he would have preferred Moon; her cruel death rendered him desolate. Now he intended to achieve revenge. It was all that was left.

He studied Slitherfear from the concealment of the swamp. The Squam was sound-oriented, not taste-oriented, so could not detect him if he remained quite still. It was easy to stay still while his burns healed. Since Heem was taste-oriented, the air brought him constant news of his enemy's activity. So he had an advantage – for the moment.

Slitherfear had been wounded, no doubt about it. He moved awkwardly, and had not eaten further of Moon's body. Even so, there was a certain sinister grace about him. His metallic scales overlapped, allowing his body to flex. He moved by pressing against objects and irregularities in the ground. He only unfolded his three limbs when he had use for them – moving some object, operating his machinery, clipping sections from plants.

Why would any creature want to clip sections from plants and run them through machines? Did the machines need to eat too? Strange, morbid mystery!

'Obviously surveying the vegetation, among other things. Taking samples, analysing them, classifying and storing the information. Environmental impact study, perhaps—'

When the Squam was moving, he was sealed in his scales, invulnerable. But when he brought his limbs out, the grooves where they had been lacked scales. What would a needle of water do right in one of those joints or crevices?

The Squam could hear when its limbs were put away. Heem had some understanding of hearing; it was a refinement of his own awareness of vibration. A shudder in the ground or air that he could detect at close range, the Squam could detect at distant range. The sense seemed quite crude when compared to taste as a primary mode of perception. How could the flavour of one individual of a species be distinguished from another? How could mere vibration be adapted to communication? No wonder the Squam depended on machines to generate taste!

Did it hear all over its body, as Heem did, feeling the vibration in its skin? But Heem's body was soft and sensitive, while the Squam's was hard. So probably the creature had a specialized sensor, a point receptor. If Heem could locate that, and strike it with a needlejet, perhaps a hot one—

Here, Heem was forced to admit, the perception of taste was less than ideal. Through taste he could analyse the nature of things carefully, even when the things had departed from the locale. But it was extremely difficult to pinpoint something. For that, he would have to approach and bounce an analytic needlejet off it, reading the changes the subject wrought. He hardly dared come that close to Slitherfear!

Yet there were indications. The Squam normally folded his arms for travelling – but not always. Once when he travelled towards the cave, folded, a vibration had come from the swamp, as of a flatfloater dropping to the water. Immediately Slitherfear had paused, lifted his foresegment, unfolded all three arms—

'How did you know it was three, not two or one arm? You could not see them.'

He knew because of the variations in the taste pattern carried by the wind. A single obstruction had a typical configuration of taste: two had another, and three another. This had matched the three-configuration perfectly, and the typical taste of the Squam's interior-space, stronger than the flavour of the external scales, had come—

'You could determine that sort of detail from taste alone?'

Yes, he could – once he had thoroughly familiarized himself with the nature of the Squam. Heem had had many

151

days in the swamp, lying quite still, healing his body, with no distraction save his study of that monster. He had become highly attuned to the nature of his enemy – an attunement that had enabled him to deal with Squams much better, late in life. Very few HydrOs ever had an opportunity to study any Squam in such detail, and fewer yet ever availed themselves of it when that opportunity came. Because HydrOs were afraid of Squams, and avoided them whenever possible.

So now he knew the Squam could hear while folded and travelling, but not well. For full definition it had to pause and open out its arms, becoming vulnerable. That was an important piece of information!

So the organs of hearing were in the arms, or in the grooves the arms covered. Those organs had to be vulnerable, otherwise they would have been situated more conveniently for use while travelling. A needlejet could probably damage them. And a deaf Squam would be like a tasteless HydrO: virtually helpless.

Slitherfear's typical taste had changed. There was the flavour of stomach about him, emanating from the aperture where he extruded his innards to digest his prey. That aperture was at the end of his snout, his foremost extremity; normally closed, it now periodically emitted bursts of taste. Another aperture at the rearmost extremity excreted decomposed material.

How, then, should Heem attack? For there was no question of fleeing; he intended to kill the foul Squam, even if that effort cost Heem his own life. His burned skin had sloughed off and healed in these past days; soon he would be back in full health. Then—

Then Slitherfear readied a machine that had the aspect of a flatfloater. It jetted massively, clouds of mechanical gas tasting faintly of combustion.

A flatfloater machine? That must mean the Squam planned to ride it – and depart the valley. Because he had run out of HydrO prey, or his business here was finished,

152

or his injury in the stomach was causing him to starve. Whatever his reason, his departure would mean a reprieve from Heem's vengeance. Heem had to roll now!

The Squam was just sliding on to the floater. Heem rolled forward violently, jetting as hard as he could, using the full accumulation of water he had amassed while recuperating. He wanted to arrive before Slitherfear unfolded his three arms. But the Squam heard him, sound travelling faster than taste, and snapped open as Heem arrived.

They collided. They were of similar mass, and Heem's impetus shoved the Squam partly off the floater. One triformed pincer closed on the surface of the floater, another clamped on Heem's flesh, and the third waved about randomly. Heem was fortunate: he had caught the monster by surprise, without his burning weapon.

The floater took off. It had the same brute power the living floater did, but it was really a cold metal platform. Heem jetted to maintain his orientation, lest he roll off, but he was held in place also by the Squam's cruel claw-pincer grip. He tried to needle the floater to establish control, but the metal was unresponsive. They sailed up and away, across the valley of Morningmist.

Heem tried to orient to needle Slitherfear, but still that awful grip interfered. Heem was accustomed to rolling, to get his position, so he could aim his needlejets; now he could not roll. He became dangerously hot trying. The Squam was horribly strong, gripping him with devastating authority. How foolish it had been to engage this monster in direct combat!

Then Heem realized: Slitherfear's hold on him was not the grip of authority, but the clutch of desperation. The Squam was afraid of falling off the floater, and was holding Heem so that the two would fall together. Heem actually had the advantage. He had caught the Squam weaponless, unbalanced, in the air: now it was body-to-body strife, elemental, with death to the one who first fell. A true rolldown between them!

153

This gave Heem confidence. He was desperately afraid of the Squam, and afraid of falling, but he would be satisfied to die himself, so long as he killed the Squam too. Since Slitherfear obviously preferred to live, Heem had a powerful tactical advantage.

He jetted more carefully, causing his body to exert rolling force in one direction and then another. The Squam's single claw hurt him as he put force against it, but he felt it give. As he reversed his thrust again, the enemy was forced to bring his free appendage down to grip the surface of the floater, lest his whole body be dislodged. The floater had irregularities suitable for the attachment of three-digited appendages. Heem was pursuing an initiative, forcing the Squam to react!

Now Heem's taste informed him that the groove from which that arm unfolded was in range. He oriented carefully and fired his sharpest needle directly into that cleft. The water was so hot it was starting to vaporize, like a jet from a floater. The effect was instant: the Squam snapped that limb back into its groove.

Encouraged, Heem jetted into the groove of another limb. This was an imperfect shot, glancing, but the effect was similar. He was not certain whether it was the impact, or the wetness, or the heat that was responsible, but he could provide plenty of each. The claw released him as the limb retracted. Now Slitherfear was clinging only to the floater, not to Heem.

Heem needled the third limb. But the position was wrong: he could not reach the groove from which it folded. Nevertheless, that limb quivered. The Squam lost his remaining grip on the floater and began to slide off it.

Heem, acutely aware of his advantage, jetted forcefully, rolling his body into that of the Squam, trying to shove it off the floater. The Squam was solid; a fall should hurt him as much as it would hurt Heem. Perhaps more.

But Slitherfear slithered forward and hunched his body, and it was Heem who overbalanced and fell off. He tasted the floater zooming ahead, while he angled down. He tasted vegetation below – and a streak of open water to one side. Heem jetted explosively on one side, nudging his body towards the water – and plunged into it with a terrific splash. His consciousness departed.

'So you survived,' the alien Jessica said. 'For a while there I wasn't sure!'

'I survived – but so did Slitherfear. I failed to kill him, and he escaped the valley.' And Heem was savagely sorry.

'But you were young then, inexperienced! He was a representative of a technologically developed species. It was not an equal contest.'

'It was still failure. The penalty is—'

'You take failure pretty seriously, don't you.'

'It is more than that. To fail in this competition is doom for me. To fail to kill the Squam—' He let his taste dilute into amorphous suggestion.

'I don't see why,' she persisted annoyingly.

'It was not merely personal failure. It was treason to my species.'

'That's nonsense! How can it be treason, when you tried as hard as you could?'

'Because no successful reseeding of Morningmist Valley could occur, while Slitherfear was there – or while he could return.'

'Of course it couldn't. You were quite right about that. But you didn't want to seed the valley anyway.'

'Therefore, treason – and now at last I pay the penalty.' He tasted ahead, admiring the looming blot of the Hole. 'Soon, now, we will spiral into the range of the killer tide, and be torn apart. Already I feel the first twinges.'

'This is ridiculous!' she cried. 'You can't equate the black hole to some prior failure! You can't accept death just because you were unable to do the impossible!'

'Equate it as you will. It is the end.'

'But *I* didn't fail! Why should I die too? I have a right to fight for my life!'

Heem considered. 'There is a certain alien justice in your view. But how can you save yourself, if I perish in the Hole?'

'I can't!' she admitted, suppressing waves of anger, frustration, and terror. 'But at least if I must die, I want to know why. You haven't said anything that makes sense to me.'

'It is clear enough. I refused to reseed the valley. Then I failed to kill the Squam.'

'That is as clear as homogenized mud!'

'Any creature of my culture would comprehend.'

'I am not of your culture! I'm an alien thing! Your rationale is insanity to me!'

Again, she had some justice. But there really was nothing he could do to alleviate her situation.

They watch-tasted the looming Hole. Already they were beyond the ship's propulsive recovery; even if he turned the ship and expended all their remaining fuel in a jet, going straight out from the Hole, it would not suffice. The doom had been committed. Increasingly he felt the nag of the tide within his body.

'Do you know,' she said after a time, 'I have had a recurring nightmare, like yours, only mine isn't a bad memory, it's a bad anticipation. You know how I've been masquerading as a man, to match my clone-brother, keeping our secret?'

'I know,' Heem agreed. At least she wasn't screaming.

'I hate that masquerade. Yet I understand it. I must maintain it, until the time is right. Yet I keep wishing I could end it, or have it ended for me, so I would not be guilty. So in this dream—'

'A dream of ending it would be a good dream.'

'No, because of the social situation. To end it at the wrong time, in the wrong manner – that would be disaster and shame. In my dream, I'm attending one of these damn clone balls, those masterworks of frivolity and waste, and this strange, huge yet handsome man comes up and rips off my dress and exposes my nakedness, and everyone sees me for a female, and they all laugh and I'm so mortified I want to die . . .'

'Ridicule before your peers,' Heem agreed. 'This I comprehend. Violation of cultural mores.'

'But the strange thing is, now that my nightmare wish is being granted and I know I am going to die, really going to die, that dream doesn't frighten me anymore. Here I've told it to you, and it doesn't bother me at all. You could laugh, and I'd just laugh too. Because showing or not showing my natural body is a pretty silly thing to get tight about. Because I don't really want to die. I'd be happy to suffer such shame, if only I could live.'

Then she was crying, and now Heem comprehended this too, and her alienness diminished in his perception. She seemed less like a Squam and more like a Moon of Morningmist, whom he had wronged by his denial, until her death made it too late. Now he wished he could spare this feeling female, even at the price of shame.

But he could not. The abyss was absolute.

All he could hope to do was to make her understand. Heem made a special effort. 'My kind must seed any suitable habitat. This is how we propagate our kind. Any isolated region of sufficient size is suitable – when it is vacant. When Meen and I were the only remaining HydrOs in Morningmist, we had to seed the valley and depart. She was ready. I refused.'

'I've got that,' Jessica said.

'But there was an exoneration. The presence of Slither-fear made the valley unsuitable. I had therefore to eliminate him. Then the valley would be suitable. But I failed. Thus I neither seeded the valley nor enabled anyone else to seed it in my stead.'

'But you tried! You risked your life attacking that monster twice. No one could ask more of you than that!'

'*I* could.'

'And anyway, you weren't going to reseed the valley, even before you fought the Squam, and there was no other male to do it, so your failure to kill Slitherfear made no difference.'

'Therein lies my treason. Had I been willing to seed, but found it necessary to eliminate Slitherfear first, my failure would have been honest. But as it was—'

'I begin to see. Your failure may have been because you wanted to fail, just as my nightmare was a reflection of my desire to be exposed. So your failure became an extension of your treason.'

'Now you roll it.'

'I wanted to roll it. To grasp it. It is like my own shame. I am not truly afraid of nakedness or exposure of my nature; I'm really sort of proud of my sex and my body. My true shame is in my desire to abrogate my responsibility to my estate.'

'And if you so abrogated, *then* you might truly wish to die.'

'So I might. I know my brother wished to die, and he is me.' She was silent for a time, her thoughts too complex for Heem to follow. Then she addressed him again. 'I'm glad I understand, Heem. Because now I can say without fear of successful contradiction that your whole death wish is unfounded. You committed no treason.'

'An alien could hardly be expected to comprehend civilized rationale.' Yet he was disappointed; he had wanted her to understand, and thought she did.

'I am a civilized alien! You have to understand that the HydrO way is not the way in the universe. What is treason to you could be honourable to me. Honourable to the majority of sapient creatures in the Milky Way Galaxy. Your horizons are too limited.'

'You prevaricate charmingly. But this is my occasion for truth. All my quasi-adult life I have concealed the flavour of my treason; now in death I can finally cleanse myself with the truth. I should have seeded Morningmist.'

'No, you're wrong! I mean you're right! Right not to seed Morningmist!'

Heem issued a confused jet, thinking he had misunderstood her. 'Right – to commit treason?'

'It wasn't treason! You suffered terribly in your juvenile state, not knowing where you came from or what your purpose was, all your brothers dying one by one. That's a barbaric way to raise children! You resolved not to perpetuate that horror – as any sapient creature would. *I* would never reproduce in such a fashion. It is the standard of your society that is treasonable, not you.'

Amazing! 'You – now that you know the truth – do not condemn me?'

'Condemn you? Heem, I applaud you! Despite all the urgings of your culture, you held to what was right.'

'This cannot be true,' he jetted disbelievingly. 'You grasp – you roll the wrong, you have similar horror in your own experience—'

'It cannot be false! How could I lie to you, being resident in your mind? My own horror is not similar; it is a private wish to see my own lot improve at the expense of my estate. A selfish wish. You, in contrast, stood up for what was right despite the pressures of convenience and social opprobrium. You held to what was proper despite personal sacrifice. There's a world of difference!'

She had to be right. She shared his brain, his nerves. He might not understand her nature, but he knew her emotion. She was speaking truth, as she understood it.

Still, it could hardly be. 'Because of me, neither Morningmist nor Highfalls was seeded. I violated the cardinal rule of our species.'

'You upheld a cardinal rule of *our* species, and of many others, perhaps the majority of all sapient species: not to throw babies to the wolves. I think you acted honourably.

159

Maybe it is against your culture's law or custom, but it remains a fundamentally decent attitude. If I have to die, I'm glad I am dying in support of such an attitude.'

She meant it. She was an alien sapient, and she endorsed his secret shame – as an open virtue. She was not revolted.

'And did it ever occur to you, Heem, that you were not really depriving those valleys of HydrO litters? Meen may have crossed over into Highfalls and found Hiim and seeded it; or two other HydrOs could have come in from elsewhere and seeded both valleys. The future of your species was not at stake; those valleys were bound to be populated. The only question was, by whom? So you elected not to participate; that was the fortune of someone else, not treason. Nothing was changed, except your affirmation of your own morality.'

'This is stupid,' Heem needled himself. 'What is it to me, what one alien thinks?'

But it was the first such affirmation he had ever had. He cared.

5

Threading the Needle

'Now you don't have to die,' Jessica said. 'You have no guilt to expiate.'

Heem was still sifting through his gratified amazement, but he had not lost the taste of reality. 'I may have no guilt to expiate. Therefore I can die satisfied.'

'You could save yourself, if you really wanted to. I'm sure of it.'

'Foolish female! The Hole cannot be escaped – and if it could, there would remain the problem of the competition, whose cut we have missed, and the incarceration that awaits me at home. I still prefer the Hole.'

'I've been thinking about that, Heem, while I worked on the problem of vision, while you fought the Squam in memory. I think we just might win that contest!'

'I have accepted the inevitable. You evince grandiose hopes.' Yet there was an insidious lure to it. The fact that a single sapient creature believed in his decision not to seed the valley – this had an extraordinary effect on his will to live. If one believed, wasn't it possible that others might also believe?

'This black hole – it's really a shortcut to Planet Eccentric. We are cutting across the Holestar System disc, instead of orbiting around it the way the other ships are. And the combined pull of Star and Hole is giving us tremendous velocity. If we could just zip through and come out the other side, we'd be first there, wouldn't we?'

'We are already within the point of no return for this spaceship. We cannot—'

'But we can loop *between* Hole and Star! Don't you see, Heem – the point of no return would be much closer to the

Hole, when opposed by the Star, since the Hole is really orbiting the Star. And if we go on through, all our present velocity counts *for* us, not against us, and will translate into velocity *away* from the Hole on the other side. We have not really been captured at all! We can thread the needle through!'

Heem was amazed at the audacity, simplicity, and naïveté of this proposal. 'To attempt such a thing is almost certain death!'

She was, of course, correct. At this stage there was absolutely nothing to lose.

'Still, it is hopeless,' he sprayed. 'The interaction of tides and stellar wind and radiation, velocity vectors – this is beyond my power to assimilate and control, in a ship of this simplicity.'

'You only think it is beyond your power. You have more resources than you appreciate. Think of it as a huge Squam to be challenged: you can beat it if you only try hard enough.'

'I am an experienced pilot, among the best of my species,' he sprayed. 'I am not modest about my abilities in this regard. I may no longer be able to defeat a Squam in fair combat, but my piloting ability is undiminished. *No* HydrO could navigate clear of the Hole from this point; therefore I cannot.'

'Well, a Solarian could!' she retorted. 'And I think that your piloting *is* diminished, because if you lost talent in personal combat, you must have lost it generally, if only in little ways you aren't aware of. And you know what you lack? It is sight. Vision. If you could see what you're doing, you could pilot this ship right between the Hole and the Star, balancing their gravity wells against each other so we don't fall into either.'

'For a species who sees, you evince little respect for radiation. To pass that close to the Star would be to be blasted by intolerable levels. Even if the ship were precisely

162

on course, we would emerge dead.'

She pondered that. 'I'm not so sure. There's a lot of gas and dust spiralling between Star and Hole. It could act as a radiation shield, preventing the ship from getting too hot or absorbing too much in the lethal ranges. It would not be a long passage. Maybe a little key manoeuvring. All you'd need to do is watch for suitable clouds, and go through them.'

She was so foolishly determined! 'It is theoretically possible. But I cannot see, so—'

'But I can! I can show you how. I can do it for you. I'm transfer half of the team; together we can do it!'

Her ridiculous enthusiasm burgeoning along his nerves was contagious. His new urge to live caused him to consider even such an extreme. 'Such a thing – it would be an extremely long roll.'

'Versus the short roll of dying without fighting!'

Heem yielded to her encouragement. 'We have nothing to lose by making the attempt.'

'Oh, Heem, I'm so proud of you, I could kiss you!' And she sent an oddly stimulating impression of physical contact through his awareness.

'What was that?' he demanded, astonished.

Abruptly she was diffident. 'Just an expression of – of encouragement. About navigating the channel—'

'Your memory-dream,' he persisted. 'The copulation ritual of your species – there was that action therein. Token contact of bodies—'

'Like your needlejets of greeting between sexes. I suppose it is analogous to – to your nonreproductive sex.' There was a warm flush of taste in the background of her thought, an embarrassment that was not unpleasant. 'I think I'm blushing.'

'What is that?'

'Never mind. Now I want to get us oriented on vision. Are you with me?'

Heem let her carry it. 'I am with you, alien.'

'Good. Now what we have to do is get your nerve-signals translated into visibility. I am sight oriented. You have piloting ability. We have to merge your pilot reflexes with my sight reflexes, and navigate by sight. It is reflex, not information, that is the key. The mode of interpretation. Because the human hand-eye coordination – well, this should greatly facilitate our manoeuvrability.'

'I will humour you,' Heem sprayed. He did not want to admit that he now found life appealing. And that kiss—

'Good. Now try to look through my perception. You've done it before, some; this is just a bigger dose. Identify with me; think the way I do. And *look*.'

Heem tried. He recalled the brief flashes he had had, seeing things. He wanted to succeed. But it was quite fuzzy.

'Now look ahead to the space between Star and Hole,' she continued brightly. 'Maybe you'd better taste it first and I'll translate. Then you pick up on my perception.'

Heem tasted the jets of his perception net. Jessica fumbled with them, struggling to reformulate the information in her imagery. 'See, the star tastes bright, uh shines bright, light, beams, hurts eyes there on the left. Oh, you roll, you don't have up or down or left or right so much. Well, I do; orient mine. Hole is black is nothingness, there to right, a gap in the optic. Like heaven and hell, but they're both hell for us, two gross gravity wells and we have to thread the needle – do you know what a needle is? No, of course not. It's a sliver of metal or something that pokes through material, carrying a line along after it, that's the thread, that's our lives in this case – we thread the needle through right where the light impinges upon the night, that shade of grey. Omigosh, that's not just light, that's a storm! Huge swirl of gas or dust or something, marking the no-man's-land zone, and we've got to go through it, it marks our channel, it is the material to be sewn, it will shield us from the killing radiation I hope, I hope . . .'

Heem tasted it, trying to shunt through her interpolation. It didn't work.

'You're resisting, Heem, I can feel it,' she said. 'Are you still upset because I'm female?'

'Yes. I don't belong in your mind any more than you belong in mine.' But again, that kiss . . .

'Look at it this way, Heem: how would you rather die, as a private individual, or with a snooping alien female in your mind, knowing your most secret, final masculine thoughts and guilts?'

'I am already subject to the latter,' Heem jetted tightly.

'But you haven't died yet. Wouldn't you prefer at least to die clean, by yourself?'

'I would.' Yet though she had expressed it well, it was not as true as it had been. He objected to her sex, but now he realized that there could be an intriguing aspect to it.

'Then you'll have to share my mind in order to get rid of it. I can't say I like this any better than you do, but maybe females are more acclimatized to male intrusion of one sort or another. *I want to live* – and if that means I have to suffer my mind to be violated, then so it must be. Maybe I felt otherwise, before I actually faced death and sifted out my realities. Now get in here and use my synapses, my perceptions – or we'll both be stuck with the least private of destructions.'

Heem could not refute her. He tried again, forcing his perception to mesh with hers, allowing his taste to be distorted into alienness. His whole system revolted, yet the alternative of an unprivate death loomed worse, now that she had pointed it out.

Yet, oddly, he suspected he would not have been able even to make the effort, if she had not endorsed his fundamental treason. She appalled him – less than before. So he could strive to free himself of her, because his alienation from her had diminished. It might not be total anathema to die with company—

165

'Heem, are you paying attention?'

He oriented on that nebulosity between the extremes of Star and Hole, for that was indeed the region they had to traverse, where the two gravity wells balanced precariously and the storm buffered the terrible radiation. It tasted turbulent, a tidal storm, shifting as the swirling matter of the two monstrous origins shifted.

'No, you're tasting it,' Jessica protested. 'You've got to see it. Here, follow me. I have two eyes, so I can see depth – at least I could when I had eyes – never mind. I'm not seeing too well myself, yet, but I know it can be done. What counts is that I have the mind for it, for visual perspective and detail. *You can see depth* – fix that in your mind. What is further away looks smaller, though you know it isn't. There's debris ringing the Hole, because there's no solar wind to waft it out; a comet would have no tail, coming in here. So a lot of gas is pushed out from the Star, and clouds in around the Hole; it can't just fall in, see, because of the angular momentum, just as *we* can't fall in. We have to spiral in – and therein lies our salvation, because if there's one thing that can counter the power of a black hole, it's the power of a larger star. That Hole is really quite small, only a few kilometres across, I'm sure, could we but see it as it is, smaller than a mere planet, smaller than a moon, but intense, yes, oh, yes, intense, while the star is thousands, maybe millions of times as large. The gravity well of the Star is bigger, much bigger, it actually surrounds that of the Hole, in fact the whole Hole is in orbit about the Star, or at least they orbit a common centre – am I repeating myself? – and we must pass through that centre in a straight line—'

'Not a straight line, babbling female,' Heem corrected her. 'A parabolic curve, perhaps, balancing the forces. See, the interstitial nebula curves partly about the Hole, enclosing it in a—'

'In a quarter moon—'

'We have to navigate that curve at high velocity.'

'You saw it!' she cried in a delayed reaction. 'You said "See"!'

'I – saw it,' Heem agreed dubiously. He had been distracted by her patter and he had jetted carelessly. Yet he *had* used her mode of communication.

'Concentrate, Heem! Make it come clear! You're so close – oh, I could kiss you again!'

'Don't do that!' Heem sprayed. But not as forcefully as he might have.

She laughed. 'I'm teasing you. I wouldn't really do anything as awful as that. See – see that moonshell area, that sort of bowl cupping the Hole – if you can see it, you can navigate it, because you are an expert pilot. All you need are information and reflexes. You can do it, I know you can!'

Heem tried, but the momentary flash he had had, had faded. 'I am not certain I really – whatever it was, is gone.'

'But you did have it, Heem! I'm sure! Try again!'

He did, but got nowhere.

'Very well – we'll have to approach this obliquely,' she decided. 'Let's – I'll tell you what, we can exchange images. You were beginning to see in the memory passages; you can take it further now.'

'First allow me to orient the ship,' Heem jetted. He manoeuvred carefully, aligning the ship with the nebula-bowl taste, then let it drift. He was conserving fuel, now that he might have need of it.

'Now – I'll visualize key scenes from my past, and you taste scenes from yours, and we'll try to get them both aligned with sight,' she said. 'I don't know if this is scientific, but I have a gut feeling about it. Once you can see your own past, you should be able to see anything – and there's our key to survival. Maybe I'll be able to taste my own past too, and get some idea what is entailed.'

'It must be accomplished before we reach that cup-nebula,'

Heem jetted. 'Once there, I shall have to guide this ship through, and prevent it from falling into either gravity well. Small adjustments will be critical. If I fail, all else is for nothing.'

'How much time do we have?'

Heem did some translating. 'I judge two chronosprays – about an hour, as you reckon time. We have been approaching steadily, and are now accelerating in free-fall; our approach will be extremely rapid, compared to our past velocity.'

'An hour!' she exclaimed. 'Well, let's get right on it, then!' She delved into her first vision, rolling him along.

Jessica faced her brother defiantly. 'Jesse, I absolutely refuse to go through that ever again! That awful cow – how could you?'

Her clone-brother spread his hands placatingly. He was a slight but handsome young man, with dark blue hair falling in curls to his light blue neck, his eyes a matching blue. His features were even, almost nondescript in their regularity. There was nothing typically aggressive or masculine about him. Which was, of course, a blessing, for her facial features were identical. Yet when she donned a feminine wig, she was fully female.

'That cow is quite a conquest, Jessica. If you were a man, you'd understand. Not the sort I'd care to stay with, but hoo-hoo! What a place to visit!'

'Well, I'm not a man, and I *don't* understand! Why should *I* have to cover for your slumming? I've got a life of my own to lead, you know!'

'Not as my clone, you don't.'

'Damn you! You always bring that up! Suppose you had been *my* clone? It's easier to delete an X chromosome than to add one.'

He raised one eyebrow. 'That depends, clone-sister dear, on the technology. In this case they found it more feasible to merge the X factor from another sperm cell in the same

168

bank with the cloned embryo, so—'

'I don't see it,' Heem complained. 'I taste the dialogue, but the colour of fur – of hair – it isn't working.'

'It's just the beginning,' Jessica told him. 'Just the initial alignment. Go into your memory, and I'll try to – to make it visible. We'll keep switching back and forth, until we connect.'

The arena was in neutral territory: the tropic region of the Erbs. Erbs filled the spectator section, their roots twining eagerly into the supportive soil. They enjoyed watching Squams battle HydrOs.

Heem rolled out to encounter his opponent. The dispute concerned five valleys along the boundary: were they to be controlled by HydrO or Squam? Squams had been surveying the region, presuming they would possess it; Heem had experienced part of that effort. Which was why he was here; he had a very special motive. This match would decide whether Slitherfear's labour paid off for the Squams.

It was not, unfortunately, Slitherfear who was to fight this duel, but another Squam champion. The creature slithered forward with confidence, almost disdain, knowing that no HydrO could hurt a Squam. But no Squam had encountered a HydrO with the motive and experience Heem possessed . . .

'No, not *that* memory; that's too much action and not enough scenery. We need strong visual imagery, colour, texture. Go back to Highfalls.'

Heem went back to Highfalls, though he would have liked to show off his victory over the Squam champion – the event that had made Heem a hero among his kind. For a while.

He recalled the taste of his awakening under water, realizing that he had survived his encounter with Slitherfear, but had failed to kill the Squam. The taste of the surrounding water was soured by his awareness of that failure.

'But water can be seen, too,' Jessica said. 'It's greenish, sometimes blue—'

'Tastes green,' Heem jetted.

'No, no! *Looks* green. Like this.' And she conjured the vision of the small lake on her human estate. 'Green.' She made an annoyed mental headshake. 'Oh, now I've taken over the memory! This is supposed to be your vision. I'm just the observer.' She concentrated. 'Here, I'll retreat to the background – ah, like this.'

That was an interesting effect, that shifting of taste nuance. 'Like this?' Heem repeated, imitating her retreat.

'Get back to your memory!' she snapped.

He rolled clear of the water, trying to taste its greenness or see its wetness. He returned to Slitherfear's camp. As he had feared, the Squam was gone, along with all his equipment except for the broken machine Heem had knocked over. The cave was empty.

But perhaps he could find the Squam again, and kill him. Heem now knew other valleys existed, and knew how to make flatfloaters carry him there. And, perhaps, he knew how to fight a Squam. Manoeuvre the creature to an awkward place, where a fall could occur, and disable his appendages, then shove—

'The scenery, Heem – what does it look like?'

Heem concentrated on the taste of the ground, water, and plants. Some oily substance had leaked from the fallen machine, flavouring the dirt.

'*Look* at it. Like this!' The taste of purple pines with green-scented needles came, superimposed over the valley of Morningmist. Or purple needles with green-flavoured wood.

But when he tried to see it, he merely slipped into that scene. Jessica and her brother were going through the forest of their estate, garbed as females. Jesse was honouring his deal with her, covering for her in the guise of

170

a female. However, it was evident that he was far from appalled at the prospect; he regarded the episode as a game.

'No, I don't want to go into that!' Jessica protested.

'But I think I am beginning to see—'

'No!'

'For one who needled me to sacrifice my mental privacy—'

'Oh – I suppose I deserved that. All right, Heem, if you can see it, you can watch it. My first sexual tryst, as a female.'

'I can't see it,' Heem admitted. 'There are strong currents of taste, but—'

'It wasn't much anyway,' she said, relieved. 'Jesse teased me for months after that about cows and bulls, geese and ganders, sauce and saucy. He had a point. I did it, but I didn't enjoy it. Casual sex – it just isn't my – I mean, there should be some depth of emotion – oh, you're a male, you wouldn't understand!'

'Correct.'

'Later on, he covered for me at a clone's party. We got along better after that: we understood each other better. You'd think that clones would understand each other from the outset, but our experiences were diverging, and the sexual difference . . .' She faded off.

'I wish I could see – you,' Heem said.

'Why, Heem!' she exclaimed, flattered. 'Even though you think of me as a Squam?'

Heem rolled away from that. He now thought of her as a person; actual vision of her would merely confirm her alienness. He had thought to set her back, knowing her aversion to being perceived without her apparel, but he had set himself back. He *did* want to see her, and not as a Squam. He had little interest in alien sex, so her episode was not important, but to perceive her more clearly as she was – why did the notion attract him?

171

He retreated to his own memory. As he left the valley of Morningmist and came up over the mountain ridge to a broad highland of distinctive flavours, and perceived the traces of unfamiliar HydrOs, he suffered disorientation. He slowed the flatfloater, then rolled off it. What was wrong? He was unable to concentrate, to function, but it was an internal rather than external malaise. He rolled to a halt.

For a long time he lay where he had stopped, his awareness fading in and out. His mind pulsed with strange concepts. What . . . why . . . ?

'Heem – what's the matter? Are you ill?'

He did not respond to the nagging thought. His whole past seemed to be swirling about him, vaporizing and coalescing confusingly. His youth in the valley of Highfalls, the deaths of his siblings, his entry to Morningmist, Slitherfear . . .

'Heem, that nebula is getting awfully close! If we don't achieve vision and put the ship under power soon—'

Moon of Morningmist, the joyous discovery of copulation, tragedy, the campaign against the dread Squam . . .

'I can't do it myself! I'm no pilot, Heem. You've got to snap out of it!'

Heem tried to marshal his thoughts. Increasingly it seemed to him that he had been operating on too immediate a basis, dealing with the details instead of the whole. He had fought a single Squam, physically, when he should have nullified the entire framework that brought such an enemy to a HydrO valley. He had refused to seed the valley, because that would have repeated the horror of his own development; he should have sought the origin of the Squam, so as to halt all such invasions. There could be some parent-of-Squams somewhere, sending the creatures out in myriads to decimate valleys; *that* was the place to strike! In fact, immediate personal action seemed generally futile; understanding had to come first. Had he understood the nature of the Squam at the outset . . .

172

At last he was discovered by other HydrOs. 'This tastes like a recent metamorphosis,' one sprayed.

'Verify it,' the second jetted.

The first jetted directly at Heem. 'What is your identity?'

'Heem of Highfalls,' Heem jetted weakly, remembering a taste that had almost faded.

'What is your purpose?'

Purpose? Heem strove to remember. There had been something about a deadly enemy, killing – but it faded as he sought it. 'My purpose—' Somehow, everything seemed irrelevant. Formulate, formulate! 'My purpose – is to facilitate understanding.' Was that right? Somehow he was unable to orient on anything specific. He couldn't remember . . .

'Welcome to adult status, Heem of Highfalls,' the HydrO sprayed. 'Roll with us, and we shall introduce you to civilization.'

'Metamorphosis!' Jessica exclaimed. 'Yet—'

'That's it!' Heem sprayed. 'I must metamorphose again. Into awareness of sight!'

'But I don't understand. In our Sphere, caterpillars metamorphose into—'

'All HydrOs metamorphose into adult stage, forgetting the events of their juvenile stage. Thus no mature HydrO has any subjective awareness of youth or age, of inception or destruction. At metamorphosis he enters a new universe of sight.'

'But you *do* remember—'

Abruptly, he was into her. His awareness coursed through her aura. She made a little scream of violation, but stifled it. For this was what she had been urging him to do.

And he could see. The immediate tastes of the little ship became immediate sights. The control buttons had elevations and shadows and depths, highlighted by the glow from the ambient-radiation-detection port, the glow of the light of the Star. The walls had nozzles and irregularities and—

173

'Colour, too. See it in colour, Heem!'

And shades of grey, with patches of green, left by the receded acceleration bath.

'I meant outside. Look at the cup-nebula.'

Heem concentrated – and in another vertigo of sensation he perceived the nebula, *saw* the bowl. The thing was opaque, cloudy, nebulous – as of course it should be! – but he perceived it with a clarity impossible to taste. He saw depth; the near side really did seem larger than the far side, yet this distortion lent a grandeur he could not otherwise have appreciated. He saw convolutions of gas and dust strewn out by the opposing forces of the gravity wells, ranged in partial orbits about the Star and Hole. Their Star sides were bright, their Hole sides dark, and they seemed to be roiling like the bodies of monstrous, deformed Squams, their motion frozen in this moment of his looking.

'I see it,' Heem jetted. 'It is a new dimension of perception, alien, horrible, beautiful.'

'Now you can navigate it!' Jessica exclaimed. Her voice lacked the definition it had once had, for he had taken over much of her aura, but her diminished presence was encouraging. 'Just as you navigated the concept-pattern to get this ship! You can steer this vessel right through the twilight zone and out the other side.'

Heem almost believed he could. Certainly it was a worthy challenge! Still, he had to caution her: 'This will be an extremely difficult passage. It has never before been accomplished by my kind.'

'Because your kind never had sight before!' she said enthusiastically. 'Vision is the language of astronomy. Even when you're tasting the sprays of the ship's instruments, you're really seeing – because the ship's sensors are optical. They have to be. In my own body I could see the stars directly. So now we're doing a double translation, from sight to taste and back to sight. And we can do things with sight you just can't do with taste, because it is virtually instant. So I know we can—'

'Enough,' Heem needled. 'The odds remain unfavourable.'

But now he had his chance and his challenge. Heem concentrated, using her vision, making it his own. He saw the glints of the planetary fragments orbiting about the Hole; in fact there were great rings of it, illuminated on the Star side, crystalline faces sparkling prettily. There were perceptible currents within these rings, bands of discolour that reflected the stresses acting on them. Well out from the Hole, the rings were rough and bright, as of large fragments; in towards the horror-sphere of non-light, the rings were fine powder, their rocks ground to minute particles by the catastrophic force of the tide. For the law of the tide dictated that the closer to the primary an object orbited, the faster it had to move, and in a gravity well as intense as this, the near sides of rocks had to move faster than the far sides, sundering the whole.

And the ship, too, would be sundered by that dread force, if the ship got anywhere near that radius. Might be torn apart anyway, if the conflict between Star and Hole was too great. Unless they passed the critical zone rapidly. Rapidly enough.

They were falling in towards the Hole, accelerating in a free-fall spiral. Heem oriented his jets and put the ship under power. First, he had to correct the direction of fall, so as to intercept the bowl-nebula of the interaction zone. Second, to pass as fast as possible. Even if the tide were not devastating, the radiation would be. He could see it now, that intense, burning brightness from the Star. This was no region for living creatures! Fortunately, a little power went a long way, when the merging gravity wells of two stellar objects were drawing the ship in.

Now the great rings of matter began to shift, as the ship's motion changed the angle of view. Perspective – the marvel of changing view, suddenly doubling the reality of the

175

sight. The rings wound about like monstrous pythons – Jessica's image of a Squamlike Solarian monster – seeming to take on life. Both Star and Hole expanded ominously. But so did the nebula-storm. It was apparent that Heem could score on it. With perception like this, guidance was no problem at all. But now that turbulence seemed more formidable. Could they survive those awful forces of interaction?

'Of course we can!' Jessica replied to his doubt, her voice faint but hearty. 'Goose it up to top speed and thread the needle, Heem!'

She certainly had confidence! This was flattering but foolish; that needle was needling through colossal opposition.

The radiation was growing worse. Much of it, Jessica clarified, was not in the visible spectrum, so her awareness of it was no greater than Heem's. But it was there, heating the ship, hurting his body. He would have to select a course that put as much dust and gas as possible between the ship and the Star – and that meant skirting perilously close to the Hole. The smallest misjudgement would lock them into the Hole, where not even the proximity of the Star could cancel its power.

As they approached the critical nexus, the view changed more rapidly. The turbulence nebula, dwarfed by the monstrous blinding disc of the Star, in turn dwarfed the tiny Hole. But it was the Hole that was their greatest danger. Heem nudged the ship slightly towards it, to skirt it as closely as he dared, driven by the intolerable radiation.

Wisps of dust passed to the starward side, putting the ship in shadow; even so, the heat was oppressive. His body really had no adequate way to dissipate that heat, since it penetrated from the outside. The tide, too, half-neutralized by the conflicting pulls, added its subtle discomfort. His body was not being torn apart, but he well knew that an intensification of this sort of stress could do it. More likely, it would break the rigid ship apart, exposing Heem's soft body to the rigours of unshielded space. That made the sensation more uncomfortable than it was, objectively. Subjectively. The little ship was not designed to withstand stresses of this type.

The nebula loomed. Now Heem saw every detail of its ominous configuration. It was virtually still, on this scale, but his motion helped him to perceive it as if it were in motion on his own scale. Matter and energy were leaking out from the Star and swirling into the Hole; the nebula was merely the region of indecision, with material piling in on one side, but also falling back to the Star. But more of it fell into the Hole, leaving the hollow of its loss. What was it like, inside that bowl?

'Oh, the heat!' Jessica cried. 'Maybe it's cool in there!'

Then they plunged inside the bowl, still accelerating. Abruptly the light was gone. Heem, so recently introduced to vision, suffered momentary shock. 'I can't see!'

'I know the feeling,' Jessica agreed. 'But you can still taste your other indicators. It's just a cloud, blocking off the external radiation, but nothing inside the ship has changed. Meanwhile, the cloud is shielding the ship, letting us cool, cutting off the deadly radiation.'

The ship shuddered and rocked. 'A storm-cloud!' Heem sprayed.

'We won't be in it long,' she said reassuringly. She was amazingly calm.

And they were out. But not in light. They were in the great shadow of the cup. On one side the turbulent clouds reigned; on the other side a ring of stars showed. In the centre of that ring the stars turned reddish, pale, fuzzy, and finally disappeared. Their light could not pass closer than a certain range, so there was nothing. Just a great black blot. The Hole.

Heem drew his attention away from that dread well and focused on the stars. He had never seen them before. Not this way, with direct vision. They scintillated in their myriads, mostly whitish, some bluish or reddish, some bright, many dim. They filled the universe—

They were gone. The nebula had closed in about the ship again, cutting off everything, for his arc was broader than that of the bowl. Again a storm of current shook the ship, and Heem had to look to his controls. The balance between Star and Hole remained precarious.

Then he became aware of something else. Something missing. 'Jessica?'

As from a distance she answered. 'I am here, Heem.'

'Are you well? Your presence seems marginal.'

'I – think so. When you entered my aura, I – there's nothing of me here except aura, so – I think I'm suffering sacrifice of identity.'

'Alien, I did not intend to destroy you! I understood you wanted me to—'

'Yes, yes, I did, Heem. I urged you to use my perception, all of it, right through to the colour. I just didn't realize – how thorough it would be.'

'I will withdraw.'

'No! You must see! You must guide the ship out of here before the opposing gravity wells and tides and radiation and storm currents destroy us!'

The ship emerged from the nebula. There was external sight again. 'I will try,' Heem agreed. 'We remain under acceleration. Now I must maintain the balance, far enough from the Star to avoid destruction by radiation, far enough from the Hole to retain escape velocity. If I do that accurately, and the fuel lasts—'

'Oh, you can do it!' she cried. 'I know you can. I'll just get out of your way and let you pilot.'

'Agreed.' This was remotely similar to column manoeuvring, but the alternatives were more deadly. If he did not perform within tolerance, one menace or the other would engulf them.

The key, now, was fuel. He needed to win free of the well

178

of the Hole and still be able to close and land on a planet. It depended on the accuracy with which he had threaded the needle. There was no safe side; Star and Hole were waiting to claim him, depending on the side he veered to. Now that he was no longer driving in, he would not fall in immediately; there would be a decaying orbit about Star or Hole, but the end would be inevitable.

Now he had to discover just how accurately he had navigated, utilizing his new sense of sight. He cut the drive. The ship continued on in free-fall, moving away from the nebula but losing velocity. Soon his instruments would indicate deviation, and the bad news would be in. The damage had already been done, either by his misjudgement or by the turbulence of the nebula. He was waiting for the extent of it to manifest.

And – the signs looked good. The Star-Hole complex retreated, more slowly each moment, but he had considerable residual velocity. The radiation eased. The ties subsided. It seemed that his velocity was sufficient – if his direction were correct.

As the ship moved on, the signs became clearer. He was off to one side, towards the Hole. But his new vision and its attendant judgement showed him that the ship's trajectory would carry it far enough beyond the Hole so that the larger ambience of the Star would dominate. He might even have to skirt the Hole more closely. Thus he had a conflict between his normal awareness and sight-awareness. It was not merely a different perception, but a different mode of comprehension. Jessica's human mind had an alien system of logic. Heem decided to gamble on it.

As he concentrated on the trajectory, watching for the opportune moment to make a course correction, stray wisps of memory fleeted past his consciousness. The death of the estate-holder, a grandiose funeral service, inheritance of the title – yet these things meant nothing to him. His kind had no subjective awareness of death, not in adult life, therefore no rituals of passage. HydrOs had no property, therefore no inheritance. These were memories of the Solarian mind. He had infused it so thoroughly that Jessica's memories were like his own.

Very like his own – for his were forbidden. No true adult HydrO remembered his juvenile state. Heem's metamorphosis had been incomplete, and that made him a non-adult. Similarly, the memories of a female alien should normally have been forbidden to him.

Now her state merged with his and with the present problem. In space there were deadly forces exerted on the fragile ship; only by balancing them could the ship pass safely. Heem had been drawn by the force of his cultural crime, balancing it against his species' need for his special talents. Jessica and her clone-brother, hiding the secret of their alternate-sexedness from their associates, had suffered loss of material resources. The estate was bankrupt; they had discovered this upon inheritance. So Jesse had got a job – the entire concept was devious for the HydrO mind, but equated roughly to Heem's own assimilation of this present challenge. When Jesse had been unable to complete his commitment, Jessica had done it for him. Balancing one set of needs and risks against another. It all merged into the present; it was all consistent.

And – his instruments shifted slowly, at last coming into conformance with his visual intuition. He had been correct to trust his new perception; the ship had been on course. A prior correction would have thrown it off, wasting fuel, perhaps eventually sending it into the Star to be destroyed. With a surplus of fuel, a second or third correction could have been made, but in this instance the tolerance was too narrow; *any* wastage of fuel could be fatal. Only through Jessica's perception, and the coordination of a mind to which that perception was natural, could this guidance have been accomplished. He had needed vision to verify that he needed to do nothing.

'We have won,' he announced. 'Vision enabled success. We shall be able to make planetfall.'

There was no response from the alien.

'Jessica,' he needled, alarmed. 'Where are you?'

He felt a faint presence stirring, but there was no vigour in it. Oh, no! Had the tide and radiation and stress damaged her aura, fading it out before its time? Or had she yielded up what remained of her being to enable him to see, to make his final judgement? At what price had he accomplished his victory?

'Alien female!' he sprayed. 'We have our differences, but I did not mean to abolish you! I – I value your presence. How may I restore you to health?'

Still she did not respond. Heem checked the ship's course once more, then turned all his attention inward.

'Jessica, I took your sight; let me give it back. It is a fine perception, it saved us, but it is yours. I took your aura; take it back. I affronted you; I apologize. You are no Squam, you are a valiant and feeling entity. Do not fade out. I need your companionship.'

At last she spoke, as from beyond the Star. 'I think I – overextended myself, and lost consciousness. Are we – how is the—?'

'We are successful!' Heem sprayed joyfully. 'We shall survive! Your vision did it.'

She was stronger now. 'Oh, I was so afraid.'

'But you were so certain I could do it! It was your confidence that kept me going!'

'Thank God for that!'

'Do you mean you thought I could not do it?'

'Oh, no, Heem. But I did fear, foolishly—'

She had feared strongly, and not foolishly, he realized now. Yet she had bolstered him with confidence, enabling him to do what he would otherwise have felt impossible. That realization stirred something strange in him. When he thought her absent, he had experienced a sensation of loss

181

of surprising intensity; now he experienced a gratitude that verged on – but the concept was amorphous.

'I appreciate that feeling, though,' Jessica said. 'We have been through a terrific experience, together.'

But he was too tired to explore that. He had expended considerable energy of his own, and with the let-down of effort the fatigue hit him. He had to rest, and so did she. He withdrew from her ambience, and the last of the sight-awareness faded from him. 'The ship is on course; we can rest for some time,' he sprayed, and allowed himself to roll to the stasis of complete relaxation.

'Yes,' she agreed, and there was something ineffable about her manner, and pleasant.

He dreamed, and now the dreams were visual. He saw a hillside decorated with pretty flowers and tall purple pines, and beside him was a presence that reminded him of Moon of Morningmist. But he could not see her, quite.

They intersected the column of ships at an angle. Using their new vision, Heem observed the tokens through the ship's perception. The situation was not good for the HydrO hosts; the first three ships were Erbs, and the next six alternated Squams and Erbs. Then, far back in the column, the HydrOs became more prominent.

'Sight makes a potent difference,' Heem sprayed. 'Erbs have sight, and they dominate the race. We can only consider ourselves fortunate that the remainder of the race will be onplanet, where taste is an advantage.'

'But they aren't really Erbs and Squams and HydrOs,' Jessica said. 'They are only hosts for the other entrants of Thousandstar.'

'Still, if HydrO hosts do not perform well, it will be a negation for our species, and our influence in Thousandstar politics will diminish,' Heem jetted. 'We can be sure the true Erb and Squam representatives are present in that lead column.'

'And the true HydrO representative is about to be,' she said. 'Our shortcut really worked! Where will we place?'

Heem surveyed the column critically. 'Twentieth. That is comfortable.'

'Not as comfortable as first would be.'

'*More* comfortable than first. The earliest arrivals will have to contend with the vagaries of the equipment and the landscape. There will be accidents, foul-ups, delays. Those best qualified to race in space will not be best on rough planetary terrain. I warrant that none of the first ten pilots will finish in the first ten to reach the Ancient site.'

'None but you, Heem! You have wilderness experience!'

'I do. But I want to be lost in the pack, profiting from the leading contestants' follies. Then, at the later stage, I will exert myself. There is still a lot of racing to be done.'

'That's for sure!' she agreed.

Heem jetted a course correction so that the ship angled to merge obliquely with the column. The ship remained in free fall, thus decelerating without the use of fuel. But as it converged with the column, fuel would have to be expended, for the retreat from the Hole was over.

'Do we have enough fuel left?' Jessica enquired worriedly. 'I know you said we did, but now that we're at the point—'

'We have plenty,' he assured her. 'Thanks to your vision, I judged the nebula passage so well that I used only half what I might have. We could decelerate late, and move safely up to fifth or sixth place, but I prefer not to advertise the extent of our success. So we will phase in with absolute minimum deceleration, somewhat shaky, obviously so battered from our pass between Star and Hole that we represent no serious competition.'

'Heem, that's unscrupulous!'

'Yes. But legitimate. The longer we seem to be a minimal threat, the better will be our chance of eventual success. This is not a polite social matter. This is a savage competition for possession of an Ancient site.'

'You have the mind of a Solarian.'

'I presume you regard that as a compliment.'

'I do.'

'Then it must be one.' The emotion he had experienced before, and put aside, came back more strongly. 'I dreamed of you, but could not see you.'

'I know.'

'Physically, you most resemble a Squam, with your limbs and hearing and the appalling habit of eating. Squams are anathema to me. In addition, you are female.'

'I am.'

'Yet I find myself – not sufficiently appalled. Your mind – is more like mine, despite the grotesqueries of your species. When I feared you had departed from me, I suffered.'

She was silent, but he could tell from her mood that she understood. It was beyond reason for a HydrO to approve of anything remotely resembling a Squam, but in this case something less stringent than enmity was in order. Maybe he should regard her more as he did the Erbs, alien but neutral, no real threat to him. She shared the perception of sight with them, after all. Yet she was not neutral. And not really alien, anymore. Why did he think of her now as he had once thought of Moon of Morningmist? It could not be simply because she was female, because he was largely indifferent to most females.

He had the feeling that she understood more about this than he did, but was holding her reaction aloof. Why?

Now Jessica spoke. 'The Erbs – you have thought very little about them. But we'll be encountering them personally, on Planet Eccentric, won't we? Along with the Squams?'

'Correct. We have had the intellectual challenge, and the piloting challenge; on planet we shall have the physical challenge. It will have its grim aspects.'

'I believe it! I have some notion what a Squam is, thanks

184

to your flashbacks, and I think I can help you there. Because I do, as you have so kindly pointed out, have certain points of resemblance. But I know nothing at all about the Erbs. If you could visualize one for me—'

Heem tried. He juggled their new sight to formulate a vision of a single Erb: a plantlike creature whose roots gathered water and minerals, a massive stem, and a splay of leaves that could fold into a dense cone.

'That's all? A sunflower with a folding flower? How does it live? I mean, it can't live on just water and minerals, can it?'

'HydrOs live on just hydrogen,' he reminded her.

'I still haven't quite accepted that, either,' she admitted. 'But if this Erb is a type of plant, it needs light too—'

'It opens its leaf-disc to collect starlight.'

'Sunlight, you mean.'

'A sun is a star, yes. When there is wind, it catches this on the leaves, achieving torque, and stores the energy for future use.'

'Like a windmill, I guess,' she said uncertainly. 'What about self-defence? Say a nasty Squam attacks it—'

'It folds its disc into a wedge and drills into the Squam's armour, splitting it apart. It is a rare Squam who can withstand an Erb.'

'But then HydrOs – you don't seem to fear the Erb—'

'HydrO bodies are soft. The drill has no purchase. We merely fire hot needlejets into the Erb mechanism, disrupting its operation, or holing its stem. Erbs represent no threat to us.'

'I see,' she said dubiously.

They limped into mergence with the column, in twentieth place.

'H-Sixty-six. Heem of Highfalls – is that you?' the taste net enquired. 'How did you escape the Hole? We thought you had suicided.'

'Salutation, H-Forty-six, Swoon of Sweetswamp. I perceived I could not achieve the first fifty, so I needled through the interstice between Star and Hole.' Heem knew the other ships were tuning in on the exchange, so he made the most of it. 'I fear the radiation and the tide—' He let the taste fade out.

'Oh, that's sneaky! Jessica said. 'They'll never worry about you now!'

'This is my hope.'

'Heem, something about the way you say that – your attendant emotion – you're not doing this just as a tactic, are you. You're hiding!'

'I knew it was disaster to have an alien female in my mind,' Heem jetted.

'Oh, come off it! We did just great together, even if I am still a little weak-kneed. After the Hole, what is there to worry about, in a mere competition?'

Heem made a mental spray of resignation. 'My liability is now of concern to you. It is proper to inform you of it before it manifests on the planet.'

'Oh-oh. There is something I still don't know? Heem – does it relate to your problem fighting Squams?'

'It relates. I deceived the competition management. I cannot defeat a Squam in fair combat. And I will surely have to, to remain in contention for the victory.'

'I don't follow that. You learned how to overcome a Squam before, didn't you? You proved this, didn't you? Winning those five valleys for HydrO hegemony, one of which was Morningmist? You proved you were correct; your litter would never have survived in Morningmist, had the Squams taken over that region.'

'I did all that,' Heem agreed. 'Yet this was a sign of my ultimate failure. I was able to use what I had learned as a juvenile, to defeat that Squam in ritual combat, and I became a hero of my kind. But the memory that enabled me to succeed was illegal. When someone betrayed the guilty secret of my past, I was abruptly an outlaw. Yet no one had known my secret, not even me – for all memory of

186

juvenile state is wiped clean in the metamorphosis to the adult stage.'

'But you just said – now wait a minute – you *do* remember! That's bothered me before. You're telling me all the things you aren't supposed to remember!'

'This – is the other facet of my secret,' Heem jetted reluctantly. 'My metamorphosis turned out to be imperfect. At first I remembered nothing; then the horrors of the Squam seeped through, and I knew I had to – to master the Squam. I began to remember how. To needle into the limb-grooves with heat, causing the limbs to retreat preventing the creature from attacking. Rolling it off a height so it would be crushed in the fall. There was varied terrain in the Erb arena, simulating a natural environment. I used it well. Thus I did what hardly any other HydrO could do: I defeated the Squam in combat. Only when I saw it defeated, and the Erbs were drawing it half-drowned out of the water, did I realize that it was not skill and tactics so much as memory that had done it. That I was not truly adult. Were this known, I would be banished from my society until my complete metamorphosis occurred.'

'Illegal memories!' Jessica exclaimed. 'Our kind thrives on memory! I remember my childhood—'

'You are not a HydrO.'

'So you became a hero and qualified for the competition,' Jessica said. 'That much I can see. And you did it by cheating, according to your culture's definition, because you aren't supposed to remember. But since you still do remember, you should still be able to handle a Squam, shouldn't you?'

'No. When the truth became known about my treason, more memories came, until I remembered it all. And with full memory of my juvenile state came—'

'Yes?' she prompted eagerly.

'Awareness of mortality.'

'You mean adult HydrOs really don't know they're

going to die? That doesn't make sense! Swoon of Sweet-swamp, just now, mentioned suiciding—'

'They know it objectively, not subjectively. It lacks personal force. We do not fear death, or consider it among our alternatives. Therefore Swoon remarked on this as a misjudgement of mine, attempting a tactic so risky as to be suicidal; she did not really contemplate death as a termination. *I* did – but I am not, am no longer, an adult; I am deficient.'

'Heem, this is ridiculous! Every creature has to die sometime, and—'

'Awareness of death as an immediacy does not come until the senile metamorphosis, when the concerns of a lifetime are put aside. Then the events of the adult stage are forgotten, and the entity is equipped to contemplate termination.'

'That's amazing! No concern about death, no awareness of youth or age! Subjectively. Like human beings always thinking the lightning will strike someone else, not themselves. You mentioned something about that before, but I didn't think it was literal!'

'When my adult metamorphosis became flawed, my awareness of demise returned. *I knew I could die.* My power departed, because I became a coward.'

She was silent awhile. The ship decelerated, keeping its place in the column. Then she said, 'Heem, I can't accept that. The way you handled that concepts contest, and the first part of the spaceship race, and the Holestar navigation – you've got good nerve.'

'These are all natural HydrO facilities. Fighting Squams is not.'

'Still, you could rise to the challenge, as you have in other cases.'

'No. I tried to needle with the accuracy required, once, on a mock-up of a Squam. I could not do it. My needles lacked sufficient accuracy. My fear ruined my aim.'

188

'That's not so!' she cried. 'You can't fear the Squam more than you fear the Hole. Fear didn't stop you when you were juvenile. I've been sharing your nerves, your mind. I know you are no coward!'

'I tested my needlejets again before I entered the competition. They remained inaccurate. My fear—'

'You knew you couldn't navigate the Hole, too!' she said. 'But when the time came, you threaded the needle perfectly!'

'Only because I borrowed your sight and your confidence. Your reflexes. No HydrO could have done it without those assets.'

'And no HydrO can overcome a Squam!' she exclaimed. 'But with sight you could do that too, Heem. I didn't have confidence; I merely urged you on, while my own terror nearly wiped me out, and you had to revive me after the danger was over. You were the strong one, Heem, not me! I just told you you could do it, and you were fool enough to believe me, and then you *could* do it. Don't you see – it isn't cowardice that stops you, it's lack of perception! You were lucky in your prior encounters, but you were wounded too, and though your skin healed, your needlejets suffered loss of accuracy. You were burned twice, Heem! There must be scar tissue interfering with your aim, or with your perception, so that you aren't aiming where you think you are. Your skin just doesn't function as well as it did before you were hurt. Once you learned more, you knew you could not depend on luck, and your jets weren't fine-tuned, so you became afraid. Your fear was a natural response to your incapacity, not the other way round. With sight, you could do it, applying your knowledge of tactics, just as you did threading the needle of the Star-Hole. And you *have* sight now, Heem! For as long as I am with you. You can beat your Squam! I'm sure of that!'

'And you expect me to be fool enough to believe you, again?'

'Yes! Because this is not something new, like skirting a black hole. You've handled Squams before.'

Amazed, Heem reflected. 'This is possible. I *am* aware of mortality, but I *did* navigate the Hole – with your help. Why should I not navigate a Squam – with your help? It just may be—' He paused. 'How is it that your kind remembers its juvenile state? *All* your metamorphoses can't be flawed!'

'We have no metamorphosis,' she said, surprised. 'Didn't I make that clear before?'

'But how do you know when you're adult?'

'By your age! When we achieve the required number of years of life, we are by definition adult. There is no break of continuity, no loss of memory.'

'By your age! This is incredible.'

'Sometimes it seems so,' she agreed wryly. 'Actually, there are also some physiological changes that signal maturity, but age is the legal criterion.'

'But then you all remember the horrors of your juvenile state! All your siblings dying—'

There are no horrors, Heem. Our parents take care of us, or some other responsible party. No human child is left to fend for himself, and few of us die in childhood. In our case, our parents died before we were grown, and the family retainer, Flowers, took over and saw to our security. It is like this in every Solarian family.'

'That cannot be so! In a few generations you would overrun your habitat. There has to be a natural control of numbers, so that a given species neither overpopulates nor dies out. Every suitable location must be seeded, but there must be no reseeding of populated regions.'

'I can see the logic of your system, Heem,' she said. 'But it is a cruel one. We produce only one or two offspring at a time, and make sure they survive. The end result is the same – and we suffer no traumas requiring the oblivion of metamorphosis. For you, remembering – Heem, it's

190

terrible. You really *do* have horrors to forget! No wonder you have traumas. I would, too, if I'd been alone with two hundred sisters, with no parents, in a valley filled with deadly menaces, and watched my sisters die, all but me, knowing that only luck accounted for my survival—'

'Your rationale and mode of life have their appeal,' Heem jetted. 'I believe I would prefer to propagate your way, rather than the HydrO way.'

'Now don't start jetting treason,' she said, touched. Then she shifted the topic. 'One thing still bothers me. If you were the only survivor of your valley, and in any event metamorphosis wiped out the memory – how did anyone know you had refused to reseed the valley of Morningmist?'

'That bothered me also,' Heem admitted. 'It fostered my illegal exploration of my own buried memories. The valley of Morningmist was empty, but that was no necessary indication of the crime, for all HydrOs could have been killed before a male came across to assist the reseeding. It had to be someone who had been there, and knew me personally, who knew that male and female had occupied the valley together, and left it empty.'

'Meen of Morningmist!' Jessica exclaimed. 'She was not killed. She crossed to Highfalls, didn't she? She knew, and she could have—'

'She would have had to incriminate herself, for she too left Morningmist without reseeding. Even though she wanted to, her failure would have made her suspect.'

'Yes, I have encountered that aspect of HydrO logic before.'

'I do not believe she would have exposed me, even had she not lost her memory through metamorphosis. I am in fact sure she did not, for when they quested for the truth of this matter, they located her, and she did not remember.'

'But there was no other person!'

'There was one.'

She was amazed. 'You don't mean—?'

'Slitherfear.'

'The Squam! But—'

'When I became known for my success against a Squam, Slitherfear became aware of my identity. He knew the geography of that region; after all, he had surveyed it. The name Highfalls sufficed. He thought he had killed me in the valley, when I dropped off the machine-floater. Now he knew I had survived. He suffered internal illness because of the needling I had done to his stomach; though his kind used their other machines to restore him somewhat, he suffered both physical pain and the humiliation of being driven from his post by a HydrO. He was as angry with me as I was with him. He communicated with my people, betraying me. They had to verify or refute the charge – and it was true.'

'So Slitherfear is twice your nemesis! He slew your love, then turned you from hero to criminal. You really have a score to settle with him!'

'And he with me. I understand he still manifests the faint odour of punctured membrane, which causes him to be held in ill repute among his kind and prevents him from mating.'

'Good for you!' she exclaimed, clapping mental hands. Heem realized that her digits were not really Squamlike; they were soft-shelled rather than hard, and possessed five extremities rather than three.

'Slitherfear has motive to thrust for fame,' Heem continued. 'His work was undone by my victory in the arena, so he too is a failure. I believe he has entered this competition. He is an adventurer, with a liking for infiltrating distant regions and a dissatisfaction for remaining with his own kind. This accounted for his original mission to Morningmist.'

'Where he blithely ate the young HydrOs!'

'It is the Squam nature. So I suspect he will be among the

192

hosts on Eccentric, vindicating himself and preying on the helpless. I hope he is; in this fashion we may meet again.'

'But if you were afraid to battle a Squam—'

'I am afraid. But it is necessary to make the attempt, to finish the business I started in Morningmist. Slitherfear must be killed, and I wish to be the one to kill him. Somehow.'

'And you call yourself a coward!' she breathed in wonder.

Her attitude was rolling better with him. Heem realized that it was merely the result of her alien culture, but still it had its merits. Perhaps he should have been conceived an alien.

Heem decelerated jerkily, managing to lose another place in the column. There were Squam ships near him; he was sure they had satisfaction in perceiving his difficult descent. When he oriented for the planetary set-down, he fouled it up some more. When the ship finally settled to the landing site, it was twenty-third.

'That's playing it comfortably close,' Jessica said. 'Let's go get our tractor, and hope we don't lose the race by two places.'

He was about to oblige, as the acceleration bath drained – for, of course, he had had to use it for the final push – when one more communication came from the space net. 'Do not hurry, Heem of Highfalls,' the cynical taste translation sprayed. 'I thought you might enter this competition, but doubted you would make it this far. I think you will not get far beyond this point, weak as you are. Do not die yet; allow me the opportunity to complete unfinished business.'

'Slitherfear!' Jessica exclaimed. 'You were right!'

Heem, abruptly faced with the conflict he had half sought, was unable to respond to his nemesis.

'Do you dissolve in your ship, stupid HydrO?' the

Squam demanded with sardonic flavour. 'Do not fade out completely until I land; I mean to destroy you with my own pincers.'

Jessica, finding Heem unable to answer, took over his communication system and responded for him. 'Thank you for the good news, slayer of juveniles,' she sprayed. 'It will be my pleasure to destroy more than your stomach, this time, monster.'

'What are you rolling?' Heem protested inside. 'I can't—'

'I'm psyching him out,' she replied. 'Making him uncertain, so he'll be nervous, make mistakes. It's good policy.'

'Wait for me at the landing site, and we shall discover what shall be destroyed,' Slitherfear replied.

'Oops,' Jessica said privately to Heem. 'I don't think it worked. He's either not scared, or he's a good bluffer.' Then, into the net, she sprayed, 'Why should I delay my mission for the likes of you, Squam? Catch me if you can.'

'I shall, coward.'

Heem suffered a surge of foul-tasting shame. Here, before all the contestants remaining in local space, he had been challenged and branded a coward. 'We must wait for his ship!' he needled.

'Don't be ridiculous,' Jessica said. 'Obviously the Squam had some reason for his certainty for wanting the showdown here. Otherwise he wouldn't have tipped his hand by broadcasting on the net. Maybe he has an acid-gun in his ship, or maybe he wants it where there will be several more Squams to help him out. We have to avoid him, or meet him in neutral territory, where we have an even chance. Let's get out of here, Heem.'

She was rolling along most logically! Of course the Squam would not fight fairly, if he had any means to cheat.

Benumbed by the rapid roll of events, Heem moved out.

6

Planet Eccentric

The surface of the planet was bright, with white washes of vapour against a blue welkin, a line of dark green at the horizon.

Heem rolled to a halt. 'How can I see all that? I have no light-receptors! In the ship we were translating machine-input that derived from a visual source, but now I can only taste and feel. There can be no direct input from the sky.'

'I confess, I cannot tell a lie, this time,' Jessica said. 'I filled in the imagery from my own awareness. I know what day on a planet looks like; I have made holograph paintings of it many times. I just don't feel comfortable, blind.'

'But if your picture differs from reality, and I am deceived—'

'That could be quite a problem when you encounter Slitherfear,' she agreed. 'I hadn't thought of that. When you fight the Squam, you have to have an exact notion of every detail. I think we can translate from your taste-input, but we'll need more work on it. So we'd better stay away from Slitherfear until we have it down pat.'

Heem was relieved to agree. He had to fight the Squam, but he wanted to do it in the most favourable situation for him.

'Still, I do have some direct input,' Jessica continued. 'I feel the sunlight on your flesh and the heat of the air; it has to be midday. So I know that whatever is visible, is visible.' And she strengthened the image.

Heem contemplated the scenery. It was lovely. He liked seeing, now that he had discovered how. His taste was unimpaired; he was aware of the pavement, the fumes of

195

the ship's emissions, the nearby alien vegetation, and the line of tractors at the edge of the landing area. There was no harm in the vision.

Suddenly the tractors appeared, as Jessica caught his thought. Gross black machines with huge ballooning tyres and metallic grills and complicated appurtenances.

'Oh, stop it!' he needled at her. 'There is no taste of composition wheels or controls. The diffusion of taste indicates smaller sources than you show.'

'Oops.' The balloon wheels were replaced by metal ones, and the tractors shrank in size.

Heem rolled rapidly across to the nearest one. As he touched it, and picked up the flavours of its immediate vicinity, the oil spots and fuel drops, the taste and visual pictures merged. It was a treadlaying vehicle, with a single front wheel, just large enough for a sapient body. The controls were multiple, so that HydrO, Squam, or Erb could operate it. Heem rolled up the sloping side ramp and settled into the control chamber, familiarizing himself with the details. It was a standard model, with the jet-buttons organized in the normal HydrO mode. He could not decipher the Squam or Erb controls, but did not need to.

The next ship was coming down; Heem felt its vibration. Jessica, indulging her artistic propensity again, filled in the image: a sliver of bright metal balanced on a thin column of orange fire against a deep blue backdrop—

The fire cut off.

Heem jetted at the tractor controls. His engine wooshed into life. Fluid drove into wheel-chambers, and the vehicle lurched forward.

'What are you doing, Heem?' Jessica cried. 'Jackrabbit starts waste fuel!'

Heem did not answer. He aimed the tractor directly into the jungle at full acceleration. The vegetation loomed up, clarifying as Jessica interpreted the taste emanations of it: green stems rising from the ground, flaring into side-stems,

196

which in turn flared into more side-stems. 'Watch out for those ferns! Jessica cried. 'Heem, there's no need to careen off like this—'

Then the concussion came. The fern-trees swayed with the blast, and the tractor jumped momentarily from the ground.

'What was that?'

'The descending ship. Didn't you see it run out of fuel? It had to crash.'

'Oh, someone played it too close.' She was chastened. 'No wonder you got out of the way in a hurry! We could have been—'

'Destroyed,' Heem finished. 'As that contestant was.'

'This competition – isn't supposed to be fatal, is it? I mean, the losers shouldn't—'

'Those who play it foolishly close can die. That pilot should have opted out, merely orbiting the planet until picked up. But he elected to risk it, hoping he would not crash too hard – and had he had moments more fuel he might have survived. It was a far lesser gamble than the one we took passing the Hole.'

'Yes,' she agreed weakly. 'Do you suppose it could have been Slitherfear who crashed?'

'Hardly. Slitherfear is too canny for such a basic error. He was several ships back, while this one was the next following us. Slitherfear will only die when I kill him.' *If* Heem killed him, instead of getting killed himself.

'Are you allowed to – to attack another contestant?'

'No. It will have to seem like an accident, or it could disqualify us if we win the competition. If we do not win the site, it will not matter; there can be no real enforcement of regulations here.'

'But after what I said in your name on the space net, everyone will know that—'

'They will assume that was bluff. There are many such bluffs in such competitions, considered part of the byplay.

197

Had I not been daunted by the sudden presence of my enemy, I should have acted as you did.'

'Well, I'm still not sure it's proper,' she said. 'Promise me you won't attack Slitherfear.'

'But you were baiting him yourself!'

'Well, I changed my mind. It's a female prerogative.'

Heem could not admit that he was afraid to attack the Squam anyway. Maybe his new perception of sight would enable him to prevail, but he was hardly confident. It was one thing to contemplate revenge from the safety of distance, but another thing to roll it into practice. 'I will, for your sake, try to avoid Slitherfear.' He felt mixed relief and frustration. If only he had the power to destroy the Squam! Secure power, not just a hope. It wouldn't matter if he lost the competition for the Ancient site, if he settled with the Squam. He could die satisfied.

'Let's reverse those priorities. We will concentrate on winning the race. If we lose it, and all is lost, and we know I will die and you will be imprisoned, *then* we can go after your enemy. That would be the right time.'

That made excellent sense. At times the Solarian found channels of logic that were quite valuable.

Heem concentrated on his driving, using the jet controls to guide the powerful little machine through the jungle. These fern-trees differed from the plants of his home-planet; they only had partial respiration, depending on a network of roots to draw sustenance from the ground. He had studied this process and understood its alien nature.

The fact that Jessica's visualization enabled him to perceive the plants with an alien sense only complemented the effect. Already he was used to vision, and even beginning to think visually.

There was a track in the jungle, circling the landing area. Heem guided the machine to follow it, picking up speed. This was not so very different from space piloting, in spirit.

'But how do we know where we're going?' Jessica asked.

Heem needled the tractor's information bank, and it sprayed a display of variegated flavours. 'This is the pattern of the landscape,' he advised her. 'The keyed tastes mark fuel deposits, hazards, safe passages—'

'Oh, a map!' she exclaimed. 'I'm good at maps. Let me visualize it – there.' A coloured picture-chart formed.

They contemplated it. The map indicated that they were on a large island girded with volcanic mountains, long rivers, broad plains, and deep jungles. At the centre of the island was the destination, the object of the competition. The Ancient site. Heem felt a thrill of excitement run through him as he saw/tasted it, and was not certain whether it was his reaction or hers.

'Both,' Jessica said. 'The fascination of the Ancients appeals to all the sapient species of the Cluster. Even if it wasn't a race, I'd have to hurry to that site.'

'You know of the Ancients in your section of the Galaxy?' Heem enquired, teasing her.

'Of course we know of the Ancients! What do you think we are, savages? It was the Solarian Flint of Outworld who saved the Milky Way in the First War of Energy by penetrating an Ancient site. And I am descended from that great man, and my home is the castle where he liaisoned with Good Queen Bess and started my family line.'

'Roll cool, alien female! So a Solarian has tasted a site. Who knows, some century the Solarians may even achieve sapience.'

She fired a mental needle-kick at him. 'You bastard! Just like a male!'

'You invite it. Just like a female.'

She needled him again, but this time it was a more friendly jab, with a faint and intriguing flavour of sex appeal. Alien she might be, but she was reminding him more strongly of Moon of Morningmist. He remembered those first happy hours in the new valley, of association and copulation.

'Just as though there is nothing in the universe except sex,' Jessica said severely.

'Is there?'

'Oh, pay attention to your map! You're running into a mountain.'

So he was, in a manner of tasting. Heem guided the tractor to the side, skirting the ridge ahead. 'According to the map, this is one trail of five threading through the terrain site. The problem is, with fifty tractors and narrow trails, it may become crowded.'

'Crowded? It must be a thousand kilometres to the site! That's one tractor per fifty miles, average.'

Heem struggled with the alien measurements, unable to reconcile them with each other or with his own frame. He had knowledge of Solarian time-scales, but not distance-scales. 'It is about two days' travel by machine, if there are not too many interruptions. But the tractors will not be evenly spaced; they are beginning clustered and will proceed at similar rates, since all are set at the same level of propulsion. There will be blockages at the difficult passes. If we get trapped behind such a block, the tractors on all the other trails will proceed bey⌐ ⌐ us. Then we will lose, regardless of what else happens on our own trail.'

'Oh, I see. So we'd better pick a trail that isn't much used – or go cross-country.'

'No cross-country. Taste these intense lines on the map? Those are lava runnels. This planet is actively volcanic. We can cross only at the bridges.'

'So there is still a good deal of luck involved,' she said. 'Those who happen to be in the wrong line, lose out.'

'We must arrange not to be in the wrong line. That way we mitigate chance.'

'Gotcha. Let's study that map more closely.'

Heem pulled the tractor off the trail and parked it behind the large clump of ferns. 'We dare not proceed too far on this trail until we are sure,' he jetted. 'I dislike delaying, but since the trails do not intersect again until after the fuel depots—'

'Fuel depots?'

'We shall have to refuel once. Machines are not civilized; they must consume physical chemicals constantly, like Squams.'

'Go ahead and needle it, chauvinist! Like Solarians too! Machines *eat*.'

Yet her words were pleasant, in contrast to her thought. He liked that counterpoint. In fact, despite what he knew of her nature, he liked her. She seemed so much less like a Squam than she had, now that he was well past the superficial points. After all, there were quite a number of species in the Cluster that consumed physical substance. Not all creatures who ate and had limbs were inherently evil.

'I should hope not,' Jessica said.

He kept forgetting that she could taste his superficial thoughts. Not that it mattered, anymore.

'The most direct route seems to be this one,' Heem jetted, mentally indicating a line on the map. 'Almost level, no swamps, only two lava bridges. Therefore a disproportionate number will follow it.'

'Which makes it a bad route,' she said. 'Now here is the longest, windingest, hilliest route, with six lava crossings. No one will take that one!'

'Because anyone who does, will lose the race. Unless all four alternate routes get clogged.'

'Which they might, if all the traffic goes on them. But what's to stop spaceship arrival number one from taking the shortest tractor route, and zooming along it without opposition, since no other tractor can catch up?'

'That is an excellent question. It simply cannot be that simple. These races are not designed for that sort of victory. There has to be something that prevents a rollaway victory for the first lander.'

'I certainly don't see what – oh, do you mean monsters or something, lurking for the first arrivals?'

'No, this is supposed to be a low-hazard competition, which means the worst hazards are the ones we bring with us, like other competitors. There are very few animals on Eccentric, because of its climate. There may be undiscovered monsters in the wilds, but not on the marked trails.'

'Then it seems to me it's backward. Each tractor that passes will chew up the ground some more, until it is virtually impassable. So the first tractor will just keep gaining.'

'That depends on the nature of the soil and of the treads. With laydown tracks like these, that approximate the sensible locomotion of HydrOs, the path may get better and safer each time—'

'That's it! she exclaimed. 'The caterpillar treads beat down the brush, press down the rocks, make a bumpy trail become a highway! So the later tractors will gain on the first ones, and save fuel.'

'And guarantee pileups,' Heem agreed. 'Yet if we can only gain by being behind, we can't win—'

'Yes, we can! The key is the same as with the spaceships! It's not where you are, it's how much fuel you conserve. If you run economically, you'll pass the others in the end. Look at those fuel depots on the map – they're nearer the landing field than they are the Ancient site. How much do you want to bet that every tractor will run out of fuel before the end, on that last stretch? So any who haven't caught on by then, and who continue to waste fuel by forging new trails or jamming into each other or simply speeding—'

'This verges on genius, alien creature! That *is* the key! A trap for the stupid or unthinking. What use to lead the pack, if your tractor stalls out before the others and you have to roll your own power while the others pass you by in their machines? The strategy is to use the most-used trail,

202

proceeding slowly and efficiently, then go ahead at the end.'

'Unless we get hung up behind a two-day-long traffic jam,' she amended. 'Better stay up near the front while the fuel depots are ahead, and—' She paused. 'Oops – I just thought, Heem. Is there enough fuel for all the tractors, no matter when they come?'

Heem checked the coding on the map. 'These deposits, in the aggregate, have enough fuel to refill only half the tractors.'

'So there is the other shoe.'

'The other what?'

'The other part of the trap. Go too fast, you run out of fuel early. Go too slow, you can't refuel. So you're out either way.'

'This is the kind of manoeuvring I understand! We must proceed rapidly to the depot, then economize on the remainder.'

'I wonder – could that also be a trap? Everyone racing to the nearest depot—'

'It could be. Yet if we do not race—'

'I'm still suspicious. There's something too pat about this. How is that fuel distributed? I mean, is there the same amount at each depot – maybe enough for five tractors? This vitally affects our strategy.'

'It does indeed,' Heem agreed. This alien was smart! 'The map seems to indicate that all depots are even. The same amount of fuel at each station.'

'So the depots on the most popular route will run out first, and the latecomers won't be able to cross to some other depot, will they! Because they're too far apart. So we'll lose about half our tractors at the first round, including some of the leaders – and the smart contestants who arrive late will do best to go on the least popular trails, in the hope that a fuel refill remains that will put them back into the race. The last could very well be first.'

'Possibly. Except that a smart leader should still be able

to stay ahead of a smart follower. Something more is required.'

'This bad route,' she said. 'It's so *very* bad, no one in his right mind would take it unless he were already so far behind he knew it was the only one with fuel. But look – there's a crossover strip here; you could start on the bad route, then cross to a better one after the fuel depot.'

'Yes. We must do that. This delay for reflection may have gained us much more than we had hoped.' Heem started up the tractor and directed it towards the bad route.

'Still, I wonder,' she mused. 'Why should they design a route that bad, then put an escape trail? I'm getting paranoid again. Heem, is there any way to take extra fuel at the depot and store it for the end stretch?'

'No. Doubtful. The depots deliver a set amount by closed connection. Otherwise the first tractors would steal it all.'

'So you can't store it up. You have only one tankful at the end, no matter which route you're on?'

'True. Perhaps some fuel from the initial tank can be conserved, to stretch the second; that is all.'

'Heem, look at this bad route. It crosses several lava runnels, then climbs right over a mountain!'

'Yes. Virtually all our fuel would be expended in that ascent.'

'But from then on, it is all downhill. We could coast almost to the site!'

Heem studied the route, surprised. 'That is a better route than it seems. It provides elevation at the expense of fuel, but it conserves that elevation until the end, when the ride down is free. Provided the tractor achieves the final height.'

'So let's stay on it, Heem! It's a gamble, but there's a lot to gain. No traffic, no fuel shortage, and we can take our tractor closer to the Ancient site than any other way. Because the tractors on the other trails, going on the level, will have to continue under power, while we can turn off the motor entirely between climbs.'

'I agree. We will be among the first ten tractors, then, even if we must travel far and slow at the outset.'

'All because we paused to consider, instead of rushing blindly ahead.' She was pleased.

Other tractors were moving, as the spaced-out ships landed. Here the trail was wide; Heem navigated past two vehicles going in the opposite direction. One was a sinister Squam, the other an Erb. If they were surprised to note the tractor going the wrong way, they did not show it. Probably they felt that every fool who lost his way was a net gain for the others.

Heem located the bad trail. Sure enough, it was virtually unused; only one or two tractors had gone before. The path was rough, but far better than straight uncharted wilderness. He moved along it at the maximum speed he judged safe.

Jessica filled in the imagery with growing detail, until Heem almost found himself thinking visually despite his knowledge that it wasn't real. The clumps of ferns had thickened into a dense jungle, their leaves interlocking so that no tractor could pass between the plants; there was no choice except to remain on the carved trail.

'Yet no big trees,' Jessica remarked. 'These all look as though they just sprang up this season.'

'They did. The eclipse-winter wipes out everything. The air freezes and settles to the planetary surface, and all organic structures shatter and are reduced to powder. In the spring there is only nutrient dust, with the seeds of the new life embedded.'

'All new, every year!' she said. 'But how can animals grow from seed?'

'Your kind does not grow from seed?'

'Not that way. We give live birth.'

'I do not comprehend.'

'The offspring are born from the body of the mother.

205

Some other Solarian species lay eggs, while – how do HydrOs do it?'

'We seed.'

'You mean like vegetable seeds? In that case why couldn't your seeds survive the winter here, buried in frozen mulch the way the native seeds do? You could colonize the planet.'

'Not like vegetable seeds. HydrOs are always animate, conscious, though we soon forget our earliest moments, even before metamorphosis. My illegal memories go back only until the time I was half grown, when the majority of my siblings had already perished. Freezing would kill us. We must have hydrogen to consume, and be warm enough to process it.'

'How *do* you draw energy from gas? I've never been clear on that.'

'It is a natural process requiring no intellect. I suppose it is no more complex than the way you Solarians process physical food. Some heat is released, which we regulate to facilitate the process, and on occasion when we require hot weapon needlejets—'

Another tractor was coming up on them from behind, gaining on them as they had conjectured would be the case.

'We should let it pass,' Jessica said. 'Then we can follow, saving fuel. If the refuelling is a set amount, there must be about twice that capacity in the tractor, so that units will neither run out early nor overflow. Anything we save now will contribute that much to our progress at the end.'

'True. But if we simply draw aside and let the vehicle pass, that entity will be suspicious, and may decline to take the lead. We must yield the lead only with seeming reluctance.'

'Say, yes! You really are smart, Heem!'

Flattered, Heem did not respond. She was quite intelligent herself, once he allowed for the facts of her alienness and femaleness.

The pursuing tractor came close. Now Heem tasted the environment of its occupant. 'That's an Erb,' he jetted. 'Nothing to worry about.'

'An Erb could win this race, you know,' Jessica warned him. 'An Erb in a tractor could run you off the road just as easily as a Squam could.'

'Never,' Heem sprayed, unworried. 'Erbs cannot compete with HydrOs. They're only plants.'

'Plants?' she demanded incredulously. 'That's not the way I remember it from our last discussion on the subject. You told me they were sapient, with movable leaf-umbrellas they used to fetch in light energy, and that they could defeat Squams in combat. That's quite a bit for a plant!'

Now the other tractor was right behind them. Heem manoeuvred to block its forward progress, as though afraid it would pass them. 'They draw nutrients from the ground, like other plants. These tractors have mulch-beds bottoming the occupation compartments, so as to be serviceable for the Erb's roots. That is also why the compartments are open; the Erbs need access to light.'

'I'm still grasping, Heem. I understand all this intellectually, but I want to form an image for us to look at right now.'

Heem concentrated, trying to convert his taste-impression to a visual one. When Jessica was doing the imagery it came easily, if inaccurately. For him it was much harder.

'Here, I'll help you. Like this?' She made a picture of a giant green fernlike thing, its fronds waving gently in the breeze.

'No, not at all like that,' Heem sprayed. 'Erbs are not green. They don't wave. They—' He focused on the taste. Actually since he had never seen an Erb – no HydrO had! – he could not be sure of the colour, but knew it did not match that of most vegetation.

The picture fuzzed and changed as they adjusted it.

Suddenly the real Erb drew alongside; Heem had not paid proper attention to his manoeuvring. He tried to crowd, too late.

'Let it by,' Jessica murmured. 'That's what we want, remember?'

Heem had almost forgotten. He allowed his tractor to lost ground slowly, and the Erb wrested the lead from him. As Heem fell behind, he picked up a clear medley of tastes carried back on the wind, and suddenly Jessica's picture firmed.

It was of a golden column swelling into a splay of tendrils below and a cone opening out above, formed of overlapping metallic petals.

'I see,' Jessica said. 'It gathers light by spreading its leaves into a full circle. But what about days when there is no direct sunlight? It can't store enough energy from the sun to maintain an active life-style, can it?'

Heem struggled with the picture, adjusting it. The Erb's cone opened into a disc, the disc tilted to face the wind, and the petals angled separately to form vanes. The wind caught them, driving them in a circle about the axis; the force of the wind was being transmuted into torque that spun down into the body of the plant. 'A windmill!' Jessica exclaimed. 'Now at last I see it! You tried to explain it before, but—'

The Erb's tractor was now ahead, and proceeding slightly more slowly on the less-beaten track. Heem edged off, allowing his own tractor to fall slowly further behind so that the Erb would not realize the truth. In the process, Heem increased his fuel economy significantly.

'But how does the Erb defend itself from a horror like the Squam?' Jessica asked. 'You said Erbs could beat Squams' didn't you? Something about drilling?'

'The leaves mass into a drill-cone,' Heem sprayed, modifying the picture again. He was getting better at this. The secret was to formulate an extremely detailed conception, then project that detail. Any aspect that was vague in his mind, was vague in the image. This was good discipline! 'Visualize a Squam attacking the Erb.'

Jessica obligingly conjured the image of a Squam. It looked somewhat alien, as she was to a certain extent drawing on her own experience of fanged reptiles, but it sufficed. The Squam slithered towards the Erb, its triple arms extended, each triple pincers open.

The image-Erb rotated to aim its wedged leaves at the Squam. The mass spun on its axle-stalk as the windmill had, but now it was driven from inside. As the Squam came close, the cone angled to point at the Squam's torso and drove forward.

The screw-thread configuration bit into the body, catching under the scales and jamming them apart. In a moment the body of the Squam was split open, its hard scales unable to resist the overpowering leverage of the spiralling wedge. The Squam was badly injured and would soon die.

'Now at last I understand that too,' Jessica agreed, blanking out the vision. 'Torque wins the day! And I see how the drill would not work against the protean body of a HydrO. It really is scissors-paper-rock.'

'It really is what?' Heem asked, confused by her flurry of concepts.

She explained, carefully illustrating with pictures. 'Scissors are closing sharp edges that sheer through paper, defeating it. But paper wraps rock, smothering it. And rock smashes scissors. So each beats the other, in a vicious circle. That's what it is with the Squams, HydrOs, and Erbs. Squams have scissors-pincers that cut through the soft paper-flesh of HydrOs, but the rock-hard drill of an Erb smashes the scissors. And the HydrOs – how do the HydrOs overcome Erbs? I know you told me before, but—'

'We wrap them,' Heem admitted. 'We surround them and jet them with hot water. They can block the pincers of the Squams, but not our liquid.'

The tractor forged on, readily handling the curves and rises of the tail. 'You know, the more I learn of your way of life, the more I appreciate it,' Jessica observed. Then she corrected herself. 'No, I don't really like it; I much prefer my human mode. But yet your scheme of things has its appeal – let me isolate this – something attracts me—'

'Your Solarian existence remains alien to me in most respects,' Heem jetted. 'But in your mode of raising offspring, and you yourself – I find myself wishing that you were a HydrO.'

'Well, I *am* a HydrO, for the nonce. I'm occupying your body, aren't I?'

'A separate HydrO. One I could copulate with.'

'One you could – what a thing to say!' she exclaimed, a sort of pleased anger washing through her aspect of his mind. 'Every time I think we are making progress, you come up with—'

'I regret,' Heem jetted quickly. 'I forgot that your kind regards copulation as indecent. I withdraw the thought.'

'Heem, you can't withdraw a thought! And my kind doesn't regard – well, I don't, anyway! I – you just caught me by surprise. We Solarians don't – I mean such things are not baldly stated, but I guess they are felt. In fact, my clone-brother, who's really me in a male disguise, a Y chromosome in place of an X – I – I guess what you're really saying is a natural urge—'

'I regret offending you. I feel towards you somewhat as I felt towards Moon of Morningmist, and I now am more familiar with you than I was with her when she—'

'You knew her a few days before she died,' Jessica agreed. 'I have been with you a similar period, and we have solved a concepts-riddle and raced in space and bypassed a black hole already. How could anything you say cause me offence? I'm – I'm clarifying my own feelings to myself now, more than to you. I'm surprised, but – deeply pleased, Heem I – I do want your respect. Because I have come to respect you. You are really quite a man in your fashion.'

'I am a HydrO, not a man.'

'Yes, yes of course, Heem. I spoke figuratively. What I meant was, I – I – oh, God, my culture makes this hard for me, and I thought I was liberated! But I want to be honest. I – I wish I were that lady HydrO. So I could – I know sex isn't serious with you, but often it isn't with us, either. Not reproduction-serious. Sometimes it's just a mutual recognition of feeling, and—'

'But we are of differing species,' Heem protested, intrigued. He had been appalled by the presence of a female mind in his; now he preferred it.

'Are we really, Heem? Is that so important? Our physical bodies differ, but our minds agree on the fundamental things, like not leaving babies alone to die. If I could occupy the body of a separate HydrO, a female, would it be wrong – what we might do?'

'No!' he sprayed explosively. 'It would not be wrong!'

'After all, creatures in transfer do all sorts of things. That's the nature of transfer. It leads to understanding, reduces alienophobia, spreads information. When in Rome—'

'When in what condition?'

'Condition?'

'I did not recognize the condition of Rome.'

'Oh. That's a city on ancient Earth, the Solarian home-world. My planet circling Capella is just a colony, as your Planet Impasse is. What I meant was that when one is in transfer, one does what the host does. Expresses oneself in the manner of the host, though it differs from – I mean, when I'm in HydrO host, it should be right to—'

'But you are in a male body.'

'I wish I weren't. I want a female body. Truth is, I might as well have been in a male body back in System Capella, since I had to act male anyway. This isn't so much of a change

211

after all! But I hate it. I wish I were female, so I could – could at least greet you in the HydrO manner. As Moon of Morningmist did. Before I went home.'

Before she went home. Heem abruptly realized that his aversion to her intrusion into his private mental space had not merely dissipated; it had been replaced by positive feeling. He liked her very well, and no longer wanted her to go. Yes, she was alien, and female – but she alone did not condemn his shame of the valley of Morningmist. She had provided him with the useful new perception of sight, that would be lost when she went. Only a mind geared to vision could make it work. She wanted to go, but he wanted her to stay.

'Why, thank you, Heem.'

Heem sprayed an explosive epithet. That damned un-privacy of thought . . . was also becoming more appealing. He was not alone.

'Look, Heem, I feel the same. I was aware of your reactions when I kissed you, and I didn't want to tease you, so I shut up. But I do – wish I could stay. I *can't* stay; we both know that. We have to win this competition and get me transferred back. Otherwise you'll be in jail, and I will perish as my aura fades. So there is absolutely no sense in – in our getting involved with each other, because even if it were possible it would still be impossible.'

She made a certain female sense. If they failed to win the competition, both would die. Slowly, horribly, suffering stifling confinement of one kind or another. If they won, they would separate, and live half the Galaxy apart. Even if Jessica could mattermit in her own physical body to his world, or he to hers, they would be of two completely alien species. Meanwhile, they were together – and could do nothing, because they had between them only a single body. So she was exactly correct; even if it were possible, it would be impossible. Therefore it was pointless and foolish even to speculate on alternatives; it was a dead issue.

Yet somehow it did not feel dead. Suppose they failed in the competition, but remained free on Planet Eccentric? At least they would be together, and could wait for the killing winter in company. He wanted her with him, even on that basis. It was an emotion he had not felt before, this willingness, even desire, to sacrifice everything else for the mere sake of the company of another creature.

'Maybe your species doesn't have that emotion,' Jessica said. 'Your couples don't seem to stay together after reproducing. Among our kind it is called love.'

'I have never tasted that concept before,' Heem admitted. 'It must be another crossover from your being, like the ability to see. I do not know how to deal with it.'

'You shouldn't have to, Heem. It is unfair to make your kind react to an emotion it doesn't possess naturally. I'll try to blot it out—'

'No! I do not comprehend it, but it relates to you and I must keep it. It is a torment that I like.'

'Oh, damn, Heem!' Yet she was pleased.

Then he had another realization. 'The competition – we do not have to win. I will yield myself to the authorities, and they will transfer you back—'

'And imprison you. I will not have my freedom that way.'

'But if I am doomed anyway—'

'You are *not* doomed. You can have the rest of the summer season of Eccentric free, then perish as you prefer, by the action of the Hole. Reaching to claim you in the form of the eclipse. It is right for you, Heem, and I would not deny you that.'

'I do not want freedom if you die!'

'Heem, if you go to prison, my heart goes to prison with you, no matter where my body is, or my aura. You try to turn yourself in, and I will paralyse you with my screams. We are not going to separate that way. Only if we win, so that I know you have a future – then I can go home.'

And she was not bluffing. She was as foolishly principled

as he. 'Then we must win.'

'We won't win if we don't pay more attention to where we're going. Why don't you stop trying to argue with females and get to work?' But she sent him a kiss.

According to the map, they were nearing the first bridge. The tractor emerged from the jungle, and there was an awful flavour of molten rock.

'Flowing lava!' Jessica exclaimed with a thrill of horror. 'So it really is true! The volcanoes really *are* active here!' Working from his taste, she made a visual picture: a cleft in the ground, brimming with glowing red liquid rock that sizzled its way downhill.

A tractor ground up from behind. Two tractors, three. The later arrivals were taking to this 'poor' route in greater numbers, evidently reasoning that it was, after all, the best prospect, just as Heem and Jessica had. Heem concentrated and then picked up the tastes: the new contestants were a HydrO, a Squam, and an Erb. They quickly spread out on the wider path beside the lava channel and raced towards the bridge ahead.

'We'd better move, if we want to keep our place,' Jessica said.

'We know one Erb is ahead of us,' Heem responded. 'I judge from the nature of the flavour of the trail that there were no more than two tractors ahead of that one. If we assume there is fuel at the depot for five tractors, we can let one of the following machines pass us, no more – and our path will be easier if we do let that one ahead.'

'That's cutting it close, Heem.'

'We must cut close to win. We must conserve fuel, building up reserve. In the final stage, those who have planned most carefully will prevail – and we must be among the first five.'

'First five? Why that number? There is no cutoff here, is there?'

'I believe all tractors will exhaust their fuel before the

214

finish, as we surmised. The leaders will be strung out, perhaps widely. We shall have to proceed without machines. There should be a chance to pass a few – but if we are not near enough the lead, we shall have no chance. I deem five to be the only ones having a fair chance.'

'I see. You're right, of course. You thought it through better than I did. Very well, we'll play it close now, so we'll have the edge when it counts.'

The three tractors were not conserving fuel at all. Each was racing to be first. It was now evident that there was no absolute limit on tractor velocity, contrary to Heem's assumption. But the faster a given vehicle moved, the more wastefully it expended its fuel. Either these drivers had not calculated as precisely as Heem had, or they did not know precisely where the limit was. Each wanted to be sure of obtaining refuelling.

No – they were not merely racing, they were fighting. The Erb was in the centre, with the best track, but as it drew ahead the others closed in from the sides to bang against it, disrupting its progress. Jessica patched together her picture from Heem's taste and vibration perceptions, showing the three tractors skewing along.

'I think we had better stay clear of that,' Heem jetted, accelerating their own tractor. 'There is no fuel economy to be gained in that mêlée.'

But there was another clang of contact. All three pursuers skewed, and the Erb bounced ahead. Heem had to veer out of the path to prevent it from bumping him. That put him in front of the other HydrO, and he had to steer on out to the jungle to avoid it. The foliage entangled his treads, and he had to slow.

All three tractors shot past him. In one miscalculation, he had lost his place. Instead of crossing the bridge ahead of the three, he would cross behind. 'Food!' he swore.

Jessica, as tense as he, broke into hysterical mental laughter. 'To you, the foulest concept is food,' she gasped.

'To us, it is excrement, or—'

Heem angrily manoeuvred the machine back on to the centre path. 'Or what?'

'Or copulation.'

Now it was his turn to signify mirth. 'You Solarians are truly, wondrously alien! Copulation is your foulest concept?' The tractor resumed speed, moving well, gaining on the others – but Heem knew he would have to pass two of them, somewhere between the bridge and the fuel depot. That would be difficult, and cost him fuel. He should have crossed the bridge first, then allowed one tractor to pass him when all were conveniently spaced out.

'It is sort of silly,' Jessica admitted. 'We have good terms and bad terms for the same things. Things that are quite natural and necessary. Your way makes more sense. Your expletive relates to a function alien to your metabolism.'

Now the bridge came into clear perception. It was, by the taste of its ambience that Jessica translated into another picture, a narrow span of hardened lava arching over the channel, wide enough for one tractor at a time. It seemed to be a natural span; easier for the Competition Authority to direct a path to it than to build a bridge over flowing stone.

The Erb charged up and on to it, lifting above the liquid lava. The passage had to be quick, because the air was quite hot in that vicinity. Both HydrO and Squam skewed to a halt. 'The weight of two tractors might collapse it,' Heem explained, slowing his own vehicle. 'No use to crowd past if it only means destruction; we have to let the Erb clear first.'

'At least we know it's safe for one, because the first Erb crossed it.'

Then, as this Erb reached the apex, the bridge collapsed. Lava-rock and tractor plunged into the boiling river. The channel was narrow; blocked by this mass, the lava foamed up and overflowed its bed. Hastily, the three remaining tractors spun about and accelerated into the jungle, getting clear of the widely spreading liquid. The vegetation it touched burst into flame.

Soon the blockage melted, and the lava overflow receded, returning slowly to its channel. Much of if remained, cooling and hardening, unable to flow. A small new lava plain had been formed. But the bridge was gone. A small section of hardened lava had formed at the height of the overflow, and now represented the beginning of a new bridge. This demonstrated how these things occurred, but it was hardly safe to use now; it would have to cool for many days.

'What do we do now?' Jessica asked dispiritedly.

'We follow the Erb into the flow,' Heem responded, his own hopes destroyed.

Her spirit revived abruptly. 'Oh no we don't! There's got to be a way to continue!'

The Squam tractor moved slowly towards them. Heem wondered whether it could be Slitherfear, and prepared himself for a battle in tractors, but soon the taste-pattern showed it was a stranger. A peculiar rapping came from its occupant: the sign-signal of truce.

'Um, let me handle this,' Jessica said. 'I'm closer to the Squam type than you are. We're all in the same boat, now.' Heem acquiesced, not wishing to converse with the monster, and she used his body to needle a tractor control. The tractor made a similar knocking sound, agreeing to the truce.

The other HydrO echoed the sound, and came close.

'HydrO,' the Squam sprayed, using its tractor's short-range communicator. The broadcast message emerged from Heem's unit in HydrO translation, since he had been using HydrO controls. The Squam, of course, had not really sprayed. 'We are competitors, but face a common problem. Unless we can proceed, all have lost.'

Extremely true. 'Agreed,' Jessica jetted into their own tractor's unit, knowing that the receiving Squam unit would translate it into the series of noises that was its language.

'Know you who passed last this bridge?'

217

'An Erb was ahead of us,' Jessica jetted.

'Could that Erb have sabotaged the bridge?'

'Trust a Squam to think of that!' Heem sprayed internally. 'Of course that happened! It must have knocked out part of the rock from the far side, weakening the structure. So that no one could overtake it.'

'We believe it did,' Jessica jetted to the Squam. Now that it was close, her picture was clear. It reposed coiled in the compartment, both extremities below, its three limbs extended upward from the elevated centre section. Three pincer-fingers on each limb were spread. The creature's hue was dark, its scales glinting metallically, and its nether portion was very like a serpent. There was no Solarian analogy for the rest, so the picture became fuzzy.

'Our map suggests another potential natural crossing, downstream where the lava spreads and cools,' the Squam continued. 'But the terrain is rugged, probably too arduous for a single vehicle. Will you assist, so that one or two of us may re-enter the race?'

'No!' Heem sprayed.

'Yes,' Jessica agreed even as he objected.

'Cooperate with a *Squam*?' Heem demanded. 'This is impossible!'

'Yes,' came the other HydrO's spray.

'It is possible and necessary,' Jessica told Heem internally. 'The Squam is being positive; we must be the same.'

'No Squam can be trusted!'

'We are not sure of that. Surely Squams differ, just as Erbs do. As HydrOs do. We had not expected such vicious tactics from an Erb, had we? And the other HydrO does not seem to fear Squams the way you do. You have Squam-phobia, Heem; it may be unjustified.'

'Unjustified! A Squam killed Moon of—'

'*A* Squam, yes; *this* Squam, no.'

'We shall have to use lines to anchor our vehicles to each other, to navigate rough terrain,' the Squam communicated.

'Shall we agree to resume the race in the same order we reached the bridge, at such time as we achieve crossing?'

That left Heem's tractor last. Still, it seemed fair. 'No, it isn't fair!' Heem protested. 'All three of us will be well behind the pace.'

'That's not the Squam's fault,' she reminded him. Then, to the Squam: 'Agreed.'

There was a brief dialogue between the Squam and the other HydrO, determining who was first. Then the quest for the natural crossing commenced. They all knew that speed was of the essence.

Off the path, progress was a challenge. The ferns crowded in as close to the lava channel as the heat permitted, leaving little room for the tractors. They proceeded in single file, slowly.

Then the channel became shallow. The lava overflowed in disciplined fashion, thinning and slowing and hardening. Flood plains had formed and turned to solid stone and been overrun by new floods, so that there were many step-layers. Several new channels had been cut through this landscape, but even the cool rock was extremely irregular.

The Squam's tractor halted. 'We must survey,' the Squam communicated.

All three occupants dismounted from their tractors. The two HydrOs met the Squam. Now no linguistic communication with the Squam was possible, but it wasn't necessary. They knew what they had to do.

They spread out, surveying the lava-beds. The rock was warm in places, hot in others; they had to discover a route that was cool enough and stout enough to be firm under the weight of a tractor.

In one place the lava formed a veritable mountain, as though it had made a vast bubble when hot, which firmed and was overlaid with subsequent lava. The far side of this dome was across the original channel; Heem could taste the vegetation beyond. The burningly hot lava flow plunged out of perception somewhere beneath this dome. This was a giant bridge!

They returned to their vehicles, consulted, and agreed: they would try to cross this dome. It seemed firm enough to support the weight. But its sides were steep.

'A winch,' Jessica said. 'One tractor here, pulling, the cable guided over the curvature. The other tractor there, pushing the third. Once the third is over the hump, it can winch the others up the incline.' She returned to their tractor's communicator so she could make this clear to the Squam.

The Squam agreed. Since Jessica had suggested it, she and Heem had the privilege of making the first attempt. Each tractor had a winch – they were multi-purpose vehicles – but the reach was not long enough. They had to hook two cables together end to end. Then the Squam parked as close to the hot-lava flow as possible, and used his pincers to string the linked cables over the dome, catching them in a crevice so they would not slip off sidewise. The other HydrO, a female, nosed her vehicle forward to push.

'If this does not work,' Heem sprayed morbidly, 'we shall be first into the flow, after all.'

'Or stuck on top of this dome,' Jessica said cheerfully.

Push and pull. Heem put his treads in motion. They skidded, for the incline here was almost vertical. Then the cable carried the front end up. The tractor tilted alarmingly and tried to skew to the side ; then the treads caught and helped it lift up the slope. The angle would have been impossible without the winch.

Heem stopped at the top, where the bubble was level. The Squam, the only creature facile at this sort of thing, slithered up to disconnect the winch. Then Heem turned his vehicle around, on top of the dome, while the Squam drove around to the spot Heem's tractor had started from. They reconnected the winch, and Heem backed his tractor down the far slope until the rear treads struck the ground. He was across!

220

Now the other HydrO nudged up to push the Squam, while Heem started winching in. The Squam's tractor-nose came up. The stiffest haul was while the vehicle's treads were skidding, for the cable now went entirely over the dome, with a fair amount of friction. Almost, it seemed, Heem's own tractor was about to be hauled up instead, though he had his treads locked. Yet the powerful winches kept drawing in. Heem worried about the fuel expenditure.

Then, abruptly, the cable went slack – and taut again, yanking Heem's tractor momentarily off its back treads. Then the cable snapped, and the tractor dropped. Jessica screamed.

'Don't *do* that!' Heem sprayed, trying to damp down the searing emotion. He shut off the motor and rolled out of the tractor. He found a channel and moved up the slope of the dome with almost the dispatch of a flatfloater.

The Squam's tractor had broken through a portion of the dome and fallen below. Now it lay in what Jessica's picture showed as a pool of light from the hole, overturned.

'One Squam departed,' Heem remarked, not unduly disturbed.

'We don't know that!' Jessica said. 'Get down there and check. It's a living creature who has helped us; we must help it.'

'But it's hopeless. Even if the monster lives, the tractor is defunct.'

The other HydrO joined them. 'That crust was weaker than we thought,' she sprayed. 'The changed angle of draw—'

'Get down there, Heem,' Jessica repeated warningly.

Heem yielded. The notion of helping a Squam was still new to him, but he found it hard to protest what Jessica really wanted. She was so beautifully righteous in her emotion. 'We must verify the condition of the Squam,' he sprayed to the HydrO.

'Why?' she asked reasonably.

Heem hesitated. 'If you don't answer, I will!' Jessica told him.

'The Squam is a sapient creature,' Heem sprayed reluctantly. 'He was helping us. We were operating under truce. To neglect him now would be to assume complicity in his destruction, violating that truce.'

'Perhaps so,' the HydrO agreed distastefully.

The rubble of the collapse descended at a navigable angle down from the HydrO's tractor. They rolled carefully down.

'Squam,' Heem sprayed. 'Do you survive?'

In a moment the other HydrO's tractor sprayed the reply. It seemed the Squam spoke into his own unit, which was still broadcasting. Thus the taste, a bit blurred by distance, wafted down from behind them: 'I am crushed, yet I survive. I shall not live long without assistance.'

Heem hesitated again, but Jessica needled him. 'What assistance may we proffer, Squam?' As his jet reached the other HydrO's tractor, Heem felt the harsh vibrations of the Squam's tractor-unit translating.

Then the indirect response came back. 'Only to notify the Competition Authority. I require serious medication.'

'I doubt our radios will reach,' Heem sprayed. 'They are intended only for short-range communication, as now, and we are far off the charted route. I believe there is a call-in at the fuelling depot. But only my tractor is across; I would have to leave you both here and go to it alone.'

'This is the luck of the situation,' the other HydrO sprayed. 'I am out of the race.'

So she was. There was no way to get her vehicle across. Heem addressed the Squam again. 'May we help remove you from your vehicle?'

'This would be appreciated,' the Squam agreed, 'I am in some pain, and greater freedom would enable me to alleviate it somewhat.'

They used the other HydrO's winch to haul large fragments of lava-rock away, then jetted the sand and dust clear.

222

Jessica watched with interest; she admitted to wondering how handless creatures moved things, and now saw the technique of jetting out small debris from beneath so that large pieces could roll.

In due course they had excavated a tunnel under the inverted tractor. The Squam dropped down and hauled himself along by means of two limbs. The third was broken, and a section of his body was indeed crushed, with ichor leaking slowly from it.

They helped the Squam get set up beside his tractor.

'This is an unanticipated kindness, from your species,' the Squam remarked.

'We operate under truce,' Heem reminded him. 'You were assisting us, now we assist you.'

'It is good that you are not like so many of your kind, who hate my kind without reason.'

Heem felt like needlejetting the monster's remaining limbs, but Jessica restrained him. 'He is not Slitherfear! He has played straight with us! Don't you forget that!'

'There is honour apart from species,' Heem sprayed. 'I am not partial to your kind, but there is also your transferee to consider.' *And my own!* he thought savagely at Jessica.

'Then I will assist you,' the Squam replied. 'My transferee is Trant of Trammel, who has made a study of the habitats of sapients. He informs me that this cave has the aspect of a suitable breeding locale for HydrOs.'

The female HydrO reacted. 'I am Geel of Gemflower. In what way is this cave proof against the ravages of winter?'

'It is heated by the subterranean lava-flow,' Trant of Trammel responded via the Squam. 'Protected from exterior storms, it maintains a survivable ambience even in the depths of the eclipse. Note that fungoid growth exists here that is several seasons' culmination. Your kind, independent of light and food, can survive here – at least for the brief period of extreme cold on the surface.'

'It is true!' Geel sprayed. 'By happenstance we have come

223

upon the means to colonize this planet! We must seed it!'

'Brother!' Jessica remarked. 'Talk about single-minded females!'

Heem suddenly felt tight. Thus abruptly, the issue of reproduction was upon him again. 'It is not a vacant region,' he protested. 'The Squam is here.'

'We are aware of your concern,' the Squam communicated. 'Squams have been known to prey on the young of your kind, though this is forbidden by the articles of compromise of Planet Impasse. I point out, however, that even were I an outlaw individual, I am largely immobile, probably incapable of catching a rolling HydrO of any size. In any event, if you notify the Competition Authority of my presence here, I will be removed, and the cave will then be secure.'

How neatly the creature had refuted his objection! Heem was forced to confront again the issue that had destroyed him before. Should he allow himself to reproduce his kind, or remain firm in his negation? If he refused again, even victory in the competition would not absolve him; but if he acceded—

'Oh, go ahead, Heem, do it!' Jessica said.

That was a shock. 'I thought you agreed with my position!'

'I do agree. But this is a different situation. There are no natural predators here. You can seal off this cave, and after the competition you can return to rejoin the female and raise your offspring yourself. Heem, you have a chance to do it *right*, this time – and in the process to make a good life for yourself if you don't win the contest. You won't have to die in the Eccentric winter!'

This was a new flavour! She was correct. He could alleviate his major objection to the HydrO mode of reproduction, and exonerate his treason – without sacrificing his chance in the competition. Still, he hesitated. 'You cannot survive, if—'

'This makes no difference to my survival, Heem! If you win

224

the competition, I live; if you lose, I die. The only thing you can safeguard is your own survival and status.'

'If anything happened, and I could not return—'

'Geel of Gemflower will still be here, won't she? Her tractor is stuck on the wrong side of the bubble; she can't cross, and probably doesn't have enough fuel to make it back to the spacefield. She *has* to stay – and what mother wouldn't?'

'*My* mother wouldn't!' Heem needled. 'Neither parent remained in Highfalls – or in Morningmist. Adult HydrOs do not remain where they seed; they leave it empty, letting the offspring suffer without protection, without information. Geel will depart with the Competition Authority when it comes to pick up Trant of Trammel and his Squam host.'

'Well, maybe so, for her. But this time it will still be different – because you'll be in charge, Heem.'

Something was still bothering him. 'You – how can you, a female in my mind, that I supposed was interested in – how can you favour—?' His thought became inchoate.

'What do you think I am – a jealous bitch? Don't answer that! You want the truth, you deserve the truth. I *am* jealous – but I am also mighty curious about exactly how the HydrOs reproduce. I can't learn it from your mind, because you honestly don't know all of it. I want to know, because—'
Here she paused, and a flavour of defiant shame washed through them. 'Because I might want to do it myself someday, if there were ever an opportunity. I know that will never be, so it is academic, a pipe dream, but if I admit that, I'm really admitting that I'm not going to survive . . . hell, Heem, maybe I just want a surrogate experience. It might be better than nothing, which is what I face otherwise. Or maybe I want to see what it's like from the male view, watching you. I've had to fake the male view for so long, I – I don't claim my motives are all pure and innocent and uncomplicated. Maybe I am a voyeur at heart. Anyway, I really think you should do it – then get on with the

competition. Because I'm not forgetting for a moment that I'll never get home unless you win!'

Yet Heem could not come to a decision. Something still bothered him about this. 'We must inspect the cave,' he sprayed externally. 'It may prove to be less suitable than anticipated.' The cave – or the situation?

He and Geel rolled around the cave. It was large, with many bypasses and alternate chambers, but there seemed to be no exits not blocked by hot lava rivulets except the one the tractor had made. The cold would undoubtedly enter that hole, in winter, but there seemed to be a number of alcoves beside hot lava that would remain warm regardless. There would need to be a constant source of hydrogen, and the hole would provide that; frozen gases would enter and evaporate and suffuse the passages. Fungus grew profusely in many places, and there were no predatory creatures. Then, in the spring, the great outdoors would come to life, an entire world open to the emerging juvenile HydrOs. It was, by HydrO definition, ideal.

'So what's bothering you?' Jessica demanded. 'Still shy about letting me snoop on your act of procreation?'

'Perhaps,' he admitted.

'Well, do it anyway. You can't let foolish foibles restrain you.'

Then he had it. 'They will all be of one sex. Where will any of them find mates?'

'The first visiting HydrO of the right sex from Impasse will take care of that – if there is a suitable place,' she pointed out. 'If not, then it hardly matters; HydrOs don't reproduce unless the locale exists.'

Heem tasted no alternative. Urged from without and within by these two females, and pushed by his own nature, which did indeed feel the imperative to seed so suitable a place, he had to do it. Yet he did not like being trapped by circumstance. 'If ever there is occasion for me to needle one of *your* fundamental shames—' Heem thought viciously at Jessica.

'When that time comes, I'll take my medicine like a good girl. But it won't. You'd have to catch me in human guise and rip my clothes off in public while everyone laughed, just as in my nightmare, and there's really no way, let's face it. Now you stop stalling and do what has to be done.'

She was baiting him, and they both knew it. Still, there was a bitter taste of wrongness in Heem. He feared some catastrophe, yet could not define it.

Gradually, as he explored the caves, Jessica's logic prevailed. His objections to his species' mode of reproduction had been alleviated. If he failed to win the competition, he could still return here, secure from his own kind, and attend to the growing offspring. He could warn them about the coming winter, if they did not know, so that none would be caught outside. He could alert them to the threat of Squams, and instruct them how best to defend themselves.

'And if you lose the competition, I remain with you until my aura fades,' Jessica reminded him. 'I will help you raise your juveniles.'

And how could he tell her no? If he sent her back to her own body, he would be prisoner, and not be able to return to his litter. The trap was inevitably closing.

They returned to the tractor, where the Squam waited. 'You were correct, Squam,' Geel sprayed. 'This region must be seeded; it will preserve our litter through the winter, and in spring they can spread again across the planet.'

'Only be sure that you have me removed,' the Squam replied. 'Then you need have no concern about the natural menaces.'

Smart Squam! He no longer had to take the assistance of the HydrOs on faith; he *knew* they would see to his rescue. Was that the real reason he had identified this ideal habitat?

Heem found himself at the point of decision – and found that it had already passed. He was ready to seed this cave. This readiness was a phenomenal relief to him. It had not been easy or comfortable to oppose the tradition and urge of his culture and kind.

Geel of Gemflower rolled close to him, spraying out her copulative flavour. It was not as enticing as that of Moon of Morningmist, but it was quite adequate to the occasion. 'So that's what females do to males,' Jessica remarked. 'I always thought of the sexual come-on as a game, but the game is much more serious from the male view.'

Heem ignored her. He responded to the overture by jetting a more intense taste at Geel. She caught that taste and sprayed it back to him, modified to signal receptivity. No conscious decisions were required; nature was well familiar with the mechanism.

'Why, it's beautiful! Jessica said. 'The dialogue of complete commitment.'

Abruptly, involuntarily, Heem needled Geel with his signature: the precise taste of his being, from which his individuality could be reproduced. In casual copulation this signature was always withheld by the male, or rejected by the female. Geel accepted it, merging it with her own essence throughout her body.

'This is just like human reproduction. The male essence joining the female essence in the body of the female, sperm meeting egg, fertilizing it—'

Geel exploded. Fragments of her splattered the tractor, the floor, the cave roof, and flew far down the main passage. Several struck the Squam and Heem himself. Nothing of her original body remained.

The Squam was astonished. 'She is destroyed!'

'What happened?' Jessica demanded, horrified.

For an instant Heem thought some other Squam had come upon them with a weapon. But there was no such intrusion. Numbly, he understood. 'The parts of the female – become the seeding. That is why no female HydrO remains to care for her offspring. And the male – must become part of civilization. That is why there are more adult male HydrOs than females. Neither can remain – lest they betray the truth to the new generation, and add yet one more horror to the process.'

'I regret I did not know,' the Squam communicated, still

going through the unit on Geel's tractor. 'I lacked intent to destroy the female. Perhaps my transferee knew – yet we operate under truce.'

'None of us knew,' Heem sprayed. 'Certainly Geel did not.' Yet had he, Heem, suspected? That bitter taste that had restrained him before – had that been it?

'Heem, I'm sorry,' Jessica said, and her emotion was strong and real. 'It's my fault. I meddled when I shouldn't have, pushing you into it.'

'You did not know, because I did not know,' he jetted trying to reassure her. But it was a weak effort, in the roll of this disastrous revelation. Geel's transferee had perished too, unknowingly. All the horror he had felt before had been restored to him. This time the Solarian and the Squam shared the guilt.

'Now we know that your sibling Hiim was dead,' Jessica said in a feminine irrelevance. 'Because Meen of Morningmist would have mated, had she found him – and she survived to become an adult. You saved her life, at least, Heem.'

Yet this locale had been seeded, in the fashion of his kind. Heem now understood another reason for metamorphosis: to erase the knowledge of what was entailed in seeding from the memory of the male, so that the species would innocently continue to propagate itself. Since it was always done in the absence of other HydrOs, and only the male survived, the secret was thus fairly safe.

He no longer felt the urge to return to educate his offspring, who were now picking themselves from their falls and making their first uncertain rolls. He would help as many as possible to get down from the ceiling safely and from any crevices in which they had lodged, and set them rolling in the safest section of the cave, but after that it was up to them. What could he teach them, that they would want to know? Let them grow in innocence.

'In innocence,' Jessica repeated. She was crying.

Nether Trio

They managed to transfer surplus fuel from the two other tractors to Heem's machine, and proceeded at wasteful velocity to the depot. Heem reported the location and plight of the Squam, and received assurance that the creature would be salvaged. Then they moved across more lava-bridges and on up the mountain, following the trail.

They came to the place where the cutoff could be made to the better trail. But the map had been deceptive: it was a steep bank. It would be possible for the tractor to slide down it, but the risk of disaster was great, and no travel in the opposite direction was possible. No one could cross *to* this path.

'I'm suspicious,' Jessica said. 'Why should they make it possible to get off this bad trail, but not to get *on* it?'

'Because others might realize, late, the significance of the elevation. No one who has not selected this trail at the outset can achieve its benefit.'

Which meant there would be little competition here. There might be three tractors ahead of them, no more, and none coming from behind. But this could be deceptive, for the real competition could be on the four other paths.

They climbed. By the time they reached the top, their fuel was low. Heem had sacrificed time in favour of fuel, adding to the reserve he had built up before, but not much of that remained. He hoped he had more fuel now than the tractor ahead of him. He wanted very badly to pass the bridge-sabotaging Erb.

The downward slope of the hill enabled him to turn off the motor and coast for fair stretches, conserving more fuel. Now this choice of routes was paying off. They had to be gaining on the tractors on the other trails, and he hoped also on the three ahead of him on this trail. Any traffic blockages occurring elsewhere were to his advantage. But he had lost time in the cavern-dome; was his present progress enough?

They glided up to a stalled tractor. 'Out of fuel!' Jessica exclaimed. 'Stopped by that little ridge ahead. It's working, Heem; we're outlasting the others!'

So it seemed. Heem caught the taste of Erb: the other driver. The one who had bypassed him, and set the trap of the bridge.

'Leave him alone!' Jessica warned. 'He's out of the race, harmless to you now; just let him stew. Don't risk your own tractor by trying to ram him.' She had caught Heem's thought and somewhat guiltily he agreed to pass on by. That should be satisfaction enough. After all, this Erb had showed him that these creatures could be dangerous too; he had taken Erbs too lightly before.

But as they approached, the other tractor came to life and lurched into their path. Heem swerved, but so did the other. Jessica screamed as the two collided, sideswiping each other.

Suddenly angry, Heem accelerated his tractor, drawing on his skill in piloting. He shoved the other vehicle back. 'Now don't get male impetuous!' Jessica cried uselessly.

But the Erb was skilled too, and was not thrown out of control. Now they were racing down the slope under power, side by side, the path barely wide enough.

'But why is the Erb doing this?' Jessica demanded plaintively.

'He thinks to prevail by destroying all who follow him.'

'But that's crazy! He needs to gain on those ahead of him.'

'Erbs are a crazy species. Vegetable synapses are not the best.' Heem was too occupied by his driving to argue the point with more precision. 'We must disengage before we are both destroyed; this is wasting precious fuel. But the pattern of tastes ahead is unclear.'

'I'll help! This is a slope – feed that pattern to me, for

231

visual adaptation – that's right! I can see it now. The path curves ahead; there's a sidewise slope to it that reverses—'

'I can see,' Heem agreed. He accelerated again as they approached the first tilt, shoving the other tractor, then braked suddenly as the Erb shoved back. The shove and reversing tilt caused the other tractor to cut in front of Heem momentarily. Then Heem banged its rear, forcing it into the vegetation at high speed.

The Erb ploughed into the ferns, lost momentum, and stalled. 'He will not get out of that soon,' Heem sprayed with satisfaction. 'He will waste much fuel. I'm sorry I did not overturn him.'

'Me too,' Jessica agreed. 'We tried to pass him by without trouble, but he wouldn't have it that way. He's responsible for killing one of his own kind, injuring a Squam, and—' She did not rethink the seeding matter, quite; it was just a flavour-colour of numbness. 'You know, Heem, I don't dislike the Squams the way you do. I mean I am more like a Squam than you, but that one at the cave seemed basically decent. I think Squams differ just as other sapients do, and there are some good ones and some bad ones. To judge the whole species by a single individual, or by the mere fact it can defeat your kind in—'

'That's it!' Heem sprayed. 'The Erbs hate HydrOs, as HydrOs hate Squams. Because HydrOs can kill Erbs, and Squams can kill HydrOs. That Squam had no animosity towards us; it did not fear us, even when critically injured. But that Erb knew we followed it, so it set traps for us—'

'I believe you're right, Heem! A three-way psychosis of hate! Squams must hate Erbs, too!'

They had come to a new understanding, but had wasted more fuel. How were they to gain on the tractors ahead, on this path and on the others?

'We'll make do, because we have to,' Jessica said.

Heem kept the tractor rolling downhill, motor off. It had a new vibration he did not like: some result of the collisions

232

with the Erb's tractor. This would decrease its efficiency of rolling, and waste yet more fuel on the ascents.

'Do we have to make do?' he enquired. 'After the episode of the cave, I wonder whether it would be worthwhile to rejoin my society at all.'

'Of course it is, Heem! Your species' mode of propagation may be brutal, but you do have a high level of adult civilization, unfettered by the traumas of youth. You don't want to throw that away. That would be destroying the good along with the bad.'

'But the bad is inherent in our kind! Every living HydrO, in fact every HydrO who ever lived, has done so because of the destruction of a parent. *I* exist because of that. I survive at the expense of my parent and every sibling of Highfalls, and now I have propagated at the expense of my mate. HydrO civilization is predicated on this anathema—'

'No, Heem! I don't believe in Original Sin! You must join your society so that you can more effectively protest this mode!'

Again he was gratified by her support. But that support was unwarranted. 'There is no way to change the reproductive nature of our species. Better to let it die out entirely.'

'That's no answer, Heem! It's not really so much different from others. In my own species, the Solarians, the male produces so many seeds they could impregnate virtually all the nubile females of a planet in one day, yet all but one of these is wasted. And the female produces eggs, one a month, enough for maybe three hundred babies in her life, were they raised ex-utero. At most ten of these will be used, and usually only a couple, and often none. Sometimes she herself dies in childbirth. So the ratios really are similar, with only a very few offspring surviving. At least your way gives these offspring some small chance to determine their own fate, while ours determines it almost randomly at conception. A different route to a similar end. And we do need different routes, because there are so many different worlds with different environments—'

'I think you are spraying nonsense,' Heem jetted. 'Yet you make me feel like continuing the struggle.'

'Oh, good, Heem, I admit I am selfish, because I want to survive myself, but I do think you have a lot to offer your culture, and—'

'You alien thing, I think I – what is that concept you have?'

She was startled. 'What concept?'

'As a male for a female, beyond the term of convenience.'

'Beyond the – oh, you must mean love.'

'Love, yes, as we discussed before. It is a concept limited in my kind, because it cannot be fully associated with propagation, since—' He flooded out that concept, but part of Geel's explosion seeped through to awareness anyway. 'But just as I am coming to comprehend the alien perception of vision, now I am coming more properly to feel—'

'No, Heem, no!' she protested. 'You can't love me! I'm alien—'

'Does the concept now repulse you?'

'But when we discussed it before, we didn't know how – what happened to HydrO females when – we really are so different, Heem, and not merely physically!'

'And your discussion just now of the wasted sperms and eggs of your kind – that was not true?'

She capitulated. 'No, Heem, it was true. I think maybe I love you too, impossible as it is. I mean, even if we could physically meet – there's just no way – and here we are stuck in just one body – oh, this is ridiculous!'

'So we remain at impasse.'

'As always.'

'Yet the emotion is to an extent independent of the body. Your Solarian body would be a horror to me. But you, yourself—'

'I know, Heem. I feel the same.'

234

That was as far as they could take it. Once more, there was nothing to do except drop the subject.

They moved on. The fuel dropped lower in the machine's tank, until there was enough only for very limited manoeuvres. 'We are not going to travel a great deal farther in this vehicle,' Heem sprayed, disappointed. 'We may have gained on the others, but not enough.'

'We're not out of it yet,' Jessica said reassuringly. 'According to the map, we're nine tenths there. Only one bad ridge to cross—'

'We shall have to roll it along – and that will be very slow.' Heem ground the tractor up over another elevation. As he crested it, the motor choked to a stop. The fuel was gone.

They coasted down until the path levelled. 'That's it,' Jessica said. 'One thing in our favour: that ridge is not far ahead, and it crosses three of the routes. I doubt any tractor will have enough fuel to get over it. The other two routes are blocked by a large river. Do Squams or Erbs swim?'

'No. They will have difficulty crossing.'

'So we're still in the game. Let's roll!'

They rolled. Heem jet-rolled up the next incline, then free-rolled down the next decline. As he passed the lowest point, he jetted to speed up, so as to continue his roll on over the next crest with minimal effort. Since the route was generally declining, they made good progress.

'This is really a pretty efficient mode of travel,' Jessica admitted. 'You conserve momentum, and really move quite swiftly. As fast as the tractor did, I believe.'

'In terrain like this, HydrOs are among the fastest travellers in Segment Thousandstar,' Heem jetted with a certain pride-of-species. 'But the tractor helped in gaining me the elevation necessary to roll efficiently on my own. It would be very slow if I had a prolonged uphill slant to traverse.'

They passed a stalled tractor. It had the flavour of Squam, but was empty. The Squam had slithered forward under its own power, and could not be too far ahead. 'I believe we are

235

about to pass another contestant,' Jessica observed. 'Don't pause to quarrel, now. We don't have your sight well enough coordinated, yet, to handle a Squam.'

'You assume I am a quarrelsome male!'

'Of course. The terms are virtually identical, aren't they?'

He needled her with a mental jet that lacked more than tickling force, and she screamed a small scream that shook no nerves. Things were back to normal.

They continued along the trail. Soon they did overhaul the Squam, who was slithering with fair dispatch up the incline but could not match Heem's accumulated velocity. True to Jessica's stricture, Heem did not pause. He did not even squirt an insulting needle at the creature as he rolled by. This was not Slitherfear, after all, and there was a certain limited merit in the Solarian's opinion about differences between individuals.

'*Limited* merit?'

But a short distance thereafter he had to stop. Another tractor was stalled in the path – and the path itself terminated ahead of it. Heem tasted and Jessica looked, and they could not perceive any trail beyond. In ended in a blank wall of stone.

'That is more of a ridge than the map suggests,' Heem sprayed.

An Erb stood beside the machine, surveying the situation. It had a map, and Heem could tell from the disturbance in the taste-pattern that it was playing its gaze over this map. The Erb's light receptors were on little stalks at the centre of its flower; when it folded its petal-leaves to drill something, its eye-patches were protected, though its sight was then limited. In this case its petals were spread, and rotating slowly.

Heem had not brought his map along, of course, but retained a good memory of it. HydrOs seldom had to carry things with them, since they had no need of the food or shelter other species required, and retained in memory most of what they had use for. Only in special situations, such as the transfer of fuel between tractors, did HydrOs ever need to transport objects – and in that recent case, the tractor's winch had done the work. Heem's memory-map indicated that the trail proceeded straight ahead. Obviously the Erb was similarly baffled.

'It occurs to me that someone in the Competition Authority made quite certain the tractors would not make it all the way to the Ancient site,' Jessica said. 'They wanted this to be an all-round challenge, so they put little surprises in the map.'

'I could climb that mountain,' Heem sprayed. 'But it would take so long I would surely lose the race. It would have been better to choose a route that terminated in a river.'

'Had we but known,' Jessica agreed. 'HydrOs can roll under water, right? Drawing hydrogen from bubbles in the water? But that's the luck of the draw.'

Heem considered. 'We cooperated with a Squam before, to cross the lava-flow. I wonder whether it is possible to cooperate with an Erb – or what we might gain from it?'

'Heem, you are becoming astonishingly liberal! But yes: they have true sight, don't they? And they can drill things. I think we could benefit from those talents.'

'But Erbs hate HydrOs.'

'Easily solved. Let the transferees do the dealing. This is not supposed to be a contest against Erbs and HydrOs, but of all the Thousand Stars against each other, using particular hosts.'

Dubiously, Heem agreed. 'You do the communicating.'

'Fine. We alien things must stick together.' She paused. 'Oops, I forgot one detail. I don't know the language. Will the tractor transmitter translate?'

'Not unless it receives a signal. The impulses are coded, and translated into the operator's language.'

'This is crazy. It will translate a broadcast, but not a direct dialogue? Before, we did okay.'

'At the lava-crossing we had two tractors, translating each other's broadcasts. Here we have only one.'

'Maybe we could use it to broadcast, then play back its own message in translation. Trick it into becoming a translator.'

'Doubtful. We had better try Thousandstar common code.'

Jessica probed his thought. 'Oh – like that truce-knocking the Squam did before. A small vocabulary of set signals for any species. So how do we proffer truce to the Erb? It can't taste us and we can't see it, not directly.' She was, however, forming a picture of the creature.

'We roll in the truce-pattern,' Heem sprayed. He initiated the roll.

The Erb drew back, scuttling along on its little roots, its stout stem swaying. 'That needs no translation,' Jessica said. 'It's afraid of you.'

'I am not surprised. Erbs are skittery creatures.'

'What about that one who tried to run us down?'

'In a tractor, it is a different matter. Your point about variation between individuals—'

'Well, try again. Move slowly, so as not to alarm it. We need to make contact.'

Heem started the truce-roll again, performing it slowly. This time the creature held its ground.

But before the Erb could respond, the Squam arrived. 'Is there difficulty in communication?' a device sprayed.

'You have a translation unit!' Heem sprayed back. 'Three languages?'

'I try to be prepared,' the Squam replied. 'I anticipated problems in this competition. Are you amenable to a truce for the purpose of advancing mutual progress towards the site?'

'Yes,' Heem agreed. 'At the site itself it must end. But if we do not make progress now, none of us will be in contention for victory. I have been trying to signal the Erb to this effect.'

238

The translation unit rendered his spray into flashes of light for the Erb. Now the creature acceded. 'However, I prefer not to associate too closely with the HydrO,' it amended. 'That breed is not to be trusted.'

'Not to be trusted!' Heem exploded. 'You hypocrite of a plant! Back there in the trail—'

'Truce, truce!' the Squam interposed. 'We have been in competition, but must abate that temporarily.'

'And I prefer not to associate with a Squam,' Heem sprayed. 'But we must associate with each other if we are to travel. Let us agree on this: if one of us attacks another, the third will be obliged to attack the aggressor. That way we are all protected; only peace will help us all.'

'Say, that's a neat device!' Jessica exclaimed. 'Whoever starts trouble will regret it. I'm glad to see you are now able to view Squams rationally.'

'Equitable,' the Squam agreed. 'Shall we review options and assets? I am Sickh and Sleekline, an unmated female who—'

'Female!' Heem interjected.

The Squam swivelled to orient her pincers on him. 'You object?' her translator needled.

'*Do* you?' Jessica needled from within.

Heem rolled back. 'Merely surprise. I had thought few females would enter this highly competitive mission.'

'A number of the species of Thousandstar have highly competitive females, and their representatives reflect this, and require female hosts,' the Squam responded. 'You, a male, have inadequate means to appreciate the devious qualities of the mystique.'

'Ha!' Jessica exclaimed.

Heem was silent/tasteless externally. Internally, he sprayed, 'This Squam sounds just like you.'

Jessica was chagrined. 'Not really?'

He had mercy. 'Not really. She believes she has a mental as well as physical advantage over me. It will be best not to disabuse her.'

'You're learning, Heem! I'll watch closely. We may make a better team than we knew.'

The Squam resumed her introduction. 'I am a specialist in geological manifestations, and my transferee is an archaeologist. I believe we can fathom an excellent route to the site, recovering time, but it is apt to be hazardous for a single entity.'

That was a potent combination for a mission like this. Geologist and archaeologist would be extraordinarily quick to perceive signs of the Ancients that others might miss. Theoretically this was a race to a marked site, but one could never be certain, with the Ancients. Also, the prior Squam had made quite an accurate guess at the prospective hazards of leaving the prepared path; this one's warning of hazard could be well conceived.

'Yes,' Jessica agreed. 'Awful smart girl, there.'

The Erb flashed at the translator, and it emitted a spray for Heem and sounds for Sickh Squam: a versatile instrument. 'I am Windflower, also female at this stage of my growth. I am a student of the material and theory of the Ancients, and my transferee specializes in transfer technology.'

An even more potent set! The Ancients were the past masters of transfer – one reason their sites were so eagerly sought. But how much did these specialized fields help in the actual competition to reach the site? It seemed the experts had not been quite practical enough. This was, Heem understood, a common failing of experts throughout the Cluster.

Heem's turn. 'I am Heem of Highfalls, male, a specialist in space piloting and combat. My transferee is an analyser of patterns.'

'Excellent,' the Squam said. 'Now let us consider how we may forward mutual progress. The routing delineated by the map is suitable for tractors; it would be possible to shape a

240

ramp against the face of the cliff and employ the winch to assist the steep ascent, but this would expend both fuel and time. Windflower's machine cannot have much fuel remaining.'

'True,' the Erb agreed. 'Insufficient for such purposes. We drove well and carefully, but the map deceived us.'

Well and carefully indeed, Heem thought. This tractor must have come farther and faster than any other. These two creatures had to be among the most skilled and clever in the competition: a fact not to be forgotten.

'Therefore, we must proceed independently, either following the marked route or devising one of our own. The marked route curves somewhat; a direct approach could cut the travel distance to a third.'

'The direct route is over the most extreme elevation of the ridge,' the Erb flashed.

'Therefore not feasible. But my preliminary analysis suggests that this ridge is porous. There should be caves penetrating it, some of which could emerge quite close to our objective.'

'This is one smart creature!' Jessica repeated.

'My kind depends on the ambience of light, except in quite close quarters,' the Erb protested. 'We have no liking for nether regions, and are not competent therein.'

'This is one reason you can benefit by cooperating with us,' the Squam pointed out. 'My kind is quite facile in subterranean situations, so long as they are dry and reasonably firm in structure. We utilize sound to explore the reaches. We are shaped conveniently to traverse small passages. However, there may be constrictions too narrow for me to pass—'

'My kind is adept at fracturing rock,' the Erb flashed.

'My kind can squeeze through almost any aperture, given time,' Heem sprayed.

'There may be sections flooded with water,' the Squam continued. 'I do not care for water.'

241

'No problem,' Heem sprayed. 'My kind can travel beneath water, so long as hydrogen is associated with it, and this is usually the case.'

'There may be steep elevations and descents, or channels of hot lava, that can only be traversed by hauling over by means of a line, or other manual exercise. My own kind is apt at this sort of thing.' The Squam paused, clicking a pincer in a signal of decision. 'I believe, acting together, we can surmount most obstacles – if we trust one another.'

'I do not trust the HydrO!' the Erb flashed.

'And I am not entirely at ease with you,' the Squam replied. 'And the HydrO is wary of me. Yet if we do not trust each other, none of us have a chance to win through to the Ancient site in time. We are not here to quarrel; we are here to bear our transferees to that site expeditiously. We would be reneging were we not to promote that interest first. I suggest that we need more than a guarded truce; we need confidence in each other. Else we dare not proceed together.'

'It may be academic,' Heem sprayed. 'You have speculated caves in this ridge, but I taste none.'

'Then I must prove myself. My study of the formation indicates a thin wall here.' The Squam slithered to a slight indentation and tapped it with one pincer. 'A smash by the tractor should break it open.'

'I have enough fuel for several smashes,' the Erb flashed. 'I will try it.'

She climbed into her vehicle. Jessica assimilated a picture of the roots of the plant twining up into crevices of the machine, tendrils clinging, manoeuvring the creature up.

The tractor moved. It charged the wall, colliding. The stone face collapsed, and when the taste of dust cleared somewhat, Heem perceived the flavour of confined air escaping from the ground. There was indeed a cave there.

Still, Heem had doubts. 'You have demonstrated your geological expertise,' he sprayed. 'But I have had bad experience with your kind before, and an Erb sabotaged a

242

bridge I was about to cross. How can I be certain either of you are better than these?'

'Sabotage?' the Erb flashed. Jessica had finally formulated an image of this: the creature angled its leaf-vanes at the primary source of light, reflecting and concentrating beams to make the meaningful patterns. It could direct a beam at a specific receiver, such as the Squam's translator, or cross an arc to include several entities. 'Provide the identity of that individual, and he shall be subject to retribution of law.'

'He occupies the last tractor on this trail,' Heem jetted.

'What was the nature of your experience with my kind?' Sickh enquired.

Now Heem could not describe this without revealing his illegal memory. 'To hell with that!' Jessica exclaimed. 'Squams don't care about HydrO metamorphosis!'

True. Squams were of the more primitive species who did not metamorphose. 'A Squam came to the valley where my prospective mate resided, and preyed on her sisters, and slew her.'

'Squams do not belong in your valleys!' Sickh protested. 'The Covenant of Impasse is most specific.'

'This one came – and is now a host in this competition. We call him Slitherfear.'

'That designation does not register with me,' she said. 'But I assure you, if I encounter that individual, I will seek a reckoning. We are civilized; we do not violate the covenant, or tolerate those who do.'

'I find this credible,' the Erb flashed.

'So do I,' Jessica said. 'I vote to trust her, Heem.'

'Because she is female?' he asked her cynically.

'No, that is no recommendation. Not all female Squams are alike, you know. It's just an intuition of mine. It makes sense that a sapient, technological species has ethical values too. There will be outlaws, of course – you are one yourself, and I am too, really – but mostly the individuals will be civilized, especially the highly educated ones. For us, this is a

243

much better gamble than it would be *not* to cooperate, and wash out of the competition. So let's trust these ladies, and treat them fairly, following the golden rule.'

'Metallic law?' Heem enquired, not quite grasping the concept.

'Do unto others as you would have them do unto you.'

'I accept this,' Heem sprayed externally.

'Then let us agree that we shall navigate this passage in company, and that no one of us will seek access to the Ancient site until all three are through the mountain ridge,' the Squam said.

'Agreed,' Heem sprayed and the Erb flashed.

The Squam removed a length of metallic line from the Erb's tractor and wrapped it about the central portion of her body. Heem had to admit that this ability to grasp and carry things was a great asset in a situation like this.

The Squam slithered into the aperture first. Heem was aware of the vibrations she made, scouting the interior by sound emanations and echoes. Heem followed, rolling down the slight incline, tasting the air in more detail. The Erb followed him, scuttling on her roots.

The air was moving. That meant the cave either had an exit elsewhere, or was so extensive that the natural processes of heating and cooling caused expansion and contraction of the air inside, therefore motion. Heem could not be sure from the flavour; it was all earth-interior taste, but with a certain strangeness.

The passage slanted almost directly into the ridge, then intersected another at right angles: This was odd; caves normally curved and changed without such precision.

The Squam halted. 'Does the suspicion occur to you, companions?' she enquired, the translator spraying and flashing.

'This is no cave,' the Erb flashed back. The translator emitted a steady interim glow that she could use for reflection, and this also helped her to perceive the cave.

Heem knew this by the way she moved and reacted, and Jessica obligingly filled in the picture this way. The technical absence of light made no difference to Jessica's images, since they were recreated from background information and his taste-awareness. 'It is artificial, but old, very old.'

'Perhaps as old as the Ancients,' Heem agreed.

'Had the map been accurate, I would have recognized its nature,' the Squam said. 'When I approached it in person, I became almost certain the ridge was artificial. It is possible that this entire structure is a monstrous earthwork thrown up by the Ancients. Do you agree?'

'The Ancients were great earthmovers,' Heem agreed.

'My geological expertise becomes suspect, here,' Sickh said. 'There could be danger of collapse, in an unnatural structure.'

It has remained intact for three million years, it should remain a day longer,' Heem sprayed. 'And if we have here access to the Ancient site – an access the Competition Authority is not aware of—'

'It would not be valid,' the Erb flashed. 'This is not a competition of discovery, but of dominance. The Star who first reaches the designated site will assume legal control of it. We must strive for that spot.' She paused. 'In addition, this is not a true Ancient site. The structure is not typical of recorded examples. I could detail this—'

'No need,' Heem sprayed. 'You are the expert on the Ancients.'

'Then let us continue,' the Squam decided. 'We may have a more ready access than we had hoped.'

They continued. After a time the passage levelled out. Then it debouched into a huge chamber, larger than the lava-bubble, level on the floor and vaulted in the ceiling.

'This place is considerable,' the Squam said. 'But barren.'

Heem agreed. His taste detected no boundaries to it other than the near one. 'Must have been a storage room,' Jessica hazarded. 'Maybe a barracks for their troops.'

245

'But if this is not of Ancient construction—'

'But there *is* an Ancient site nearby. Maybe the Ancients took over a building built by a prior species.'

'A species prior to the Ancients?'

'There *were* other creatures! We just call the highly technological one the Ancients, for convenience.'

They continued across, and in due course found a passage leading away from the opposite wall. But it slanted down, not up. 'I distrust this,' the Squam said.

So did Heem. The competition objective would be on the surface. At this rate, they could pass right under it – and lose the competition.

Yet where could they go, except on? To backroll and follow the tractor trail now would be ruinously slow.

Then the passage slope increased, dropping abruptly into water. 'Oh, no!' Jessica moaned. 'The sewer system!'

'This appears to be a drainage conduit,' the Erb flashed. 'The Ancients did not employ such devices.'

'My transferee agrees,' the Squam said. 'Many older civilizations have employed such systems, but the Ancients do not seem to have utilized liquids in sufficient quantity to require any drainage system. However, this seems typical of a configuration we recognize, in which case there should be access vents on both sides of a submerged conduit.'

'I will investigate,' Heem sprayed. He rolled past the Squam and into the water. The taste was old, yet not stagnant; there was some circulation, and enough dissolved gas to sustain him. This water had originated on the surface not long ago; perhaps it was the residual drainoff of a recent storm. Into what lower chamber it might flow he could not guess.

Then he encountered a network of metal. It was a grate, preventing access by large objects. He shoved at it, but the thing was secure. No passage for travellers here! He himself might squeeze through it, slowly, reforming his tissues on the far side, but neither Squam nor Erb could do that. 'And we are not going to leave them stranded,' Jessica reminded him firmly.

He rolled back, emerging into the air passage. Jessica, filling in illumination in her mental image where there was none, showed the Squam and Erb, waiting expectantly for the news.

'The way is barred,' Heem reported. 'The flavour of the water indicates access to other air passages beyond, but there is current and the taste of other grates. I might pass, but you cannot.'

'My sonar indicates no more direct route towards the Ancient site than this,' Sickh replied. 'We must force passage. Windflower, are you able to function beneath water?'

'I am,' the Erb replied. 'In fact, my roots are dry, and in need of immersion. I will force passage through the grate.'

'Then if you will accompany Heem to that grate, he will lead you beyond it to the next exit to air.'

'Know what?' Jessica remarked. 'She is using our given names, and that makes us seem more like people than alien creatures. That Squam is really trying to get us to work together.'

'I do not like being alone with the HydrO,' the Erb protested.

'Heem's needles cannot harm you in water,' the Squam pointed out.

'True!' Windflower flashed, surprised.

'If you will also carry the end of this cable, you can draw me through to air,' the Squam continued. 'I am unable to function effectively or endure long immersion. I must inhale oxygen and other gases to sustain my life processes.'

'In addition to eating?' Heem enquired.

'We all have our failings,' the Erb flashed tolerantly.

The Squam accepted these remarks with excellent grace. 'My life will be in your care.'

The Erb, encouraged, fastened a loop of line about her

247

main stem and moved to the water. Heem followed.

At the grating, the Erb twined her roots into the sediment below, anchoring herself more securely than any animal could, then closed her petals into the formidable power-wedge. The drill rotated and shoved forward into the grate. There was a skin-shocking vibration, and the bars ripped out of their moorings. No wonder Squams were afraid of Erbs! Heem had known intellectually that the plants had good torque, but had never imagined the extent of it personally.

Windflower dropped the twisted grate into the deeper water ahead. It sank down into the crosschannel, and Heem tasted the flavours of the sediment it stirred up. Soon he had a clear picture – Jessica's image was helpful again – of the whole local section of this intersection. He rolled himself down into the other conduit, flattening himself against the current, and came up into the mouth of the pipe on the opposite side. The grate here was firm, too.

The Erb joined him. But now there was a problem. The grate was too high for her to reach from the floor of the large conduit, when her drill was formed. Heem could not communicate with her linguistically, in the absence of the translator, but tasted the problem clearly. They were balked again.

'Could she stand on you?' Jessica enquired.

There it was! Weight was not much of a factor, here in immersion. If the timid Erb would trust him enough . . .

Heem nudged down beside Windflower's roots. She yanked them out of contact as if burned. He flattened his base, fitting it to the caked floor of the conduit, and humped his body. And stayed there, motionless.

The Erb was intelligent. Soon she realized what he was offering. Tentatively she touched him with a root. Heem remained firm. She brought another root. Finally she climbed on top of him, anchoring her roots uncomfortably in his soft skin. He did not like this contact any better than she did! Yet there was an alien delicacy in Windflower's touch that had a strange appeal.

'She's female,' Jessica said. 'Males like the female touch and you *are* a soft touch for – if I were only physical—' She stopped, having reminded herself of the futility of such speculation.

'In Solarian hosts – people touch closely?' Heem enquired. 'Not merely jetting each other from a distance but making tight contact – like this?'

'They do. Not precisely like this, as we don't have physical roots, but close, yes. It is called an embrace.'

'Disgusting!' Heem said involuntarily.

She laughed. 'It really can be a lot of fun, Heem; you'd know that, if you could ever try it.'

'Perhaps,' he agreed, becoming curious. After what he had learned about the alien sense of sight, and about cooperation with assorted alien creatures, he was becoming more liberal about alien values.

Suddenly his whole body was shaken. The Erb was starting her drill. Heem braced himself despite the cruel grip of her roots in his flesh. There was a terrible wrench that half tore him from the floor. 'Hang on, Heem! She's drilling the grate!'

He knew that. Heem hung on. The wrenching seemed intolerable. Vegetable fibres were really tough, to absorb this kind of punishment. Then, abruptly, it eased. The grate was free!

Windflower cast the grate away. She extricated her roots from Heem. This, too, was painful. But he had survived the worst, and his skin had not really been damaged.

They proceeded up the passage until they emerged in air. They were through the sewer system! Windflower still dragged the cable after her. Now she anchored herself in the dirt of the new passage, but was unable to draw in the cable. Her upper tendrils were adept at holding, but not at hauling.

'We can handle that,' Jessica said. 'Put the line on the floor, and roll along it, drawing up the cord in a pulley action – know what I mean?'

'No.' Heem had not used such a cord before.

She formed a picture, and suddenly it was clear. Heem positioned himself atop a slack section of cord, then rolled it along until it entered the water. Here there was a loop where the weight was off it. He inserted his body into that loop, formed a crease the length of his topside, and let the loose cord fall into that groove.

'Like a yo-yo,' Jessica said, flashing another image. 'Now curve around, hanging on to that string, until you can draw it away from the water.'

Following her image-instructions, Heem did. He was able to turn, carrying the cord along with him in the groove. When he rolled away from the water, the slack was taken up. Now as he pushed forward, the taut line had to loop over his body, getting pushed down to the floor, where his weight held it in place. He was, indeed, like the pulley she visualized, drawing on the cord without ever truly grasping it. Or like the tread on a tractor, passing around the forward wheel. This was hard work, abrasive on his skin, but he knew it was necessary. He heaved, and heaved again, and again.

Finally the Squam emerged from the water beside the Erb. One set of pincers were clamped on the end of the rope; another grasped her translator. Her front and rear extremities dragged behind. 'My appreciation to you both,' the unit sprayed and flashed, none the worse for its dunking. 'I could not have navigated that water alone. My sonic orientation is completely unreliable in fluid.'

'Which is one reason your accurate needles can mess up a Squam,' Jessica remarked. 'Squams depend heavily on hearing, and water in the wrong place shorts them out.'

The Erb withdrew her roots from the floor and stretched her limber stem, relaxing. She had been detectably nervous the whole time she had been alone with Heem; now the presence of the Squam gave her relief. The two of them, Erb and HydrO, had worked well together, but without the translation unit and personal reassurance of the Squam, the Erb never would have done it.

250

'Compliment her,' Jessica advised. 'Make her like you. All females like to be complimented. It will make her easier to get along with.'

Heem decided to accept this advice of the local expert on female nature. 'Windflower was primarily responsible,' he sprayed. 'She tore out two grates and anchored the line, despite hardships.'

The Erb did not comment. 'She's paying attention though,' Jessica assured him. 'She knows you did a lot of work, and gave the credit to her.'

Sickh rewound the cord about her body, and they moved forward. The tunnel now tended upward. Were they near the end?

'I hear something,' Sickh said. 'There is a living presence in this passage.'

'Oh-oh,' Jessica said.

Heem concentrated. Yes, the drift of air carried a sinister flavour. 'Animal, not plant,' he agreed. 'Yet I had understood there were no dangerous animals on Eccentric.'

'Oddities occur in the depths,' the Squam remarked. 'Small creatures, feeding off fungus, could exist here, their eggs protected somewhat in winter.'

The proof was not long in arriving. A swarm of furry-bodied little things came down the tunnel. Heem tasted the hair of their torsos and the callouses of their feet spreading out before them.

'They emit light,' the Erb flashed. 'They are vision oriented, but unlike my own kind these produce their own beams, though these are faint. There are many of the creatures, perambulating on three appendages with a root behind that assists in balance. They appear to be an eating species.'

'Bad news,' Jessica said ominously. 'Those eating species are in bad repute in this neck of the Galaxy.' Heem had no doubt the other transferees were remarking to their hosts similarly.

'Perhaps they merely pass through, on their way to water,' the Squam said.

251

Forlorn hope! In a moment the horde was upon them. 'They have weapon-orifices,' Windflower reported. 'Cutting edges formed of horn or bone.'

'Teeth!' Jessica said. 'I believe these most resemble what we call rats. We're in trouble!'

There was a flash that translated into the taste of pure horror. Heem could not perceive the Erb's reflections directly, but Jessica's image made it seem real. 'They feed on me!' the Erb screamed.

Sudden pain struck Heem. 'And on me!' he sprayed. A rat had used its crude toothed orifice to puncture Heem's flesh.

'Don't just sit there hurting; needle it!' Jessica cried.

Heem needled it. The creature made a vibration and drew back, wounded. Its companions pounced on it and tore it apart with their own teeth. Heem tasted the tearing of flesh, the spilling of juices. 'This is worse than what Squams do!' he sprayed, forgetting the undiplomatic nature of the remark.

'They are consuming undigested flesh!' Windflower flashed.

'Appalling,' Sickh said. 'Digestion should always take place outside the body so that the waste products can be eliminated.'

Two more rats came at Heem. He needled both, destroying them. Meanwhile, the Squam slithered to join the Erb, who seemed to be largely helpless before this attack. Sickh's pincers clicked; Heem felt the vibration, tasted the squirting rat-juices, and knew that the Squam was protecting the Erb's tender roots.

But there were more rats charging down the hall. They were small, but there was something peculiarly horrible about that footed travel. 'The commotion has attracted the whole neighbourhood of monsters,' Jessica said. 'They'll never stop coming. We've got to get out of here before they overwhelm us.'

'They don't like water,' Heem announced to the others. 'They shy away from even my glancing jets. We must retreat to the sewer.'

They retreated. Heem got nipped several more times; the creatures darted in so swiftly it was hard to needle each one in time. He was sure the Erb was having a similar problem. Only the Squam was immune – which was fortunate, because the Squam could not remain long in the protective water.

They reached the water and immersed themselves. The rats lined up at the edge, flashing their little beams, balked.

'It seems we are secure for the moment,' Sickh flashed. 'But how are we to progress to our objective?'

'You can progress,' Heem jetted from that part of him that remained above the water. 'They cannot penetrate your armour.'

'I may not progress alone; this was our covenant. We must free all of us – or none of us.'

'She means it,' Jessica said. 'There's nothing holding her here but honour.'

'Honour in a Squam!' he sprayed, marvelling.

'It was not so funny in the lava-dome! You're still trying to judge a whole species by a single individual.'

'We can retreat the way we came,' the Erb flashed.

'And yield our chance in the competition,' Heem jetted.

'These vermin are discouraged by water,' Sickh said. 'Our friend the HydrO fathomed that, most astutely. Perhaps we can make further use of this.'

'The monster is seeking to compliment me,' Heem sprayed internally to Jessica. 'Exactly as you had me do to the Erb.'

'And you like being on the receiving end, don't you – even from a Squam?'

Heem made a taste-wash sigh. 'Yes. I am an easy wash for female folk.'

'As I have known for some time.' But her spirit was

momentarily light. 'Underneath all that gruff jetting you're a pretty nice guy, Heem.'

'Now *you're* doing it!'

'Well, Squams of a feather . . .'

'Feather?'

'Never mind.'

'Would it be possible to flood the passage?' Windflower enquired. 'This might eliminate the vermin.'

'Excellent notion!' the Squam agreed. 'Yet it could be difficult to do what the eons have not done.'

'We might employ the grates we removed, buttressed by other materials, to block the main drain, forcing the water level to rise,' the Erb continued. 'It would be difficult, perhaps hazardous. But for me, too-long-continued confinement in darkness is also hazardous and most unpleasant.'

'I know exactly how she feels!' Jessica said.

'There will also be a problem making the water barrier tight,' the Squam agreed. 'Yet the alternative—'

'I can make it tight,' Heem sprayed. 'With my body, spread over a mesh.'

'With your body!' Sickh exclaimed. 'We would not require such sacrifice!'

'I intend no sacrifice,' Heem needled at the translator. 'The HydrO body is constructed to withstand slow pressure, and to adapt shape to need. Were a suitable framework in place, such as one of those grates, I could spread across it, sealing it, cutting off the flow of water until such time as it were advisable to release the flow.'

'How would you escape, when that time came? The pressure would hold you firm.'

'No, the HydrO body can also pass through a mesh, slowly. I have but to allow holes to open—'

'Then you could have proceeded without us,' the Erb flashed. 'You did not need to have the grates removed.'

'Not so,' Heem sprayed, embarrassed. 'Our covenant—'

'Yes indeed,' Jessica said smugly.

254

'What I cannot do,' Heem jetted, 'is set the framework in place.'

'I can do that,' the Squam said. 'But I could not remain to anchor it as the water rose. I must have access to air.'

Strange, Heem thought, how he, who lived entirely on gas, could immerse himself indefinitely in water; while the Squam, who was only partially dependent on gas, had to have it regularly. This was worth noting, should he find himself in conflict with a Squam near water. Even a brief immersion might seriously handicap the creature.

'I can anchor it,' the Erb volunteered.

'Then I believe we have a feasible course of action,' Sickh concluded. 'If we can flood this passage high enough to drive the vermin completely out, we may be able tó traverse it before they return. If we then cannot win through to the surface near the site, we shall have to retreat to the tractor and await assistance by the Competition Authority, for we will be out of the race.'

Heem moved down inside the main conduit, exploring by touch and taste. They were in luck; the tube narrowed shortly below their crossing. There seemed to be a huge old valve, half buried by sediment, whose operation was beyond their power, but whose constriction provided a certain lodging site for their grates. He rolled back and reported.

'Two grates are sufficient?' the Squam enquired.

'One grate will cover it,' Heem assured her. 'But there are holes in the grates Windflower removed, where her drill lodged. Better to use both grates, overlapping, to cancel out the holes and make it more secure. They will have to be held in place until pressure builds behind them.'

'And when that occurs, pressure will diminish in front of them,' Sickh said. 'There will be air there, perhaps.'

'There is a pocket of air at the valve now,' Heem jetted, remembering. 'Trapped where the conduit bulges and narrows. It is usable; I tasted it.'

They worked out the details quickly and went to work.

Windflower lifted and carried the grates slowly to the valve and leaned them beside it. Then she hauled Sickh down on the cable – actually, the Erb anchored it, and the current brought the Squam along. Sickh helped move the two grates into precise place, then fastened her pincers on them and held her air intake high so as to reach the pocket of air. Windflower set her roots firmly in the sediment below and twined her smaller upper tendrils into the grates, anchoring the metal upright. And Heem spread himself flat, forming a wide but shallow disc across the face of the grates-network, preventing the water from passing through.

Immediately the pressure rose. There had been a fair current here, signifying a considerable flow of water. Now this water was backing up, rising in the side passages. Because the slant of those passages was slight, a small rise should advance the water considerably along those tunnels. But how far would it have to go to remove all the vermin? If it flooded in the direction of the large central hall instead, they would never get their smaller passage cleared. They had to hope that the small passage ahead was at a lower level than the one behind them. Heem thought it was.

'It seems we must wait a time,' the Squam said. 'Shall we distract ourselves by conversing? If you, Heem, are able to spray from your dry side, and if you, Windflower, can angle a vane through here—'

They managed it. The Erb poked a vane through a space between grate and curved wall, while Heem sealed over the rest. They were in physical contact with each other, but were accustomed to this now.

'I am curious, Heem, how your kind developed space technology,' Sickh remarked in what Heem presumed was a standard interspecies conversational gambit. 'We had assumed, until experience with the sapients of other Stars showed otherwise, that it was necessary to possess an accurate vibration or radiation perception, and to possess well-coordinated manipulative extremities. Yet HydrOs have neither. I realize you are quite competent with spaceships, tractors, and other tools – but how were you able to construct these in the beginning?'

'This is not obvious?' Heem sprayed, surprised.

'Of course it's not obvious, dope!' Jessica said from within. 'We Solarians always made similar assumptions. How can you grow, hunt, gather or prepare food, for example, if you don't have – oops.'

However, this provided Heem with the key for his reply to the Squam. 'HydrOs are not burdened with the liabilities of food consumption or need for shelter that certain other creatures are,' he sprayed delicately. 'Consequently the whole of our attention may be freed for intellectual and tactical challenges. We can move objects of considerable size by pushing or rolling them, but preferred to develop machines to do such brute work for us.'

'Yet how did—' the Squam began.

Heem found himself enjoying this. 'We taste-analysed a variety of substances, and found that some possessed traits that would serve. Jetting certain stones with certain force caused them to yield trace electrical currents we could taste—'

'Semiconductor diodes!' Jessica exclaimed.

'And certain metals conducted currents from one region to another, with particular arrangements causing this flow to change its nature, dissipating itself in the heat or causing an attractive force for other substances!'

'Wires, transformers, resistors, magnets,' Jessica continued. 'There you have the basis for the electric motor!'

'And the appropriate combination of such substances and currents led to the first crude electrical machines. It really was not difficult, since we could taste the nature of each circuit and flow quite readily. Our small machines were employed to construct our larger machines, in a progression extending ultimately to space itself. It had been a matter of conjecture to us how creatures possessing no refined analytic taste, so as to be unable to comprehend the finer properties of matter, could ever achieve a similar level of technology.'

'You are marvellously lucid,' Sickh said. 'I grasp now that you proceeded from the molecular level to the macroscopic level – a sensible procedure. My kind went the reverse route, utilizing the principles of gross leverage and exploitation of combustible substances to fashion large, crude machines, which we then refined to smaller, more precise ones. We progressed most rapidly in sonics, but did in time achieve some competence in other technical fields.'

'As her multi-species translator attests,' Jessica remarked. 'That's a pretty neat gadget, you know, considering its small size.'

'And we Erbs,' Windflower flashed, 'commenced with optics. We were aware of the stars of the universe from earliest times; indeed our constant observation of these nocturnal phenomena may have been the primary stimulus for our achievement of mobile status. We desired to explore those lights more closely, and early realized that each was as bountiful a source of life-giving light as our own near Star. We commenced with optics; from simple reflection, such as we do in ordinary communication, we progressed to laser technology, then spread our leaves to intercept the illumination of other disciplines. We were amazed to discover that sapience was possible without vision. Yet it would seem, in retrospect, that sapience can arise from virtually any form, when conditions are otherwise appropriate.'

'Even among species who are sighted, limbed, and consume food,' Heem agreed.

'I'll get you for that!' Jessica said.

'We do seem to achieve the ultimate unity in sapience, however divergent our origins,' Sickh agreed. 'It is possible that not all of us will survive. In the event I do not emerge from this situation, I ask the survivors to let it be known what happened to me and my transferee, who has of course supported our effort and assumed identical risks. She is Hov of Star Salivar; her species, she regrets, somewhat resembles the vermin of this passage, physically, but she is a very pretty personality.'

'Physical substance means nothing,' Windflower flashed. 'There are plants that focus light indiscriminately, burning everything about them, and other plants who are constructively sapient. We are glad to know you, Hov of Salivar.'

'Appreciation, Windflower of Erb.'

'My transferee also wishes to be known,' the Erb continued. 'She is Wryv of Star Ffrob, a fungoid sapience.'

They exchanged polite greetings with Wryv.

Heem's turn. 'Should we inform them?' he asked Jessica.

'Oh, go ahead! I want to be known too – at least to these friends. Spill the beans.'

Heem was momentarily repulsed by her image of food, but proceeded. 'I am the HydrO species representative,' he sprayed. 'My transferee is not of Thousandstar. She is Jessica of Star Sol of Segment Etamin, similar in biology to the Squam, but possessed of sight, and female.'

There was a pause. 'Do I miscomprehend?' Sickh enquired at last. 'I know of Segment Etamin of the barely known Far Galaxy, and vaguely of Sphere Sol in the stellar wilderness. But I had understood you to be male.'

'It is unusual, but we do have a female transferee in a male host,' Heem sprayed.

'Unusual!' the Squam cried. 'This is the understatement of the—'

'Why then,' Windflower flashed. 'I should not fear you. A sighted female—'

'This is female illogic,' Heem jetted. 'Typical also of my transferee.'

'All *right*!' Jessica snapped. 'If it gives her comfort, let it be.'

Sickh was more serious. 'Does this remarkable juxtaposition account for your transition from the robust personality of Ship H-Sixty-six to the thoughtful individual who summoned assistance for one of my kind? There would seem to be the touch of the female there.'

'I was not inclined to assist your kind,' Heem admitted. 'She urged me to it.'

'Let her flash with us!' Windflower pleaded.

Heem turned over the body of Jessica. If these creatures supposed he had been pretending, and thought to trap him by means of female dialogue, they would be disappointed.

'Hello, girls,' Jessica said. And they proceeded to a merry trialogue while Heem snoozed.

He was jolted back to awareness by a question addressed directly to him. Jessica had returned the body to him. 'Is the water level high enough?' the Squam enquired. 'We cannot afford too much passage of time, lest others reach the site ahead of us and bring our entire effort to nothing.'

Heem tasted the water. 'The flavour of the drainage indicates that a considerable expanse of formerly dry passage has been covered, and some vermin have perished. But there seem to be more remaining.'

'Let us wait a small delay longer,' Sickh decided. 'The vermin must all be removed.'

'Not too much longer,' Windflower flashed. 'I have been some time out of light, and have expended energy; I weaken.'

'And I begin, pardon the expression, to hunger,' the Squam agreed. 'Yet there will be inadequate time to feed. Do you suppose, then, that it is safe now to let the water ebb?'

'Safe, no,' Heem opined. 'But if the vermin are subsapient, they may not realize when the flow reverses, and will remain clear for a time.'

'Let us gamble, then. We face a crisis of another kind if we delay too long.'

The crisis of a hungry Squam? Heem drew in his body, letting the water leak through the valve. He wanted to drain the reserve rapidly, to give the vermin less time to discover the change.

This turned out to be no gentle flow. A fierce current manifested, tearing at their bodies. Heem tried to slow it by spreading himself again, but was unable; already the grates were being shoved sidewise, and he had to disengage quickly or be carried away himself. He flattened himself against the wall of the valve instead, half surrounding the Erb. Something clamped painfully on his flesh, giving him taste-memory of his fight with Slitherfear on the Squam's machine-floater so long ago. He hung on as the turbulence tore at him. All their tedious labour, about to go for nothing, as they got carried down the conduit! Because of a single error of judgement on his part.

'Don't blame yourself, Heem,' Jessica said. 'Nobody anticipated this.'

'But I am accustomed to fluid dynamics. I should have been careful!'

'How often have you dealt with million-year-old sewer systems? We all make mistakes, especially when we're in a hurry. Just hang on!'

He hung on, as she put it. At last the turbulence eased. The water was returning to its original level, though not to its original taste. The sediment had been swirled up and resuspended, changing the flavour. Heem also tasted the juices of dead vermin, carried along by the current. At least something had been accomplished.

He discovered that one of Sickh's pincers was clamped on his flesh. That was what he had left, in the mêlée. The grip was painful – yet he knew it had been desperation, for otherwise the Squam would have been carried away.

The Erb moved up towards the side tube. Heem started to follow – and was balked by the Squam. 'She is unconscious,' Jessica said. 'Maybe drowned. We've got to get her out of the water, Heem!'

Heem tried. The cable was gone, and the translation unit; he could not even ask the Squam to let go – and if she did, she would be lost, for he could not carry her. He rolled forward, jetting forcefully through the water, heaving her body around and over him. The water made her light; he could do it. When she was before him, he rolled over her; no way to crush her armoured body! Then another heave. This was excruciating, but he was making progress. He wrestled Sickh around the corner and up the exit tube. At last they emerged into air.

Windflower was there, but could not see them in the dark. Her tendrils ran over them worriedly, finding the clamped pincers. Then she knew. Her drill formed the hard point nudging into the pincers, and suddenly they spread. Heem was free.

The Erb picked up the Squam's body with an effort of convolution, and shook it. Water dripped out of its orifices. Sickh stirred, responding weakly.

'She's alive,' Jessica said, relieved. 'It would have been terrible if she'd drowned.'

Heem had to agree. He would not have believed he would ever feel that way about a Squam, but of course he had never interacted with a lady Squam before. This one had complimented him with obvious artifice, yet he had been swayed.

Now they were here in the vermin-passage, without cable or translator. They had to go on. Heem hoped there would be no more problems; the present ones were almost overwhelming.

Sickh recovered enough to slither. They moved forward as rapidly as they could. Heem led the way, knowing that the Erb could no longer see, while his own perception was unimpaired; he could discover any hazard in time to block her off from it. The Squam could perceive well too, but was not strong now.

The vermin were gone; the flowing water had vanquished them. The water had also cleared the floor of the passage somewhat, facilitating travel.

The passage inclined upwards. They passed the water line and moved from damp to dry pavement, but no rats came. Heem tasted their traces; many of them had scrambled past here, but they seemed to have been terrorized by the pursuing water. A good sign.

They came to another great empty chamber, much like the first. They hurried across it, confident that they were approaching another termination. They found the opposite passage, followed it past an intersecting tunnel, and came at last to—

A chamber at the end, terminating in a blank wall. Just like the one they had broken into, beginning this nether trek.

'A barracks, for sure,' Jessica said. 'Individual sleeping quarters, and a central mess hall – two units, for two battalions, mirror images of each other, with a common drainage system. Only problem is, how do we get out?'

'The Erb drills us a hole,' Heem replied.

'Have you been watching Windflower lately? She's been without light a long time; she's wilting on her roots. I don't think she can do it.'

To make it worse, the rats were returning. Perhaps these were strangers who had not encountered the rising water, so remained bold. Fortunately there were fewer of them; foraging must be worse at this periphery. So far. But with the Erb unable to see them, and very tired, and the Squam not much better off, this was bad.

The rats were getting bolder. There would be worse trouble than losing the competition if the three of them did not get out of this labyrinth soon.

The Squam acted. She fastened a pincer on the Erb gently, and guided her to the outer wall. She tapped against it meaningfully. The Erb would have to try to break through, tired or not. Their lives depended on it.

A rat charged, sensing that Windflower was the vulnerable target. Heem rolled to intercept it, needling it accurately. The thing rolled over, its three legs kicking in air. Heem positioned himself behind the Erb, guarding her from further attack, while the Squam guided her drill.

They were cooperating efficiently – without the translator. Because they knew each other, trusted each other, and because they had to.

The drill started. Even Heem could tell it was not going at

proper strength. It bit into the wall. The taste of rock dust sprayed out. Then chunks of rock were split off and dislodged. The face of the wall cracked. She was doing it!

The drill stalled. Windflower leaned down. Heem surveyed her, alarmed. There was a taste of spoilage about her.

'She's wilting!' Jessica cried. 'Her last strength is gone! She's got to have light, fast!'

The rats, aware of their advantage, scuttled in. Heem needled three at once, amazed at his facility; few HydrOs could perform that well. 'It's the vision,' Jessica said. 'Remember how it helped you thread the needle of Holestar? Now you can *see* the rats, and wipe them out. It's excellent practice.'

So it was. Never had Heem had so precise a control, for more than a single needle at a time. But he wanted to be sure of his new power.

More rats were pressing close. They had discovered the fringe of his range, and crowded just beyond it; even with enhanced accuracy, there were limits. Soon they would charge, in too great a number for him to withstand – unless he kept them occupied by extending his range.

The Erb sank to the floor. The rats nudged near her extremities. Heem spread himself half over her, needling outward, protecting the length of her. It seemed futile, since they were trapped here and would inevitably perish, but he had to fight to the end.

And – he rather enjoyed this target practice. He *was* getting better, scoring on individual rats at twice his normal distance, forcing the whole horde back uncertainly. He was decimating them from a distance, and might eventually eliminate them all – if more were not constantly skulking in from the rear passage.

The Squam slithered to the side. Two rats attacked her, biting her torso. They could not hurt her, but she was evidently annoyed; she picked one up in each pincer and crushed them so that their juices squirted, and hurled them bleeding into the mass of their kind. She was stronger now;

she would survive the rats. But she could not pass the sewer alone, so she too was doomed.

Sickh tapped the wall with a pincer. She slithered farther and tapped again. What was she doing? 'She's sounding it for the thinnest section, for fractures,' Jessica explained. 'The Erb weakened it; if impact at one place will break the rest of the way through—'

Satisfied, the Squam did just that. She tapped harder, until she was smashing all three pincers together at the wall. Bang-bang-bang – Heem felt the small vibration of it, building.

There was a larger shudder as something fractured. 'She's doing it!' Jessica cried, with the same excitement Heem had had before. 'She's found the fracture point! Now if only she can exploit it.'

Sickh slithered out into the centre of the chamber. Then she moved rapidly towards the wall, hurling her armoured body at it. This time the impact was much greater. Again the wall shuddered, and chips of rock fell down. But there was no breakthrough. 'If only we had a tractor, as before,' Jessica said.

The rats were becoming alarmed by the vibration. They were evidently very sensitive to collapses of stone, as they were to flooding of passages. They scuttled wildly about the chamber. The Squam paused.

'She can't get up proper speed with those rats in the way!' Jessica said. 'We'll have to clear them out. Let's see what we can do, Heem.' She formed a picture of the creatures, and imagined little concentric-ring targets on each body. 'Target practice – final exam.'

Heem oriented himself, gathered his fluids, and fired an amazing fusillade of needles in one salvo. Jessica had spotted seven of the rats, precisely, and he needed all of his uncanny new accuracy now. Any he missed would get in the way again while Sickh was moving. Long distance, he scored on six rats. The seventh was only wounded; quickly Heem reoriented, and this time he finished it. This was not only his best effort to date, it was the most accurate multiple needling he had ever tasted of any of his kind performing. He was a super-HydrO!

'Now don't get a swelled head,' Jessica cautioned him. 'If you could jet through that rock wall, *then* you'd have something to crow about.'

He was getting used to her irrelevant vernacular. But she was right; he owed his expertise to her vision, not to any merit of his own.

The way was clear. Sickh charged across, smashed into the wall, and fractured it. A section of the wall fell in. There was an abrupt if small change in flavour. The rats retreated, frightened. 'That's the taste of light!' Jessica cried. 'Striking the dust, drying the water. *She's broken through!*'

But now the Squam fell to the floor, inert. The collision had damaged her. She moved one pincer weakly, then folded herself together and lay still.

'So close, so close!' Jessica moaned. 'Either of them, just a little more – and we who retain our strength cannot exert it here. The irony!'

'Light!' Heem sprayed. 'The Erb – she needs light. If we can get her in it, she might recover.'

He tried. The rats were no menace for the moment. He devoted his full attention to the task, shoving part of himself under Windflower's body, then jetting as if for an uphill roll. His advancing surface shoved her forward before she slipped beneath him. 'Try it again, Heem!' Jessica cried. 'Get her into that beam of light!'

Heem shoved again, and again, each time moving her a small distance. She was not firm, like a rock; she was irregular and bendable, hard to get any purchase on. The job was tediously slow. But at last they came up beside the Squam, and Windflower's stem slid into the light.

The Erb stirred. Her leaves moved as if blown by wind; the

266

taste-ambience shifted. She curved around, seeking that light, absorbing it.

The rats came back, acclimatizing. They were, after all, visual creatures; they made flashes to see. The more forceful radiation from outside startled but did not actually hurt them. 'Keep them off,' Jessica said. 'We've got to give Windflower time to recover her strength. Maybe she has reserves she can draw on, when she sees light at the end of the tunnel.'

'She can see it,' Heem said, though he suspected Jessica had not meant precisely what he had understood. He kept the rats off, still practising his marksmanship. But his own strength was waning. His constant effort had heated his body; his hot needles were effective, but he needed to cool or he would start to destroy his own tissues. His reservoir of fluid was diminishing; he was using up the free hydrogen in this region faster than the slow air circulation replaced it, and every needle used yet more. Some fresh air was coming in through the crack in the wall, but not enough. He was moving into a hydrogen-deprivation stage, and it was uncomfortable.

'Don't give up, Heem!' Jessica urged. 'Windflower is recovering. Just keep the rats clear a little longer—' And she washed him a kiss of encouragement.

Heem kept them off a lot longer. He was losing consciousness, focusing only on the immediate menace. A rat would charge, he would needle it, it would fall. Another would charge, be needled, and fall. But the range of his needles was diminishing, and the semicircle of rats was constricting. If the stupid creatures ever realized how vulnerable he was now to a mass charge—

But every time Heem sank into a misery of inattention, Jessica roused him by her pleading, threats of screaming, and murmurs of confidence and affection. After a while these things became merged in his mind like the composite

267

taste of a crowd, but still he suffered himself to be roused. He was vulnerable not only to the rats, but also to the encouragements and threats of the alien, and had to perform.

The Erb drew herself slowly to her roots. She was standing again! She formed her wedge and put it to the crack in the rock. She applied her torque – and suddenly the rock was wedged apart, sundered, blasted. Dust flew, and large fragments of stone dropped to the floor, half burying the Squam. A huge, strong beam of starlight came in, bathing them all in its warmth.

Heem collapsed. Light made little difference to him, but the warmth of it brought his already overheated system to the verge of ruin. He had done what he could, and could do no more. He had to sag down and take in hydrogen. The Erb, at least, was free.

But Windflower did not go. She enlarged the hole, then climbed awkwardly over the rubble towards the interior of the chamber. She found Sickh – for of course the Erb could see, now – inserted her drill in the pile, and hurled out the rocks. The rats scattered yet again as the shower of material crushed down on them. What power there was in an Erb in light!

Sickh stirred. She had been inert for some time, and was now reviving. She slithered over the rocks towards Heem, towards the hole in the wall. Two would escape.

The Squam clamped a pincer on Heem's tender flesh and hauled. It hurt, but it was good; she was drawing him towards the hole.

Towards – what?

'Idiot!' Jessica berated him. 'Your crazed mind is confusing the hole with the Hole. Relax!'

Heem relaxed. This was not demise, it was rescue. Up and out they moved, into the beautiful taste and fresh hydrogen of living day. Three had escaped!

8

Site of Hope

The rich, cool air soon restored Heem, and the intense light revived Windflower to full tumescence. The two relaxed, regaining strength, while Sickh returned to the chamber to feed on the dead rats. Windflower stretched out a root and touched Heem's flesh in a gesture of trust: she knew how he had protected her from the rats, and was signalling her gratitude. Natural enemies had become friends.

In due course the three of them resumed their trek towards the Ancient site. How much time had they gained or lost? Were they now among the leaders, or was the competition over?

They did not have far to go. There was a valley beyond the ridge, then a low hill. The fern-foliage had abated; only low brush hampered progress. From the height of the hill, which they all climbed slowly, the Erb began flashing. Without the translator, Heem was only vaguely aware of the pattern of radiation reflected across his body, and assimilated no meaning.

Then Windflower moved laboriously in the interspecies language. DESTINATION – NEAR, she signalled. OTHERS NEAR.

Clear enough. The truce was over; they were at the verge of the site.

Heem wished he could bid proper farewell to his companions, but this would be time-consuming in sign language and superfluous. They all knew how they related. He set off towards the site at a swift roll.

The ground became rougher in the valley, forcing him to move cautiously, so he lacked sufficient velocity to crest the next rise. But it did not matter. A Competition Authority checkline was there. As he crossed that spread flavour, a machine spray challenged him: 'Identify competitor.'

'Heem of Highfalls, HydrO host. Jess of Etamin, transferee,' he sprayed. Now it would come: how far back were they?

An inspection beam played over him. 'No physical apparatus may be conveyed across this line. Proceed, contestant; your legitimacy is verified. You are fifth to cross.'

Heem rolled on. Fifth! Right where he had to be! Their excursion under the ridge had indeed gained them time, despite their problems and delays. Now they had a fighting chance to win. He tasted entities behind him, and knew that Sickh the Squam had arrived at the checkline, and would be the sixth to cross, with Windflower the Erb not far behind. They were in competition with each other now, but Heem preferred to have them challenging him, rather than strangers.

'That's for sure,' Jessica agreed warmly. 'They're good people.'

The hill continued, and soon the Squam overhauled him, making a swerve to indicate greeting, and moved on ahead. 'We are now sixth,' Jessica said. 'But there must be another slope to roll down, soon.'

Heem checked the map, but it lacked detail within the checkline circle. Soon, however, he verified it: a nice, clear, even slope. He tasted the ambience of a body of water, overlaid by a faint flavour of alien metal. The Ancient site – across a lake.

Jessica conjured the map again, and was similarly frustrated. 'They are being deliberately obscure,' she complained. 'They're not giving us any hints what to expect here. But I can make a reasonable guess or two. I think the site is on an island in a small lake, so that every contestant has to overcome the challenge of water. Seems to me this whole region is a depression, a concavity – it may all be part of the site. A great circular excavation, with the entrance at the centre. The Ancients did things like that; most of their known sites are pretty massive. There's some coding in this circle on the map I can't quite make out—'

'It indicates a structure,' Heem sprayed as his rolling gathered momentum. Now he tasted the ambience of two other entities ahead, besides Sickh: an Erb and a HydrO. He would not be able to pass the HydrO, who could roll as well as he could, but was gaining on the Erb. 'A building, and we must achieve its apex first, to win the competition.'

He rolled past Sickh, giving her a swerve of greeting. With a lake at the base, he could afford to build up speed. Water was less bruising than land.

'How will Sickh cross?' Jessica enquired, worried.

'Fool female! We're racing against her now! We do not want her to cross.'

'I suppose. But it seems unfair, since she can't traverse deep water.'

Heem rolled by the Erb and splashed into the lake. It was shallow, hardly covering him. 'Squams can ford this, holding their air tubes above,' he sprayed. And dropped into a deep hole. 'Of course, they will have to negotiate it with a certain care, to avoid problems.'

'I think she can swim a little, but she's too solid to float, so she's got to have shallow water within range. I guess she'll make it.'

This concern for a rival struck Heem as almost humorous, yet it was a facet of Jessica's personality that he found he liked. She was a gentler creature than he, despite her wild Solarian background; she had fewer hurts and savageries.

'I suppose that's right,' she agreed. 'You could use an ameliorating influence, and I could use an aggressive influence. We make a good team—' She broke off, and her hurt washed through him.

'What did I think this time?' Heem demanded. 'I did not attempt to sadden you.'

271

'Not your fault, Heem,' she said. 'It's that very soon now it will be all over, one way or another. Win or lose, we shall part – and I don't want to part.' And her emotion flooded his being as thoroughly as the lake flooded his environment. 'Oh, God, I don't! I want to be with you forever!'

And it could not be. The grief saturated him, and he knew it was not hers alone. She was a difficult, alien, and disembodied female, totally unlike anything he had imagined before she joined him, and the perceptions and emotions she brought were strange and almost beyond comprehension. But necessity had forced his comprehension of vision, and the emotion had followed. He wanted her too, for the moment and the eternity. And could not have her.

At least they could win the competition, and promote his welfare and hers, though these things were no longer as important as they had been. They would retain their memories of their mutual experience, and that was a partial good.

'Yes,' she agreed. 'Or was that my own thought?'

'I don't know. Does it matter?'

'I don't know.'

Thus, inconclusively, their reflection ended. Heem was now forging out the other side of the lake. He tasted the other HydrO more clearly now. A female, rolling up from the opposite side of the island. It was Swoon of Sweetswamp!

'Old home week,' Jessica murmured. 'She may not be much on riddles, but she certainly rolls a good race.'

However, several creatures were already at the structure: two Erbs, a Squam, and a HydrO. The four who had preceded him into the final circle.

'But we passed one of those,' Jessica protested. 'An Erb, just entering the lake. There should only be three here.'

'Erbs can function in water. It must have used its drill to draw itself through the water extremely rapidly, and pass us again.'

She visualized an Erb with rotating propeller-leaves,

272

moving so rapidly it left a turbulent wake in the water. 'Must be.'

None of the early arrivals were trying to climb the building; instead they were fighting each other. This was a vicious circle; the Squam was pinching the HydrO, the HydrO was needling the Erb, and the second Erb was drilling the Squam. Since each had to keep out of the way of the creature who could destroy it, there was more motion than action. Heem rolled to a stop, tasting the situation as well as he could from a distance. Swoon of Sweetswamp paused similarly, on the other side of the island.

'I don't understand this,' Jessica said. 'Why aren't they trying to climb the building? This is supposed to be a race, not a battle!'

'The HydrO management did not select a combat specialist randomly,' Heem sprayed. 'They anticipated this. If my practice with your vision and sight-needle coordination suffices, I need give way to neither Squam nor Erb. Still, I would prefer not to fight; there is really little to gain from it. Especially if we can ascend the structure while the others are preoccupied.'

'Agreed. Let's sneak through.'

They rolled forward, cautiously, keeping a taste out for Swoon, who could reach the building just as fast as they could. They also kept track of the battle raging.

The Squam tore a piece out of the HydrO – but in the process got caught by the Erb. In a moment the Squam's armour had been wedged apart, and the creature lay broken and dying. 'You monsters don't fool around!' Jessica exclaimed, making a graphic picture of it. 'We Solarians take some time in our fights, as in our love-making, usually, having to strike repeatedly. Well – no, in swordplay it can be very quick. And my clone-brother makes love in a flash. So it depends. Still—'

The HydrO, saved by one Erb, needled the other. The Erb wilted, its mechanism jammed and leaking sap. 'That's gratitude for you!' Jessica said indignantly.

'That is free-for-all for you.' But Heem was not pleased.

One Erb remained uninjured. It used stem and tendrils to shove the helpless creatures away from the structure, including the HydrO, who had collapsed after its final needle. But the Erb did not attempt to ascend itself. Why?

Heem was wary, but Swoon was rolling up rapidly, so he had to accelerate himself. The two converged, and the Erb hastily moved away. 'Odd,' Jessica said.

The structure turned out to be a tower, round and smooth. It stood somewhat taller than a fern-tree, with a spiral ramp ascending it. Simple enough for any of the contestants. But why had the Erb, obviously in a position to be first to the top, backed off? 'There's not supposed to be danger here, is there?' Jessica asked.

'Not from the Site,' Heem jetted grimly. 'But we cannot trust the other competitors.'

Swoon reached the ramp first. She was an exceptionally swift roller, faster than Heem – which explained how she too had passed him on the approach within the checkline circle. She must have been selected for this quality, as well as for her superior piloting. In the vehicle or alone, she could move. She rolled right up the ramp – and slid down again, surprised.

'Our turn!' Jessica exclaimed.

'No, wait,' Heem sprayed. 'There is something wrong here.' He rolled to the base of the ramp and stopped.

Swoon recovered from the impetus with which she had been ejected, and approached. 'It dumped me!' she sprayed indignantly. 'It's roller-surfaced, impossible to mount. I wondered why the Erb backed off.' Then, in an aftertaste: 'Oh, greetings, Heem of Highfalls.'

'Greetings,' he sprayed noncommittally. He inspected the ramp, touching its substance with his own, tasting it carefully. There were no perceptible rollers, but there was certainly a roller effect.

The Ancients had been the Cluster's finest craftscreatures; they obviously had wanted this ramp to be too slippery to ascend.

There would be no way to change that except by conforming to whatever approach the Ancients had desired. There was really no way to deal with *any* Ancient artifact except by its own rules, which were usually obscure. The Ancients were not merely a riddle from the distant past; they were an exciting challenge in every taste of the concept. Which was why every Star of Thousandstar was fascinated by this well-preserved site. It was not mere intellectual curiosity; there could be fantastic technological wealth here. This was the site of hope.

'I don't know,' Jessica said, also highly intrigued. She loved puzzles; Heem could feel her being coalescing around this mystery. 'Generally the live sites have aural keys, not physical ones. Could it be that this was a usable ramp for them?'

'A small flatfloater could mount this readily,' Heem agreed. 'Or any of the jet species. But why should the Competition Authority require us to ascend to the top, if there is no way for any of the host species?'

'I think we have here another riddle,' Jessica said, delighted. 'One set up by the Ancients, and used by the Competition Authority. To make this a real multi-level challenge, so that mere guessing at the outset, or racing ability in space or on land or in water, is not enough. The winner of this competition will be lucky, swift *and* smart. Deserving in every respect. The early arrivals here merely have more time to solve the final riddle, but if they are not smart enough, they have no chance to win.'

'I do not taste it precisely that way,' Heem sprayed. 'A smart late arrival will never win through the stupid early ones, who will kill him rather than allow him to prevail. We shall have to solve the riddle before more competitors arrive, or we shall have to fight merely to hold our place in line.

275

Recall what happened to the first three arrivals.'

Jessica retouched her image of the three wounded and dying creatures. She needed no reminders. Lives were now at stake.

Already, Sickh was arriving, emerging from the shallow water.

'There is a globe or something at the base of the ramp,' Jessica said. 'Focus your taste on it, Heem – I want to see it clearly.'

He was more concerned with the ramp and the arriving competition, for he knew how smart Sickh and Windflower were. He did not want to needle either of them, which meant he would simply have to solve the riddle before they reached the tower. But he obeyed Jessica's directive rather than argue.

She formed a picture of a small sphere, with a line hovering inside it, balled on one end. Both globe and line gave off a faint radiation that made it possible for him to locate them accurately; he doubted it was taste, because if the particles of their substance were being constantly emitted, they would have eroded entirely away in the time since the Ancients departed. Yet it seemed like taste. Synthetic stimulation of his perception? Another indication of the sophistication of Ancient construction. Even minor details were crafted to last virtually forever, performing in manners the technology of moderns could hardly match.

Heem moved nearer the globe, touching it with a small section of his skin. The line moved, its ball swinging to point at the place of tangency. He slid his skin to the side, and the line followed.

'That's a dial of some kind,' Jessica said. 'A three-dimensional indicator. See – it points to you where you touch the globe, then remains where put when you retreat. You can set it where you want.'

Sickh was near, and Windflower was motoring through the lake. Another Squam was coming within perceiving

276

range, too. Already this place was getting crowded, with two of each host-species in the neighbourhood.

The nearest Erb set his drill, orienting on Sickh. 'Oh-oh,' Jessica said. 'That Erb gave way to us, because it is afraid of HydrOs – but it is not afraid of Squams! We'd better help Sickh.'

'You keep forgetting she's competition too! She may solve the riddle before we do!'

Jessica responded as he knew she would. 'Sickh is also a lady – and a friend. Remember how she broke open the first crack in the wall, and how she hauled you out into the fresh air so you could recover. Without her, we would not be here at all. If we have to lose to somebody, let's lose to a friend.'

Heem acceded. Jessica had a more sophisticated conscience than he did. 'The dangerous one is Windflower, she's the specialist in Ancients. She will know how to get up that ramp.' He rolled towards the male Erb, who retreated expediently.

'You're letting a Squam in?' Swoon of Sweetswamp needled incredulously. 'At least facilitate your own kind!' And her concluding message was flavoured with a strong savour of sex appeal. But she gave way to the Squam, as she had to.

'Why that brazen vixen!' Jessica exclaimed. 'She's trying to seduce you into giving *her* the advantage!'

'One female really resents tasting her technique being employed by another,' Heem sprayed with a certain resigned mirth.

'So?' Jessica demanded indignantly. 'When did *I* ever employ – don't answer that!'

'Too bad she's competition,' Heem continued. 'She has a most enticing flavour.'

'All *right*! I'd have flavour too, if I were – never mind. Just get back to your business.'

Sickh slithered up, investigated the ramp, and examined the globe. She seemed to be able to fathom the dial as readily as Heem could; the indicator probably gave off sonic vibration too. Remarkable device!

After a moment's experimentation, Sickh aimed the ball end of the line at the Star. She slithered on to the ramp – and up it.

'The key!' Swoon sprayed, rolling close. She brushed against the globe, causing the line to change orientation – and abruptly Sickh slid to the base of the ramp.

'That's the key, all right!' Jessica exclaimed. 'I wish *I'd* fathomed it! Set the pointer on the sun, and the ramp freezes. Could be like a time clock, since the position of the sun indicates time of day. Move that indicator, and you roll, ready or not. Oh, do you roll!'

Sickh made a pass at Swoon with one pincer, and Swoon retreated in haste. Sickh reset the pointer, started up the ramp – and Swoon rolled in towards the globe. Sickh halted, and Swoon halted. They were at an impasse; if the Squam mounted the ramp farther, the HydrO would arrange to dump her down again.

'I begin to appreciate the dimension of the problem,' Jessica said. 'No one can make it to the top without the cooperation of those at the bottom – who will lose if they do cooperate. Very neat challenge!'

'So the early arrivals aggravated each other in exactly this fashion, and got embroiled in a fight, the conclusion of which we tasted,' Heem agreed. 'Only the Erb survived – and he dared not betray the secret to us, so had to retreat without attempting the ascent. Yet why didn't he merely set the dial and rush up before we arrived? He was waiting for us.'

'I don't think we've fathomed the whole mystery yet,' Jessica said. 'Maybe we should make another deal with Sickh.'

'Maybe so,' Heem agreed reluctantly. 'But we can't communicate with her, without translation. Not technically enough, fast enough.'

'Oh pooh! She will understand.'

Heem moved to the base of the ramp, blocking off Swoon.

'Fair warning,' he jetted at her. 'We are in competition, and my transferee means to compete. Roll back.'

'But the Squam is on the ramp!' Swoon protested.

'You are perceptive.'

'I refuse to sit still for this!' Swoon rolled towards him.

Heem needled her with a long-distance, accurate shot. She rolled back, surprised at his proficiency; she was well beyond normal needle-range. Conversational jets required little physical cohesion, as their flavour alone counted; needles lost their force much sooner.

Sickh, realizing that Heem was guarding the dial, giving her a chance, slithered rapidly up.

'You are rolling away my chance, and yours!' Swoon jetted. 'You are betraying the Star you represent. I can offer you so much more than any Squam can!' And she sprayed him with sexual flavour.

She certainly did have a tempting taste! No doubt she had been selected for this quality, too. Her offer would have been quite attractive, except for two things. First, Jessica's cynical laughter was echoing through his system – a strange effect for one who could not hear. Second, he knew what happened to a HydrO female who reproduced. Swoon was suggesting copulation, not reproduction, but still the memory disturbed him. Heem stood firm, preventing her from interfering.

Suddenly Sickh came sliding down the ramp. Yet no one had touched the dial. 'I begin to glimmer why the Erb did not race up,' Jessica said. 'The rules change halfway up. This is no minor, one-stage challenge.'

Sickh slithered up beside Heem, her forepart aiming away from the tower. 'She is giving us our turn,' Jessica said. 'I told you she would understand. She will guard the dial for us, now.'

Heem rolled to the dial. It was now misset – not a little, as might happen in time as the radiation from the Star changed its angle, but a lot, as if jogged entirely out of place. Yet no one had touched it. Sickh did not believe that he, Heem, had moved it either; her attitude suggested that she had failed, not he.

He reset the dial to point at the sun; Jessica's visual image helped. The ramp firmed, and he rolled up it. 'We're on our way – maybe!' Jessica said.

Halfway up the tower – one loop of the spiral – there was another globe. 'Uh – I don't think we can safely ignore it,' Jessica said. 'Obviously we have to set it too, or the whole thing bounces out of whack. But I doubt it aims at the sun; someone must have tried that already.'

Heem agreed. 'But what else should it orient on?'

'I've got it! Is there a moon for this planet?'

'There are three. Only one is readily perceivable, however – and none have taste for me.'

'Um. You have a mental ephemeris, don't you? A table of System bodies and times? You can calculate where that moon is, even though you can't see it. The biggest, closest one. Yes.' She delved into the ephemeris Heem remembered. 'Let's see – it should be about there.' She added a glowing mood to her vision of the sky. 'It should not glow like that by day, but who's going to know the difference? I love this mental painting. Is it correctly placed?'

Heem verified it by his calculations. 'Yes.'

They set the indicator to point to the moon. Nothing happened. Heem rolled on up – and the ramp turned to rollers, dumping him helplessly around the tower and down to the ground.

'So much for that,' Jessica said. 'The Ancients weren't much for looking at the moon. Not much romance in their hearts.'

'What has a moon got to do with romance in a blood-pumping organ?'

'Nothing.'

Windflower had arrived. Heem rolled out of the way, giving her a turn. Swoon made a spray of muted fury, but kept her distance. 'She's the expert on the Ancients, isn't she?' he jetted rhetorically.

The Erb flashed at him enquiringly; Heem felt the reflected starlight on his skin, and Jessica formulated a momentarily blinding glint of light. These visual constructs were intriguing! Heem made a little spray of acknowledgement, but did not move. He and Sickh guarded the base of the ramp.

Windflower tried the ramp, and got nowhere. She investigated the globe. She oriented the indicator on the Star, and travelled up the spiral. 'Just like that!' Jessica marvelled. 'She certainly *does* understand the Ancients!'

But in a moment Windflower came down again. She was not rolling, but twining along on her own power. Why had she changed her vegetable mind?

The lady Erb came to stand beside them. After a moment Sickh went up the ramp again. Then she returned, under her own power, as the Erb had.

'Must be our turn,' Jessica said. 'I'd really like to know what's going on!'

Heem rolled up the ramp. He reached the second globe and checked it. The indicator was oriented, but not on the moon, or anything else they could fathom. Heem moved beyond the dial – and the ramp was firm.

'Windflower set it correctly!'Jessica exclaimed.

'Then why should she back down, instead of going on to the top?'

'Because she wasn't the first to arrive. We were asking her advice, so she gave it. She showed us where to set the second dial. Now she has repaid us for the chance we are giving her.'

'Where *did* she set it? It seems random to me.'

'It must be something she could guess from her knowledge of the Ancients. Something obvious. If the first dial points at the sun, the second—'

'The Hole!' Heem sprayed.

'The Hole!' she repeated. 'Of course!' She considered momentarily. 'We can't go on up; she was only showing us. We have to give her first turn. It's only fair.'

Heem did not argue with her. He rolled down the ramp.

Now Windflower went up. She made it almost to the top

of the tower – then slid down rapidly, barely staying on top of her roots. 'She must have tripped a third relay,' Jessica said. 'One that's more difficult than the others.'

'Now we know how to approach it. The three of us will keep taking turns, until one of us scores. That gives us one chance in three to win – with the assurance that a friend will win if we do not. This seems worthwhile.'

'Heem, I love you.'

The simple statement almost dissolved him. It was serious; there was no banter in her emotion, no teasing. They were now at the crisis point, within range of success or ultimate failure, either of which meant separation.

Heem made no overt response, because he was unwilling to reconcile himself either to victory or defeat when both meant the end. He merely accepted her statement. That was enough.

Windflower set the bottom dial and moved clear. Sickh and Heem checked it, noting the setting: the one the Erb had tried at the top. The wrong one. This was necessary information – but they could not tell what the dial pointed to. It seemed random, and it assuredly was not.

Sickh reset the dial for the Star and mounted the ramp. She paused at the second dial, then went on, approaching the top. And slid rapidly down. She set the dial, allowing them to see her wrong guess.

'Another moon,' Heem decided, checking against his ephemeris. He was still bothered by his inability to fathom the rationale of Windflower's guess, which had surely been an educated one. A wrong guess did not necessarily indicate failure; it might merely be the elimination of a viable but unapproved alternate.

It was Heem's turn again. 'There's got to be some rational setting,' Jessica said. 'Some pattern I can grasp. Windflower understands the Ancients as well as anyone can, but hasn't guessed this one. That means it is either random, which I don't believe, or relates to something we have not yet understood.'

'We need to grasp the purpose of this installation,' Heem

282

sprayed. 'Then we might know the correct direction.'

'Yes. But what *is* that purpose?' They were at the third globe now, close to the top of the tower, almost directly above the base of the ramp. They had spiralled twice around the cylindrical structure, and were a fair height above the ground. So near to victory, yet so distant!

Heem thought of rolling rapidly, gaining momentum, so as to achieve the top of the tower regardless of the friction of the surface, but was sure that would not work. The ascent was too steep and curved, and the Ancients surely had designed their site to prevent so simplistic a solution to the challenge. The low retaining wall outside the ramp might dissolve, sending him hurtling fatally to the ground . . . well, no, the Ancients weren't generally vicious in that manner. But they had their ways to enforce their alien directives.

'Can't take time; the others must have their turns, before more contestants arrive.' Indeed, from this elevation Heem perceived the faint flavours of one, perhaps two more Squams, and another Erb. Two creatures could not protect the ramp for long; the savage fighting would break out again. Because the only way any contestant could be quite sure of his chance was to eliminate all competition.

'Maybe straight down,' Jessica suggested. 'Star – Hole – Planet.'

Heem set the pointer accordingly. He essayed the ramp beyond – and was sent sliding around and around to the bottom. 'I'd enjoy the ride, if it weren't so serious,' Jessica exclaimed.

He rolled back to the lowest dial and set it to point down: his failed guess.

Windflower ascended again. 'Come on, we have to figure this out while we're waiting, not while we're actually on the ramp,' Jessica said. 'What was this site used for? It can't have been a mere camp, or a city, or even a spaceport; the tower is set in the centre of an island—'

'There might not have been water here originally,' Heem pointed out. 'That must have filled in the depression later, as drainage from the surrounding hills.'

'The depression – yes, of course! It's all part of the site, as we thought before. With the barracks further out. This could have been a major research station, with a monstrous reflecting telescope—'

'Telescope?'

'A visual device, like a huge – a huge eye. It gathers light or other radiation in a sort of cup and focuses it at a central point—' She paused as the meaning burst upon them both. 'Like the apex of this tower. Heem, this is an observatory!'

Heem grasped her picture. 'Our experts have used such devices to gather the radiation-taste of the wider universe. But our collectors are mobile, so as to orient on distant phenomena despite the eccentricities of local planetary motions. This is fixed.'

'Well, some big reflectors are fixed – but yes, I see your point. This is more suited to maybe sending a signal out, though why so big a disc—'

The two new Squams were approaching. Heem felt a roll of tension: one of them was his nemesis Slitherfear! He wanted to fight that monster, yet he was also afraid, uncertain his needles were accurate enough. The Squam knew of Heem's prowess, and might be on guard against it.

Windflower slid down. Quickly she reset the dial, and quickly Sickh and Heem checked it. They all knew time was shortening. She had oriented this time on the planet of Impasse. That had been wrong.

Heem and Windflower stood at the base, orienting outwards, while Sickh slithered quickly up. 'Not the other habitable planet of this system,' Jessica said. 'What would an observatory orient on?'

'Or a beacon,' Heem amended.

'A beacon! That's it! Like a lighthouse, shining a huge beam to warn ships clear, so they won't founder. To warn spaceships away from the Hole! The rotation of the planet would make that huge bright beam flash around the sky, a quite obvious signal! Maybe it wasn't light, but some special type of radiation – or, there are infinite possibilities. The pattern would spell danger, and it might have operated for centuries, millennia—'

Heem considered. It did make a certain alien sense. 'Yet this does not tell us where the third dial should point.'

The two Squams, becoming cognizant of the situation, slithered in towards Heem. But Windflower formed her drill, catching one Squam on the armoured body. Once scale was ripped out; the creature retreated, leaking ichor.

Slitherfear encountered Heem. The Squam seemed less formidable without his machine-weapon, and Heem felt a spray of confidence. 'No – don't let him know what you can do,' Jessica cried. 'He may think your prior victory over a Squam was a fluke, and not be properly prepared. Wait till you can wipe him out with one shot, when he's not on guard.'

Heem heeded her advice. Surprise was important, and betrayal of his power – assuming he really had it – could cause him trouble at this stage. He must seem to be a typical HydrO, so the Squam would hold him in contempt. For the moment. Objectively, Slitherfear knew Heem was dangerous, but subjectively he might not.

He needled ineffectively at the Squam's armoured torso. But the needle struck precisely where he had aimed it. Thanks to Jessica's image, he was ready; he could meet Slitherfear on an even or more than even basis. When it was time.

Windflower oriented on Slitherfear now, and the Squam retreated. But Swoon of Sweetswamp rolled swiftly in from the side and needled the Erb through the stem. It was a devastatingly accurate shot, at close range. Windflower whipped back, hurt.

Then Sickh slid down the ramp. She slithered with such force it was a virtual leap, her pincers reaching for the HydrO. Swoon rolled hastily away.

Heem moved to Windflower, wanting to help but unable. She had been punctured, and there was the flavour of her sap on her stem. It did not seem to be a fatal wound, but she was already wilting, unable to fight. Probably she had not fully recovered from the light-deprivation of the tunnels, so was more vulnerable now to such injury. She would have to withdraw from the competition, retreating to the lake, where she might endure in sun and water until the

Competition Authority came to help. 'Damn Swoon!' Heem sprayed angrily, borrowing from Jessica's vernacular. The concept 'damn' as he understood it meant consignment to an unpleasant region.

Windflower half fell across him. Heem remained still, not knowing what to do. It was his turn to mount the ramp, but he could not simply dump his friend and leave her in this hostile group. Yet neither could he help her, he lacked the resources.

One of Windflower's leaves moved along his skin. It withdrew and moved again, slowly. Then a third time, the same line. 'She's telling us something,' Jessica exclaimed. 'Those are not random lines. I think I understand! This is more than a lighthouse – it is a marker, a surveyed-in point, for general navigation. So ships travelling the Galaxy can use it as a reference, knowing exactly where they are. There must be other survey markers – and we must point to one of them, to show that we know what we're doing, before this one lets us in. Windflower must know where such a site is, because she's studied the Ancients. She may have tried Planet Impasse just in case, but now she *knows* it's another site somewhere else, and she's showing us where.'

'This is far-fetched, even for your female-alien lightleaping mind! So many unverified assumptions—'

A fourth time the Erb made the line on Heem's surface. Then she collapsed.

'Got any better notion? Jessica demanded, her mental voice chill.

'No, but still—'

'We've got to use it, Heem. She gave it to us!'

That he could grasp, almost as if he had her hands. The Erb's guess might be wrong, but it was her final gift, and had to be honoured. Heem rolled carefully from under Windflower's body, letting her slide gently to the ground, and rolled to the globe and set it. Sickh blocked Slitherfear. Another Erb was coming near; that would mean trouble for Sickh. He had to hurry, to win or return to help his friend. 'Right,' Jessica agreed.

He paused, one spiral up, to set the second dial and taste

the situation below. Slitherfear was trying to get at the globe, but Sickh balked him. Then, as Heem moved up the second spiral, the new Erb lunged his drill at Sickh, chipping off a scale – and Slitherfear caught one of her flailing limbs in his pincers and cut off her pincer. Even Heem was able to feel the vibration of her agony as more of her life-fluid welled out. Sickh, too, had not fully recovered from the ordeal of the tunnels, and could not defend herself adequately.

'That bastard!' Jessica exclaimed, furious. Her image was of a member of her species generated without proper cultural sanction; this seemed to be a gross insult. 'He attacked his own kind!'

'This is fair, in this competition,' Heem reminded her. But he was angry too. His worst enemy had unfairly wounded one of his friends.

Slitherfear mounted the ramp. 'We could dump him,' Jessica said. 'But we'd dump ourselves too.'

They came to the third dial. Heem set it in the direction Windflower had indicated. He knew of no significant system or stellar object in that region of space, but if the Erb did—

The upper ramp held. They had found the final key!

But Slitherfear was gaining on them. He could really move on this firm surface, pressing against the small retaining wall for additional leverage. Heem, jetting hard to roll up the steep incline, was slow.

He was tempted to wait and fight the creature here, but yielded to Jessica's imperative and rolled on up. He tasted the stranger-Erb pursuing the Squam, and Swoon was following the Erb. How he wished it could have been Sickh and Windflower on the ramp instead of these enemies! But of course it made no real difference; only the first could be the winner.

He reached the top – victory! – and halted. He had won the Ancient site for Star HydrO – and for Jessica's survival. But where was the Competition Authority representative that was supposed to be here to verify the identity of the winner? The top of the tower was a level platform surrounded by a low ridge, with a metallic dome raised above it. That was all.

Slitherfear charged up. 'Heem – with no entity here to keep score – no competition monitor – suppose the Squam doesn't stop?'

Suppose? Obviously Slitherfear would be governed by no law other than force. The Squam intended to throw Heem off the tower and claim the site for his own Star – which Heem was sure was Star Squam itself.

'Why, the utter freak!' Jessica exclaimed indignantly. 'He's going to cheat!'

'We have resources,' Heem assured her. 'I can hold him off with my accurate needles, and there's an Erb behind him.'

'The thing to do is change the dial setting,' she said. 'Dump them all at the botton, while we stay up here.'

'He is already beside the top dial; we cannot reach it.' Heem braced himself. Slitherfear came forging to the top, limbs folded.

Heem needled the most convenient extremity, but it was not extended and the overlapping scales protected every part of the Squam in this position. From the side Heem might have been effective, but endwise there was no purchase for a needle.

'He has to breathe, doesn't he?' Jessica asked even as Heem needled.

Good notion! Heem jetted voluminously at the creature's air intake, which was a small tube projecting from the top of the central hump. The Squam choked. He halted at the edge of the platform, unfolding all three arms.

Heem jetted again, not with needle force, because the angle was still wrong. But the Squam deflected the water with one pincer. 'We can't stop him on the ramp,' Jessica said. 'His armour is too strong. But if we let him up here, where we have more room to manoeuvre for position—'

'He's got his own problem. That Erb is on his tail.'

Slitherfear realized this. He pulled in his limbs and slithered rapidly forward. Heem could do nothing to stop him. The Squam nosed into the open chamber that was the apex of the tower, under the dome.

The Erb was right behind. As it arrived at the top of the

ramp, its drill formed. Now the Squam had to unfold his limbs again, lest the plant catch him and destroy him. For a moment the three of them paused, dispersed in a triangle about the enclosure.

'And it *is* a triangle, or a vicious circle, with each entity capable of destroying another,' Jessica said.

'I think we have an advantage,' Heem sprayed. 'We know how to fight the Squam.'

'Still, Slitherfear is treacherous, unscrupulous, and dangerous,' she said darkly. 'And there's something funny about that Erb. Isn't his stem sort of thick?'

Heem checked. The taste of the stem was strange. 'He's wearing a protective shield, so he can't be needled there!' Heem jetted. 'That means he will not be easy to eliminate.'

'It is not surprising that some pretty tough characters are in this competition. I wonder how he smuggled that jacket in? Maybe tossed it over the line, then picked it up . . .'

'In addition to that – what use to clear off the others, if more keep coming up the ramp? We need to reverse the ramp, while we wait for the Competition Authority to arrive and verify. But now the Erb stands near the dial, blocking us off.'

'I'm not sure we can reach that dial anyway, without getting on the ramp – and then *we* would get dumped.' Jessica raised a mental pair of hands to tug at mental hair. 'Why, oh why isn't a representative of the Competition Authority here to verify the winner? This whole thing is amazingly sloppy.'

Heem could only agree. Had the competition been properly organized, the present predicament would never have arisen.

The three creatures remained poised, no one taking the initiative. It was clear why: anyone who eliminated another would be vulnerable to the third, since the circle would then be broken. The Erb held the Squam in check; if the HydrO needled the Erb, the Squam might then be the winner. Except for Heem's special talent: the ability to fight a Squam. And the Erb's evident protection against a HydrO. That complicated the issue.

'You're right, Heem; first we'd better secure the top of this tower against further intrusions; then we can worry about the other two up here. We don't want to weaken ourselves fighting these two, only to get wiped out by the next one up the ramp. Maybe if it remains a standoff long enough, the Competition Authority representative will get off his lunch break and report back for duty.'

Heem made an involuntary spray of mirth. What an insult she had dealt the errant representative, implying that he was a food-eater!

And – the next competitor was already coming up the ramp. Swoon of Sweetswamp, who had evidently paused along the way to note and memorize the dial settings. How would her presence further complicate this situation?

The Erb, feeling most immediately threatened despite his shield, was first to act. He lunged his drill at Swoon. The attack caught her by surprise; Erbs hardly ever initiated hostilities against HydrOs, since the result was almost certainly disastrous for the Erbs. She didn't realize that this one was no ordinary Erb. She paused at the top of the ramp.

The Erb lunged again. Swoon retreated. The globe was immediately behind her. Suddenly Heem recognized the Erb's strategy: to force Swoon into the globe, by her contact changing the setting – and dumping her at the base of the tower. That would eliminate one competitor for a time – perhaps a long time, if she had trouble remounting because of competition below.

Heem could have warned her, but held his jet. He did not want her competition either. He wanted as few creatures up here as possible. In this he was in agreement with the Erb. With only three here, he could act against the Erb, then turn his full attention to the Squam.

Swoon banged against the globe.

The bottom dropped out of the platform they stood on. HydrO, Squam and Erb were in free-fall, dropping down inside the tower.

'From above, it reverses!' Jessica explained. 'Instead of down outside, down inside!' She had a mental picture of her Solarian body, blue hair floating upward with the force of the fall, legs kicking beneath the cone of material that

290

surrounded them. Her dress, skirt, slip, clothing, apparel female Solarians wore was supposed to conceal the upper sections of her lower legs, lest observing males of her species become unduly intrigued. Alien it was, but now Heem found the image peculiarly attractive. She was probably a creature of considerable physical appeal to her own kind.

'I would be, if I ever had a chance to be myself, instead of a fake man. But I guess it was out of the frying pan and into the fire.' Now her image was of the falling Solarian female descending from a large rimmed disc into the leaping flames of some nether conflagration. 'From male apparel to a male host.'

The flames were consuming her dress, exposing more of her upper legs. Heem found those legs quite interesting. Now the upper section of her garment was also disintegrating, exposing—

'Heem!' she cried, and he broke off his mental gaze. 'Heem – we're still falling!'

So they were. But they were falling slowly. 'This is not free-fall – it's counter-gravity!' Heem sprayed.

'There is no such thing as anti-gravity!' But her protest lacked force, as they floated down. Ancient science seemed to mock the limitations of the moderns.

They came to rest in a cylindrical chamber beneath the base of the tower. Its walls were of a material similar to that of the dial-globes outside: they were clearly perceptible to all senses. Five passages led out from the central plaza. There was no dust, and the air was pleasant.

Here it was – an entire, functional Ancient complex to be explored. A treasure of a magnitude found only once in a millennium in any given galaxy. But they could not explore it; they had to settle which Star had the right to exploit this site. For that Star would shortly be the dominant one of this Segment. The vicious triangle remained.

Not quite. There was another creature present. Its torso was vaguely like a stem, but thicker; at the base were several little feet, not roots; at the centre were several manipulative appendages, not Squam-limbs; and the apex terminated in a complex spiral wire.

'An Ancient?' Heem sprayed, startled.

¿Hardly!¿ the creature jetted back at him. ¿I am the Competition Authority Representative, a native of Segment Fa¿, selected as an objective arbiter for your Segment's activity. I was examining a decorative globe near the access ramp, when I was precipitated here, and was unable to return.¿

Heem relaxed. 'So that's what happened to the Representative!' Jessica exclaimed. 'He must have been brought by floatercraft, and not realized the significance of the dials.'

The creature carried a translator, from which emerged the jets and other modes of communication. It was evident that the Squam and Erb understood him also. ¿Which of you was first to achieve the apex of the tower¿

'I was,' Slitherfear answered immediately.

'You falsify!' the Erb flashed indignantly. '*I* was first.' The representative oriented on Heem. ¿You make a similar claim?¿

'Brother!' Jessica exclaimed. Heem only sprayed agreement.

¿We shall then await arrival of the Competition Authority Vehicle, and convey the three of you to an interrogation station, where the truth shall be ascertained. Analysis of your aural printouts will immediately—¿

The communication was cut off by Slitherfear's action. The Squam lunged into the Fa¿, knocking him down. One limb reached for the apex-spiral, and the pincer clamped on it and wrenched it out of the body.

Both Heem and the Erb moved forward, but Slitherfear was already slithering away. One pincer grasped the translator. 'There will be no aural printouts,' the Squam said. 'I have nullified the Fa¿.'

'You have not nullified *us*!' Heem jetted, his shock at this horrendous deed converting to cold anger. '*We* know the truth, not the Fa¿.'

The Squam's body heaved. His stomach extruded – and it was no living membrane, but a fibre sac. That meant that Heem's action, there in the valley of Morningmist, had been effective; the Squam had had to have his stomach amputated. He probably lived on artificial infusions of chemicals.

From the sac tumbled a cylindrical object. The fibre stomach was then sucked back in, and Slitherfear picked up the object. It fitted neatly in one set of pincers, the three surfaces holding it without slippage. 'So nice of you to allow me leisure to extract my tool. You, HydrO, will murder the Faȥ by needling him through the torso; he is only comatose while his spiral perceptor is disconnected. I will then have to kill you and the Erb in defence of self.'

'This is so dastardly it's crazy!' Jessica exclaimed. 'Heem, you're not about to murder the Competition Authority Representative!'

'I believe you are overly optimistic,' the Erb flashed at the Squam. 'I was not first to the apex of the tower, but if you kill the HydrO, he will be eliminated by death and you by disqualification, and I will become the legitimate winner. My aural printout will show the validity of my claim. I believe you have already disqualified yourself by your attack on the Faȥ.'

Slitherfear aimed his cylinder at the prone creature. A needle of water shot out, piercing the Faȥ. The torso humped in agony, the limbs thrashing; then it subsided. The taste of mortality suffused the air. 'As you can perceive the Representative has been needled to death,' Slitherfear said. He put a second pincer to his weapon, clamping on it and breaking it apart. He threw it to the floor.

Abruptly the weapon burst into flame. The heat was fierce but brief; then nothing remained but the dissipating taste of combustion. It had been a self-destruction item.

'This remains unclear to me,' the Erb flashed. 'You may frame the HydrO and kill him – but you cannot also kill me. And if you could, you would still be subject to the aural printout yourself.'

'This is part of my expertise for this mission,' Slitherfear said. 'I am the Star Squam representative; I have no transferee. Instead I have an aural scrambler. No clear printout is possible. The truth cannot be had from me.'

'An aural scrambler!' Heem jetted. 'This would affect the scruples, even the sanity of any entity who employed it for any prolonged period.'

'Like a pact with the devil,' Jessica agreed. 'The devil

293

takes your soul in return for material gain.'

The implication had not been lost on the Erb. He flashed at the translator, but his message was for Heem. 'HydrO, we compete with a mad creature. I think you and I had better form a—'

The translator crashed to the floor. Its message ceased. The Squam had destroyed it, too, before Erb and Hydro could come to an agreement.

The Erb formed his drill and moved purposefully towards the Squam. Slitherfear retreated quickly into the passage behind him. His sanity was evidently not so far eroded as to make him that foolish. He had to kill the Erb, but could hardly do so in a direct, fair encounter. He would avoid contact until he could obtain some illicit advantage. Perhaps he had another weapon hidden in his pseudostomach.

'Do you think we can trust the Erb?' Jessica asked worriedly. 'He can only win by seeing us both killed.'

'True. He did try to falsify his order of arrival to the Competition Authority Representative. He may balk at murder, but we cannot safely assume so. He may even be a decent sort, like Windflower, but he's not here to be decent. We had best stay clear of him. We don't need to attack him, even assuming we can penetrate his protective shield. All we need do now is survive until Competition Authority reinforcements come; then we shall be adjudged the victors.'

'Maybe it would be smartest simply to retreat for the time being,' she said. 'Let the other two fight it out, while we wait for the Authority. You don't have to kill Slitherfear directly, even if the Erb doesn't catch him; just by surviving, you will finish him, because he is guilty of murdering a neutral sapient entity. You can be sure he won't get off *this* rap; it would make an inter-Segment incident. His scrambler will do him no good, if you are present to testify.'

'True.' Was he being sensible, or merely yielding to his fear of the Squam?

'You're not afraid, Heem! You never were a coward, and now with your needles sharp you're as formidable as any HydrO can be. There's just no profit in charging blindly into battle. Besides, we'll have a better chance if we familiarize ourselves with the locale. We might even set an ambush for the Squam, since he has to come to us if he wants to win.'

Good tactics! Slitherfear would indeed come for them, for to fail to do so would be to lose. They could prepare a fitting reception.

Heem rolled down the passage most nearly opposite the one the Squam used. It opened shortly on another chamber, also with five branching exits, including the passage they had come on. 'Uh, you know we could get lost here, if the rooms are all the same,' Jessica said nervously.

'If we are lost, the Squam cannot locate us,' he reminded her. 'But we shall not be lost; I will know the taste of my own trail when I cross it, and can follow it back.'

'Nothing here,' she said, reassured, forming the image of the bare chamber. 'The Ancients really cleaned it out when they left. But if they knew they were leaving, why didn't they turn off the tower mechanism?'

'It is hard to fathom the rationale of the Ancients! Perhaps they expected to return – and were caught unawares by their abrupt demise.'

'But this is *so* clean! It's not just mothballed for later use, it's *empty*. The way you leave a house when you're moving for good.'

'A what?'

'Oh, never mind! Just keep rolling along.'

Heem rolled along, down the opposite passage. They came to another chamber, and another. 'It's a labyrinth!' Jessica exclaimed. 'But what's its purpose? It just doesn't seem to make much sense.'

'If we were able to make sense of the Ancients, we might achieve their level.'

'I don't know that there's much here to exploit. The mechanisms of the tower, that's all. Some sites have had important transfer technology, but if this was just a survey marker station . . .' She let her thought fade into tastelessness.

Then, abruptly, a passage opened into a much larger chamber. All about the perimeter were point flavours, in the same multi-sense technique as the tower globes. 'The stars!' Jessica said. 'This is a planetarium! An astrotarium—' The

Ancients liked the stars; they had representations—' Her image replaced the taste-pattern, as it had when they threaded the needle between Star and Hole. The stars became bright constellations, scintillating on a black background.

They rolled to the centre of the chamber, and it was as if the galaxy spread out about them. The stars were not mere dabs of taste or light, but tangibilities in full dimension. Depth, intensity, colour – all were present, wonderfully.

'Why are some stars keyed wrong?'

Heem realized she was correct. He had considerable mental awareness of the configuration of local space. This multi-dimensional map was far more detailed than what his mind could hold, and highly accurate. It was, of course, Ancient-old; but most stars did not change very much in such a period. There was a wrongness about their representation that the passage of time could not account for.

'Heem – you're familiar with this galactic locale. Is there – are the stars all there, in the picture?'

'There are more stars than any mind can track,' he jetted. 'But all the habitable systems are keyed in, in a shade of colour-taste, and all—' He paused, as the significance of the elementary keying opened to him. 'All *inhabited* systems are keyed in. Star HydrO, Star Erb, Star Squam, the other Stars of this Segment – all my mind can verify are present. But not Holestar.'

'Of course not. *This* is System Holestar, and it had no sapient life-forms three million years ago. Except for the visiting Ancients, of course, and the barracks-builders, who were probably also of non-System origin. The only native life would have been plants and maybe low-grade animals. Even the rats of the tunnels are probably imports, vermin who sneaked in on spaceships and took over after the premises were vacated. They could not have evolved on Eccentric, since there were no non-lava passages before the sapients colonized it.'

'A variant keying indicates other inhabited systems, as many as the ones we know, but this is wrong. I recognize a

296

number of these. System Extirpate, where a nova seems to have wiped clear all life—'

'*Seems* to have?'

'HydrO technicians explored it long ago. There were a few artifacts suggestive of technological sapience on the two planets there, but both planets had been so badly burned by an ancient nova—'

'Three million years ancient?' she asked, catching on.

'Yes. Only Star Extirpate is not a nova star, so could not have been the source of obliteration. It does not seem likely that another star could have been near enough to do this, and then vanish entirely. It is one of the mysteries of space. And other lifeless systems—'

'Are listed on this Ancient map as supporting potentially sapient life?'

'Unless I misinterpret the key.'

'Heem, this is horrible! Could there have been twice as many life-forms three million years ago as now, and half of them were obliterated?'

'This is my understanding. This must have been a survey station too, accurately mapping all sapience in this sector of our Galaxy. The other markers we conjectured may have mapped other sectors.'

'And then half of that sapience was brutally destroyed. Could it have been war – war on a galactic scale? And the present-day life-forms are the survivors?'

'But we lacked technology then! We HydrOs were presapients, not yet evolved to our full powers, lacking all knowledge of the extra-planetary universe. The same was true of our neighbours in Thousandstar – and I believe it was true also of the rest of this galaxy generally. None of the contemporary life-forms had entered space then. We could not have defended ourselves from technological species such as the Ancients.'

'Nor could we Solarians,' she agreed. 'We were barbarians, hardly mastering the use of fire, then. Some among our kind might conjecture that we rose to heights long ago, then reverted to barbarism after some colossal catastrophe, but archaeology does not support this. We were primitives.

Yet we survived, and you HydrOs survived, and all the others, while the civilized Ancients perished.'

'And this station knew precisely which survived and which perished – for the keying differs, and not coincidentally.'

'But this station is part of the culture that perished! It could not have recorded its own demise so neatly!'

'Only if it saw it coming. The Ancients might have vacated, leaving only the tower and planetarium operative, still surveying data for those who might follow.'

'And no one followed, for all civilization in the galaxy had collapsed, leaving only vermin-species like ourselves.'

They contemplated the grim galactic map, mystified and appalled. The mystery of the Ancients became greater with each discovery relating to it!

There was a vibration, followed by the spreading taste of metal. 'Something is happening!' Heem sprayed, alarmed. 'Perhaps the Competition Authority has arrived!'

'Must be! The Fa¿ should have signalled them before he died, though why he didn't have them come to get him out of the depths – let's get over there to stake our claim before Slitherfear does something worse yet!'

Heem rolled rapidly towards the source of the commotion. He could guess why the Fa¿ hadn't summoned help; he would have thus exposed his own incompetence. It was also possible that the Ancient site shielded transmissions, making external communication impossible.

They passed through several of the pentagonal chambers and came at last into another larger one. The Erb entered from another passage ahead of him, and a third presence manifested: a HydrO. Swoon of Sweetswamp had managed to follow them down into this complex.

Slitherfear was in the centre of the room, his pincers gripping some kind of machine mounted there. It was from this device the vibration and taste emanated. It seemed to be an Ancient artifact, operative but somewhat irregular after its long hiatus. The Ancients had been the Cluster's finest builders, but the inordinate period since their passing had made even their machines unreliable.

The Erb charged at the Squam, his drill formed and

turning. Slitherfear rotated the machine until a lens pointed at the Erb, and struck a globe-control with one pincer.

The taste of alien power jetted out from the machine. The Erb collapsed.

'It's a death-ray generator!' Jessica exclaimed. 'An Ancient weapon! Must have been too awkward to move, so they had to leave it.'

'And Slitherfear found it, discovered its operation and made a commotion to lure the rest of us here to be killed! We should have stayed hidden, instead of succumbing to his trap!'

Heem rolled at the Squam from the side. Slitherfear, aware of him, swung the machine about on its mounting, but Heem had the advantage of velocity, thanks to the time it had taken to kill the Erb, and crashed into the Squam before the machine could orient. Slitherfear was shoved away, half rolling on the floor. He was up immediately, pincers extended – but now Swoon of Sweetswamp was there, almost colliding with him herself. She needled him, rolling back.

'His tough luck that we all arrived at once,' Jessica remarked without sympathy. 'Had we been spaced out more, he would have finished us all, just as he planned.'

Slitherfear, enraged, slithered after Swoon. 'Heem, he'll kill her!' Jessica cried.

'He can't catch her,' Heem jetted. He also remembered the way Swoon had needled Windflower. That had pretty much abated any sympathy he might have felt for the HydrO. 'We must inspect this machine he found, because it represents the greatest immediate threat to us.'

'You're right,' she said reluctantly. 'At least let's check the Erb. Maybe he's not actually dead. Stunned—'

Her and her concern for living creatures! They checked the Erb, while the Squam chased the HydrO into another passage. The Erb was not dead, but he was not living either. 'His aura,' Heem sprayed, dismayed. 'I believe his aura is gone.'

'Aura! Of course! The Ancients were the consummate experts in aura! This must be a transfer device, moving his aura to some other host, perhaps across the Galaxy!'

Heem rolled back to the machine. Its control-globe had the balled-line inside, similar to the globes outside, but in addition there were three symbols on the ball's surface. Jessica pieced them out, translating Heem's taste into vivid pictures. One was an empty circle, O; another was a two-knobbed line, .___.; and the third was a circle with a dot inside, ⊙. That was all.

The only other controls seemed to be the activator-globes: one opaque, which the Squam must have used to turn the machine on, the other empty, but apparently trigger for the transfer, since it was the one Slitherfear had banged to destroy the Erb. 'We'd better not fool with either of these,' Jessica said nervously. 'We know so little about this thing, and it seems just about ready to blow itself apart. We don't even dare try turn it off, because we can't be sure how the off switch works.'

'But so long as it remains functional, we are threatened by it,' Heem pointed out. 'If we leave it unattended, and Slitherfear returns—' He focused his taste on the fallen Erb, meaningfully.

'Um, you're right again, Heem.' They studied the marked globe again. 'Maybe if we changed the setting – what do you think these symbols mean?'

'It is set now on O,' Heem sprayed. 'That could mean vacancy of host. A body without an aura. Like the Erb.'

'Horrible – and probably correct. An aura destruction setting. I don't think contemporary science has anything like that, and I'm not sure it should. What does that make the ⊙ symbol?'

'An aura-creating setting? No, even the Ancients could not have created an aura from nothing! But if they had an aura available—'

'I think I've got it, Heem! This is no weapon – it's a research tool! This was a laboratory attached to the observatory or the beacon or whatever, with many cubicles for researchers to occupy, like a big office building. They were analysing auras, classifying them, separating the sheep from the goats—'

'The—?'

'Never mind! And the sheep they keyed in one fashion and the goats in another, for their big map of the Milky Way, or at least this segment of it. Now maybe it was a very subtle thing they were studying, so they had to transfer a given subject aura into a blank host, to maintain it while studying it in a controlled environment. And sometimes they had to superimpose it on an occupied host, as my aura is superimposed on yours. So they would have needed some blank hosts, and some occupied ones. So they used this machine to blank a given host, and the O is the setting for that. And—'

'This is awful!' Heem protested. 'To blank creatures, probably sapients—'

'No worse than vivisection! If you want to know about something, you have to work with it, take it apart, analyse it. The Ancients did not advance their science of auras to the pinnacle they did without doing a hell of a lot of lab work, believe me! So the ⊖ setting must be to superimpose an aura on a given host, maybe one that's already occupied, maybe not. The same thing we do today, for travel and inter-Sphere communication. And the .__. setting—'

'That might be neutral. Just an aural scan, no transfer, necessary to verify the situation before acting.'

'Maybe,' she agreed dubiously.

They had no more time to consider. Swoon was rolling back, still pursued by Slitherfear. She was leaking water from a wound; he had evidently caught her and gouged out a small chunk of flesh with one pincer. 'Help me, Heem!' she sprayed. 'He will kill me, then you, unless we fight him together. I cannot roll much more.'

'Help her,' Jessica decided. 'She is no threat to us! *He* is!'

'First this, just in case,' Heem sprayed. He touched the machine's control-globe, moving the indicator to the neutral double-knob-line position. Then he rolled out to intercept the Squam.

Slitherfear immediately turned his attention to Heem. He knew where his most formidable opposition rolled. Swoon rolled around behind the machine and settled, trying to stop

301

her leakage of fluid and recover strength. 'Be alert for him, Heem!' she jetted. 'He caught me by moving slow, then leaping suddenly forward. He's invulnerable! I tried to lead him over the edge of a drop I found, but he was too cunning.'

'I thought we were going to fight the Squam together,' Jessica grumped. 'She's turning the whole job over to us.'

'Will the machine abolish him?' Swoon sprayed, nudging up to it. Her wound seemed to be closing nicely.

'That machine is too dangerous to use!' Heem sprayed, alarmed. 'It may react against the operator.' But his keenest worry was that she would try to use it against the Squam – and catch the HydrO instead. Because he and the Squam would be moving quite rapidly and erratically. Her 'help' could be disastrous!

'Especially since we aren't sure about that setting we put it on,' Jessica agreed. 'It may be neutral – but it could be something else. Like self-destruct.'

Slitherfear leaped, his whole body flexing, propelling himself from the floor. All three appendages extended forward, pincers closing.

Heem rolled adeptly to one side and fired his sharpest, hottest jet at the most accessible juncture; the emergence of limb from torso.

He scored. The effect on the overconfident Squam was devastating. That limb went lax, not even able to fold properly into its slot. 'You thought you had an easy mark, did you,' Heem sprayed, not caring that the creature could not understand him without the translator. 'Now we settle it, killer of juveniles!'

Slitherfear was wounded, but not stupid. He oriented on Heem more carefully now, keeping his two remaining pincers close to his body, allowing Heem a fair shot only at the useless limb. Naturally Heem did not waste his effort on that. He rolled around, but the Squam turned with him, on guard. It was necessary to get close to score a crippling shot – but then he would be within range of the pincers.

Slitherfear lunged at him. Heem rolled back, this time finding no opening. He had beaten the other Squam, so long ago in the arena, by forcing him to close up completely, so that he could not fight, then nudging him into deep water. Slitherfear refused to be cowed, and in any event, there was no water here. The monster lunged again, cautiously, and Heem retreated again, seeking an opening that did not materialize. This was no easy contest!

'The only easy contests are those in which Erb tears up Squam, or Squam tears up HydrO, or Hydro needles Erb,' Jessica said. 'By developing your finesse with needles you have merely achieved parity. You still must find a way to defeat an equivalent adversary.'

Some encouragement! Again the Squam lunged, and again Heem dodged. 'Look out!' Jessica cried, as Heem banged into the base of the Ancient machine. He had been paying attention only to the Squam, neglecting his environment. He rebounded from the metal – and Slitherfear leaped twice as fast and far as before and caught him with one pincer-set.

'That's what he did to me!' Swoon sprayed, rolling back. She was not much help either.

The pain was terrible, but Heem focused on the necessary. Because the pincers were anchored in his flesh, they could not be retracted or moved quickly. He aimed carefully and slanted a single hard needle into the vulnerable juncture.

Again, the effect was gratifyingly immediate. The pincers went slack. The Squam had lost another extremity! One more and he would be helpless, and Heem would be able to orient his needles at leisure, drilling in between the scales until he punctured the vulnerable interior. He was not merely a match for this monster, after all; he had an easy victory! His visual accuracy and coordination were devastatingly effective.

The Squam lunged – for the Ancient machine. *That* had been Slitherfear's objective! He had been manoeuvring for this approach, not really trying for Heem – and now all three limbs were back in action. 'Heem, we've been suckered!' Jessica cried with dismay.

Heem was completely unrolled. All his practice, for nothing! All his confidence, false! The Squam had known what Heem would try, and pretended it was working.

Heem had deceived himself, thinking he could—

'Heem, we haven't lost!' Jessica screamed. 'We've just taken a small tactical setback. He expects you to give up now, but you won't. Get back in there and fight!' And she drove him forward with the image of a booted Solarian foot, swinging at him.

Heem jetted so violently he virtually hurtled across the chamber. He smashed into the Squam – but this time Slitherfear held firm, braced for the impact, trying to maintain possession of the machine. Heem needled at all three extremities simultaneously, utilizing the salvo accuracy he had practised against the rats.

And for once the Squam really *had* underestimated him. Slitherfear fell back in pain. His limbs had not been nullified, but the needles had obviously hurt. Heem rolled after him, needling again in the same places, deepening the hurts. He also shot a jet at the air-intake hole. The Squam choked again, but fastened one set of pincers firmly on Heem's flesh, near enough to the spot just injured to prevent Heem from needling effectively. Heem tried to pull away, but could not without leaving his flesh behind. This time he was really caught.

He felt something awful. Not just the fact of his predicament, but a kind of sickness suffusing him, fuzzing his awareness, causing him to hate his very existence. All his civilized values seemed meaningless; it was better to deal on a purely selfish basis, to destroy all opposition ruthlessly, to—

'Heem, it's the scrambler! It's scrambling your aura too, and mine, where they overlap his. It's driving us both crazy! We've got to get away!'

But he couldn't get away. The pincers were inexorable. They held too big a section of his flesh. If he ripped free, he would die. Yet if he did not—

'Remember Sickh!' Jessica cried. 'How you moved her out of the water!'

What did Sickh have to do with this? Oh. Heem thought it impossible, but he tried. He jetted himself into a violent roll, drawing the Squam along after him, and the creature's body fell over his own and crashed to the floor beyond. It was

304

after all possible! But the triple claw retained its cruel grip.

Heem rolled on, over Slitherfear, needling him in passing, keeping him distracted while velocity built up. He rolled beyond, drew the Squam up again, and slammed him over again, and needled him again. Slitherfear might have been able to stop it by shifting his weight at the appropriate moment to counter Heem's effort, but did not understand what was happening. HydrOs always tried to pull away from Squams, not to roll over and under them!

Heem found a looseness developing between scales, where the Squam's body was being wrenched about, and needled there repeatedly. A third time he hauled the Squam up, this time slamming him into a wall. He needled the gap between scales again, using his hottest water.

'Heem—' Jessica cried.

He heaved Slitherfear up yet again, to slam him again.

'Heem, I think you can stop. I think he's dead.'

He paused. He no longer felt the sickness of the scrambler; his mind was clearing. The claw still gripped, but it was a death grip; the animation was fading from the body of the Squam. The creature could only take a certain amount of shock, when its whole body was involved; its armour became a liability. Heem had killed his enemy by beating him to death.

Heem shifted his body cautiously. Now he was able to draw himself free. 'I think he was weak, too,' Jessica said. 'From the rigors of the race, and his unnatural stomach, and that awful scrambler. He thought he could win by treachery and brutality. When you showed that you could fight him—'

'*You* showed him,' Heem sprayed. 'You drove me, you guided me when I was defeated. You saw clearly the paths I could not find, that made victory possible. Without you—'

'I had faith in you,' she said. 'Because with all your alien foibles, such as lack of limbs and sight, you're still a better man than any I know at home. I—'

'No, my turn! I love you, alien female! Without you I could not have won. Without you I could not endure.'

'Heem of Highfalls!' It was Swoon of Sweetswamp, near the Ancient machine, recovered enough to hail him with a jet. She was of course unconscious of his internal dialogue. 'Do you survive?'

'I survive,' he sprayed. 'The Squam is dead.'

'Then you are the winner of the Competition. Yet if I had not distracted the Squam, weakening him by the chase—'

'True,' Heem agreed, feeling generous. 'Your presence helped. It got him away from the machine, gave me time to study it.'

'So you understand the operation of the Ancient device?'

'Somewhat, perhaps, thanks to your—'

'Then would it not be fair to share the victory with me? The honour to Star HydrO would be unabated, and there is enough in this complex for more than a single Star to exploit. The mechanisms of the tower, the machine – there must be other things too, of similar value.'

'There are other treasures,' Heem agreed, thinking of the planetarium. 'Yet the rules of the Competition specify—'

'The rules specify that the winner takes the site,' she sprayed. 'But who is the winner when it has taken more than a single entity to achieve it? This becomes in effect a relay race, and all who participated in the winning effort should share in the profits of that victory.'

'She does have a point,' Jessica agreed internally. 'I think you could afford to agree. The agreement might not have force with the Competition Authority, but that would not be your fault. Offer her a quarter share of the proceeds of the site.'

'Would you consider a quarter share for your Star?' Heem asked Swoon.

'I would prefer a half share,' Swoon sprayed, 'I could be most appreciative, Heem, in the name of the Star I represent. My transferee can promise you rather substantial long-term personal recompense—'

'She trying to bribe you, Heem!' Jessica exclaimed indignantly.

'And I myself can offer you quite immediate short-term pleasure,' Swoon concluded. She jetted a supremely evocative erotic flavour at him.

'And now she's trying to seduce you again!'

'It is an attractive enough offer,' he sprayed to her internally. 'There is no finer pleasure than—'

'Damn it, don't tell *me* about that!' she cried angrily. '*I* can't – oh, hell, I'm just being a jealous female! I get so tired of participating in these things in the male costume instead of the female.'

'Yes, of course,' Heem sprayed, chastened. 'I will decline her offer.'

'No, don't do that. I have no right to—' She couldn't finish the thought. 'I'll be leaving you soon anyway. I love you, Heem, whatever happens. I would not deny you your pleasures. I would not be the dog in the manger.'

'The what? Where?'

She flashed him a picture of a four-legged, tooth-faced creature standing in dehydrated vegetation, threatening another creature who evidently desired the vegetation. Heem could make little sense of it.

'What it means is that I can't be the kind of female you need, but I don't want to be a female canine either. There is a special word for that.'

But Swoon was spraying again. 'Perhaps your offer is sufficient, Heem. My Star might be satisfied with no more than this machine. Do you know what it is, how it operates?'

'I believe it is a research tool set to banish auras from given hosts, or to superimpose auras on occupied hosts. Be careful not to jog the activator-globe.'

'Which globe is that?' she jetted, alarmed.

'The clear, empty one, I believe. That is the one the Squam touched, to banish the Erb.' He rolled closer. 'Now if you'd like to celebrate our agreement in the HydrO fashion—' It was not serious, in that he had no intent to reproduce – no, never that! – yet he wished it could have been Jessica. It was the alien female he was holding in his mind and longing for, as he sprayed romance at Swoon.

But this time Swoon did not return that kind of spray. She was now behind the Ancient machine, orienting it on him. 'I believe we can dispense with that, Heem. I have what I need.'

307

Alarm shocked through Jessica. 'Heem, look out!'

Heem froze, horrified. 'What are you doing, Swoon?' But he already had a notion. Betrayal.

'I am taking the entire site, Heem, since you were foolish enough to yield to me the key to victory.'

'But I thought you wanted to share, to indulge in—'

'Ha!' Jessica exclaimed bitterly. 'She only used her sex appeal to get what she wanted from you: information about the operation of the machine, so she could use it without killing herself. She's a conniving bitch – and I fell for it too, because I wanted you to be happy. Men often make concessions for sex alone; women seldom do. I only regret I allowed my own concern to interfere with my logic. I failed you, Heem – in the one thing I was really equipped to help you in. Protection against deceitful, cynical, excellent-tasting females.'

'I'm sorry about this, Heem, I really am,' Swoon sprayed. 'You're a tough, apt HydrO who did help me get my ship, and I'd love to copulate with you. But I have so much more to gain by winning the Ancient site for my Transferee's Star.'

'But you can't win!' he jetted at her. 'The aural printout will show you were not the first.'

'I'll take that chance. You were the first – but you killed another competitor, the Squam. That makes your victory suspect. We none of us are clean, Heem, but the Competition Authority will not be eager to roll to the enormous trouble and energy to run this competition again. In the end, the race goes to the fittest, and the fittest is the survivor – and I am that survivor. It's certainly a better chance than what I'd have if you live. The Competition Authority would not have honoured our deal.'

'I think they would!' Heem sprayed. 'The rationale of the relay race, of more than one contributor to the victory – I believe such a compromise is better than the alternative of condoning murder! I accepted your rationale – why can't you?'

'You are charming, Heem, in your naïveté.' She extended a section of herself towards the machine's globe.

Heem rolled for her, but she was too fast. She banged the

activator-globe. Power lurched out from the lens, bathing him, but a flashback also bathed Swoon. There was a terrible wrenching.

In a moment – perhaps more than that, for Heem could not judge how long he had been unconscious, if indeed at all – he recovered his orientation. He remained on the floor, and Swoon remained at the machine. His aura had not been abolished! The neutral setting—

Then he became aware of something else. He was whole, yet there was an absence, a loss—

'Jessica!' he sprayed desperately.

There was no answer. He felt for her presence in his being, and found nothing. He was alone.

'Oh, alien female!' he sprayed. 'That Ancient machine did function – weakly! It did not abolish me, it abolished the less-entrenched aura. It wiped you out!'

Yet self-preservation still motivated him. No, not that; rather it was the need for vengeance. Swoon had murdered Jessica; Swoon must pay the penalty.

Heem surveyed the physical situation. Swoon still hunched by the machine. A backlash of power had encompassed her; she had evidently been stunned. He could kill her now. He did not care about his own ultimate fate. He intended to punish Jessica's murderer. He would needle her at close range, without mercy.

He rolled in close. Swoon stirred. He readied his needles – but had to orient carefully, because now he lacked the visual coordination he had come to depend on. He was blind. His needles would not have their former accuracy and timing. He must do this with extreme concentration—

'Heem,' she sprayed weakly.

'Do not plead for mercy,' he sprayed savagely. He knew he should simply needle her, but was compelled by his nature to communicate, to justify himself, even to his enemy. 'You killed my love; I shall kill you. You took the light from my perception; I shall destroy your perception. You betrayed—'

'Heem – wait. I am Jessica.'

'Do not seek to deceive me again!' he raged, his spray so

309

hot it vaporized close to his body. 'I believed you once. I am not twice a fool!' Then he froze. *How had she known of Jessica?*

'Heem – I was retransferred,' she sprayed. 'The machine setting – the two-balled line – it must have meant not neutral, but exchange.'

He hardly dared believe, yet he so much wanted to. 'Prove this to me.'

'Your nightmare of the Squam – your illegal memories—'

'You could have guessed of those! You may have suffered another incomplete metamorphosis!'

'Then *my* nightmare, as a Solarian – clone masquerading as a male – a strange man tearing off my garb, betraying my secret in public—'

Heem's doubt collapsed. '*No* one else could know of that! Yet how could you have been exchanged, and not me? And not the two female auras of Swoon's host? They are not with me.'

'Because we are all females, Heem, and you are male. The two other auras bounced; they remain here in this host, stunned by my forced arrival. You also bounced, having no male host available within the focus of the machine. Only I was female, with a female host to transfer to. Only I was able to move when compelled. You and I have been through something like this before; we recovered from the shock more quickly. I have assumed control of this body.'

A tremendous relief washed through him. Jessica had survived! He had revenge on Slitherfear. He had won the competition, and would be restored to favour among his kind. All his frustrations had abruptly been abated. Never had he felt so good!

'Oh, Heem!' Jessica continued. 'Now at last I can spray love with you! Quickly, before the Competition Authority arrives and transfers me back to Capella. Come, my love—'

But Heem's awareness was fuzzing, the tastes overlapping each other. The Ancient complex seemed to be rotating around him, expanding and contracting, its strange half-flavours confusing him.

'Heem – what's the matter?' Jessica sprayed, alarmed. 'Are you badly injured? Oh, Heem, I'm sorry! I didn't mean to tax your energies beyond—'

He marshalled himself with a desperate effort. 'It is the metamorphosis,' he sprayed. 'It was incomplete before, because I had unresolved compulsions. Slitherfear—' He found himself sagging into incomprehensibility, and tried again. 'Murders not avenged would not let go, undermined the memory-blank of maturity. Vengeance is immature, yet there is justice. I became a juvenile masquerading as adult, much as you masqueraded as male. Now all is resolved, and I am whole, and my metamorphosis is becoming complete—'

'But then you will forget all that has happened here!' she protested.

A third, fading effort. 'I – will forget. The rigours and complexes of the juvenile state are too strong to permit maturity, must be cast aside. But you must inform them—'

'Oh, Heem, I will, I will! I'll tell them how you won, for Star HydrO. Swoon's Star gets no share; she betrayed you, she forfeits. But Sickh and Windflower were true – the re!· race hypothesis is valid, Heem, I'm sure of it. Do you mind if I include them for shares? Heem, can you hear me? I mean, can you taste me?'

Heem tasted her, and sweet she was indeed, but no longer could he answer. Consciousness was departing, and with it his entire immature existence. He was about to be adult.

'Oh, Heem, I'll never see you again! Not as I have known you! You won't even remember me, and I can't remind you because that might undo your maturity.' She paused, in the far and fading distance. 'Yet maybe that is best. Our love was hopeless from the beginning. We should never have allowed it to happen. This way you, at least, will not suffer, and I'm glad for that.'

Then she was gone from his awareness, except for one especially strong concluding needle of flavour that momentarily banished his opacity: 'I love you, Heem of Highfalls. Farewell!'

Epilogue

Jessica, in male guise, greeted each clone-pair arrival at the entrance to the main ballroom. The motif was HydrO-clone, but as co-hosts the Jesses remained human. This ball was in nominal celebration of Jesse's successful mission to Thousand-star; no Capella-clone had ever before made such a coup. The financial aspect was theoretically unimportant; it was the notoriety that counted. (Yet the completion payment had been welcome, buttressed as it was by appreciation bonuses from Stars Salivar and Ffrob, who had been granted partial shares in the enterprise.)

A pair of mock-HydrOs arrived in bulky costume that almost concealed the extremities. A concealed bulb squirted Jessica in the face. 'HydrO you do!' a clone exclaimed genially.

Jessica made an insignificant gesture with her little finger. A torrent of warm water shot out of a supposedly decorative nozzle set in the wall, thoroughly dousing both jokers. 'The warmest, wettest welcome to you, HydrOs!' she said calmly.

'To be sure.' But their enthusiasm for the humour seemed somewhat dampened.

A pair of Squams arrived next, their tails carried over their third arms. They had noted the foregoing exchange of pleasantries. They glanced with concealed non-Squam eyes at the enormous decorative pincers also set in the wall, and elected not to attempt a practical joke. Jessica smiled somewhat grimly as they proceeded directly towards the mock-up of an Ancient site in the centre, where the refreshments were being served. The old retainer, Flowers, was in charge there, keeping a benign but discreet eye on the proceedings. He was garbed as a dominant sapient of Segment Faζ, with many little hands and feet, and a spiral not want a good marriage; she wanted love. For a brief period she had had both adventure and love – and lost them. How could she remain in an alien body across the Milky Way Galaxy? How could she love a creature who resembled a squirting jellyfish? It was all impossible, and properly over – yet there was now little flavour to human existence. *Heem, Heem!*

The sound of one more dragon-coach came. Another guest, arriving late? Jessica checked her tally; all the usual crowd were accounted for. She pushed another button on her hand unit, reminded poignantly of the way a HydrO would have needled that button with a jet of water, and got the readout: Morrow.

Morrow? He was an older clone, married, not given to attending the basically juvenile functions of the young clones. If there were such a thing as metamorphosis among human beings, Morrow had passed it, and put aside childish things. Also, his attractive clone-wife would not approve of this frolicking among the nymphs at this stage.

The sound of the approach became loud enough for all to hear: not a single-dragon coach, but a grandiose four-dragon chariot. Only a man like Morrow had either the money or the nerve to use such an artifact; dragons could get quarrelsome in teams. But Morrow – was Morrow.

Jessica walked over and consulted with her brother. 'Morrow coming; know what to make of it?'

'Morrow!' he exclaimed. 'So soon out of mourning!'

'Mourning?'

'Where have you been the past fortnight? Across the Galaxy? Morrow's wife got hit by a runaway dragon-et she thought was tame. They destroyed the animal, of course, but she was too badly injured; she took euth.'

'Euthanasia? She died?'

'Successful euth usually is fatal, yes, brother,' Jesse agreed. He never called her 'sister' in company. '*Some* clones have consideration enough to honour such a request, instead of gallivanting off to far places on vacation.'

'Some vacation!' she muttered, hitting him lightly on the shoulder in masculine fashion. She was glad she had saved her brother, and not been a murderess, and knew he was glad too; that lightened her mood. She had gambled and won, in this respect, at least.

Flowers moved across from the refreshment site as well as his several little feet permitted. Flowers put up with a lot of indignity for the sake of his charges. Without his discretion and help, Jessica could never have managed her transfer ruse. Flowers had insisted on taking care of the vacant host at home, so that the Society of Hosts had no knowledge of the exchange or of Jessica's sex. Had the truth come out, Flowers could have been disbarred as a retainer, but he had taken the risk – for the sake of the estate. Other clones had in the past proffered very good terms for his service, but he had been loyal to this estate, and to the Jess-Clones.

'The Lord Morrow grieves for his cherished wife, but needs another,' Flowers said gravely. 'His estate is large, and his son is yet a child.'

'He could hire a nurse,' Jessica pointed out. 'God knows he's rich enough! He certainly doesn't need to preempt another clone-female from an already critically short supply.' She felt a genuine indignity.

'Lord Morrow is not a reasonable man,' Flowers replied, in a typical understatement. There had been stories of Morrow in his younger days, taming rogue dragons, substituting for a gladiator in a genuine contest and winning, travelling the Cluster in transfer for the mere sake of adventure. Neither caution nor finance had ever stopped him from indulging his mood of the moment, until his slip of a wife had twined him about her finger. Morrow's weakness had at last been exposed: he could not deny the woman he loved. Now it seemed he had been loosed again, having been also unable to deny his wife her demand for death.

Jessica remembered another male who had been that way, to a certain extent. Tough to the point of foolishness, but

316

weak against females of any species. Heem . . .

'Actually, it will be a good deal for the one he chooses,' Jesse remarked. 'Even if he takes a child bride, he has a lot to offer, both physically and socially. I understand he's very gentle, at home.'

'But an ogre in public,' Jessica amended. She nerved herself, and glided to the ballroom entrance to greet the widower.

Morrow was a huge, dusky man, black of beard, with muscles like those of the gladiator he had impersonated. It was rumoured that he still exerted himself with archaic barbell weights by way of entertainment or meditation. Certainly no runaway baby dragon would have crushed *him*. Jessica was daunted by his gruff power that seemed to radiate from his body.

'Welcome to HydrO-clone Ball, my Lord Morrow,' she said formally, showing the deference due an elder clone. Actually, he was only a decade older than she, but age was not the only distinction. 'This is an unexpected pleasure.'

The giant stared at her, his eyes narrowed appraisingly. 'I like your costume not,' he said. 'Remove it.'

Jessica smiled in her masculine mode, though she felt an ugly chill. There was something about this man, a barely leashed violence. 'My Lord?'

Morrow shot forward a monstrous hand, catching her forearm with a punishing grip. 'Off with the mask, hypocrite!'

Jessica choked off her scream, for it would have betrayed her nature instantly. She struggled ineffectively to free herself. 'My Lord Morrow!'

The entire ballroom quieted. The clones were watching the scene, smiling, assuming it was a programmed skit for their entertainment. Only Flowers realized that this was no skit, and knew the possible consequences. He started forward, his extra feet bumping against his real ones.

Morrow grasped the lapel of Jessica's suit with his other hand and exerted his horrible muscles. The flimsy material tore lengthwise down the front, exposing her strapped halter.

317

'What is this?' Morrow demanded, as the smiles of the clones broke into appreciative laughs. Nakedness was nothing, but *involuntary* nakedness was exciting, even in a skit. 'A bandage on the uninjured man?'

'Yes,' Jessica cried, numbed. 'An injury—' An injury to her spirit more than to her body.

Flowers arrived. 'My Lord, if you please—'

Morrow hooked two fingers in the strap and ripped down. The material tore, and suddenly both Jessica's breasts were bared. Now she screamed.

'See what we have hiding here!' Morrow bellowed, tearing away the remainder of her suit and turning her around for all the clones to view. Flowers tried to cover her with his jacket, which he had providently collected on the way, but Morrow shoved him gently but forcefully away. 'I would not hurt you, old man; I seek your service for my own estate. But stand clear.' And the retainer had to withdraw.

'See!' Morrow repeated, half cupping one of Jessica's breasts with an open hand.

For a moment the clones stared in disbelief. Then one whistled. 'Those are real!' he exclaimed, laughing. Jessica found herself too numb to protest.

'Yes, it is funny, is it not?' Morrow roared. With a bound and reach of surprising swiftness he approached and caught the laughing young man. 'We laugh as we strip away our pretences, do we not?' And he tore the man's Squam-costume lengthwise.

The young clone, cowed, clutched his tattered costume to his body.

'Laugh!' Morrow bellowed, ripping away more of it.

The lad laughed, somewhat hysterically, now standing naked.

Morrow lurched to the side, catching a girl in a HydrO costume. He ripped it off her. 'Laugh!' he commanded. She shrieked her embarrassed laughter.

The huge man whirled on the rest of them. 'Off, off with it

all! Laugh! Laugh! It is funny, is it not?'

And in moments he had the whole room naked, himself included, everyone laughing nervously.

Morrow returned to Jessica, who had remained frozen. Her nightmare had finally become literal, and it was every bit as bad as she had ever feared. 'You I claim,' Morrow announced, like a dragon roaring over a fresh kill. 'I found you, and you are female and you are fair, most fair, and what shame remains to you that these others do not share?'

'You think that's reason to marry a monster?' Jessica demanded, flushing to the waist. How had this brute known her secret? Why had he come for her, instead of for one of the nymphs who would have been glad to have him? Not that he was unattractive, or his attention unflattering, but—

'Not entirely. Yet I promised you this needling of your fundamental shame, and you promised to accept it in the proper spirit. Do you renege, alien female?'

'Alien female!' she repeated. 'What address is this?'

Morrow drew her inexorably in towards him. 'Do you forget so quickly, creature-who-eats? Did you lie when you claimed your kind suffered no metamorphosis? After we solved the riddle of concepts, threaded Star and Hole, and fought the monsters? You taught me vision, you taught me love, you addicted me to these things, that I can never experience as a HydrO, and now I come to spray with you – do you dare reject me, image-of-Squam?'

'Heem!' she cried, belief and disbelief colliding. 'But it can't be – you metamorphosed—'

'Alas, it reverted again. The first time the immaturity of the need for vengeance nullified it; the second time, the alienness of love, I could not yield that emotion, and so it undermined my maturity, and I remembered, and I knew what I had lost, and so I travelled in transfer to seek out my second nemesis and conquer her.'

She felt dizzy. 'But what of Morrow?'

'You also taught me how truce could be made, even with

319

aliens, even with creatures of anathema, who are no longer evil when understood. I promised the sufferer a good wife, one he would appreciate when his grief abated; he promised me the first month. Thereafter we share. He is a good creature, though he eats; but he is bereft of his love, as I am.'

Flowers drew near again. 'Jess, is this man hurting you? I have fetched a laser weapon—'

She faced her old retainer. She took a deep breath, for the first time unashamed to show her bosom in public. 'Flowers, don't ask questions. Just pick up the largest bowl of pseudofruit punch you can heft, bring it here, and dump it over our heads. Now!'

Bewildered but loyal, Flowers did as he was told. As the other naked clones stared, the sweetened fluid washed over their two heads and bodies, soaking them with its flavour.

'Now we spray together,' Jessica said, kissing the creature she loved.